I0664121

Celeste & the White Dragon

a novel by

D. Michael Martindale

Worldsmith Stories
Salt Lake City, Utah

ISBN: 978-1-970065-02-2

Published by
Worldsmith Stories
1042 Ft. Union Blvd. #109
Midvale UT 84047

info@worldsmithstories.com
https://worldsmithstories.com

What readers have said about D. Michael's novels

"I found Martindale's writing exciting and compelling. He created a world of nations, customs, and peoples that blends magic with the gods of the lands. It's an exciting read, carefully constructed with sequences and twists to sustain a series. I'm looking forward to the second book of the series."

— Doug Gibson, writer, blogger

"Exciting, clever, and action packed. A great story and a great ending. This is going to be such a hit!"

— Sharon Dodge, database administrator

"The story drew me in right from the beginning. I was so engrossed in the first chapters when I read them that I knew I wouldn't be able to put the book down again."

— Karen Crapo, caretaker

"Jack London once made my heart pound, but Michael Martindale is the first writer to rock me back in my chair in wide-eyed amazement."

— Preston McConkie, journalist

"Like Stephen King, Martindale captures the earthy rhythms of daily life as the characters get caught up in bizarre, harrowing events."

— Christopher Kimball Bigelow, author and editor

"Outrageous, provocative, insightful, courageous and thoughtful. Michael Martindale reminded me of the sensitivities of Orson Scott Card in his novel *Saints*."

— Eugene Kovalenko, blogger

"Martindale's frank sensuality...is not salacious; it's simply a matter of fact. A lesser book would have found a way to ignore it completely. It is frustrating when people, in life and in fiction, say what they think should be said instead of what they feel. In that light, Martindale's relative profundity is refreshing."

— Sam Vicchrilli , In Utah This Week Magazine

"Martindale...paints a scenario at once believable and shudderingly delusional."

— Kim Madsen, readers group coordinator

"The story still lingers in my mind. It was a real page-turner!"

—Eileen Stringer, reader

"Reading this fast-paced and quickly changing story is like embarking on a river rafting trip that starts out in placid shallows, never suspecting that around the next corner whitewater rapids wait, anxious to engulf you. The ride never slows down until the last few pages."

—Jonathan Neville, writer

"One of the things that a novelist, especially one who writes fantasy fiction, is required to do, is get the reader to suspend disbelief, and then sustain that suspension... This is where Martindale succeeds hands down."

— David Birley, reader

"His captivating storytelling keeps the plot moving without being predictable or trite. His descriptions ring true."

— Wife of reader

"Skillfully written, creating a realistic, complex, difficult world where everything is not as it initially seems. It's a page-turner, a real heavy weight."

—Mahonri Stewart, playwright

"D. Michael has an incredible talent for writing. I was utterly wowed by his characters' inner thoughts."

— Brian Sheets, digital media specialist

"I had a hard time putting it down, and as a result I read it surprisingly quickly. I had to know how the whole mess was going to end. It's deep, well thought out, and opens up some interesting and thought-provoking ideas."

—Lee Penrod, systems programmer

To Natalie
who, like Celeste,
rose from the darkness
to become a shining light.

BOOKS BY D. MICHAEL MARTINDALE

Brother Brigham
Twisted Mind
Celeste & the White Dragon

TABLE OF CONTENTS

Map of Cueldea

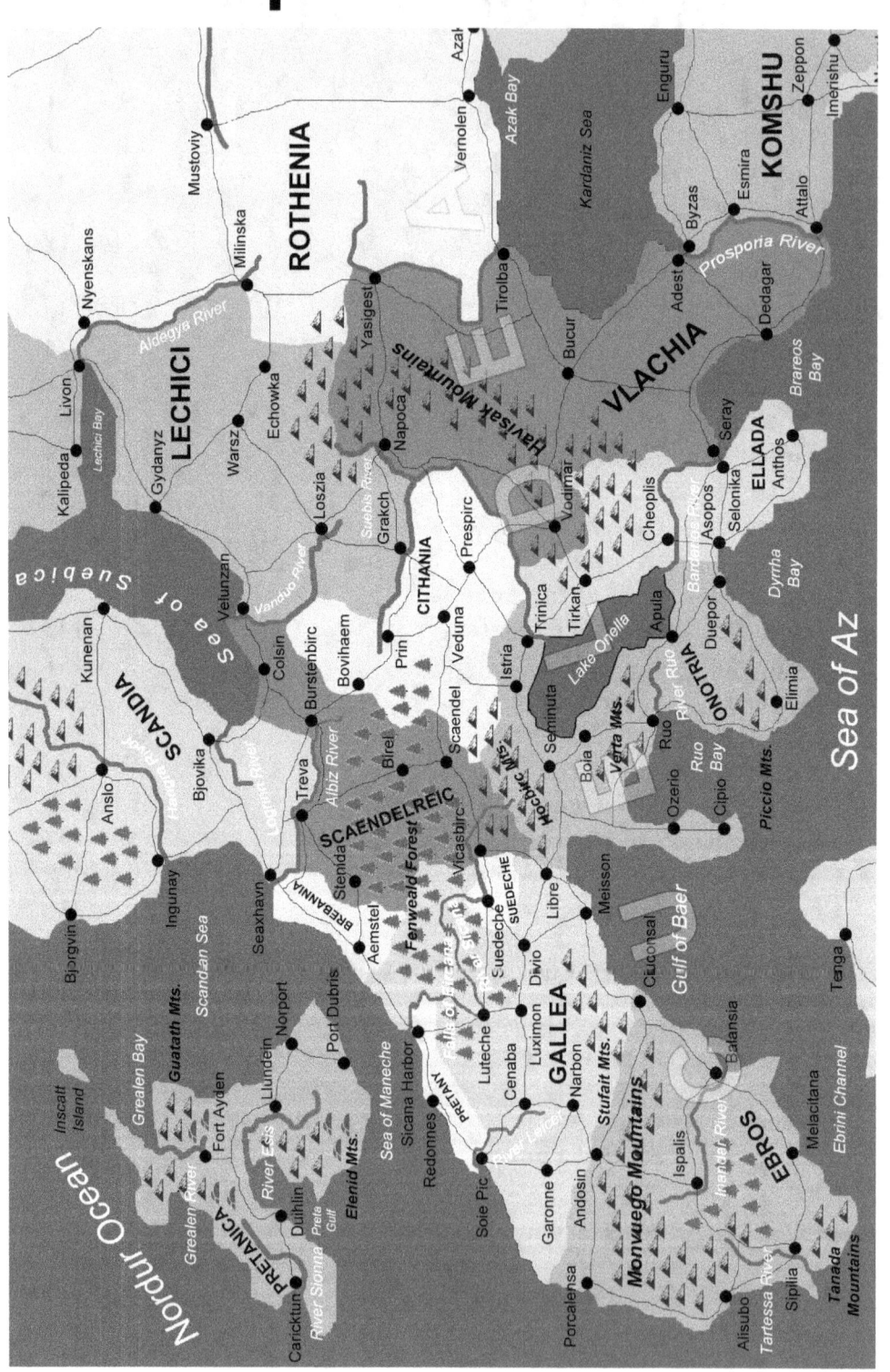

Map of Ifran

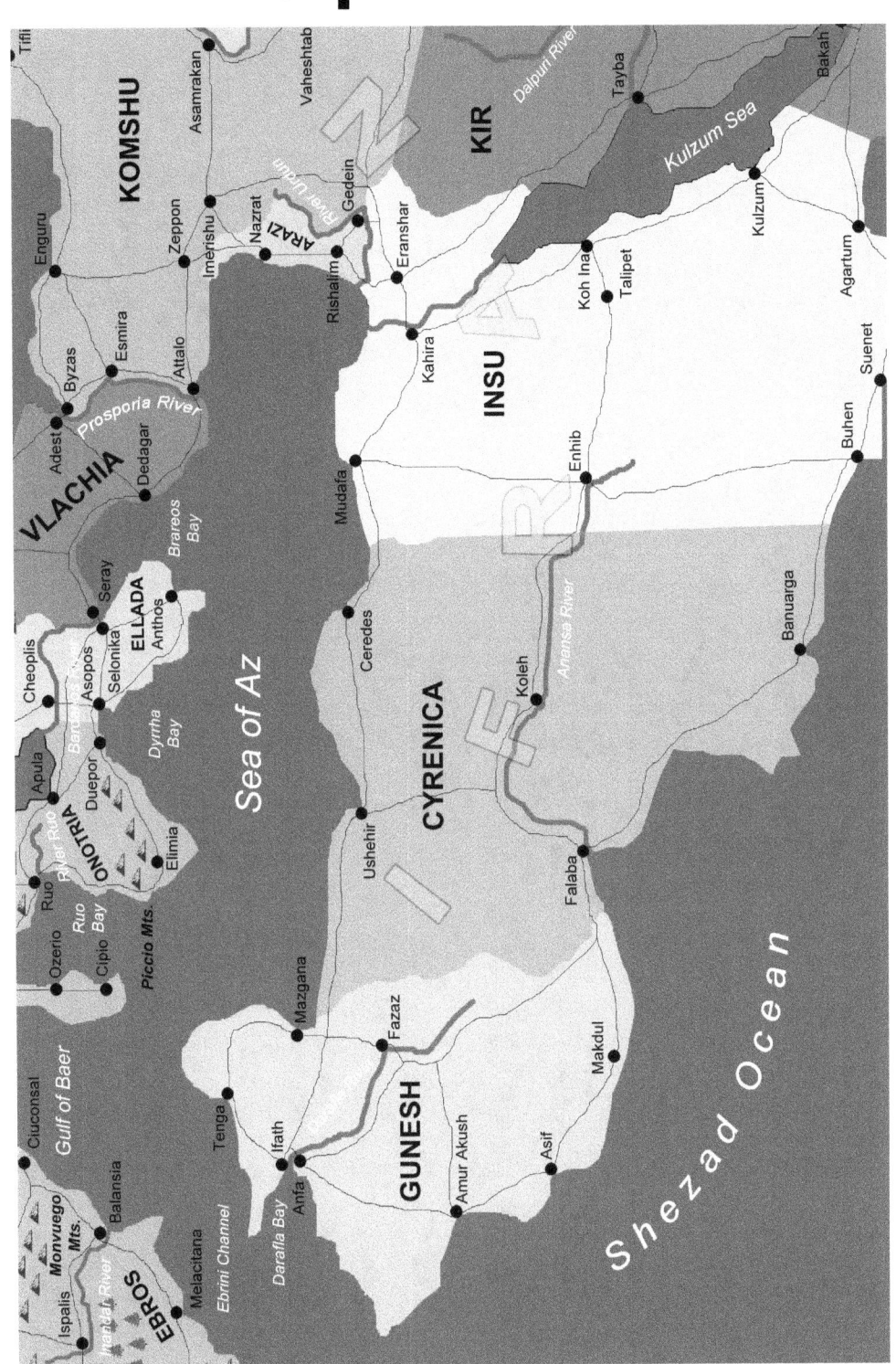

Chapter 1

Tamara

Zenia woke up in a pool of sweat with darkness surrounding her. It was a dream that woke her up—a Truth Dream. The one she'd cast a fortnight ago for this full moon.

Both queens were going into labor.

She flung the downy blanket from her body, fetched her clothes, and struggled to put them on. Her hands could hardly work the fasteners, they trembled so much. She could hear the moan from Mariam, the false queen, sleeping in the next chamber. She prayed to Mother Goddess that Tamara, the true queen, moaned from labor at the same instant.

Another spell Zenia cast those many months ago should have synchronized the pregnancies of the two women, but it was an experimental spell Zenia had pieced together from her limited knowledge. A part of one spell that synchronized events to the phases of the moon, a part of another that linked the fates of two people together, a part of a third that blessed the progress of a pregnancy. Typical village witch magic, but she wasn't smart like Eloise, her adoptive mother who'd taught her everything. Eloise probably could have fashioned the experimental spell with skill, but Zenia had no idea if her effort had succeeded.

If it had, not only were the two queens going into labor at this moment, but every event from their water breaking to each stab of contraction of their wombs to the crowning of the infant's head would coincide with one another.

If it failed, this whole night would be a disaster, and she and her beloved queen Tamara would be dead before dawn.

Zenia crept through the darkness, feeling her way to the supplies she'd prepared for this moment. She hung the string of the pouch around her neck, gathered up the bundle of clothes wrapped in a linen cloth, and retrieved the small flask. She slid a sheathed dagger into a pocket in her skirt, hoping she'd not have to use it.

She needed to hurry before Mariam's moans woke anyone else. Entering the false queen's bedroom, Zenia spoke softly, "Mistress, I'm here. What's the matter?"

"The baby's coming," Mariam said through her panting. "Too soon!"

Zenia kept her breathing as calm as she could. This was her only indication that the spell might be working. Tamara became pregnant a month before Mariam. If the two pregnancies were synchronized, Mariam should give birth a month early, just as she was doing now.

She prayed fervently it was true.

"I brought something to ease the pain." Zenia held the tiny flask up before Mariam's eyes. "Drink this."

"Thank you!" she said as she grabbed it and swallowed. The pain must be making Mariam appreciative. She normally treated her old chambermaid dismissively.

Zenia waited as the potion seeped into Mariam's system. Even though she treated Zenia with condescension, Mariam trusted her because Zenia had never given her reason to do otherwise. Her longsuffering paid off now.

Mariam gazed at Zenia and smiled warmly as the potion worked, calming her, easing her pain, and finally dulling her mind. Since Zenia was the first person Mariam locked eyes with, Zenia was the one the potion caused her to obey. She could see Mariam's eyes glaze over, her facial expression slacken, and knew she was charmed.

"Stand up," Zenia hissed. It felt good to treat her like the servant. Mariam complied, pausing a moment to steady her balance with the effects of the potion. Around her loins, her nightgown was wet and odorous with fluid from her womb. "You know where Tamara is, don't you?"

Mariam nodded.

That reassured Zenia that the spell's connection between the two queens was working. Zenia took her arm with one hand as she clutched the bundle of clothes with the other and brought her out of the queen's chambers into the large corridor. "Take me to her."

Mariam began to shuffle forward, slowly and deliberately. Her pace tested Zenia's nerves, and she looked about for any movement in the dim light of the occasional torch on the wall. Zenia's hand through Mariam's arm began to tremble. This was the moment she would learn for certain if her efforts had been in vain. If her spell had failed, Mariam would lead her nowhere. Tamara would give birth, then be killed. Zenia would be found leading Mariam around in a magic-induced trance, a pouch of magical globes around her neck. She would be executed as well.

If her spell had succeeded, the connection of childbirth between Mariam and Tamara would draw the two women together. Mariam would lead her to wherever Tamara was hidden, and with the help of Mother Goddess, Zenia's plans of escape might actually work.

Mariam led her along the corridor toward the large staircase that descended to the Great Hall. This was the most dangerous moment in the entire plan. Someone could find them suspiciously wandering the castle. She'd cast her spell so the births would align with the full moon when it rose high in the sky, late in the night, the only thing she could think of to avoid encountering anyone. But it was a gamble. She prayed the servants and lords and ladies of the court would all be sound asleep in their beds, and only a handful of the King's Guard would be located at key points.

She fingered the pouch around her neck.

The first set of guards stood at the bottom of the stairs facing away from them. "Stop," Zenia said in a whisper.

Mariam complied. Zenia pulled her into the shadows, then took a globe from her pouch, copper in color, an inch and a half in diameter. She set it on the top of the stairs, uttered some words in the Ancient Tongue, and gave it a push. Quickly she joined Mariam in the shadows.

The globe rolled over the edge onto the steps below. *Clink! clink! clink!* it went as it descended.

The guards turned and spotted it, then looked at each other with apprehension. They backed away, drawing their swords, as it hit the floor and rolled toward them.

One of them reached out with the tip of his sword and stopped the globe. The surface of the globe sparkled, then cracked open in a puff of blue smoke that swirled around them. Their eyes rolled up in their heads, and they slumped to the ground.

Zenia waited a moment to make sure the noise attracted no attention from anyone else, then whispered, "Move."

She led Mariam down the stairs past the sleeping guards, then let Mariam guide her again. They made their way through the Great Hall toward the flickering dimness of the corridor that led to the guardhouse. Zenia tensed with alertness. She knew there'd be more guards there.

Mariam moved slowly but unwaveringly down the corridor until she neared the entry chamber to the dungeon. Zenia counted two voices speaking from inside. She stopped Mariam with a word and whispered, "Are we going to the dungeon?"

"That's where Tamara is," Mariam said.

"Gwendolyn promised me she'd be kept in a comfortable place."

Mariam stood peering at her without expression.

"Answer me," Zenia whispered, then realized she hadn't asked a question. "Why is Queen Tamara in the dungeon?"

"She kept trying to escape."

Zenia's heart sank at the thought of her queen hidden away in that dank place, but being confined within the walls of the castle keep simplified her plans.

She quickly peeked into the entry chamber. Two guards sat at a table against the wall, rolling dice and slapping coins down. She pulled out another globe.

She glanced again, gauging the distance, then jumped out, flung the globe against the wall where they sat, and leaped back out of sight, hoping they'd be too startled to recognize her.

The crunch of the globe against the wall and the sound of a chair falling over told the tale. Zenia peeked again and found one of them slumped over the table and the other on the floor next to the overturned chair.

The two women crept past them into the dungeon.

The air was dank and musty. Dark stains, green moss, black mold decorated the stone walls. They passed several sealed cell doors. The flames from too few torches attached to the walls gloomily lit the corridors. They came to a place where the corridor T-boned in two directions. Zenia waited to see which way Mariam would go. She went left.

Zenia slid a third copper-colored globe from the pouch around her neck. They passed no cells here. Ahead the sound of gurgling water made her pause. Mariam kept marching forward. "Hold!" she hissed in a sharp whisper.

Zenia crept forward and peered around the next corner. She saw a widened area where a basin was recessed into the wall with a stream of water from the River Sicana spilling into it. A guard seated at his station lolled his head back in sleep. Beyond that, another corner.

Gingerly Zenia approached the basin and laid the bundle of clothes on its edge. The constant stream of water echoed through the hall.

"Wait here," she whispered to Mariam, then crept up to the snoring guard, rolling the globe in her fingers. She took in a deep breath, held it, and lifted the globe to the guard's nose. Using both index fingers and thumbs, she crushed its shell like an egg. The bluish vapor swirled about and whooshed into the guard's nostrils as he inhaled. A shudder ran through his body, then calmed. The snoring became louder.

She blasted the air out of her lungs and panted a couple breaths. She eyed the ring of keys hanging from the wall near him. The vapor induced deep sleep, but it was still only sleep, and the guard could be awakened by a loud noise—like the jangling of keys.

Mariam's body twitched with a contraction, but she made no reaction to the pain beyond a short grunt. A soft moan floated from around the corner.

It must be Tamara, having a contraction the same time Mariam did. Her spell had worked! Tears glistened as she expressed thanks to Mother Goddess.

She reached for the ring of keys and lifted them from the hook as gently as she could. The guard slept through the faint jingling. "Follow me," she hissed at Mariam in a sharp whisper.

She rounded the corner and saw Tamara in a cell behind bars, sitting on a cot and bent over with her hands clutching her belly. Tamara's eyes lifted, wet with tears, and widened. "Zenia! Thank the Goddess," she whispered loudly.

Zenia rushed to the gate and kept trying keys until one of them worked. The stench of the dungeon cell assaulted her. To think her poor queen had to live in these conditions!

She had to force the key to turn the rusty lock. It clacked open louder than Zenia would have wished. Mariam plodded up behind and waited listlessly.

Zenia pulled on the gate and stopped immediately as the creaking echoed through the hall. This will not do! She decided to yank the gate fast and get the noise over with. She shivered at the metallic whine, but it died quickly, and the gate was open wide enough for one person to pass through.

She stopped to listen. The guard's snores continued.

"Walk into the cell," she ordered. Mariam's eyes twitched as her body obeyed. There wasn't much time left. The potion was starting to wear off, and a part of her deep inside tried to rebel.

Zenia squeezed in after Mariam and helped Tamara to her feet. Her belly was huge, and Tamara supported it with both her hands. "Thank the Goddess you're here," she uttered, then buckled over as another contraction hit.

Mariam's body trembled as an identical contraction hit her womb. Her eyes squinted as she grunted.

"We need to hurry," Zenia whispered. "Take your clothes off."

Tamara nodded.

"Take all your clothes off," she repeated to Mariam. The several seconds of delay before she obeyed disturbed her, but obey she did, her eyes dark and locked on Zenia. The gossamer royal nightgown dropped to the dungeon floor, and Mariam stepped out of it.

The two queens stood naked in close proximity to each other. Zenia paused an instant to gaze at both youthful bodies. Tamara was seventeen years of age. Mariam looked the same thanks to Gwendolyn's Illusion spell, even though she was several years older.

It was the first time Zenia had seen the two together. Even though she knew the sorceress Gwendolyn's spell had made Mariam look like the true queen, the resemblance still astonished her. Even down to the same moles on the same places on their bodies that no one but the king or the chambermaid would ever see. The only difference was the dungeon filth on Tamara's body and the disheveled appearance of her hair.

Zenia bent over and scooped some dirt from the floor. Mariam glared at her and gave out an abortive snarl as Zenia smeared the filth over her naked body. She then rubbed her hands in Mariam's hair, mussing it up.

"Put those on," she said to Mariam, pointing to the tattered clothes on the floor Tamara had just removed.

Mariam's teeth grit as her body grudgingly obeyed. She was fighting hard now. Only moments remained before the charm potion would fade and Mariam would cry out in her piercing, shrewish voice. Not even the enchanted vapor would keep the guard asleep then.

"Come, my Queen. I have clothes for you by the water basin."

Tamara nodded, eyes gleaming with unfallen tears of pain.

Zenia grabbed the royal nightgown Mariam had left on the floor and led Tamara out of the cell. The poor queen lumbered with the weight of the baby. Zenia nudged the cell gate closed until the lock clicked, Mariam glaring at her with eyes full of hatred, then the two of them crept around the corner. She hung the keys back on the wall as they passed the guard and headed for the basin.

Zenia soaked Mariam's nightgown in the basin water. Tamara pressed her back against the wall with a contraction and a stifled cry. Mariam let out a moan in the distance. Zenia glanced at the guard in distress as he stirred. She knew they were out of time.

She grabbed the bundle of clothes and pushed Tamara into movement. "Quickly! The Charm spell is dying."

Around the next corner they stopped, and Zenia scrubbed most of the filth from Tamara with the wet nightgown, untangled the royal clothing wrapped in linen, an elegant, casual maternity dress the false queen had often worn when relaxing in the gardens. She helped Tamara into it. "I'm sorry I have to rush you when you're in labor."

"My sweet, sweet Zenia," she said as she struggled into the dress with her enormous belly, "I'm just happy you found me. I never thought I'd see you again."

Mariam cried out inarticulately. It wasn't from any contraction because Tamara had none at the moment. The potion had worn off, but Mariam's power of speech hadn't quite returned. In a moment it would, first slurred, then clearing to normal.

"What is your problem now, bitch?" a male voice growled.

Tamara gazed at Zenia with alarm.

"Go!" Zenia cried in a harsh whisper. She fastened a hook on the dress that Tamara had missed and gathered up the nightgown and the linen fabric. They pressed forward, Tamara moving unnervingly slow.

"Aaaaah-aaahm the queen!" Mariam cried with a slur.

"That again?" the guard scoffed.

The two women hurried out through the entry chamber and back into the corridor. Another dangerous moment approached—getting past the guards at the castle entrance so they could head for the royal stables and flee.

Zenia needed to get Tamara and her infant safely into the care of Eloise, hidden away from King Christian and Gwendolyn. She sent a cryptic message to Eloise a fortnight ago, warning her that she'd be coming. She hoped the message had gotten through.

It wouldn't be easy to hide them. She wasn't quite sure how powerful Gwendolyn was. Vastly more powerful than Zenia, to be sure, because Gwendolyn was a full-fledged sorceress who had studied the Ancient Magic, and Zenia had only been taught basic witch magic. Her advantage was that she'd kept her magic skills secret all these years as a chambermaid. Not even Gwendolyn knew she could cast spells. Zenia had used her powers as sparingly as she could to avoid drawing attention to herself.

They approached the gate to the castle. She could hear the hushed voices of the guards in conversation with each other. She handed the bundle to Tamara. "Hold this, my Queen." Tamara took the bundle just as a contraction hit, and she muffled her cry with it.

A distant sound of commotion came from the direction of the dungeon.

"They're coming!" Tamara whispered.

"On their way to tell Gwendolyn that you've gone into labor." She hoped it was true. She hoped the guard hadn't finally believed Mariam.

Zenia crept up to the gate.

"What do you suppose all that noise is?" one guard said.

"Probably the Royal Lovemaking."

The two guards snickered.

They were both standing outside the gate to her right, but she couldn't see them to gauge the distance. Nor did she have a good angle from inside the gate to be sure to roll the globe close enough to them.

She'd have to let them see her.

She took a deep breath, then walked out into full view.

The guards looked at her. "Chambermaid, what are you doing here?"

She threw the globe at their feet. It burst into a cloud of bluish vapor that engulfed them.

"What by the demons is that?" one of them said before they toppled to the ground.

Zenia helped Tamara across the drawbridge over the moat of water deflected from the River Sicana. The full moon lit the courtyard as they headed to the stables. The buildings along the walls of the courtyard were silent and dark—even the baking house, since the workers wouldn't be there for a few more hours.

Behind them, garbled words drifted from the gatehouse. The castle keep was coming to life at the birth of the queen's baby. Zenia trembled with fear, wondering how soon Gwendolyn would realize it was Mariam, not Tamara, in the dungeon cell. No one but Christian, Gwendolyn, and Zenia knew the switch had ever taken place, but Gwendolyn would see right through her own Illusion spell and know the wrong woman was imprisoned.

Tamara let out an unmuffled cry with another pain. "They're closer together," she moaned.

"I know," Zenia said. "I'm sorry, my Queen, but we have to hurry."

She supported Tamara by the waist and tried to rush her as much as she could, keeping to the shadows of the walls. With this full moon, the guards in the turrets above would easily spot two women crossing the courtyard.

The stables butted up against the wall. Zenia beat on the door of the livery man's quarters. *Wake up!* she cried in her mind.

Finally the door creaked open and the bleary-eyed man growled, "What is it?" His eyes became more alert. "Zenia!" A smile crossed his face. "Eager to-night?"

"This is the night, Hector! Please, we need the horse."

"We?" Hector looked past her and gaped at Tamara. He grabbed Zenia's arm and pulled her close to his face. "You didn't tell me you were bringing the queen. What by the demons is going on?"

"I don't have time to explain right now. Please!"

"Zenia, you have to tell me—"

Tamara cried out, "I command you to prepare a horse for us immediately!"

Hector stared gloomily at the queen. "It's ready now. Zenia told me—" He glanced at Zenia with a scowl. "—she said it would be soon. I've kept one ready every night."

They hurried into the stables, Tamara lumbering in pain.

"Great Gods, she's in labor!" Hector said as he swung the doors open. "What are you doing?"

"Which horse?" Zenia spat.

"Right here." He unfastened the reins and led the animal out.

She looked the horse up and down. "What is this, the worst horse in the stable?"

"Yes! I didn't know the queen would be with you."

"It's old."

"You want me to give you the king's best horse, just to make sure he'd notice right away?"

"I'm sorry. Of course you're right. Thank you for your help."

"Gods, Zenia. Why does the queen need to sneak out in the night on a stolen horse?"

"Not *now*!" Zenia said. "I'll tell you when we meet again."

He harrumphed, then helped the two women mount the horse, Tamara still clutching the bundle that Zenia had given her. "You'd better have the horse back by tomorrow night," he said as he handed the reins to Zenia, then opened the secret door through the courtyard wall used whenever the king wanted to send or receive someone quietly. He led the horse out, then slapped its haunch. The horse jumped and broke into an unenthusiastic gallop.

Tamara's breathing was heavy in Zenia's ear as she clutched tightly to her waist with both arms. When another contraction subsided, Tamara wept, "Oh, Mother Goddess, this hurts!"

Zenia wanted to fall to the ground and beg her forgiveness for putting her through this, even though she knew it was necessary to save her life.

"Zenia," Tamara whispered into her ear, "what did you mean, when you meet him again?"

"Nothing, my Queen," Zenia cried against the wind so she could be heard. "I just said it so we could get out of there."

"How did you get him to give us the horse?"

She pursed her lips grimly, and for the first time in her life did not answer a direct question from her queen.

"Zenia!"

"I...paid him."

Tamara rested the side of her head against her back. Zenia could hear faint sobs coming from her.

"Anything to save you, my Queen," she whispered to herself.

She crossed the bridge over the River Sicana and drove the horse through the quiet city of Luteche, the largest city in the kingdom of Gallea, and into Fenweald Forest on the East Highway. Her destination was her home village in the outskirts of Suedeche where Eloise lived, who had raised her from a girl barely becoming a woman when she was orphaned. It would take all night and part of the day to reach her—if this horse could survive the journey.

Gwendolyn would use all her powers to search for Tamara and her baby, and Zenia knew magic would be the only protection against her. She prayed that the magic of Eloise would be enough to hide mother and child from Gwendolyn's searching eye. She knew her own village witch magic would not be enough to protect them if Gwendolyn found them.

The rush of the air as they fled through the forest and the rush of the wind through the leaves created a steady whoosh in Zenia's ears. The chill of the night bit at her cheeks. A moth fluttered straight for her face and slapped into her forehead. The moon winked steadily through the crowns of the trees. The road was dimly lit, but lit well enough. It was the road home, and she knew it well.

Tamara's cries of pain became regular. Her breathing was harsh and fitful. With many miles left to travel, Tamara shrieked, "It's coming! Stop, Zenia, stop! It's coming!"

"Oh Goddess, no! It's too soon. We're not there yet."

"Zenia, please! The baby...I can feel it...it's coming."

Zenia searched for a clearing until she found one just ahead. She pulled on the reins and slowed the horse, steering it to a tree she could tie it to, then leaped to the ground. The bundle that had been wedged between Tamara's belly and Zenia's back tumbled onto the dirt. With great difficulty, she helped Tamara down.

Tamara bellowed with a contraction. "It's coming!"

"Oh, Goddess, why now?" she murmured. To Tamara, she said, "We need to get your clothes off," and began unfastening the dress. Tamara tried to help, but buckled over with the pain. "I'll do it, my Queen." She worked her clothes off and laid them aside.

"Crouch down. I need to feel for the baby." Zenia reached down, pressed her fingers into Tamara, and felt the scalp. "You're right, it's coming. My sweet Queen, with each pain, squeeze as hard as you can."

Tamara howled and bore down. The contraction passed, and Tamara panted heavily. "It hurts so much."

"It'll be alright." Zenia quickly gathered up some wildflowers and leaves. "If there's anything a village witch knows, it's spells for childbirth."

She held the bits of vegetation in her cupped hands and whispered an incantation, then crushed them between her palms. She took the mulch of grass and petals and rubbed them against Tamara's belly, smearing them on her skin.

Tamara shrieked with another contraction, tears streaming from her eyes and mucus streaming from her nose.

"Doesn't it hurt less?" Zenia said with consternation.

Tamara answered with a wail as she bore down.

"It should be working!" She crouched down for a better view. Already the baby's eyebrows showed beneath the sticky matte of dark hair plastered tight against its scalp. Zenia muttered a breath spell of Sight to monitor the birth.

The dark aura hit her like a blast of icy wind.

She fell back. "Oh, dear Goddess!" she gasped, putting her hands to her mouth. "I know why Gwendolyn wants this baby!"

Tamara let sobs escape as the latest contraction ended. "What?" she spat as if she hadn't heard.

"Oh, my Queen! I couldn't sense it while the baby was inside you, deep inside your life vitality."

"What are you talking about?"

"Your baby—it has some kind of power inside it." She paused to stifle her own sobs that suddenly wanted to escape. How could she say the rest of it to her beloved young queen?

But she had to tell her.

"I'm sorry, my dear, sweet Queen. Your baby has a cursed power within it."

Tamara fixed her gaze on her, a gaze that looked perplexed and horrified and enraged. "What are you saying?"

"That's why Gwendolyn wants this baby."

"This is my baby," Tamara said through squinting eyes. "My sweet, innocent baby. How can you say that?"

"I'm sorry!" Zenia looked about without knowing what she was looking for. Maybe some hint of what to do. Something in the trees or the flowers or the swish of the horse's tail to give her an idea.

Tamara's body clenched with another contraction. Zenia leaned toward her. "Stay away!" Tamara spat. "Don't come near my baby!"

Zenia ignored her and leaned forward to grab the baby's head. It was all the way out but for the chin. The scrunched, blood-stained face looked like any other baby in mid-birth, but she couldn't shake the feeling of dread that seemed to ooze from the birth fluids.

Gently turning the head of the baby as the latest contraction died, Zenia said, "One more push should do it." She didn't say the rest that she was thinking.

This baby had come fast. Fast and easy—hardly any effort at all. Too fast and easy. This baby wanted birthing quickly. It wanted to be out in this world... for what?

Tamara panted without a word, her eyes closed, her hands resting on the ground behind her to support her as she crouched. Sweat streamed down her face and glistened on her bloated breasts.

In the moment of calm, Zenia knew what she had to do. She couldn't let this baby fall into Gwendolyn's hands. She couldn't let this baby fall into *anyone's* hands who might use its power for evil. She couldn't let the baby itself grow up to use its own dark powers.

She couldn't let the baby live.

Tears streamed down her face. It would stab Tamara to the depths of her soul for Zenia to kill her baby. Tamara would hate her forever.

Another contraction began. Tamara's eyes popped open as she squeezed. Zenia turned the baby, and it slid out easily, trailed by the umbilical cord.

A wolf howled in the distance. A violent shiver washed through Zenia. The aura of darkness permeated the air around her. Even the wild beasts could sense the presence of this terrible force!

"It's out!" Tamara cried.

"It's out," Zenia said.

"Where's my baby?" The glare in her eyes was accusing.

What should she do? Her mind spun dizzily. Should she break the infant's neck? Should she hand the newborn babe to its mother to suckle? Should she turn and flee and rid herself of this whole horrifying dilemma?

"Give me my baby!" Tamara rolled forward on her knees and grabbed for it.

Reflexively Zenia pulled the baby away. She knew she could never kill it if she gave it to Tamara. She knew she wasn't ready to kill it. She had no idea what to do.

"I command you to give me my baby!"

Tamara suddenly buckled as another contraction worked on the afterbirth.

Zenia knew this was the moment to do the deed. A quick snap and it would all be over. Except for a brokenhearted queen who would despise her and probably want to kill her in turn.

Zenia looked at the baby, eyes squinted shut, lungs wheezing with its first breaths, glistening with blood and fluid on its skin, thick black hair matted to the scalp.

It was just a baby. A little girl.

Tamara cried out with another pain.

The baby's eyes opened, and Zenia shuddered. They were black, blacker than a moonless night in the darkest forest. Black with a cold stare.

Tears streaming down her face, Zenia wrapped her hand around the baby's skull and prepared to twist. The wolf howled again, causing Zenia to jump.

"Zenia," Tamara wailed, "please don't kill my baby."

"It's cursed," she whimpered.

"It's just a baby."

"Look at it!" Zenia rested the infant in one arm and thrust it forward. "Look at its eyes."

Tamara leaned forward and gazed. A smile crept across her face, then she saw the eyes. She gasped and recoiled, stumbling back onto her haunches. "No, no. Oh Goddess, no."

"I'm sorry, my dear Queen."

"No, not my baby!" Another contraction hit. She cried out.

"We've got to get the caul out," Zenia said. She tugged on the cord with her free hand. Slowly it gave way and the caul popped out.

The baby wailed weakly.

"Zenia, don't kill my baby!"

"I have to!"

"Please! Do something about it."

Zenia wrapped her hand around the skull again. The baby's tongue flicked out as the chilling eyes stared. Like a snake.

"I have to," she whispered, but she couldn't bring herself to twist.

"You're a sorceress. Can't you save my baby?"

"I'm no sorceress! Just a poor village witch."

"Zenia, please." Tamara's eyes pleaded as she leaned back on her arms, looking exhausted.

"I don't know what I can do."

"Please save my baby!"

"I...don't..." She thought hard. Was there any magic she knew that could help? Anything Eloise had taught her?

Tamara panted as her naked body shivered in the breeze. "Can't you draw the evil out?"

Draw the evil out. That reminded her of...something...a day...a terrible day when her stepmother Eloise had performed a miracle.

A young boy, barely two years old, suffering from a ravaging disease that was eating him alive. He had days to live, if that. His parents begged Eloise to save him, but the disease was too powerful—too much for her skills alone. She needed help. She needed an outside power to strengthen her magic, an outside source of purity to seep in and drive the disease out.

The mother instantly fell to her knees. "Take the power of my life and give it to my son."

Eloise pierced her with her gaze. "You will die."

"*Take the power of my life!*" the mother cried. "If my son dies, I will die anyway."

The mother nursed her young son as Eloise slowly let the blood from an artery in her neck. The boy sucked the life and purity from his mother as Eloise murmured powerful incantations and the mother drifted to sleep.

Then with tear-streaked cheeks, Eloise took the boy outside and held him up to the brilliant sky. She solicited the powers of Master Sun to suck the disease out so the purity could fill its place.

The boy lived.

The mother died.

"Maybe..." Zenia whispered in horror.

"What?"

"Maybe there's something I can do."

"What, Zenia? Tell me."

"The baby can suck the power of your life from your teats, and maybe that can purify the dark power in her soul."

"Do it!" Tamara leaned forward and reached for her baby.

"I'll have to cut you."

"I don't care. Give me my baby." Her hands touched her newborn infant for the first time, fingers grasping.

"I'll have to draw blood."

"I don't care. *Give me my baby.*"

"You will die."

Tamara paused with her hands around the baby's waist. "What?"

"I'll have to bleed you to death. Your baby will suck the purity from your life as you die."

Tamara gazed down at her baby. She flinched at the eyes, but her expression softened as she gazed. "Then I die."

"My Queen, I don't even know if it'll work."

"Do it!" Tamara grasped the baby firmly and drew it to her bosom, the umbilical cord still dangling and attached to the caul lying on the ground. "If you kill my baby, I don't want to live anyway."

Zenia nodded, feeling the echo of those words with that mother from the past. "I don't know if I can make the spell work. I saw it heal a disease, not purify a dark power."

But she pulled the dagger from her skirt and gazed at the sheath.

Tamara lay back and rested her baby on her chest. The baby nuzzled and rooted and found the nipple. She began to suck.

"I'm so sorry, my dear Queen," Zenia whispered in her ear. "This will hurt."

"Do it," Tamara said as she let her head fall back to the ground with her eyes closed.

Zenia took a deep breath and unsheathed the dagger. She gently pushed Tamara's head to the side, exposing her neck. She'd have to cut until she found an artery. She wondered if this pain would be worse than the childbirth.

There was nothing to do but cut. Zenia pushed hard as she drew the edge across her queen's milky skin. Tamara cried out, a horrible shriek of pain. Zenia cut hard and deep, wanting to get it over with fast. The rhythmic spurting of blood pulsed out. The red puddle grew quickly.

Her queen would die now.

Zenia at once chanted the incantations she remembered hearing Eloise chant those many years ago. It was a spell of Purifying that she'd never heard Eloise cast before or since. The dire circumstances then must have burned the words into Zenia's mind those many years ago, because she remembered them easily.

Tamara began to sing, a faint lullaby for her daughter. The baby slurped at the nipple, and Tamara's blood spurted from her neck with each heartbeat. Zenia prayed the incantations with all the power in her soul, hoping desperately it would work.

The wolf howled fiercely. It was much closer. She trembled with fear. The last thing they needed right now was a ravenous beast!

She glanced up at the horse. As old and dispirited as it was, it still bucked and neighed at the howl of this wolf.

"Zenia," Tamara whispered, barely audible, "will you protect my daughter?"

"You know I will. I'll love her as I loved you." She flinched as she realized she was already speaking of Tamara in the past tense.

Tamara smiled, her eyes closed, her body trembling with cold. The baby broke her suction hold on the nipple, her mouth drooping open and her eyes closed with sleep.

A last breath rattled from Tamara's body, and no more breaths came after.

A flood of tears tried to burst from Zenia's eyes, but she fought them back. There was too much to do. She grabbed the baby and used the dagger to saw the umbilical cord away. It was probably the largest stump ever left on a baby, but that didn't matter.

She lifted the baby and looked at the eyes. They were closed, and the face scowled. With the power from her Sight spell, she could feel the struggle going on inside between the purity of Tamara's sacrificed life and the dark power the baby was born with.

Would it work? The purity the baby had suckled from her mother fought to gain control over the innocent creature. Zenia saw nothing with her natural eyes, but she could sense the struggle almost as if it were a thunderstorm of lightning and darkness.

She knew she wasn't finished. The struggle was mighty and the outcome uncertain as long as the corruption remained inside the infant. Zenia needed an outside power to draw the darkness away, leaving the purity to fill the void, as Eloise had done before.

The horse jumped and whinnied at a rustling in the trees. Zenia swung around just as the wolf broke into view, growling and saliva dripping. It was monstrous!

"By the Goddess, not now!" she cried. "I won't let my queen die in vain!"

She held the baby up in full view of the wolf and shouted protective spells against wild beasts. The great struggle inside the infant washed over everything. The wind seemed to rage at its power. The trees bowed and creaked at its tingling. The wolf howled viciously and growled as it paced back and forth without coming nearer. Its hairs prickled, standing up tall and making the animal look even more monstrous. Its eyes burned with an unholy red glow.

The baby moaned—an unearthly moan—and croaked—an unearthly croak. Zenia needed to purge the corruption. She had no idea what would happen if she left it inside.

This wolf had to go!

Zenia advanced on the animal, calling out spells, holding the baby in front of her as the child emanated prickling magic.

The wolf arched up, leaped up as if it wanted to pounce, but was held back almost as if an invisible wall were between them. With one final howl, it turned and plunged into the trees.

Zenia gaped with amazement at the fleeing creature, but she had to act fast. Keeping the baby in front of her, she searched around for a power to call upon. The trees? The air? The sky?

The moon. She looked up at the shining moon, eerie with its cool light and full face. The moon had been instrumental in synchronizing the pregnancies of the two women. Its expression grinned at her, inviting her, beckoning her.

Zenia would call on the power of Mistress Moon.

She held the infant girl up to the sky. "Great Mistress Moon!" she called in the Ancient Tongue over the rushing wind. "Suck the corruption from this child as she has sucked purity from her mother's breast. Take that purity and turn her dark magic into a white magic, a power for good in this world."

The wind around her swirled, creating a vortex. Foul smoke seemed to ooze from every pore of the baby. At the same time a whirlwind of white mist funneled down from the lunar face, stretching in an ethereal finger of brilliance to earth. The dark vortex reached up and the two swirls touched. Crackling sparkles filled the sky as the air thundered with a vengeance.

The baby shuddered. The tree crowns danced as if a storm raged. The horse bucked and neighed in consternation against its reins. The air filled with fine, black particles that, one by one, shimmered into brightness. The white funnel of lunar mist flowed into the clearing and surrounded the two females. The baby, still held high into the air, seemed to breathe it into her nostrils. The pores all over her naked body seemed to suck it from the sky. As if a demon had given up the ghost in one great gnashing cry, the dark aura flew out in all directions and dissipated into the night.

The chill in Zenia's soul evaporated as a soothing warmth rushed through her body. The baby's head turned toward the sky. Her hair—once dark and matted—was dry and flowing in the wind and white blonde. Zenia lowered the child and gazed into her face.

The eyes—those chilling black eyes—now peered with a silvery blue luster. A burning aura surrounded the child and reached up in a column to touch the moon. An aura of purity warming Zenia's soul.

Tears burst from her eyes. It worked! Tamara had not sacrificed her life in vain. Her infant had been cleansed of the evil power. In its place glimmered a white power astonishing to Zenia.

She knelt before Tamara's body and held the infant before the lifeless eyes. "My dear, sweet, beloved Queen. See how your daughter shines now."

She laid the baby on Tamara's naked breasts. "My little girl, see how your mother lies peacefully. She gave everything to save you. Remember your mother. Remember her sacrifice. Oh little princess, remember your mother Tamara forever."

The baby cooed as she lay on her mother's breasts. Her eyes shone in the moonlight—the Mistress Moon that had purified her. Zenia left the child an instant to grab Tamara's dress still lying on the ground. She wrapped the baby in it—a queen's dress for the royal offspring.

This child, this princess, this vessel of brilliant power was someone Zenia had to protect at all costs. In fact she had delayed too long. The birth of the child, the death of Tamara, the appearance of the wolf, and the spectacular purification from Mistress Moon had made her forget the danger from the castle in Luteche. It couldn't be far behind! She and the new princess must leave at once.

She paused for an instant—but only an instant—for her grief at the loss of her queen and the appalling way she had to leave her nude body lying in the woods. But there was nothing she could do. If she tried to minister to the body, Tamara's death could easily become meaningless if members of the King's Guard caught up with them.

She hoped travelers would find the body. How that would shake things up in the kingdom—the queen's nude body lying abandoned in a forest!

But more likely the monstrous wolf would return and devour her.

Tears blinding her as she worked, Zenia laid the linen cloth over Tamara, covering as much as she could, then uttered what breath spells of Protection she could think of. She untied the spooked horse and struggled into the saddle with the baby in one arm. Quickly she dug her heels into its shanks and aimed it down the road. With only one hand on the reins and one hand clutching the baby, she dared not gallop too fast.

As she rode in the ghostly moonlight, letting her tears flow freely now, she kept glancing down at the new princess. "You need a name, little one."

Zenia looked at the sky, at the baby's aura rising up to Mistress Moon, and knew this child would be forever linked to the heavens.

"There's only one name for you, my sweet girl," she murmured as she gazed at the silvery eyes. "Celeste."

Chapter 2

Gwendolyn

The knock on the door startled Gwendolyn awake. It took her an instant to clear the cobwebs from her mind. The knock came again—the code knock from her personal servant Bernard.

"Enter!"

The door flung open and Bernard burst in. "The birth! It started."

She sat up with a jerk. "Tamara?"

"Yes."

Great Gods, it was happening at last! She paused to catch her breath, her heart churning with emotions. "Send the midwife at once."

"She's already there, Mistress."

She swung her legs over the side of the bed, clutching the bedclothes against her body. "The moment the birth is finished, clean the baby up and bring it to me." She took a deep breath of regret. "And slay the mother—discreetly."

Bernard nodded. Gwendolyn waited until the man had closed the door behind him, then jumped out of bed and changed into her clothes.

It seemed unreal. The birth of Tamara's child had finally come. At last Gwendolyn would hold it in her arms, feel its naked power unsmothered by Tamara's own life vitality. At last she'd become the most powerful sorceress in the continent of Cueldea.

And for the rest of her life bear the burden of guilt for doing it.

After she slid her shoes on, she leaned back in the chair and tried to gather her composure, calming the conflicting emotions in her soul.

Gwendolyn had tried to treat Tamara well, keeping her in a comfortable cottage away from the city of Luteche. That girl loved to run away whenever things didn't go her way! In the end, the isolated dungeon cell was the only thing Gwendolyn was confident could hold her.

Yet if she didn't have a tendency to flee, she never would have fled that one night and returned pregnant, and the infant about to put great power into Gwendolyn's possession would have never existed.

Who could the father be? She tried to find him using her Extended Sight spell to trace Tamara's movements the night she fled. But something had always confused the spell long before she could find him.

This was no ordinary father to sire such a child. The thought that a man might wield powerful magic disturbed her. What man in Cueldea had ever studied magic? Male wizards were a thing of the South in the continent of Ifran. In the North, women controlled the magic—village witches, sorceresses—and that's how Gwendolyn liked it. That's how the Seven Sisters liked it. Men were wild, violent, aggressive. The thought of magic in the hands of men was horrifying. It was bad enough that the lands south across the Sea of Az were dominated by wizards bearing penises.

She shuddered herself out of her meditations. There were preparations to make. She gathered up the materials she'd need to cast the spell—the herbs, the weeds, the insects, the minerals, the oil, and most important, the Ancient scroll. She'd studied that scroll dozens of times since she discovered Tamara's extraordinary baby, committing its words to memory. But she wasn't taking any chances with the most critical enchantment of her life. She would read the spell word-for-word as she burned the materials and released the vitality locked within the infant.

She spoke a breath spell to ignite a candle sitting nearby, arranged the materials carefully in the bowl on her worktable, and drenched them with the oil. She rolled the scroll out on the table where she could read it and weighted down its corners with stones. Then she waited for the baby that would empower all her plans.

She wished the price wasn't so high. To acquire the power of the newborn infant, she'd have to slice the child open and drink its blood as it died, mingling its magical potency with her own. When she first realized she'd have to do that, it tore at her. Never would she have imagined herself doing such a thing—not even to become the most powerful sorceress in the land—if the fate of the nations of Cueldea didn't depend on it.

But the domination of the Seven Sisters needed to come to an end. Their bickering and short-sightedness in the face of threats from the South and from the East threatened the very survival of them all. She'd witnessed the looming dangers in her visions. It forced her to choose this ghastly solution. She knew she must become powerful at any cost to overthrow the Seven Sisters and lead all of Cueldea to victory against the threats.

She'd agonized over this decision every day since she discovered the unborn infant. She knew at once she could use the Ancient scroll to make that power her own. It was a gift the Great Gods had led her to that fateful day she found the hiding place behind the Falls of Eircana. A gift to accomplish this very mission, and she dared not squander the opportunity the Gods had given her.

But the baby had to die in the process. And Gwendolyn anguished over that.

Tamara, that foolish girl, had to die too. She'd never forgive such an atrocity, and she'd never give up opposing Gwendolyn. There was only one way to guarantee she'd never interfere.

The power of the Ancient Magic exacted a heavy price—every sorceress knew that. Gwendolyn was willing to pay that price and let it weigh on her soul for a lifetime.

The knock came again. She commanded her servant to enter. Bernard came in, an infant boy in his arms. She rose from her chair to accept it. "Is Tamara dead?"

He hesitated, still holding the baby, his face pale. "The woman in the dungeon is dead."

Gwendolyn scowled. "What does that mean?" She looked at the naked baby lying on a blanket. "Give me that."

Bernard placed it in her arms. Gwendolyn gazed at the child, at the wispy brown hair and the greyish blue eyes. The baby let out a newborn wail. It was a small infant with no power in its voice. Like it had been born too soon.

"What is this?" she snarled. "This child is weak and sickly." She spoke the words of the Sight spell and peered at it. There was no aura of power. "This is *not* Tamara's baby." She thrust the child back into the servant's arms. "What's going on?"

Bernard's eyes shone with fear.

"Out of my way!" She shoved him aside and marched out the door. "Wake the king," she called behind her, "and send guards to the queen's chambers."

Bernard scampered away as Gwendolyn rushed through the castle to the dungeon. As she neared Tamara's cell, the guard stationed there and two other guards, Ismael and Audric, parted as she entered. The midwife cowered in the corner, staring at the body lying in the straw and the filth.

It was Mariam.

But not Mariam in the guise of Tamara. It was the real Mariam without the Illusion spell—with auburn hair and brown eyes. And a gaping wound with entrails bulging out where a sword had ripped across her belly.

Gwendolyn stared with horror. "What happened here?"

The dungeon guard jumped forward. "The prisoner gave birth, and we slew her as you ordered. Your servant took the baby and brought it to you." He gestured toward the body. "When she died, she turned into this woman." He gazed at her with nervous anticipation. "An illusion...like you told us."

Gwendolyn stared grimly at the body. How by all the Great Gods did Mariam end up in this cell? How did she give birth a full month early? Where was Tamara?

Who was responsible for this outrage?

"Yes," Gwendolyn said grimly, composing herself, "an illusion, like I told you." She gazed at the midwife, trembling in the corner in shock. Gwendolyn walked to her and gently lifted her to her feet. "What's your name, child?"

"Lezelle," she said almost in a whisper. She didn't take her eyes off the body.

Gwendolyn nudged her chin to make her look up. "Listen to me, Lezelle. I'm sorry you had to see this." She turned to the others. "All of you, listen to me. This prisoner was sent by our enemy King Gunther to infiltrate us. His sorceress Deirdre enchanted her to look like Queen Tamara."

She peered down at Mariam, trying to hide the emotions seething inside. "But I discovered the deception, and that's why King Christian threw her in this cell. She'd have been executed immediately, but he let the spy live long enough to give birth. The child is innocent—we let it survive. But the mother received the execution she deserved."

Gwendolyn led the midwife to Audric. "Take her to her quarters and make sure she gets some rest."

He nodded and placed his arm around the young woman, leading her away. As Gwendolyn watch them disappear around the corner, she thought hard.

Will that story be enough to hide what really happened? Or should she kill the midwife and the guards? She would do it without hesitation if she needed to—no price was too great to fulfill her plans—but she hated any more blood on her hands. And Ismael and Audric had been the most loyal to her among the King's Guard.

Her greatest concern was accounting for Mariam's son and a missing queen. She'd have to tell everyone that the queen died in a childbirth that came too early. A simple enough story, but the coincidence was troubling—the queen gives birth and dies at the same time a prisoner posing as the queen gives birth and dies. Would it be enough coincidence to raise suspicion? The only ones who knew about the birth and death in the dungeon cell were the ones who witnessed it.

On the other hand, adding the sudden disappearance of the midwife and the guards would raise even more suspicion.

No! No more lives than necessary. If they caused problems, she could always deal with them later.

Slapping footsteps echoed from behind, and young King Christian dashed into view, barefoot and partly dressed. With wide, horrified eyes, he gaped at the slashed body of his lover. "Oh, Gods!" He took running steps toward her, but Gwendolyn stopped him.

"You are dismissed," Gwendolyn barked at the guards. "Go!"

The two guards disappeared, leaving the sorceress and the king alone.

"Are you out of your mind?" she hissed at him. "What are you doing down here?"

"She's dead!" He rushed forward and knelt down before her, eyes watering as he lifted her head into his lap. "How can she be dead?"

"The king does not run into the dungeon to weep over the death of a spy! Are you trying to expose us?"

"You promised me she'd be my queen for life. The mother of my heir."

"Your son lives."

He looked at her with hard eyes. "Where is he?"

"Bernard has him."

He kissed Mariam gently on the lips and lowered her head to the floor . Standing up, he gazed down at her. "Why is she dead in the dungeon?"

"I don't know what happened. Someone put her there and helped Tamara escape."

Christian grabbed her arm. "Zenia. She's not in her chamber."

"Zenia?" Her mind raced. What could that harmless old chambermaid do?

"Sighurd tells me there were guards found asleep at their posts. Six of them."

"Six?" She peered at Mariam's body, peered about the cell. Something very strange was going on here. "Take me to those guards."

The six detained guards were surrounded by three others, including the Captain of the King's Guard, Sighurd.

"We found these lying next to them." Sighurd pointed at a table where metallic objects lay.

Gwendolyn bent over and studied them. They were fragile shells of copper alloy, broken into pieces like eggshells. The kind witches and sorceresses used to deliver vapors. She picked a shard up and sniffed.

Sleep vapor.

Gwendolyn cried out in a rage, startling the rest of them. Someone had recruited Zenia and armed her with enchanted aids. Zenia had switched Mariam and Tamara and escaped with the true queen, just as Tamara was ripe and ready to give birth.

"I'll have these men duly punished," Sighurd said.

"It wasn't their fault," Gwendolyn said and walked away.

Christian ran up to her. "What's going on?"

"Zenia did this—with the help of some enchanter." She peered at Christian with a scowl. "We have to find her immediately. Call your best guards. I'm going after her."

"*We're* going after her!"

"You have a new son, an heir, with no parent but you. Stay and protect him!"

Christian glared at her, then marched off while Gwendolyn rushed back to her chambers. As she pulled out her riding clothes, she uttered the words to refresh her spell of Sight. She wondered if she should cast the Extended Sight, but decided she couldn't spare the time. Each minute she delayed, Zenia fled further away. She'd have to make do with breath spells.

She directed the focus of her Sight out into the keep and courtyard of the castle, looking for any clue. Immediately she found the shimmering magical residue of the vapor each place where Zenia had used it.

She focused on the stables, assuming that's how Zenia would flee. She searched within it and counted animals. A horse was missing. She'd have to speak to the livery man about that.

She made a quick perusal of Luteche and saw nothing, but she couldn't imagine Zenia would linger so near anyway. She'd flee as far as she could. She'd flee to whoever helped them escape.

Who would want to help them? The obvious choice was Tamara's father, Duke Geoffrey of Suedeche—*if* he'd learned what Gwendolyn had done to Tamara.

And who could have told him about Tamara? There were only three people who knew. Herself, King Christian—and Zenia.

She understood now what happened. Zenia somehow got the information to Geoffrey, and he planned the escape with the assistance of a witch in Suedeche. Zenia and Tamara would flee to Suedeche to return his daughter to him.

Curse that chambermaid! Gwendolyn had been careless with Zenia. She seemed a meek, simpleminded servant. Now Gwendolyn realized it had all been an act.

Fully dressed, Gwendolyn hurried out to the stables. She found Sighurd and three of his guards ready to accompany her. The livery man stood next to Gwendolyn's horse, reins in hand. Hector was his name. She mounted, then bent down to take the reins. "I know you helped them escape," she whispered into his ear.

Hector blanched.

"Captain, we ride east," she ordered and kicked her horse into a gallop. They left through the outer gate, crossed the bridge over the river, and galloped away on the East Highway. Sighurd rode abreast of her with his men in tow.

They plunged into the thick forest. The full moon lit the way. The rhythmic bouncing made it difficult to focus her Sight, but she pushed her senses into the dark ahead, searching. She only needed to find the distinct, dark aura of the infant, unmistakable in its signature. Even inside Tamara's womb, shielded by Tamara's life force, Gwendolyn could detect the aura with her Sight spell if she concentrated. It was subtle, but she knew what to look for. And Tamara was ripe—that baby wouldn't stay inside much longer. Once outside, its dark aura would be a beacon to her.

She recoiled as her Sight suddenly came upon a dark aura more chilling and powerful than an unborn baby could possibly emit. It was of a kind she'd never seen before. Whatever fell creature it emanated from seemed agitated. It moved in a wide arc, often doubling back and doubling back again. Its aura rippled with emotion.

"Captain," she shouted over the rushing wind, "something foreboding lies ahead of us. Warn your men."

Sighurd turned his head back and cried warnings and orders, then said to her,

"Can you protect us?"

"I didn't prepare any potent spells," she replied. "We're only supposed to be chasing two women. I'll do what I can." She spoke the most powerful Warding and Protection breath spells she knew and enveloped everyone within them. She had no confidence they'd work if the thing attacked. Perhaps the spells would discourage it from approaching them.

They rode for many miles, Gwendolyn peering ahead with her Sight for any sign of the two women and for the threatening dark aura. It was off to the south in the forest, continuing its agitated pacing.

Ahead a small clearing shimmered with the residue of powerful magic. "Halt!" Gwendolyn cried as she reigned her horse to a stop.

"Halt!" Sighurd repeated, and the group bunched up behind him.

"What is that?" Gwendolyn said as she focused hard on the clearing with her Sight.

"I don't see anything," Sighurd said.

"There's a clearing ahead. Something happened in it." She rode forward, slowly and cautiously.

"There's something on the ground," Sighurd said as the clearing came into view. He led his men toward it.

Gwendolyn studied it with her Sight. The object lay within the shimmering of spent magic, strong magic. It was a body.

She urged her horse ahead and dismounted. Sighurd and his men spread out within the clearing on horseback. She crept to the body and crouched. It was covered with a linen fabric drenched with a large stain of blood. She pulled the fabric down to look at the face.

It was Tamara.

"Sighurd!" she cried as she covered the face.

He dismounted and approached.

Quietly she said, "Keep your men away."

"Who is it?"

She pulled the linen back again. Sighurd gasped. He straightened up and ordered, "Guard the perimeter!"

His men took positions at the edges of the clearing, facing away from them.

Gwendolyn examined the body. A deep gash had been cut into her neck. An enormous puddle of blood wet the ground around her. Near the puddle lay a dagger. She picked it up and examined it. Nothing special about it. The kind of weapon commoners would have.

Gwendolyn lifted the fabric higher. Tamara's flaccid belly, empty of the child, was stained with the smearings of herbs—an incantation for birth pains. The dead eyes stared into the sky. The moon reflected in them.

Gwendolyn studied the body with her Sight. The pale shimmering of Protection spells and some other enchantment encompassed it. Weak village magic, strong enough to ward off small scavengers. Maybe enough to keep a larger predator from noticing the body at a distance.

The spells would do nothing against whatever creature emanated that black aura. She swept her Sight out and found it hovering in the distance—a smaller distance than Gwendolyn felt comfortable with.

None of this made sense. All the spells Zenia had cast were nothing more than the conjurings of a village witch. All the spells but one.

That lingering residue of magic came from no witch's spell. That was a power at the level of a sorceress. If Duke Geoffrey *was* helping her, he must have recruited greater assistance than that of a village witch.

Gwendolyn stood and gazed about at the shimmering, trying to identify the spell. She regretted not casting the Extended Sight spell. But how could she have anticipated these circumstances?

"Mistress," Sighurd called, "over here."

He was bent over something lying on the ground. She approached, and her heart leaped into her throat when she saw what it was.

The caul and cord.

That caul, nine months nourishing and protecting Tamara's extraordinary child, would have powers beyond a normal caul. The intensity of the spells she could cast with it!

She chopped off the umbilical cord with the dagger and tossed it away. Carefully she sliced out a piece of the caul, an inch wide and two inches long. Handing the rest of the caul to Sighurd, she said, "Stow that away somewhere safe."

He held it between two fingers with a disgusted grimace.

Gwendolyn brought the slice of caul close to her mouth, cupping it with both hands. She spoke an incantation over it. The slice burst into a blue flame, almost singeing her face. The flame devoured the slice of caul and died quickly, barely warming her palms.

Gwendolyn's Sight sharpened and reached out. Immediately the residual shimmering brightened, a healthy glow throughout the clearing reaching up in a column to the sky.

No, not to the sky. To the moon! Someone had called down power from Mistress Moon.

The black aura blasted her from behind, twisting and roiling in its corruption. She tasted a craving for blood, a lust for the kill, rushing toward them.

"Captain, the caul—fast! Give it back to me!"

"What?" He fumbled around in his saddle bag where he had just secured it.

"Hurry!" She turned to the other soldiers. "From the south!"

The men swung their horses around as Sighurd handed her the caul. She stabbed it with the knife to slice another piece off just as a huge creature leaped from the trees onto the nearest mounted guard.

It was a wolf. An enormous, fiendish wolf with glowing red eyes.

The Beast of legends long past!

The guard's horse reared up, whinnying in terror, throwing the guard and the wolf to the ground. The Beast bit deep into the man's shoulder.

"Curse all the Gods!" Gwendolyn cried and held the entire caul up, the dagger still protruding from it. She chanted a Protection spell as fast as she could, one imbued with Purification. The caul exploded with sparks that shot out in all directions. The dagger clattered to the ground. The treetops thrashed with the force of the explosion, and the air crackled with the power of it.

The Beast shrieked and jumped back. Wolven eyes blazed with red fury, and the creature leaped back and forth, yelping and howling unearthly noises that chilled Gwendolyn's soul. The wounded guard cried out in anguish as he lay there.

The rage, the fear, the pain in those burning feral eyes! The Purification in Gwendolyn's spell had to be causing the creature torment. It pranced back and forth with frustration. She knew it wanted to attack them—now more than ever—but the Protection and the Purification in the spell kept it at bay with a massive energy fueled by the power from an entire extraordinary caul.

She cursed the foolishness of the Gods that forced her to use up the entire caul with one spell. It would last for days. But in her haste, she'd instinctively tied the spell to their surroundings. If they tried to move, they'd leave its protective sphere, and the Beast would be upon them in an instant. If she'd cast it upon herself, its protective orb would have traveled with her.

There was no breath spell Gwendolyn could cast that would protect them from this enraged creature. She looked around for anything she could use and remembered the umbilical cord lying tens of feet away like a dead snake. Its essence contained a weaker power than the caul, but it was still a power that could protect them for an hour, maybe two. Enough to get away.

But that would only do them good if the Beast didn't follow them. She was sure it would.

She had to force the Beast away, overpower it to the point where it didn't *want* to stay near. The umbilical cord might have enough strength for that.

She ran for the cord. The guards stood frozen with horror, gaping at the wolf and their wounded comrade lying writhing on the ground.

Gwendolyn approached the Beast, holding the ends of the cord and pulling the slack in the middle taut. As she neared the edge of the protective sphere glowing in the sensitivity of her Sight, she held the cord up for the Beast to see. The creature thrashed about with bared teeth, growling furiously, saliva streaming from between its fangs.

Gwendolyn spoke the words of a Warding spell, slowly and deliberately, fastening her gaze on the Beast. The cord erupted in a cloud of bluish vapor that flowed swiftly toward the Beast and surrounded it.

The Beast reared up with a bellow, danced as if on fire, and plunged yelping into the woods.

"We have to hurry," Gwendolyn said to Sighurd. "That won't keep the Beast away more than half an hour, and we've got to be far away by then."

"What about Hereward?" he said, gesturing toward the wounded man.

"It's a full moon," another guard said. "Won't he be changing any moment?"

Gwendolyn sighed at their superstitions. "Don't believe the folk stories. It takes months for the corruption to seep in enough to cause the Change, and years for a child, since a child is more innocent."

She gathered up some flowers and weeds and knelt down beside Hereward. "That was the Beast that wounded you," she said softly so no one else could hear. "I can heal you, but you've been corrupted. You have several months of normal life, then the Change will begin."

The man moaned, trembling, and his eyes glistened with fear. "Is there no spell that can save me?"

"I know of no spell that can purify this corruption. It's from an ancient..."

Realization hit her. She gazed up at the shimmering residue, at the column that rose to the moon. She stood and walked around, examining it.

It was a spell of Purification, invoking the enormous power of Mistress Moon. She looked at Tamara's body, at the pool of blood soaking the corner of the linen. With her Sight she examined the gash in the neck, cut deep to hit an artery.

She knew what had happened. This was not unlike her own powerful spell she planned to use on the infant. A baby born filled with potent dark power. The gash to bleed the mother as the baby suckled. The vitality of the mother seeping into the small body as she died. A supplication to Mistress Moon to purify the child from its Death Magic, turning it into a shining Life Magic.

Gwendolyn swept her powerful Sight down the highway to the east. There it was, burning brightly in the dark night, reaching to the moon. The aura of the child of Tamara, galloping toward Suedeche and the realm of Duke Geoffrey.

But that couldn't be their final destination. Geoffrey's duchy had only witches. It would be no sanctuary, and he and Zenia knew it. He had no sorceress in his employ.

Or did he?

Further down the highway, past the borders of Suedeche, was Scaendelreic, the realm of King Gunther. The abode of the sorceress Deirdre, one of the Seven Sisters.

Yes, everything was clear now. Geoffrey must have paid handsomely for their assistance.

She looked again at the residue surrounding her. Could this spell be powerful enough to purify the corruption of the Beast? She had no idea. That curse came from an ancient source, more ancient than the Ancient Magic of the original Seven Sisters.

She knelt back down and placed a hand on Hereward's cheek. "When the Change begins, we cannot let you roam free. You'll have to be destroyed. I'm sorry."

Tears slipped from the corners of his eyes and slid down his temples.

"If we must destroy you, I promise it'll be quick and painless. But you have several good months of life ahead of you, and for that I'll heal you now. But Hereward." She leaned forward to place her mouth near his ear to whisper. "If you flee so we can't destroy you, I'll track you down and give you a horrible death. That I promise. One Beast on the loose is too much already." She straightened back up and said, "Do you understand?"

The man closed his eyes, spilling more tears, and nodded.

Quickly Gwendolyn spoke the incantation over the herbs in her hand. They burst into flame that quickly consumed them. He howled in pain. But the edges of the torn flesh slowly grew together and knitted into a wicked scar.

Gwendolyn stood. "Help him onto his horse." The other two guards rushed over to assist him. "There'll be pain for several hours, and you'll be exhausted, but you'll live—with no more harm than a ghastly scar that you can impress the whores with. For a few more months."

She turned to Sighurd. "Captain, we have a traitor to pursue. We've already wasted too much time."

"That was the Beast, wasn't it?" he said harshly.

"We need to go."

"I thought the Beast was an old folk tale. Why now, centuries later, does it return?"

"I wish I knew. *Now*, Sighurd, before it returns to *us*!"

"What about the queen's body?"

She looked at the blood-soaked body-shaped linen, pale in the moonlight. "Don't worry. That is the most protected body in the history of humanity." She added bitterly, "I used up an entire caul to cast that spell."

They mounted their horses and galloped down the highway.

Gwendolyn kept a sharp eye on the bright aura ahead. The answer to tonight's events was obvious. It had to be Deirdre, King Gunther's sorceress. Who else would have reason to help with a mission against King Christian and Gwendolyn? Maybe Geoffrey hadn't had to pay one dirty copper coin for Deirdre's help. Maybe Gunther and Deirdre were delighted to reignite the war.

Zenia informed Geoffrey, and Geoffrey felt betrayed by his ally. He recruited Gunther and Deirdre to assist him against Gallea. Deirdre would be watching with her powers and see what the baby was. She'd want it for herself.

Great Gods, this was serious! This wasn't about a village witch and a traitorous chambermaid backed by a duke. This was a battle with Deirdre herself—perhaps with all the Seven Sisters, who never sanctioned Gwendolyn's rise as a sorceress. A battle Gwendolyn was not yet ready to wage.

Zenia had to be heading to Deirdre right now for sanctuary, where the child would be safe from Gwendolyn, but at the mercy of that sorceress. Did that fool of a chambermaid think the child would be any safer with her?

Zenia *must* be captured before she crossed the border into Suedeche.

Gwendolyn studied the aura with her Sight and tried to estimate its location. She and Sighurd's guards rode the finest horses in the kingdom of Gallea, while Zenia rode with a baby in her arms. Yes, they should be able to catch up with her before she reached Suedeche—certainly well before she reached Scaendelreic. She could still thwart Deirdre's attempt.

Suddenly the baby's aura bulged until a second aura broke off. Another aura of brilliance, identical to the first, reached up to the moon.

What in the name of the Gods had happened? There couldn't be two auras like that one. One of them had to be an illusion. But which?

The two auras moved in different directions. One of them charged north into Fenweald Forest, the other continued on the highway to Suedeche. Snarling, Gwendolyn shouted to Sighurd, "We must hurry!"

The pursuers spurred their horses and thundered down the highway.

Gwendolyn tried with all her power to see a distinction between the two auras, to determine which one was real and which illusion. She hoped the closer she got, the better she could distinguish them.

But the two auras remained identical. It was as if they were split in two from the original.

This had to be another of Deirdre's spells. Gods curse her, she had an armament! She might be able to split an aura, but she couldn't split the baby. There had to be a way to tell which aura remained with the child.

After much fierce riding, the aura that was on the highway stopped, somewhere within the borders of Suedeche. The other one kept moving deeper into the forest. What could that mean?

Soon she and the guards would reach the point where the first aura veered off. She had to make a decision fast. If she chose wrong, the baby would be lost to her and in the clutches of Deirdre.

The aura in Suedeche gathered in on itself and vanished.

Gwendolyn gaped. An aura like that couldn't just disappear! That one had to be the illusion.

She held her hand up and slowed down. The guards responded. She studied the edge of the forest as she rode until she spotted a deer trail.

"This way!" she cried to the men.

They plunged into the trees.

Chapter 3

Eloise

The slow pace infuriated Zenia. She felt the skin crawl on the back of her neck as she anticipated King Christian's guards galloping up behind her at any moment. She considered kicking the horse into top speed, and if she fatally dropped Celeste as a result, that would be better than letting her fall into the hands of Gwendolyn. The baby's power may have been transformed from evil to pure, but it was still power, and who knew what Gwendolyn would do with it?

But she couldn't let that happen. She promised Tamara she'd protect her child. So she rode on at a slower gallop and let her skin crawl.

If the worst happened and the guards caught up with her, she could always twist that tiny neck after all. It would be a form of protection—protecting Celeste from whatever fate Gwendolyn had planned for her. If Gwendolyn got hold of Celeste, she could do anything she wanted with her. No one in the kingdom of Gallea knew Celeste existed.

Even as she thought it, she knew she could never do it. They *had* to make it to Eloise. She began praying to Mother Goddess to protect them until they arrived.

There were still many miles to the tiny village of Vilnetal in Suedeche where Eloise's cottage was. Zenia wondered how soon the sun would rise. There was no sign of dawn yet.

As she rode, she wondered, where had Celeste's power come from? She couldn't imagine someone cursing her. Who would have such power? Certainly not a sorceress, otherwise Gwendolyn wouldn't need the baby. Zenia knew of no mortal being with greater power than a sorceress.

Did a God curse her? Never had Zenia known the Great Gods to be so vindictive. A demon from the netherworld? No tale ever claimed such power for demons. Had Celeste inherited it from a parent? It certainly hadn't come from Tamara. But the story Tamara told of the father, the unnamed woodsman she met when she fled, never indicated he was any different than anyone else.

It was the night Tamara discovered that Christian had a mistress. Tamara and Christian had been betrothed to seal the alliance between his father King Guillaume and her father Duke Geoffrey. But after their wedding night, Christian never loved her as a husband again—and that one time resulted in no baby. Before long, Tamara found out why he ignored her when she discovered him in the throes of passion with Mariam, a servant girl, right there in his bed.

Tamara, young and distraught and humiliated, fled into the forest on horseback in the night, ignoring the dangers. She rode for hours before she dismounted and collapsed onto the ground from exhaustion.

Early the next morning, a woodsman out hunting found her sleeping. He took her in and cared for her, cleansing her, feeding her, letting her sleep on his bed covered with the luxurious pelt of a bear. She remembered what he fed her—rabbit stew with carrots and green beans and mushrooms.

"What are you running from?" he asked her, but when she hesitated to answer, he said, "You don't have to tell me."

She never asked him his name. She didn't want to know. It was safer for him.

But he asked her name, and didn't seem to react when she uttered the name of the queen. Did this forest hermit even know who the queen was?

She didn't know what he thought, and she didn't want to know. All she cared about was that he showed her compassion and kindness throughout the day, much more than her husband had ever shown. By evening, she thought she was falling in love with him.

She wasn't quite sure how, but her nightgown slipped away. Her back was on the bed, her skin caressed by the fur of the pelt. On her wedding night there was mostly pain, but this time her whole body exploded with sensations that made her cry out.

When she awoke, the woodsman was outside swinging an axe and splitting chunks of log. "You need to go back now," he said when he saw her.

The words shocked her. She realized she never wanted to leave him.

"You're a lady, and a lady can't just disappear into the woods without someone coming to find her."

He was right. Being alone in the forest with the queen would endanger him.

He put her on her horse. "The East Highway is that way." They locked gazes for a moment, then he whispered, "Goodbye," and slapped the horse's haunch.

She rode until she reached the highway where the King's Guard eventually found her.

Tamara told the story to Zenia with a gleam in her eye, almost worshipfully. But there was nothing in it that indicated something special about the woodsman. Just a lone hermit carving out an existence in the forest.

So where did Celeste's power come from?

The horse tired and slowed down. Zenia wasn't sure what to do. Stopping was out of the question. Driving it until it collapsed no better. Traveling at a slower pace would only help the King's Guard catch up to them.

There were still so many miles to travel!

A faint blue began to color the sky near the horizon—dawn at last on its way. The moon hung low in the western sky behind her, bobbing in and out of sight as the tops of the tallest trees passed by. The curves in the road multiplied as it wound through a hilly region.

As she rounded a bend, a shadowy figure bounded out onto the road not far ahead of them, waving its arms. Her heart jumped, and she reared the horse to the side to avoid it.

"Zenia, it's me!"

She pulled on the reins to stop the horse, clutching tight to Celeste. "Eloise?"

"Quickly! Off the road!" Eloise grabbed the horse's bridle and pulled with all her might. The horse whinnied its objection, but followed.

"What are you doing out here?" Zenia asked.

Eloise brought the horse toward a spot where the trees and brush were thinner—not exactly a clearing, but room to move. She led it to another horse tied to a tree and secured it there.

"Gwendolyn and some henchmen are coming," she said as she took the baby from Zenia. "We need to move fast."

"Gwendolyn herself? Oh dear Mother Goddess!" They might be able to hide from the King's Guard, but from the sorceress Gwendolyn—never.

"She's beautiful!" Eloise whispered as she gazed into Celeste's face. "I knew she would be. A child kissed by the moon couldn't be anything but beautiful."

"How did you know?"

Eloise giggled and looked around conspiratorially. "I have a little surprise." She handed Celeste back to Zenia, then brought them to a stump with a black cloth draped over the top, covering something spherical.

Eloise plucked a corner of the cloth with two fingers, then paused. "I'm going to show you something very secret and very dangerous. You can't tell anyone about this. Are you ready?"

"Ye-es," Zenia said uncertainly. Eloise was one for dramatics, but this was hardly the occasion.

She whipped the cloth off. Zenia gasped.

Glimmering in the moonlight in the middle of the jagged stump, nestled securely between its woody teeth, perfectly round and perfectly clear, lay a scrying globe.

"Where in the name of the Mother Goddess did you get that?"

Eloise shrugged her bony shoulders and giggled, "I stole it."

"How do you steal a scrying globe?"

"The less you know, the better." She fluttered the cloth until an opening appeared—it was a sack. She slid the globe into the opening and tied it closed with a tie string. "This is a concealing sack. It keeps the globe hidden from prying eyes."

Scrying globes, concealing sacks—these were things of legend, even myth, that no village witch had any business possessing. Until now Zenia had her doubts they ever existed. Their rightful owner would never give up tracking them down, not for an entire lifetime.

Eloise had done a terribly dangerous thing!

"Please, how did you get these?"

"I'm telling you, Zenia, you don't want to know."

"Who's looking for them?"

Eloise sighed as she tied the sack to her saddle. "You won't let it go, will you? I won't tell you how I stole it. Let's just say...Deirdre would love to know who has them."

"Oh dear Goddess, not Deirdre!"

"The globe, the sack it was in, a few of her scrolls." She turned and held her arms out. "Now let me hold this delightful child again!"

She handed the infant to Eloise. "Why didn't you ever tell me?"

"My dear girl, are you mad? I couldn't tell anyone. Deirdre's searched high and low to find me, and anyone who knows anything about it is doomed. I couldn't put you in such danger."

She couldn't believe Deirdre hadn't already found her. How had she kept this hidden from the sorceress?

"But it doesn't matter now," Eloise said. "She knows."

"*What?*"

Eloise lay Celeste on the ground in a bed of leaves that were already prepared. "I cast the Truth Dream like you told me. I watched everything that happened tonight. Your escape, Tamara's sacrifice, how you purified Celeste—all of it." She looked up and smiled. "I got your message!"

She pulled a scrap out of her skirt and handed it to Zenia, who looked at the familiar words she'd scrawled:

Watch for me. I'll be coming to you. Cast a Truth Dream that triggers when I leave the castle on horseback.

Zenia crouched next to Eloise and gazed at Celeste. The infant was asleep, but stirring. She would probably awaken soon. "You saw all that through the globe?"

"That's right." Eloise pulled some materials out of her pocket and lay them out carefully on a bare spot of earth.

"Can Deirdre find you when you use it?"

"She already has. I've been very careful about using the globe. Keeping it in its sack all the time. Using it for only brief periods—and *never* anywhere near our village. Deirdre was never able to track me."

From another pocket Eloise produced a small flask of oil and poured it over the materials. "Until tonight. I used the globe the whole time to watch you. Deirdre knows where I am now."

Horror shot through Zenia. "We have Gwendolyn *and* Deirdre after us?"

"I expect so. I haven't been wasting any time watching Deirdre. I know she'll come."

"But—"

"She hasn't had enough time to be here yet, even with...well...even with all her powers."

Eloise picked up a small twig and held it up to her mouth, then whispered to it. A tiny flame burst from its end. She touched the flame to the oil. It flared up, consuming the materials.

With forcefulness Eloise cried out a strange incantation Zenia had never heard before. She opened up Tamara's dress that Celeste was wrapped in, exposing the infant's body to the cool air. She gathered up the ashes of the materials and dumped them on Celeste's body, then rubbed them all over until the child's torso was smeared with grey. Celeste woke up with a tiny bellow.

"I learned this from a scroll I found," Eloise said. "Cast a Sight spell. You'll want to see this."

Zenia muttered a quick breath spell, wondering what would happen. As the spell energized, the aura emanating from Celeste filled the air with a blinding brilliance. She instinctively threw her arms up, even though covering her eyes would do no good against Sight.

Eloise giggled. "Amazing, isn't it! The last time I looked, Gwendolyn hadn't turned her Sight this far. But as soon as she does, Celeste's aura will be a blazing fire in the pitch black night."

"Oh Goddess, what do we do? How will we ever hide Celeste with this aura?"

"Calm down, my daughter. I've been figuring all this out while you rode here. Now here's what'll happen. We need to go separate ways."

"No!"

"I need to distract Gwendolyn and Deirdre from you. I'll ride off into the forest, and you'll continue with Celeste toward Suedeche. Do you remember that spot in the forest just outside Vilnetal where I used to hide things?"

"How can you distract them when this aura will go with us?"

"Listen to me, daughter! We don't have time. Do you remember the place?"

"Yes, but—"

"I hid a chest there. Inside is a scroll you'll need to read, and that will take care of Celeste's aura—"

"I can't do Ancient Magic!"

"You already did. That's how you purified Celeste. Now there's a place I know where you can raise Celeste to—"

Zenia broke into tears. "Please, Eloise, *you* need to protect Celeste. I can't fight two sorceresses."

Eloise grabbed Zenia's shoulder. "Neither can I! I have to distract them, and you have to hide Celeste where she can't be found. That scroll will—"

"You *can't* distract them with this aura!"

Eloise smiled her mischievous smile. "That's what I'm taking care of right now.

Zenia wiped her eyes and became calm. "Then I'll distract them and you hide Celeste."

Eloise jerked her head toward her. "I heard what you promised Tamara. You need to take Celeste and raise her as your own daughter, as I raised you."

"You know I can't keep Celeste hidden forever, and I don't have the power to protect her. You know that."

"I saw the spell you cast. You worked magic that a sorceress would be envious of."

"I only copied a spell I remembered watching you cast, years ago."

Eloise smiled a half-smile. "Yes, well, I *did* work a little magic to help you remember it. That spell came from an Ancient scroll, and you cast it. You *can* do it!"

"I can't. I won't. Where are you getting all these scrolls?"

"Zenia, Gwendolyn has already found Tamara's body. She's on her way now. So is Deirdre. I'm sure they've both already seen Celeste's aura. We have to act now."

Zenia looked at Celeste. The baby fussed and whined and puckered its lips, searching for a teat. "I promised Tamara I'd protect her. The best way I can protect her is to give her to you and distract the sorceresses away from her."

Eloise stood and faced Zenia. "You can't fight two sorceresses. You said so yourself."

"It doesn't matter. Only Celeste matters."

"When they find you without Celeste, they'll kill you."

With tears forming in her eyes, Zenia whispered, "It's the least I can do, after killing Tamara."

"Oh daughter." She threw her arms around Zenia. "I'm so sorry you had to go through that. But listen to me. They'll kill you, but first they'll torture you."

"It doesn't matter. I won't know where you are."

"It matters to me! You're my daughter."

"Tamara was my queen, and I sliced her neck until she bled to death. Please, Eloise, you *have* to take Celeste. They'll figure out it was me who took her, but they don't know anything about you. You're the only one who can protect her. Please! I can't let Tamara's death be wasted."

Eloise clung tightly to her.

"You know I'm right, Mother," Zenia whispered in her ear.

"You sweet, stubborn girl," Eloise whispered, then released her embrace.

Zenia gazed into the narrow, craggy face of Eloise. Her eyes were shadowed in the dark, but she knew what those stormy grey eyes looked like right now. Warm, kind, loving—she had seen them most her life. "Love her like you loved me, Mother."

Eloise brushed a tear away from her eye. "When you go, find the first opening into the forest and ride as hard as you can."

"But how am I supposed to lure them away?"

Eloise grinned as she raised her arms up, regaining her bravura. "Watch this!"

Her palms faced each other, cupped as if holding a large pumpkin between them, and she crouched down. Celeste's aura bulged and filled the space between her palms with brilliance. Eloise drew her hands further apart, and the brilliance expanded to fill the space.

She stood slowly and turned toward Zenia. The ball of brilliance between her hands broke away from the aura.

"Remain perfectly still, please," Eloise said.

She carefully pushed the brilliance toward Zenia. It grew to surround her body from head to foot. A finger of it reached to the moon. Zenia expected to feel a warmth or burning, but the brilliance gave her no sensation.

"There! Now you look like you have Celeste's aura." Eloise beamed satisfaction.

"How did you do that? How can you give me another person's aura?"

"I said you *look* like you have it. It's an illusion."

For the first time, Zenia dared hope that Celeste might be safe. "But how do we know they'll follow me and not you?"

Her face saddened. "The less you know, the better." Tears slid down from her shadowy eyes. "Go, my sweet child. When one of those nasty sorceresses gets close, cast a simple Negation spell on yourself, and the aura will disappear. Maybe that'll confuse her long enough for you to get away."

She pulled Zenia into a desperate embrace. In her ear she said, "If they torture you, use all the powers I taught you to resist. You don't know where I'm going or what I'll do, but the one valuable thing you do know is who has Celeste."

Zenia squeezed her with all the love she felt. "May the Goddess protect you and Celeste."

The baby broke into an earnest cry, small and sweet in the wind and the rustling of the trees.

Eloise kissed Zenia on the cheek, a gentle lingering one. "I'm so proud of you for all you did to save her. What a smart thing you did! What a brave thing! I'm so sorry you had to lose Tamara in the process."

Zenia clasped Eloise tightly, pressing her cheek against the woman's bosom. She would probably never see her again. She would probably never see Celeste again.

"Time to go." Eloise broke their embrace. "Wrap Celeste back up and hand her to me." She untied the horse and climbed into the saddle. Zenia wrapped the dress back around Celeste and placed her in Eloise's arm.

"I love you, Daughter," Eloise murmured.

"I love you, Mother."

Eloise steered the horse carefully through the thick brush. She made a shadowy figure through the trees as she reached the highway.

"By the way," she called, "that spell you and I cast—the spell that purifies corruption? I stole that from Deidre too." She raised her face to the sky and shouted, "Thank you, Deirdre, for helping us save two children from corruption, you nasty old witch!" She spurred her horse down the road out of sight.

Zenia loosed her horse and mounted as quickly as she could. She felt naked and exposed with the false aura shining around her—and that's how she wanted to feel. She worked her way to the road, then trotted along it for about a hundred feet until she found a narrow deer trail cutting through the thick forest growth, heading north.

She steered the horse onto it and urged it into as fast a trot as she could. Branches of trees and brush scraped along the horse's sides and Zenia's legs. Many times she had to duck to avoid a branch slapping her in the face.

"Great Mother Goddess," she prayed, "protect Eloise and Celeste. Help them escape. And protect me too!"

Birds began to sing in anticipation of the morning. Zenia cast her Sight as far behind her as she could. It reached no more than a mile, but within that range, Zenia saw no movement.

Did she dare hope she might escape?

At least her pursuers would have just as slow a time of it. This narrow trail through the thick forest evened things out.

But the trail only lasted half a mile until the trees stopped and a large meadow stretched out before her. As she plunged out of the forest, a deer drinking from a creek startled and bolted.

The temptation to cross the meadow at a brisk gallop was great, but Zenia knew she had no chance there. Her ancient, weary horse was no match for the giant brutes the king's soldiers rode. They'd catch up to her easily in the open. Her only hope was to lose herself in the forest.

Lose herself! As if that could happen with this aura shining around her. If she spoke the Negation spell, the aura would disappear. Zenia would have a real chance of hiding. But she wouldn't do it. She had to maintain that aura as long as she dared, to lure two sorceresses to her.

"I can't escape," she said with resignation. All she could do was buy as much time for Eloise and Celeste as possible.

The forest—the thickest part—was her best chance for accomplishing that. Zenia steered the horse toward the treeline, but the animal resisted. It kept turning its head toward the creek.

"Oh Goddess, no, we don't have time for that!"

But this poor horse couldn't have much left in it, and severe thirst wasn't going to help. She knew she'd be caught immediately if she ended up on foot, and by now her own thirst was searing. She rode the horse toward the place where the creek entered the forest and let it drink as she gulped handfuls of water.

"Hurry, hurry," she murmured as the creature slurped, keeping her eyes on the place where the deer trail emerged. The sky was dark blue now. The stars were starting to fade.

A flurry of birds broke chattering from the trees into the air. Her pursuers were definitely on the deer trail.

"That's all you get," Zenia barked as she leaped back on and yanked at the reins. The horse whinnied in complaint, but complied. They galloped into the trees, and a branch banged into Zenia's forehead, almost knocking her from the saddle.

The horse slowed to a crawl as Zenia tried to shake the dizziness from her brain. It was nearly impossible to move through the heavy growth. This was her life now, stumbling through the brush until her pursuers found her—all the life she'd ever have until Gwendolyn or Deirdre captured her and tortured her to death.

Eloise rode hard until she reached the hill near Vilnetal, her home village in the outlying region of Suedeche. Celeste wailed constantly. She must be starving and miserable from the journey, and the dress she was wrapped in was stained with excrement.

"My poor girl, I'm sorry I can't do much for you right now. There's no time." She kissed Celeste on the cheek. "Just a little longer, and I'll take care of you."

She slid gingerly off the horse while holding Celeste, then scraped together with one hand a mat of leaves to lay the girl down on. "You're a beautiful little girl," she cooed, "and you have the most beautiful aura I've ever seen. But that shining aura is your doom."

Eloise took a few steps to a boulder nestled against the rise of the hill. She scraped away loose dirt behind the boulder, revealing a small wooden chest. She opened it, revealing several rolled up parchments and an amulet.

She picked up the amulet, an oval piece of jewelry attached to a delicate chain with a ruby embedded in the center. She hung it over her neck, adding it to another necklace with a crescent moon made of silver, and tucked the trinket into the blouse of her dress. She spoke the word in the Ancient tongue to activate it.

Carefully she unrolled each scroll until she found the one with the spell she was looking for. She spared a moment to renew her Sight spell so she could watch Celeste's aura. It veered far to the horizon where the moon was near setting. "Hmm," she said, wondering what that could mean, then held the scroll flat against the ground with both hands. "I'm sorry, little one, but I'll have to rob you of your childhood." She read the words carefully and loudly.

The glow of the aura released itself from the moon, shrunk tightly around Celeste, fading, dimming, then disappeared as if the infant's skin absorbed it. Eloise sighed sadly.

She picked Celeste up and cuddled her to her bosom, ignoring the fecal slime oozing onto her hand. "Your beautiful aura is now contained deep inside you where no one can see it." She kissed the baby on the forehead. "But I'm afraid all that energy bottled up with nowhere to go will make you age faster."

She gazed into the infant face with the scrunched eyes and the gaping, wailing mouth with toothless gums. "But that's a blessing. Gwendolyn and Deirdre will waste time searching for an infant."

Eloise set Celeste down and placed the scroll into the chest, then used a handful of dirt to scrub the excrement off her hand. She shoved the chest into her saddlebag. Pausing to look for the last time toward her village, seeing nothing more in the gloomy pre-dawn than the smoke of home fires drifting above the trees, she murmured, "Goodbye," then mounted the horse with Celeste and rode into the forest, away from the East Highway, away from Suedeche, away from everything.

She would never see her village again—her sweet cottage with all its memories where she and Zenia had lived—the village folk she had ministered to as their resident witch. She'd never see that boy again, much taller now—the boy she'd healed of disease at the expense of his mother's life.

She could never see any of them again, never tell them where she'd gone or why she'd left. Her life would be herself and Celeste now, living alone in the hidden cottage deep in the forest that no one knew about—the cottage she'd prepared years ago for the time she knew would one day come when she'd have to hide from a sorceress.

But in all those years, she never dreamed she'd be hiding from *two* sorceresses—or that she'd be raising another stepdaughter. And not just any girl. A princess.

She sighed again and put her past life out of her mind. A new life was beginning—a new mission. The most dangerous one of her life.

And the most important.

Chapter 4

Deirdre

The Truth Dream woke her. Deirdre recognized it at once—her scrying globe was being used again.

That nasty thief drove her to fits of rage, but she had to admire her. Deirdre had figured out the thief was somewhere in King Christian's realm, either Gallea or his ally Suedeche, and that she was a woman, but that was all. This thief was smart. She never used the globe long enough, and never in the same area. Deirdre had not been able to locate or identify her.

Tonight would probably play out the same, but she had to try. She had everything ready for this moment. She always had everything ready so she wouldn't waste any time.

She cast the special Sight spell that would connect her with the globe. In less than a moment she had the location of the thief—that was the easy part—and it surprised her. It was unusually close to one of the locations where she'd used the globe before. She never did that. Was the thief getting careless, or was she desperate?

Deirdre swooped in on the location with her Sight, hoping to catch a glimpse of the thief. As the special Sight spell focused in on the globe, it would let her see not only what the user was looking at, but who the user was.

Yet every time Deirdre was on the verge of seeing the thief, the globe disappeared—tucked away into the concealing sack she'd also stolen.

The thief knew the timing well, and Deirdre had always struggled to be just an instant faster each time—an instant enough to catch that precious glimpse of the user. Would she succeed tonight?

She pushed her Sight hard toward the globe. In mere seconds—*mere seconds*—she would connect her Sight with it, and the thief would stand out a vivid image that she could identify.

Her Sight swept into the globe, and the diffuse image of the thief formed.

This was the instant the globe always disappeared, and Deirdre waited with a mix of anger and resignation for the image to go dark.

And saw the thief.

She gasped at the image. Not only had she caught a clear glimpse of the thief, but the thief was still there, continuing to peer straight into the globe, oblivious to Deirdre's mystical presence.

This was astounding! Why was the thief so careless tonight? Surely she must know Deirdre was staring at her.

"Hello, Deirdre," the thief said. "I can feel you in there."

"Who are you?" Deirdre said, too shocked to do anything else.

"Never mind about that. I regret not being able to hide from you tonight."

Deirdre studied her. There was something familiar about her. But something of profound significance must be unfolding for the thief to not hide herself. So she didn't keep her focus on the thief to figure out who she was. She didn't swoop out of her chambers with her Flying spell to chase down this infuriating woman to take back her property and exact her revenge.

She watched what the thief watched.

Christian's queen Tamara, heavy with child and in labor, riding on horseback into the forest with some servant woman. Stopping at a clearing because the child refused to wait any longer. The birth of a monster—an infant with a dark power inside it.

What was this child?

Yet an even more astounding thing happened. This servant woman bled Queen Tamara to death as the baby suckled the life out of her. The purity of Tamara blended with the curse of the dark power inside the baby and struggled for supremacy.

Deirdre could see the dark power slowly defeating the purity. Tamara had given her life for nought.

Suddenly a monstrous wolf drew near—a cursed creature with eyes blazing. It looked for all world like the Beast of legend that centuries ago had tormented the kingdom of Scaendelreic, then Gallea. What was that horror doing walking the earth again?

Something drew the Beast to the clearing. Something about that child. It would kill them all, and it would all be over with. Just as well. If that child were allowed to grow, she'd be a menace to the balance of power in Cueldea. And if that child were to fall into the hands of Gwendolyn...

Suddenly Deirdre realized why the queen and her servant had been fleeing into the forest at night. They were removing the child from the grasp of Gwendolyn.

Then all was well tonight! The world had been saved from a terrible threat. The queen and the servant kept the child out of Gwendolyn's hands, and the Beast would end the life of them both. Deirdre took a moment to honor the sacrifice of Tamara and her servant which would save the world. She almost felt inspired enough to forgive the thief for stealing her globe.

Almost.

It was time to focus on the thief again. But suddenly the maid servant lifted the child up to the heavens and called upon the moon. Deirdre gasped again—two such marvels within moments of each other! The servant called on the power of Mistress Moon to purge the dark corruption from the child and allow the purity to prevail. Using the Ancient Purification spell from one of the scrolls the thief had stolen from her!

All the darkness within the child fled, and the vitality of the moon engulfed her, cleansing her and empowering her as no child had been empowered before.

At the same time the wolf attacked, but was held at bay by nothing more than the power within that child. The pathetic breath spell the servant cast certainly did nothing.

This was the most incredible thing Deirdre had ever witnessed. No wonder the thief felt compelled to keep watching, knowing Deirdre would see her.

The thief directed the attention of the globe westward toward Luteche. Gwendolyn was on horseback in the company of four men, in pursuit of the queen and her child. Deirdre guessed right. Gwendolyn knew about the child's power and wanted it for herself.

It was too late for Tamara. But the servant and the baby could still be saved from Gwendolyn's clutches. And Deirdre was the only one who could, since she was the only one of the Seven Sisters who knew it was happening. Yes, it was Deirdre's duty to save the noble servant and the child. Not even recovering her precious scrying globe was as important. Her revenge would have to wait for another day. Today Deirdre would save the world from Gwendolyn.

The servant and child headed directly toward the location of the thief. Deirdre could follow that blazing aura to their exact location. Perhaps she could save them *and* get her stolen treasures back at the same time.

It was time for her Flying spell. Thank the Great Gods the thief hadn't stolen *that* scroll from her!

As Deirdre prepared to cast it, she turned her Sight toward the globe and the thief again. That face, so familiar. Where had she seen it?

"Farewell, Deirdre," the thief said. "I have to go now,"

The globe disappeared.

Curse that witch! She'd put it back in the sack. No matter. Deirdre had seen her, knew her location. It wouldn't take her more than an hour to get there and have the servant, the infant, the thief, and her precious globe in her grasp.

Everything was falling into place to accomplish what the war with Gallea had failed to achieve. Gwendolyn was a rogue sorceress and needed to be disposed of, but her power had resisted defeat—even with the death of King Guillaume and Queen Delphine, Christian's parents.

But now this marvelous child kissed by the Mistress Moon could be their salvation. With the baby's power and with the thief captured and all the magic she'd stolen retrieved, Deirdre could help Scaendelreic defeat Gwendolyn. The kingdoms of Gallea and Scaendelreic would be united under the influence of Deirdre. With Gwendolyn out of the way, the Seven Sisters could unite all the kingdoms of Cueldea under their influence, and at last they could stand against any onslaught from the male wizards in the South. The world could live in peace and tranquility—under the rule of the Seven Sisters. And since Deirdre would be the one to possess the child, she'd have the power to rule over the Seven Sisters, as the sorceress of Scaendelreic by right ought to have all along.

This was too much to be chance. It had to be an omen from Mistress Earth herself. She must have arranged the events of this night for this very purpose.

Deirdre cast the Flying spell on her glittering, many-colored robe, then slipped it on. She strode to the door of her tower balcony and threw it open, stepped out and raised her arms out so the robe hung from either arm, then leaped. The wind caught the robe and lifted her up like a bird on the wing.

She loved the sensation of flying through the air with the wind in her face. Lanterns glowing beneath her like twinkling stars fell away as she left the city of Scaendel. Behind her loomed the castle of King Gunther. Ahead gleamed the marvelous aura of the infant. She aimed straight for it.

The aura split in two. One continued east toward Deirdre at the speed of a horse, and the other north, away from both Deirdre and Gwendolyn.

Great Gods, how much magic could this thief do? How much magic had she stolen, and from how many of the Sisters? Apprehension replaced the anger she felt for the thief. Could this be another rogue sorceress in the making, like Gwendolyn? As if the world needed another one of those!

Nevertheless, the splitting of the auras was an effort in futility. One of the auras had to be an illusion. It didn't matter which one. Deirdre would check the one approaching her first, and if that was the illusion, she'd simply continue on to the real one and the child.

In less than an hour she crossed the border into Suedeche. Before long she could see lights in the distance marking the location of the castle of Duke Geoffrey and the surrounding city of Suedeche with the moon glittering in the bend of the River Sicana that cut through it. The aura had stopped at a location past the city, somewhere in the countryside of Suedeche. It wasn't far now.

Suddenly the aura disappeared.

Deirdre smiled with satisfaction. Obviously that was the illusion. Now she didn't have to waste a moment checking it out. She could fly directly to the other aura fleeing into Fenweald Forest where she could seize the thief, her scrying globe, her concealing sack, and the precious child that would empower her to rule Cueldea and defeat the armies and wizards of the South.

This was indeed a wonderful night!

Chapter 5

Kasimir

Faisal stopped with his hand up. Kasimir froze, looking forward where his older brother gazed. What had he noticed?

The grove of wild and gnarled olive trees shivered as the sun shone through them. Kasimir was both grateful and regretful for the steady wind blowing, barely trembling the leaves. It soothed the intense heat of the day as it blew across the glistening sweat on his black skin, but could drown out small sounds that might signal an encounter.

Like the sound Faisal must have heard, but Kasimir hadn't.

Probably a predator. He hoped it would be a hyena. Perhaps Kasimir could capture the jinni that resided within it.

Or maybe it would be a jackal that could bring Kasimir good fortune if it crossed his path.

A cheetah would be the greatest find of all. If he could capture a cheetah and tame it, that would fetch him prestige that few young men his age achieved.

At last he heard the sound, a brushing, barely noticeable, probably against a branch. Faisal pointed to where it came from, where a mass of trees blocked the view. Faisal gestured to the right, and Kasimir crept sideways, stepping silently as he'd been trained. Faisal moved to the left.

A faint vocal sound—a human sound. He glanced at Faisal, who gazed at him in alarm. Sudden pounding on the ground caused both of them to raise their scimitars.

Through the trees crashed two sturdy horses covered with head and body armor. Strange men rode in their saddles, men of a kind Kasimir had never seen before. Their skin was a lighter color. Their eyes were narrow as if they squinted in the sun. Their armor and helmets were unknown to him. Their hands held no swords, but bows and arrows of an unfamiliar kind. And each bow had an arrow nocked and pointed right at them, as the warriors gripped their horses with nothing but their legs.

Faisal cried and charged. One arrow flew and drove into Faisal's side.

The other horse bore down on Kasimir. He dove behind the nearest tree as the warrior shot his arrow. It embedded in the tree's lowest branch.

Kasimir whirled around and raised his scimitar. The warrior turned the horse quickly and let another arrow fly. It grazed Kasimir's thigh with a sting. The other warrior shot an arrow into Faisal's shoulder, then leaped from the horse and attacked with a sword.

The warrior who attacked Kasimir turned and galloped at him with a third arrow ready. Kasimir ran out with his sword up and barely jerked his head back as the arrow zoomed past his ear. He swung his blade across the horse's shins as the warrior rode past.

As his horse buckled, the warrior rolled to the ground and back on his feet, keeping a tight hold on his bow. He nocked another arrow and let it fly. The wild aim zoomed past Kasimir, who tried to knock it away with his sword and missed.

The warrior dropped his bow and slid a long, narrow sword from its scabbard.

Kasimir charged with a cry. The warrior raised his sword and broke into a run with his own cry. Their blades crashed together with a clang. The blow was powerful and shook Kasimir, but he held steady as the blades slid apart with a ring and the two charged past each other.

They both whirled around and peered at one another. The warrior's lips were painted red, and he had a scar on them from a thin gash that had cut vertically down the middle of them.

In the distance, Faisal battled desperately with his opponent, two arrows sticking out from him. The horse with the sliced shins bellowed.

The warrior smiled at Kasimir and walked toward him holding his sword casually. Kasimir lifted his blade and panted three quick breaths to calm himself. The warrior looked him up and down with contempt and spoke a word in a strange language: "*Nanai!*"

Kasimir thought he knew what that word was. He saw it in the man's eyes. *Boy!*

Kasimir was an excellent swordsman who had trained under a master. He'd beaten many men twice his age. But there was one thing he was still a boy in. This was the first time in his young life he'd faced a man in true battle to the death. His heart beat fear.

Today I become a man, he vowed to himself.

He kept his scimitar raised and breathed as evenly as he could. The warrior stopped before him just far enough back so neither of their blades could reach. Clanging and grunting continued where Faisal was.

The warrior lifted his sword straight up before his face. His eyes crossed to look at the blade, then straightened out to gaze at him.

Kasimir brought his sword down in a ready position. Somberly they peered at each other without moving.

"Make your move," Kasimir spat.

The warrior's eyes flickered briefly.

Kasimir took one step back.

The warrior launched and sliced his cheek with the tip of the sword. Kasimir barely knocked it away with his blade before it could go deeper.

The warrior laughed and attacked. The clanging began in earnest.

Great Gods, the man was fast! Kasimir had always been proud of his scimitar, the powerful weapon of grace and strength, but this man's smaller sword was easily manipulated. Kasimir could knock it away with ease, but he was becoming weary doing so. He felt like the warrior was playing with him to wear him down, maintaining a haughty smirk throughout the process.

You don't fear me, he thought. I'm just a boy.

Kasimir had the power, but his opponent had the wiry finesse and could toy with him indefinitely. Kasimir had to make a move fast.

But all he could do was hold his own against the seasoned warrior. On the training field, that would have pleased him. In a life-and-death battle, that would end his life.

He needed an instant to think, just a brief moment of disengagement. He fell back, but it did no good. The warrior stayed with him, unrelenting.

Kasimir stepped back again, and again, and his foot landed on a rock, wrenching his ankle. His leg buckled. He toppled to the side, barely managing to catch himself from hitting hard. He lost his grip on his scimitar, which fell free to the ground.

The warrior glared at him and uttered something harsh in his language, finishing it with a pause and that same word, "*Nanai!*"

That was Kasimir's weapon! He'd be the boy the warrior thought he was.

He peered at the warrior, letting his eyes water, then moaned, "No, no, please don't kill me."

The warrior spat on the ground in front of him in disgust as Kasimir rested his hand on the hilt of his scimitar. The warrior attacked with his lightning stab, but Kasimir rolled to the side and swept his sword across the warrior's shins just like the horse. The warrior bellowed and dropped to the ground, toppling onto his side.

Kasimir looked toward Faisal. He still fought the other warrior, but he panted desperately and sweat dripped from him. The warrior swung hard, and the sword blade bit deeply into the side of Faisal's abdomen. He howled and dropped to the ground.

Faisal's warrior raised his sword for the fatal blow. Kasimir leaped to his feet and charged. The warrior turned his sword toward him, but Kasimir arrived too soon and batted the man's swing away, then sliced his scimitar down the man's face and chest and belly, cutting him open.

The warrior gurgled on blood and dropped forward, landing hard on his face.

Kasimir rushed to Faisal and crouched before him. "How bad is it?"

"Bad."

Kasimir flung off his leather mail and tore a long piece from his qamis. He wrapped it around Faisal where the wound was and tied it.

"Kasimir, your opponent!"

He looked up and saw the warrior dragging himself toward his bow. He dashed toward the man with his scimitar. The warrior's narrow eyes widened, and he scrambled as fast as he could. Kasimir raised his scimitar with a war cry.

The warrior reached the bow, nocked an arrow, and aimed while sitting on the ground. The arrow flew.

Kasimir swung his sword at the arrow and missed again. It embedded just under his clavicle. He cried out, but kept running, and reached the warrior before he could nock another arrow.

Kasimir swung with all his might. The pain in his chest exploded. His blade sliced deep into the warrior's neck, vibrating to a stop as it hit the spine. The warrior gurgled and choked as blood spurted from arteries.

Kasimir struggled to release his sword from the neck. The warrior listed to the side, holding his throat. The head lolled to the side, widening the gap in his neck, allowing Kasimir to wrench his blade free.

The warrior's breath sputtered and stopped as he dropped to the ground.

Kasimir yanked the arrow in his chest out with a howl, then dashed to the bellowing horse and whacked its neck until it silenced. He approached the other horse cautiously until he could grab its reins and lead it to Faisal.

"I won't let you die, Brother."

He struggled to pick up Faisal, grunting in pain, and set him on the horse in front of the saddle. He mounted the horse and kicked its sides.

They galloped through the grove. Each hoof fall shot pain through his clavicle and ripped a harsh cry from Faisal's lips.

They galloped to their city—Eranshar in the nation of Insu. Kasimir wasn't even sure if his brother was still alive. The wall and gate of the Ribat of Wizards loomed before him.

"Help! Help! He's dying!"

The guards at the gate swung it open. Kasimir dashed into the courtyard. He immediately dismounted and slid Faisal to the ground. "Please help me!"

Novitiates scrambled to him, some tearing off more bandaging from their own clothes, some uttering prayers and incantations for Faisal. One led the horse away.

"Call for a master!" cried Kasimir.

One novitiate broke for the Tower of Masters.

The binding of his wound complete, the novitiates lifted Faisal and carried him toward the tower. Master Izzet appeared in the doorway, the gems embedded in his face glittering in the sunlight. He beckoned to them. "Quickly, into the infirmary."

The novitiates rushed down the hall and laid Faisal on the table.

Master Izzet unwrapped the bandaging and inspected the wound. The amount of blood sickened Kasimir, but at least Faisal was still breathing.

"He won't make it," Izzet said. "Please stand back."

The novitiates stepped back with wide eyes as Izzet pulled his garment open to reveal his chest bedecked with gems. When he first became a wizard, Izzet started with forty-nine starstones—seven times seven—embedded in his skin on his chest and face. Kasimir estimated about two dozen were missing now. The scars left from plucking them out looked like the scars of a smallpox attack.

Izzet plucked a starstone from his skin, the lowest one remaining on his chest. A bead of blood formed at the site. Izzet pressed the stone against the blood and spoke an incantation.

The gem glowed with a brilliant light. Izzet held it with cupped hands to his mouth and continued the incantation. The stone burst into a blinding flash as if he held a star in his hand. He threw his hands out, and the glow swooped down to Faisal's wound.

Faisal's eyes popped open as he sucked in a deep breath. Izzet kept his hands facing out as the wound closed up and the edges of the skin knitted together into a jagged scar.

The young men gazed with wonder, including Kasimir. In his three years as a novitiate, he'd only seen a starstone used once before. He was just as amazed this time.

"Faisal needs to rest now," Izzet said, "and take some food in." He walked to Kasimir and placed his hand on his shoulder. "I'm sorry this happened on your first scouting trip, but I'm glad we were able to save him. Now tell us what happened."

"We ran into two warriors on horseback."

Murmuring broke out among the novitiates. Izzet hushed them with a raise of his hand.

"What did they look like?"

"They were dark-haired like us, but had lighter colored skin and narrow eyes as if they were pulled taut. They had bows and straight, narrow swords."

Izzet's expression was grim and his lips tight. "What did they do?"

"They attacked us. We fought them. Faisal nearly died from it. I was wounded, but was able to kill them. I rushed back with Faisal, hoping he wouldn't die."

Kasimir looked around and noticed his fellow novitiates peering at him with wonder.

"You yourself killed two warriors in personal combat?" Izzet asked.

"Y-yes."

Izzet addressed the entire group. "If I'm not mistaken, I think those were scouts from the East."

The murmuring was more agitated this time.

"Easterners scouting our land is not a good thing." Izzet pointed to three youths as he spoke their names. "Daoud, Omar, and...Amir. Prepare to accompany us to the battle site while I bind Kasimir's wounds."

Master Izzet and the four novitiates rode quietly through the grove on horseback, keeping a sharp eye out on their surroundings. A pack horse accompanied them. Kasimir tried to remain calm with nerves on edge. This was where he'd faced death, where he'd killed two enemy warriors for the first time in his life, and where he almost lost his brother.

Would there be more Easterners charging from the trees?

They arrived where the battle took place. Their first sight was the dead body of the warrior that attacked Faisal. A couple small scavengers chewed away at the body. Izzet galloped at them to scare them away.

Izzet dismounted, looking carefully around. Further down were the bodies of the second warrior and the horse. He got down on one knee and examined the nearby body, the clothing, the sword, the deep wound Kasimir had sliced from face to midriff. He drew his finger across the warrior's lips, red and scarred like Kasimir's warrior.

He stood and peered toward the other bodies. "Who killed the horse?"

"I did," said Kasimir.

"Why?"

"I wounded it in battle and...it was in pain and howling and I didn't have time to care for it. Faisal would have died."

Izzet nodded, then turned to the other three youths. "This battle has to disappear—every bit of it. Collect everything you can find and load it on the pack horse. Bodies, weapons, everything."

"The horse too?" said Omar.

"No, not the horse. That's too much."

The three boys went to work as Izzet led Kasimir off toward the dead horse.

"You've done a great work here. You honored yourself and your training with your courage, skill, and quick thinking. You saved your brother, and you lived to return and warn of us of an impending threat."

"Thank you, Master."

They reached the horse. "You inflicted the wounds on the legs?"

"I did. That caused the rider to...dismount."

Izzet smiled. "You mean fall off."

Kasimir smiled.

"Very good." He glanced past Kasimir. "Amir," he called, "don't forget that arrow stuck in the tree." To Kasimir he said, "I want you to understand why I'm doing what I'm about to do." He pulled his garment open to reveal his chest stones.

"Starstones are precious things. The gems must be mined and cut and polished. After that, it takes a full week for a wizard to capture the power of a star and store it in the gem. The drain on his own energy requires several days of rest before he can do it again. We're careful with the use of them. We use them only for matters of import, not for frivolous things."

Kasimir nodded, excited to learn more about the mysterious gems that every wizard wore.

"I'm about to use one to rid ourselves of this horse. What a mundane thing to do with a starstone, don't you think?"

"I...I guess."

"It's not! We must remove all indication that a battle was ever fought. There must be no sign that these scouts from the East were ever here. We must make their fate mysterious to the Easterners. If they vanish without a trace, that will make us appear powerful to them. That will instill fear."

Kasimir's mind swam with the implications. He'd performed an act that would appear mysterious, threatening, fearful to the Easterners? He was just a novitiate!

"So we must dispose of the horse, but it's too unwieldy to carry back with us. Do you understand?"

"I do, Master."

"Because of you, these scouts will never return to report on our strengths and weaknesses and resources. Because of you, we've become aware of how bold they are, how at last they've begun to invade our land. Because of you, we have a hint of who they are, of what their weapons and armor are, and how they battle. Because of you, their advance has been delayed. We can be better prepared. Now stand back."

Izzet plucked a starstone and pressed it into the blood that oozed. It glowed with brilliance. He spoke into his cupped hands until the stone burst into a blazing light that rushed forward and consumed the horse out of existence.

"Help the others make one more sweep of the area. Make sure nothing is left, not even a piece of jewelry, a swatch of cloth, or a tuft of hair."

"There's blood," Daoud called.

"Blood in the wilderness is a common thing. Let it go."

When Izzet was satisfied, they mounted and rode back to Eranshar, the pack horse carrying two dead bodies and their swords, bows, and arrows.

Kasimir rode tall in the saddle. He had become both a man and a hero today. But mostly, he was grateful for starstones that had saved his brother's life.

Chapter 6

Zenia

The King's Guard had clearly followed her into the forest. Zenia had no idea what Eloise had done, but Gwendolyn chased the wrong aura. She had to assume Deirdre had done the same. It was time to dissipate the illusion.

Zenia spoke the breath spell of Negation. Her Sight spell was fading, but enough persisted to see the glow of her aura disappear.

Now she needed to flee for her life. And for Eloise. And Celeste. The longer she made Gwendolyn chase her, the longer Eloise had to escape.

She doubled back and headed for the meadow again, hoping that would confuse everyone. As she broke from the trees, she pounded the horse into as fast a gallop as it could muster. If she could cross the meadow and disappear into the forest on the other side, maybe she could survive the night.

The horse puffed loudly. Zenia could feel its strength giving way. "Come on, my friend," she urged. "Come on. Just a little further."

Two-thirds of the way across, then three-fourths. The trees ahead beckoned. She dared hope she might escape.

The horse stumbled. She catapulted into the air and hit hard on her right shoulder. A sharp pain flashed and her clothes tore as she skidded across the grass and gravel and rocks. Her skin shredded along her right arm.

Her head reeled with the pain. The horse bellowed with each of its labored breaths. It lay on its side, one leg twisted unnaturally.

Slowly she sat up. The pain burned along her right side. She almost fainted, but supported herself with her left arm and refused to pass out.

The horse bellowing out in the open announced their location. Her pursuers would already have turned back this way.

She had to get to her feet and run. She tried to push herself up, but her head spun too much. She flopped back to the ground with a moan.

Riders burst from the forest and thundered across the meadow. She muttered a breath spell against pain as they neared, then prayed. "Mother Goddess, please help Eloise. Please help Celeste. Hide them from all dangers."

The horses trampled the grass as the guards surrounded her and came to a halt. One horse strode up to Zenia, stopping next to her bawling horse. She didn't look up to see who it was.

"End its misery." It was Gwendolyn's voice.

A guard dismounted. It was Sighurd, Captain of the Guard. He chopped the horse's neck with his sword. The bawling stopped.

Gwendolyn dismounted, crouched down low, and stuck her face in Zenia's. "Traitorous little chambermaid, where's the baby?"

Zenia closed her eyes and remained silent, steeling herself against what was to come. Her feeble spell had dulled her pain, but she knew it would do nothing against the pain Gwendolyn was about to inflict.

"Are you going to force me to do this?" Gwendolyn's voice sounded almost regretful.

Zenia said nothing.

"Your shoulder looks dislocated, and your arm is raw meat. That must hurt tremendously. One last time, where's the baby?"

She remained motionless.

Gwendolyn sighed with exasperation. "I hate you for making me do this."

Biting stings flared across her arm. Her eyes popped open. She bit down hard to keep from crying out. Gwendolyn had scooped up a handful of dirt and poured it across her shredded flesh.

"Who did you give the baby to?"

Zenia began sobbing from the pain.

Gwendolyn stood and raised her foot, bringing it down hard on the arm, grinding the dirt in. The granules were like shards, and the pain exploded into agony. Zenia shrieked.

Gwendolyn leaned over, her brow knotted, and examined her intensely. "What's this? A spell against pain? A ridiculous little breath spell, but a spell nevertheless." She gazed into Zenia's eyes. "None of this makes any sense."

She stood back up and ground her foot into the arm again. Zenia wept loudly.

"Why would Deirdre equip you with one powerful spell, then give you nothing more than silly breath spells for everything else?"

Deirdre?

Gwendolyn's face lit up. "*You're* the witch, playing with folk magic. You cast it on yourself. Why you little demon, you hid it from me all this time!"

Gwendolyn turned to Sighurd. "Captain, tie her and take her back to the castle. Gag her so she can't speak. And don't dress her wounds."

Sighurd pulled Zenia to her feet as Gwendolyn stared at her with a frown. The pain overwhelmed, her head spun, and she started to faint, but the guard held her up until her head cleared.

Gwendolyn studied Zenia with her head cocked. "*You* must have had the false aura. The child went to Deirdre. Somehow she hid the child's real aura. Curse both of you!"

Hid the aura? Zenia tried to think through the pain.

Sighurd spoke softly to her, "I'm sorry about this." He pulled her arms back to tie her wrists together. Her injuries burned with the worst pain she'd ever felt.

Gwendolyn gazed off into the distance. "How did she hide that aura?"

Zenia finally comprehended what Gwendolyn was talking about. She thought Deirdre had Celeste! She had no idea Eloise was ever involved. *Thank you, Mother Goddess*, she prayed. *Thank you for protecting them.*

Gwendolyn would waste days, maybe months, trying to steal the baby back from Deirdre. Plenty of time for Eloise to flee and hide.

"You're forcing me to do what I have to do," Gwendolyn hissed at Zenia. "You have no idea what I'll do. You *will* tell me everything!"

Sighurd lifted Zenia onto his horse, then mounted behind her and galloped away.

The pain was excruciating, but Zenia didn't care. It was only justice that she endure anguish after inflicting it on her queen. She could endure anything for Tamara and Celeste.

And now there was hope! Eloise had a real chance to save Celeste—a wonderful chance—a miraculous chance. All the sacrifices made tonight would not be in vain. Thank the Blessed Mother Goddess!

Zenia put all her strength into ignoring the pain. There was one more thing she could do. She could steel herself for the coming torture and hold out as long as possible. She could say things to keep Gwendolyn focused on Deirdre, when the pain of torture grew too great to remain silent.

As long as Gwendolyn spent time torturing Zenia, she wouldn't be looking for Celeste.

Deirdre swooped toward the fleeing aura. There was little time to spare. She could see Gwendolyn fast on its heels, a powerful sphere of Sight enveloping her—too powerful! A Sight so powerful it gave off an aura. Sight normally didn't radiate an aura, thank Mistress Earth. What use would it be if every time someone used it to pry around, any witch could see her prying?

Deirdre veered up and away, fearing Gwendolyn might have already seen her. But she seemed too focused on the infant's aura to notice her.

Where had she gotten all her magic? wondered Deirdre for the hundredth time. Gwendolyn was too much of an unknown—too much of a wild card. Curse that sorceress! It was essential that Deirdre keep the child away from her. But with that powerful Sight, Gwendolyn would see her instantly if she did anything to draw attention.

Suddenly the aura disappeared.

What in the name of Mistress Earth? How could both auras vanish? Where *was* that baby?

She swept around and descended into the forest. Her Flying spell would give off less aura while idle. Her feet touched the ground, and with her Sight she peered in the direction the aura had been.

There was a meadow ahead. She heard a horse pounding through it. She focused and saw the servant and horse galloping across. They'd covered most of the distance to the other side when the horse gave out and stumbled.

The servant went flying. Deirdre caught her breath, expecting to see the baby fly out of the servant's arms and mangle on impact with the ground.

But there was no baby.

The servant lay on the ground moaning with her right side torn up. The horse bellowed with a broken leg. Gwendolyn and her companions burst from the forest and charged toward her.

Deirdre leaped back into the air, wishing she could help the noble servant, but she couldn't let Gwendolyn know she was here. And she had a more urgent concern to deal with. The other aura had to be the true one. She needed to rush back to where it disappeared and see if she could find anything, anyone, any clue where the baby might be.

Gwendolyn no longer mattered. She was back to being a mere nuisance. Her opportunity to overpower all of Cueldea was gone. That threat now lay with the thief who must be the one who possessed the child. Deirdre would never stop until she destroyed this new rogue sorceress and confiscated all her magic. She had a duty to the Seven Sisters and to the inhabitants of Cueldea.

And the sweet taste of revenge was never far from her mind.

Sighurd handed Zenia off to the guard named Audric, who brought her to Gwendolyn's chambers and chained her to the wall with clasps around her wrists and ankles. She'd never been in this room before, but it was instantly recognizable as the workspace of a sorceress. Shelf after shelf of arcane minerals and herbs and weeds, bottles and vials of liquids and potions, the lingering acrid smell of burnt materials from years of casting spells. There was a worktable against one wall and a bed against another.

She shuddered, wondering why a sorceress would have chains on the wall of her private space.

Moments after Audric left, Gwendolyn entered. She went to her workspace and removed a small vial from a shelf. She lifted it to Zenia's lips. "Drink this."

The liquid's aroma wafted into her nostrils. More potent than the one she'd concocted for Mariam, but she recognized it at once. A Charm potion.

She closed her mouth tight.

"Do I have to hold your nose?"

She opened her mouth and let Gwendolyn pour it in. Immediately she spit it back out into her face. Angrily Gwendolyn wiped it off with her sleeve. "I gave you your chance to make this easy."

The torturing began.

Zenia muttered one spell after another—Protection, Relief from Pain, Warding, Purification. Chained to the wall, breath spells were all Zenia could cast. Breath spells were convenient for a quick effect, but weak because they had no materials to consume and convert into magical energy except the air from the spellcaster's lungs as she spoke.

None were strong enough to ease the torture Gwendolyn inflicted.

"Where's the baby?" she kept asking until the words were burned into Zenia's mind. "Deirdre has it, doesn't she? What does Deirdre want it for?"

The sorceress knew just how to do it. Chilling the blood, setting fire to the nerves, making the skin crawl then reattach, breaking bone after bone with a slow, agonizing twist, then healing them to be broken again—anything that would inflict intense pain without causing permanent damage.

Gwendolyn called it "compassionate torture."

Zenia wished for death. She prayed for death. She regretted she had no spells to cast that would kill herself, but she only knew the Life Magic of village witches, and death was not a part of them.

Every hour—every minute—Zenia was on the verge of talking just to make the pain stop. Then Gwendolyn could kill her, and Zenia would have peace at last.

But she had to keep Gwendolyn preoccupied for as long as she could. For every moment she was busy torturing Zenia, that was one moment she was not searching for Celeste. And if Zenia told a lie too soon, Gwendolyn would assume it was a lie. Zenia had to hold out as long as she could.

She had no idea how long she'd been chained up by the time her mind sank into a dullness that made the pain distant. It was as if she were watching Gwendolyn torture someone else. She could feel the pain, but it didn't matter. Nothing mattered. Maybe she wouldn't have to say anything. She could hang there, her breath belabored, nothing more than the clasps on her wrists holding her up, until death released her.

All of a sudden Gwendolyn fell back into a chair with an exasperated sigh. "You should have broken by now."

Zenia heard the words, recognized each one, but it took a moment to understand the sentence. She could muster no more strength than to whisper, "I...I... made a vow to Tamara."

"I know chambermaids are dedicated, but this much?"

"I was...her mother."

"What?"

"I...was her...wet nurse...her nanny. I...raised her."

Gwendolyn stood and approached her and peered into her face. "I should have vetted you better. Who knew a timid chambermaid would conceal such strength within her?" She removed the clasps from her wrists and ankles and let the chains rattle against the wall. She caught Zenia when she buckled and helped her across the room to lie on the bed.

Zenia closed her eyes and instantly fell asleep.

Gwendolyn woke her by removing her clothes and guiding her, still groggy, into a steaming bath. The sorceress caressed her face with a soaked washcloth. Zenia closed her eyes to enjoy the sensation.

"I've been going about this all wrong," Gwendolyn cooed in her ear. "I was a fool to do that to you. After all you did last night, I should have known you wouldn't break from torture."

The steam and the caresses and the soothing talk put Zenia into a daze. The absence of pain was a joy.

Gwendolyn said, "Clever of you to keep your magic abilities secret. I should have paid more attention to you."

"I was careful," she said, woozy from the soothing water and Gwendolyn's strokes and the pleasure of painlessness.

"Planning to betray me all along?"

"Not until you took Tamara."

"Did you learn all those spells from Deirdre?"

"Deirdre?" She tried to think what Gwendolyn was talking about.

"How did you meet with Deirdre without anyone knowing?"

She wished Gwendolyn would stop trying to make her think and let her drift into sleep. "I've never met Deirdre."

Gwendolyn's hand stopped. "Really?" she said with a cock of her head. She ran the cloth again over Zenia's left shoulder, then her right shoulder. It felt good. She was surprised at how good it felt on her right shoulder, but she couldn't think why.

"You're a clever woman," Gwendolyn said. "Clever enough to understand my purpose, I think. Perhaps you can be my partner in saving Cueldea. Perhaps I should have been forthcoming with you from the beginning."

The words made no sense. Partner? Purpose?

"But that spell is so expensive to cast. I foolishly thought I could get the information out of you."

Zenia opened her eyes and looked around. What was she doing here, soaking and relaxing in a tub? She looked around at the room to catch her bearings, seeing the trappings of a sorceress, and remembered where she was. Gwendolyn continued to sponge her down with the smile and affection of a mother.

"I deeply regret how I treated you," she said.

She sponged Zenia's belly, still tight after all these years. She thought of all the ravaged bellies she'd seen of women who had repeatedly given birth—stretch scars, loose skin. She'd given birth to only one child—a stillbirth—which made her a prime candidate for wet nurse for Duke Geoffrey's daughter when his wife died in childbirth.

"I know you think I'm evil with all I've done," Gwendolyn said as she worked on her legs. "But I want to show you something. I want you to see what I've seen, then you'll understand why I had to do what I've done, and why I *will* do whatever it takes to save Cueldea from the coming horror."

"Why should I believe you?"

"You won't have to believe me. You can see for yourself."

Zenia knotted her brow, and Gwendolyn leaned in close with a broad smile. "You'll experience a spell of Sight you've never dreamed of."

"A false vision," she said obstinately.

The steam floated before Gwendolyn's smile. "Come, little witch. You've experienced Sight. You know that feeling of certainty, that assurance of truthfulness in what you see."

Yes, Zenia knew that feeling.

"You'll see great distances. You'll see into the past and the future. You'll see the danger that's coming to our world. You'll see that it must be stopped at all costs. Then you'll understand."

A thrill passed through Zenia's body. She always wondered what Gwendolyn did hour after hour those many nights when she shut herself in these chambers with orders not to be disturbed. Using her Sight spell, Zenia could see magical energy emanating from the room, a strange and powerful glow she'd never seen before. Those times when Gwendolyn was preoccupied were the times Zenia dared practice magic herself.

But Sight spells were subtle things that didn't emanate an aura. If this really was a Sight spell, it must be so powerful, it couldn't help but glow. Zenia shuddered to think she'd been casting her own spells while Gwendolyn had a powerful Sight spell activated. She must have been too distracted all those nights to have noticed Zenia working magic.

But what was this thing Gwendolyn wanted her to see? What could she possibly show her that would justify killing Tamara and taking Celeste?

In spite of her suspicions of Gwendolyn and her fear for the safety of Eloise and Celeste, Zenia was curious and wanted to see what this powerful magic could reveal.

But she had to keep her wits. Gwendolyn's gentle, caring behavior was an obvious ploy to disarm her, to get her to talk. Zenia couldn't imagine anything that would convince her to betray Celeste. But she was happy to let Gwendolyn waste more time trying.

The sorceress spread the washcloth across the edge of the tub and reached for a huge, thick towel draped across the chair nearby. She extended her other hand and said, "Let me help you out so you can dry off and dress."

Zenia took her hand and climbed out of the tub. The air in the room hit her with a chill that felt good after the intense heat of the bathwater. Gwendolyn wrapped the towel around her and patted her all over. It was then that Zenia noticed her mangled arm had been healed.

"On my bed there's a robe for you. Put it on and lie down while I prepare the spell."

She complied as Gwendolyn gathered materials from her shelves. This spell must indeed be expensive! She pulled an impressive amount of materials down and prepared them.

The robe was soft and warm and white, and the bed engulfed her with loving goose-down arms. A brief image flashed in her mind of Tamara lying naked in the woodsman's bed as Zenia had pictured it when Tamara told the story. Her exhausted mind became drowsy, but perked awake as she smelled acrid smoke and heard forceful words. Gwendolyn stood beside her, flaming bowl in hand, casting her spell of Sight.

Zenia had cast many breath spells of Sight to examine something unseeable by mortal eyes, and occasionally burned the herbs needed to strengthen that Sight. But this was the power of a sorceress at work. This Sight flowed from the smoke of the burning materials and washed over her like a tingling fog. She could see the sphere of magic engulf Gwendolyn too.

The world, the skies, the heavens, opened up, filling her mind. She saw tens of millions of souls darting about and chattering in a dizzying frenzy. She felt the whooshing and pelting of dozens of storms throughout the lands. She smelled infinite bouquets of floral jungles and heard raucous symphonies of vicious beasts. Above her the skies teemed with birds of all sizes and plumage, of clouds she could look upon from below, from within, and from above where the face of Mistress Earth spread before her in a breathtaking expanse of colors.

Through the tumult of sensations from her own small Sight spells, Zenia could easily focus on the things she looked for. But this was too much...too much. Her mind couldn't grasp it.

"I know it's overwhelming," Gwendolyn's voice pierced through the cacophony. "Concentrate, little witch, concentrate on my voice. Focus on my face. I'll lead the way."

Zenia thrashed through the ocean of sensations to find the voice and cling to it. Gwendolyn repeated her instructions over and over: "Concentrate on my voice. Focus on my face." Zenia found the stream of words and followed it to Gwendolyn's mouth. Her Sight peered at the murky features of her face until they shimmered into clarity.

"That's right, my little witch, you're doing it."

The blast of sensations retreated into the background, becoming a dull roar, then a steady whisper like a brisk spring wind. Gwendolyn's form stood out clearly, vividly. The glow of the magical aura around both women was brilliant.

"This is an Ancient spell I discovered years ago," Gwendolyn said. "A scroll tucked in a clay pot hidden away. Abandoned by the original Seven Sisters of the Great Gods. Forgotten for centuries. You and I are the only ones who have experienced this Extended Sight for hundreds of years."

"Extended Sight?"

"We can see thousands of miles. We can look into the future to see what's developing. We can look into the past to see what's been done."

Gwendolyn's words boggled her mind. A spell from the Seven Sisters—not the mortal successors of today, but the demigod Pilgrims that had been sent into the world centuries ago. She wasn't sure Gwendolyn told the truth, but there was no denying the energy that pulsed through her soul, the images she beheld that stretched far and wide, the sense of truthfulness that permeated her. Whatever this spell was, it was powerful and it showed real things.

"I've spent years watching the world, piecing the confusing bits together into a picture of what's to come." Gwendolyn took Zenia's hand, a metaphorical gesture within the sphere of Sight that had no physical meaning in the real world. "Let me show you what I've learned."

There was both a sense of movement and no sense of movement as images rushed past. Zenia had no experience to help her interpret what she saw, but if Gwendolyn's words were reliable, she must be traveling far. The miles flew past as if the two women were each a wing on the same bird flying its way south in autumn. Vague, splashing images, more color than substance, as if a painter had randomly tossed vials of paint on his canvas. If they were traveling into the past or the future, Zenia had no way of knowing.

It seemed an instant and it seemed an eternity—traveling through this Sight gave Zenia no sense of time—before Gwendolyn slowed them down. "I discovered a world that no one in Cueldea has knowledge of," she announced.

The splashes of colors sharpened into clear images, revealing a world different from the one Zenia had known all her life. Vast expanses of plains and wildgrass. Tall mountains crowned with snow like the mountains of Scaendelreic that she'd heard about but had never seen. Thousands of wild horses roaming the land.

And a people Zenia had never dreamed of. A restless people that roamed as if they were wild horses themselves, carrying with them all that they owned. Cottages that were not cottages as Zenia's people knew them, but fleeting structures that could be erected or taken down within an hour when they were ready to roam again.

"These are the people of the East," Gwendolyn said, "spread across a land three times the size of Cueldea. They are a fierce people, cruel and violent toward one another."

Zenia focused on the people. Their skin was the color of the copper globes she'd thrown at the castle guards. Their hair was black as an overcast night in the forest with no moon. Their eyes were slits so narrow, she wondered how they could see at all.

But they could see! Even their children captured and tamed wild horses and rode them with a skill and passion that astonished her. They carried powerful bows and could grip their horses with their legs as they shot arrow after arrow in battle. Their aim was true.

Their battles were constant. She saw families and tribes raiding one another, slaughtering one another to steal the necessities of life in their barren land. The victors would rape the women and enslave the children. They would execute the leaders in terrible ways. Laying planks on them and standing on them until they suffocated. Boiling them alive in great pots.

"For a thousand years these Easterners were nothing to us," said Gwendolyn. "They battled among themselves with no thought for what lied beyond their lands. Their endless skirmishes kept them weak. Until the Blood King arose."

The view shifted as Gwendolyn directed the Sight far to the east toward a young man riding tall in the saddle of his horse, wearing a helmet of greater prestige than the thousands of warriors around him.

"See how his followers swear fealty to him, not with the words of a vow, but with the sword and with blood."

Zenia watched warriors kneel before him, cut a vertical slice on their lips with their swords, and kiss the feet of the Blood King, leaving a stain of blood in the shape of lips. All the warriors had a thin scar across their lips, and they painted their mouths crimson as a token of their loyalty born in a bloody kiss.

"But that's not the only reason he's called the Blood King. Behold his wife."

The vision shifted to the king on horseback as he surveyed a huge field from a prominent hill. The sky was blue with fluffy clouds and a bright sun shining down. His many thousands of warriors stood at the base of the hill before him, facing the army of their opponents amassed on the far end of the field. Nine archers stood ready at the front of the king's army with arrows nocked. Three flaming pots sat before them.

As a unit, nine warriors emerged from the army and rode out into the field. Behind them on foot followed nine other warriors each carrying a pot of clay. They stopped after a hundred feet and waited.

A woman walked out half the distance to them. She was dressed in a long tunic of blood red fabric with gold trimming and a gold sash tying it together.

She raised her arms to the sky and shouted a word in their language. The warriors on horseback dismounted, drew their swords, and with a loud cry sliced the heads off their horses. They straddled the fallen animals and held their swords upright before them with their eyes closed.

The woman cried another word, and the men with pots strode forward and poured a dark oil over the warriors and the horse carcasses, then stepped back ten feet. One final command from her lips, and the archers dipped their arrowheads in the flaming pots, lifted their bows, and shot the flaming arrows into the backs of the warriors. All nine arrows hit dead center.

The warriors sat motionless and never uttered a single cry as the flames engulfed them and their horses. The woman took a long, deep breath, then began moving her arms and body in a fluid dance that was disturbingly beautiful in the presence of such carnage.

"She's a sorceress who calls upon some divine power to assure their victory. She uses the powerful life vitality of nine men and nine horses to cast spells of Death Magic that the Seven Sisters hid from us because they were too destructive."

Powerful winds blew huge, dark, ominous clouds over the field. Rain pelted the ground. Lightning flashed and thunder roared. The Blood King's armies charged.

Bolts of lightning sizzled the grass of the field and the warriors of the opposing army. They broke in terror and fled. None of the bolts hit the Blood King's army.

"This king triumphs over all his enemies. But he slaughters only the leaders. He offers their people, even their warriors, freedom if they swear allegiance to him. He treats them better than their own leaders did. See how his empire grows!"

Zenia could see his reign spreading throughout the lands of the far East.

"First he united the tribes of his own people, then he conquered the kingdoms near his homeland. He ended the endless conflict among his people and built a powerful, united empire. He now sets his eyes beyond his borders."

"This is terrible!" Zenia cried. "What if his empire spreads until it threatens Cueldea?"

"It already has," Gwendolyn said ominously. "What I've shown you is the past. Behold his empire today."

The view fogged and shifted and clarified. The empire of the Blood King had expanded west until it reached the westernmost part of the Eastern continent. His warriors had grown into hundreds of thousands. His armies stood at the border of Komshu, the gateway nation between Cueldea and Ifran, peopled by a mixture of races from both continents, fair and black.

"See now what the future holds."

The armies of the Blood King attacked Komshu. They fought with a viciousness his armies never displayed when battling the nations of their own race. They slaughtered the men wantonly and raped and enslaved both women and children.

"We in the West are not of his race. They see us as inferior people, as animals, barbarians of extreme skin colors and wide eyes. The King extends no offer to join him. He destroys us."

The armies of the Blood King swept through Komshu, destroying its cities. They solidified their hold on the land, then invaded and destroyed Arazi, the nation on the east shore of the Sea of Az where the people revere the man-god Kristos. They moved into the country of Insu in Ifran where the Southern wizards are, slaughtering as they went.

"Please! No more!" Zenia cried, covering her eyes. It did nothing to block out the images of the Sight.

"I've shown you the future. The Blood King will devastate Insu, then turn his eyes to us. Cueldea will fall before his armies as easily as all the other nations did. I've seen it! Do you understand now why no cost is too great to stop this massacre?"

Gwendolyn pulled her out of the vision and back into the room, and the tingling of the spell receded into the background. Zenia lay on the bed, crumpled up in a protective ball with her arms hugging her legs, weeping uncontrollably. "That can't be a true vision."

Gwendolyn sat next to her and caressed her hair. "You know it's true. You felt the truthfulness of it."

She was right. Zenia had felt the glow of certainty within her bosom. No illusion could give that feeling.

Had Zenia misjudged Gwendolyn? Yes, the sorceress was ruthless and self-obsessed and hungered for power. But now that she'd seen what Gwendolyn had seen, she understood her urgency. She could almost forgive Gwendolyn's viciousness.

But no, her ambitions blinded her. Her bloodthirsty plans to murder Tamara and steal Celeste's power for herself were a justification, not a salvation. She could just as easily have shown Tamara what she'd shown Zenia. Of course Tamara would have understood, like Zenia understood now, and of course Tamara and her daughter would have voluntarily allied with her to stop the horror from happening.

Gwendolyn didn't want Celeste's power to save Cueldea. She wanted to steal her power so *she* could save Cueldea—and rule over it.

"Will you help me, Zenia?" Gwendolyn said, never stopping the caressing. "Will you bring me to Tamara's baby so we can combine its power with mine and stop the Easterners from destroying all that we know?"

Zenia was grateful for the vision Gwendolyn had given her so she could be aware of the threat coming from the East. But the old sorceress had to be out of her mind if she thought Zenia would betray Celeste. There was no need to. Celeste could be the savior of Cueldea that Gwendolyn wanted to be.

But Eloise knew nothing of the Blood King. She wouldn't know to prepare Celeste for the coming war. Only Zenia knew. For the first time since she resigned herself to death, she realized she had to do all she could to live and escape and warn them.

It was time to lie.

"We can partner together, you and I and Celeste, to defeat the Blood King. You don't need to kill her."

Gwendolyn's eyebrows raised, and she smiled a broad smile. "Is that the baby's name? Celeste? It's beautiful!"

Curse her foolishness! She revealed Celeste's name. How stupid of her!

"That's all I want," Gwendolyn said. "To stop the Blood King."

"Swear to me by the Great Gods that you will never harm Celeste."

"Of course, my little witch. I swear by Mother Goddess and Mistress Earth and all the Great Gods that, once Celeste has helped me stop the Blood King, I'll leave her completely alone until the day she dies. I swear I won't allow any harm to come to her...once the Blood King has been stopped."

Zenia peered carefully into Gwendolyn's eyes. Her broad smile remained. Her eyes gazed back unflinchingly. Her soothing handstrokes were comforting.

Zenia didn't believe a word of it. She may not be very smart, but she could see that the carefully worded oath promised nothing. Of course Gwendolyn wouldn't harm Celeste after the Blood King was stopped. She'd kill her before the Blood King was stopped to possess the power that would stop him.

But she could pretend to believe.

"Celeste is in the care of Deirdre," Zenia said. "Deirdre helped me rescue Tamara from the dungeon. She cast the spell of the two bright auras to confuse you. When I escaped into the forest, I met Deirdre there. She cast a spell to hide Celeste's aura and took the child with her."

Zenia studied Gwendolyn's face to see if she believed it. The sorceress revealed nothing of what she was thinking.

"That's all I know," she finished. "I don't know what happened after that."

Gwendolyn took too long gazing and smiling. The stroking had stopped. "Deirdre," she murmured.

"Yes."

"I thought you said you never met Deirdre."

"What?"

The smile evaporated. "You're a fool, Zenia. I gave you a chance to cooperate with me, and I'd kill you right now for making me waste that expensive spell on you. But I have another use for it. Now you'll see the real power of Extended Sight."

Gwendolyn drew her back into the Sight spell and directed them toward the castle in Luteche. "Finding things with Extended Sight is difficult with all the sensations bombarding you. But if you know where to start watching, you can follow events and find out everything that happened."

Zenia stared in horror as she realized Gwendolyn had taken her back to the night she helped Tamara escape. She saw herself waking from the Truth Dream, leading Mariam into the dungeon, exchanging her for Tamara, and riding off into Fenweald Forest with her.

"Well done, little witch!" Gwendolyn said. "You handled that perfectly."

Zenia saw herself stop in the clearing, lay Tamara on the ground, and deliver the baby. She watched herself cast the Purification spell. With tears streaming down her face, she witnessed again her queen die. She watched as the Beast attacked and was repelled. She observed Mistress Moon turn an infant monster into the beautiful Celeste.

"Amazing!" Gwendolyn whispered.

The Zenia of last night rode with Celeste until they met Eloise.

"Who is this?" Gwendolyn asked, then gasped as Eloise revealed the scrying globe.

Zenia watched Eloise create the illusion aura. She saw the two of them part as Eloise rode away with Celeste. Gwendolyn kept the focus of the Extended Sight on Eloise. Zenia trembled with fear.

"Now let's see what your powerful friend did with Celeste."

Zenia began a breath spell of Negation, hoping it would be strong enough to break this powerful Sight, but Gwendolyn clamped her hand over her mouth before she could finish. She wept and wished she could turn her eyes from the Sight, but she could only follow where Gwendolyn took her. Eloise rode to their home village of Vilnetal in the Duchy of Suedeche, then rode out into the forest where she stopped at her hiding place and pulled out a hidden chest. Within the chest were scrolls and a trinket.

"Great Mistress Earth," Gwendolyn whispered. "Where did she get those?"

Eloise took the trinket and placed it over her neck, then spoke a word of command.

The Sight jumped to some other location in the forest.

"*What?*" Gwendolyn shrieked.

She directed the Sight back to where Eloise had unearthed the chest and followed her actions again. At the same point, the focus of the Sight jumped to yet another location in the forest.

A stream of curses spewed from Gwendolyn's mouth, invoking many Gods by name.

Zenia's heart leaped with joy. She had no idea what Eloise had done, but somehow even this powerful Sight could not follow her any further.

Gwendolyn uttered the spell of Negation herself, and the energy of the Sight burst and flew away in a whirlwind of sparkles. She thrust her face into Zenia's view, snarling horribly. "*You will tell me who she is and where she took her!*"

Zenia grinned at her. "Do you think she'd be stupid enough to tell me?"

"It was Deirdre, wasn't it? She gave her those things."

Zenia shrugged.

Gwendolyn jumped to her feet. "Guards!" she bellowed, and the door to her chambers flew open.

Zenia recognized the guards that came in, Ismael and Audric.

"Strip her, bind her, and gag her," she ordered.

The two guards tore the robe from Zenia and bound her hands behind her back. Before they could slip the gag over her mouth, she cried out, "We've beaten you, Gwendolyn. You'll never have Celeste."

Gwendolyn smiled an evil smile. "You think I haven't prepared for every contingency?" She marched to her shelves and began filling a sack with items as the gag slid into place. "You should have talked while you had the chance. Now others will pay for your stubbornness."

Zenia shivered as the chill of the room and the chill of Gwendolyn's words soaked into her naked skin.

"Bring her out to the execution field," Gwendolyn ordered.

With no gentleness, the two guards dragged Zenia out of the keep and across the courtyard, through the outer gatehouse and to the edge of the forest, to the field where notorious criminals were executed by spear. A whole day had passed, and night had fallen again. Zenia blessed Mistress Moon, full and ghostly above the east horizon, for what she'd done for Celeste.

This is it, she thought. I'm being executed and it's all over. Gwendolyn still thinks Celeste was delivered to Deirdre, and now it was all up to Eloise to protect her. She wished she could warn Eloise about the Blood King, but at least the little princess had a chance—a very good chance now—to survive. One day she may still be able to stop the invasion from the East.

Zenia prayed to Mother Goddess like she never prayed before. *Please warn Celeste about the Blood King.* She vowed, when she died and entered the presence of the Goddess, to supplicate her personally.

Ismael and Audric brought her to one of the posts in the execution field. Her hands were pulled back and tied together behind the post. Her ankles were tied to it as well. The rough slivers of the post bit into her naked back.

Gwendolyn walked up to Zenia and started spreading materials from her sack in a circle around her. "You know the Beast is abroad in the land again. After all these years! It attacked us last night as well as you and Tamara."

She stopped in front of Zenia and produced a flask of oil. "Superstitious peasants don't understand the curse of the Beast. They think a sorceress can cast a spell and destroy it."

Gwendolyn carefully poured the oil around the circle, making sure it touched every weed and herb and mineral she had placed on the ground. "Do you believe that, Zenia? Are you a superstitious fool like the peasants?"

Zenia didn't understand what Gwendolyn was doing or why she talked about the Beast. Why didn't she just command the guards to jab a spear into her?

Standing before her again, Gwendolyn produced a small, straight stick from her pocket. "They don't understand, we can't destroy the Beast. Its curse comes from a source very ancient and very different than the magic we practice. Our skills can't destroy it. The most we can do is ward it off." She twirled the stick back and forth between her fingers. "Or attract it."

She spoke a short spell, and the tip of the stick burst into a flame. "That's exactly what I'm going to do."

She dropped the flaming stick onto the oil and spoke the words of a spell as it flared up quickly into a ring of fire.

"I'm attracting the Beast now." Gwendolyn looked Zenia up and down. "And there you stand naked and tied to a post. What a vulnerable position to be in!"

A bloodcurdling howl rang from the forest, and a shudder swept through Zenia's frame. A spear wasn't good enough for Gwendolyn. It was execution by mutilation. Not only physical mutilation, but spiritual mutilation—if the superstitions of the peasants could be believed. Zenia would be torn to pieces and devoured by the Beast and enter the next life accursed. That meant no chance to be in the presence of Mother Goddess.

Dear Goddess, could those superstitions be true? She'd dismissed the legends of the Beast all her life, but now that she'd seen the Beast with her own eyes, she couldn't dismiss them any longer.

"I will not betray Celeste," she said into her gag, knowing the words would never reach Gwendolyn's ears.

The flame died away, leaving charred materials behind. The howl sounded again, nearer.

"What is that you're saying, little fodder for the Beast?" Gwendolyn said in a mocking tone. "Have you convinced yourself you're even willing to sacrifice your soul to protect Tamara's little brat?" Gwendolyn approached her and spoke into her ear. "Do you know what? I believe you would. I do believe you'd sacrifice your own soul to save the child."

She turned to the guards and barked, "Bring them!" To Zenia she said, "While we were having our conversation today, I had the guards gather up some of the orphans in the city. *They* will be fodder for the Beast."

Oh Goddess no!

The guards dragged out a procession of small, weeping children, naked and dirty and tied together with ropes around their wrists to form a chain. They positioned them in a line before Zenia, facing her. The two guards drove a stake into the ground on either end of the line and tied the rope to them. The children pulled against the stakes, but they held fast.

Gwendolyn eyed her with a deep scowl. "Don't make me do this."

Rivers of tears burst from Zenia's eyes. She struggled against her bands, beat her head against the post, cried out to Mother Goddess to release her so she could save the children.

Quietly Gwendolyn said, "You can stop all this, Zenia. Just nod your head, and I'll remove the gag. Then you can tell me where Celeste is, and these children can live, unharmed and uncorrupted by the Beast. You'll also have the satisfaction of knowing Celeste's sacrifice will save the world."

She continued to struggle.

"Zenia, don't be a fool! It's best for everyone."

The Beast sprang from the edge of the trees and roared, some two hundred feet away. Zenia jerked in terror and the children screamed. They yanked against the ropes and the stakes, but the guards poked at them with spears and shouted at them to stand still. Some of the children dropped to the ground and wept. Others cried out to Gwendolyn, to the guards, to help them.

"You can stop this, Zenia," Gwendolyn shouted over the din. "Just nod your head, and I'll ward off the Beast."

The monster crept forward with a menacing growl as it eyed the guards and the children. It was the same wolf that had appeared while Tamara gave birth.

The guards drew back away from the children, clearly frightened.

"I placed a Warding on the children," Gwendolyn said. "The Beast can't make a sudden attack, but it can slowly approach them."

The monster had covered half the distance to the children, close enough to see the saliva dripping from its fangs. Its head was low and its red eyes gleamed with bloodlust.

"This is your last chance, Zenia. Do you want the lives and the souls of these children on your conscience?"

Zenia raged with all the rage and horror she felt, thrashing back and forth. She couldn't let that foul monster attack the children. "Oh Mother Goddess!" she cried out against the gag. "What do I do? Please save them!"

The Beast approached.

"No!" Zenia wept. The child nearest to the wolf shrieked and broke into a dance of terror.

"Just nod," Gwendolyn said.

Zenia howled one last howl. It wasn't just the lives of these children. It was their very souls. She couldn't let it happen.

She nodded violently.

Immediately Gwendolyn pulled a copper globe from her pocket, whirled around, and threw it hard at the Beast. The globe burst open against its face and a green smoke spewed out. The Beast yelped and reared up and jumped back. The smoke dissipated as the Beast rubbed its face with its paws.

"Get the children out of here!" Gwendolyn shouted, and the guards ran forward and sliced the ropes free of the stakes with their swords. The children were pulled to their feet and rushed away.

Gwendolyn tugged at the gag until it came loose. "That Warding vapor won't last long, and I don't have another globe of it. Tell me what I want to know now, or the children come back and I leave you all to your fate."

Zenia shut her eyes and banged her head against the post.

"Tell me, little bitch—*now!*"

Zenia wept and shook her head in despair.

"Guards!" Gwendolyn shouted.

"No! I'll tell you."

Gwendolyn peered at her with wrath-filled eyes. "Where is Celeste?"

"With Eloise."

"Who?"

"The woman you saw take her away."

"Who is she?"

"The village witch that took me in when my parents were murdered."

"Impossible! No witch has the powers she had. Who helped her?"

"No one helped her." Zenia spat out the words between her sobs.

"I'll call the children back."

"She stole her magic from somewhere else."

Incredulously Gwendolyn asked, "Where?"

"I don't know."

"*Where?*"

"*I don't know!* You don't think she'd be stupid enough to tell me, do you? She knew you'd torture me."

Gwendolyn nodded slowly. "I believe you. No matter. I'll find them."

Zenia broke into sobs. All she wanted to do now was die.

Gwendolyn kissed her on the cheek and whispered, "Goodbye, little witch. You fought a good fight. I honor your courage. But I can't have you around interfering with me anymore." She started to walk away, then turned. "I have no idea if the superstitions of the peasants are true. I hope for the sake of your soul they're not."

She walked to the outer gatehouse of the castle and disappeared. The Beast had stopped yelping and prancing in anguish. It stood quietly, its head low, its eyes glaring at Zenia, a soft steady growl coming from its throat.

This was it! The Warding vapor would fade, the Beast would advance, and Zenia would be torn to shreds and devoured. And she didn't even have the comfort of knowing she'd kept silent. She had betrayed Eloise—she had betrayed Celeste. How long before Gwendolyn found them? Years—months—days? She had no idea.

The Beast approached in the same threatening, creeping gait. The Warding vapor must be wearing off. Zenia spoke prayer after prayer to the Mother Goddess—for Celeste, for Eloise, for the fate of Cueldea, for her own soul.

As the Beast lunged and tore the liver from her belly, she prayed that the superstitions of the peasants were wrong.

Chapter 7

Christian

Christian peered grimly from his window above as the Beast devoured the chambermaid. It was disturbing that a myth from the hoary past had come alive before his eyes, disturbing that the sorceress who served his kingdom was willing to do such merciless things. But he also felt a deep satisfaction at the sight. That bitch chambermaid had caused the death of his love, Mariam.

Now he had to deal with a squalling little monster and a new wet nurse to help him. Even now, he could hear its faint wail piercing through the stone walls of the castle.

This was supposed to be a joyous time, he and Mariam doting together over his heir, the future king. He'd have been the loving father when the creature made sweet cooing noises and gave off sweet newborn aromas, and banished it and Mariam to her chambers where she and her chambermaid could deal with it when it did not.

Instead Mariam was dead, the chambermaid was dead, and all he had was the wet nurse his servants had scrambled up from the city that day. What was her name? Ah yes, Henrietta. It irked him that a scrawny, plain, peasant girl's teats filled the mouth of the prince instead of his queen's teats.

His only consolation was that the chambermaid died a horrible death that probably doomed her soul for eternity, and that the queen his parents had forced on him for political reasons had fled with whatever horror festered within her womb and was dead. Christian still had no idea why that baby was so important to Gwendolyn, and he didn't care. The understanding he had with her was exactly how he liked things. He let her worry about the details of ruling the kingdom so he could focus on his hunts and his jousts and his archery and his feasts with friends and his nights of passion with his love.

Mariam alone made his life endurable. Ever since he stole her virginity on a pile of hay in her father's stable during one of his clandestine nights out, reaping the harvest of females in the kingdom, his passion for her never died. She loved him, she adored him, she served his every whim. He wanted to make her his queen, but his coldblooded parents wouldn't allow it. They needed an alliance with Duke Geoffrey—what did they care about his heart?

But he got his revenge in the end. He arranged to have Mariam work in the kitchen and snuck her into his bed whenever he could keep Tamara away. When Tamara caught them one night and broke into a hysteria and ran off like the child she was, then came back pregnant by the Gods knew who, Gwendolyn came to him with an arrangement. He was finally able to make Mariam his queen.

Gwendolyn had to make her look like Tamara, but that was okay. It wasn't that Tamara wasn't beautiful, and he looked forward to bedding her on their wedding night. But she was no Mariam. She was as timid as a cockroach and had no idea what she was doing. It was like loving a bowl of porridge.

He flopped down fully clothed on his bed, the bed where he and Mariam had loved each other almost every night until the child in her became so large, lovemaking became more acrobatics than passion, and he banished her to her own bed until her belly and her honeypot returned to normal.

If he'd known their last lovemaking before he banished her would be their last lovemaking forever, he'd have opted for the acrobatics.

He didn't even have Tamara anymore to satisfy his urges. She was dead, and Gwendolyn was tightlipped with what happened. What happened to her baby he also didn't know, but Gwendolyn must not have it because she was in an even fouler mood than normal. All he knew was, she'd caught the chambermaid that helped her escape and fed her to a monster out of the darkest nightmare.

He lay on the bed with an arm over his eyes, wondering what he would do with his life. Go carousing at night again, searching for another Mariam? Marry another virgin daughter of some ruler that didn't seem to have a better reason to ally with Luteche?

It's not like he had an obligation to marry again. He had his heir. It was a screeching, squirming headache now, but when it got old enough to become a son, someone Christian could bring hunting and teach archery to and educate on the pleasures of girls, someone who could find his own way to the privy instead of soiling perfectly good linen, he'd enjoy his offspring then.

My son will be king one day.

The thought exploded into his head. It sobered him. What kind of king would he be?

He'd be whatever kind of king Christian taught him to be.

If Christian continued as he was, he'd teach his son to be a useless, carousing, lust-filled king, a king unfit to rule. Gwendolyn would have to be the one to teach the boy how to be a king, and that aggravated Christian. Or she'd have to quietly rule in his stead like she did now. That aggravated him even more.

What was he doing, he suddenly asked himself, letting that witch rule his kingdom? She'd come out of nowhere, and his father King Guillaume had accepted her as his sorceress out of desperation because the threat from Scaendelreic loomed. King Gunther had a sorceress to aid him, one of those cursed Seven Sisters. Without Gwendolyn, Gallea didn't stand a chance.

He sat up and swung his legs over the edge of the bed. *I'm as much a child as Tamara was!* he said to himself. He hated his parents, but he always respected the king his father was. He was a strong king, a king who cared about his kingdom and his subjects. He needed Gwendolyn, but he never let her control him. It wasn't until he and his queen died in the war that Gwendolyn swooped in as the shadow regent for boy Christian.

Well, he wasn't a boy anymore, and he'd better stop acting like one. This fiasco with Tamara's child showed he had no idea what she was doing with his kingdom. He had no idea what was so important about Tamara's baby and what Gwendolyn had intended to do with it.

As he thought those things, realization hit him. His own son was the son of a king, but a fraudulent queen. Tamara's child was the offspring of a true queen, but an unknown father. Her child and his were both illegitimate, both born the same night, and both had a claim to the throne.

Gwendolyn would love to have her own heir on the throne, one she could raise and control. That meant she had to rid herself of Tamara, of Christian, and...

He realized he never bothered to name his son—the prince, the future king. More proof that he was a child himself, *more* of a child than Tamara.

He stood up tall and said, "No more! I shall be king!"

He marched out of his chambers and into the nursery where Henrietta had her breast out feeding his child. His sudden appearance startled her, and she began to tremble. She pulled the baby from her teat and tried to stand. The child began to cry.

"No, no!" he said with his hand up. "Please continue."

She hesitated, then sat back down, and guided her teat back into the child's mouth. He sucked greedily.

Christian dragged a chair over and sat close so he could touch the boy. He stroked the wispy hair and studied the scrunched eyes. Something welled up in his chest, a feeling completely unknown to him, a wholesome joy that even Mariam had never invoked in him.

"My prince, my crown prince," he whispered. "My son."

Christian would have to think long and hard, would have to carefully strategize, how to handle Gwendolyn. He knew she wouldn't just relinquish the power she'd grown used to wielding. Having witnessed what she did with the chambermaid, he knew she'd kill without hesitation. He was about to take on a sorceress powerful enough to withstand Deirdre.

He pursed his lips as he thought. In one instant he'd gone from self-centered child to contemplating the most dangerous path of his life. Nor was it his life alone at stake, but that of his son as well. He'd have to act with great caution and great cunning.

"My son," he murmured again as Henrietta gazed at him with wide eyes. "You need a name." At once he knew what that name should be. Christian would make sure this prince would grow up to be as great a king as his own father, a king worthy of the name...

"Guillaume. Prince Guillaume of Gallea."

Chapter 8

Sighurd

Now that she was in the privacy of her chambers, Gwendolyn shook uncontrollably. That had been too close! What if Zenia had never broken? What if she waited a few seconds too long? What if Gwendolyn had missed when she threw the Warding globe?

As an abstract thought, she'd convinced herself that even sacrificing some orphan children with no families was worth the cost of saving Cueldea. But when confronted with the image of that monster advancing on the terrified children, she was horrified. She couldn't let it happen! Yet she had to let it happen. Zenia had to break.

Zenia did break. Of course she broke. She couldn't possibly let those children die either. But she took so long. Gwendolyn expected her to break immediately as soon as the children were before her and the Beast appeared. For a few agonizing seconds, Gwendolyn thought she might not, and in that moment she realized that *she* couldn't let it happen.

With every fiber of her being crying out to stop the Beast, Gwendolyn had to stand there stone cold with a passionless face, playing the cruel monster Zenia thought she was. She had to resist the overwhelming urge to look back and see how close the Beast was. The hair on her neck prickled at the thought that it may already be too late.

She stumbled to a bottle of wine, pulled the stopper, and took a deep draught.

Thank the Great Gods Zenia *had* broken, barely in time. Thank the Gods her aim was true, or all of them might have died, including herself.

She sat with the bottle, taking more swallows, letting a single smirking laugh escape her lips as she thought of the Seven Sisters and their solemn vow to never consume spirits—a vow as stringent as their vow of chastity. A drunken sorceress casting spells was not a happy thought. Gwendolyn honored the spirit of that vow herself, indulging rarely and sparingly.

But not tonight. Tonight she needed it because she couldn't calm her shakes.

As the wine did its work, she prayed, "Mother Goddess, accept Zenia's soul. You have to accept it. None of this was her doing. She was a loyal servant to her queen."

The words stole her composure. She let tears slide down her cheek. "Curse my soul if you must, but accept hers. I'm the one responsible."

A couple more swallows stilled her weeping. "Calm down, Genoveva," she told herself. "Think of what you've accomplished."

She learned Deirdre did not have Celeste. She may not even know Celeste exists. What a relief! That sensation soothed the anguish and gave her a measure of peace.

But only a small measure. Eloise had her, but who was Eloise? After the things she'd seen happen last night, Gwendolyn wondered if she was a greater danger than Deirdre. Somehow that witch purified a dark power, created an illusory aura, and made the real aura disappear—things a hundred village witches together could never do.

She thought of her treasured amulet hidden away in the secret compartment of her room, the Magic Eater. The one she'd used when she met quietly with Deirdre years ago to discuss an unofficial truce between Gallea and Scaendelreic. Was it possible a second one existed, and Eloise possessed it? Was that what the trinket was she put on?

She'd never heard of an Ancient amulet ever being duplicated, but who knew what the Seven Sisters of old had done, what artifacts they'd hidden away?

She realized maybe it would have been better if Deirdre did have Celeste. She at least was a known quantity. This Eloise, whoever she was, had access to spells that put her in the same league as a sorceress. How many other unknown tricks did she have at her disposal?

Yet she was no member of the Seven Sisters. Only one other person had power comparable to the Seven Sisters without being one of them—and that was Gwendolyn herself, Gwendolyn the Rogue Sorceress.

Until now. Another rogue sorceress had arisen, one who'd hidden herself in plain sight as a village witch. With a loyalty and a purpose that could not be guessed at.

The sense of relief evaporated. Celeste was in the hands of a rogue sorceress.

But there was still one small hope. Zenia would never hand Celeste over to someone who might be a threat to the child. She trusted Eloise to keep her safe. Zenia's plan would be to protect Celeste, not exploit her.

Unless Eloise deceived Zenia to get possession of the girl. Was that likely? Zenia knew her intimately. If Eloise were a ruthless character, surely Zenia would have noticed something long ago. Then again, no one who knew Gwendolyn in her youth when she was called Genoveva would have ever dreamed she'd become the person she was today.

She sighed in exasperation. The situation was too volatile. She needed more information. Even her Extended Sight failed her there, with that strange power deflecting it to random spots.

That flamed her anger, and with the alcohol affecting her brain, she decided to try once more. She gathered up and prepared the materials needed, taking longer than she normally would with the spirits affecting her mind, and cast the spell.

The Sight deluged her senses. Mixed with the wine, she felt a touch of nausea. Why had she drunk it? She could only sit and close her eyes and take deep breaths. Closed eyes didn't shield Sight, but at least they kept the room from spinning.

Finally her brain sorted through the sensations and found clarity. She sought out the location where Eloise had dug up the chest. Maybe if she concentrated hard enough, she could break past the deflection.

It took her a few seconds this time to realize that her focus jumped again. She laughed at herself. How foolish to talk about concentrating after imbibing wine!

She cursed herself for getting drunk and wasting more of the rare materials on a useless attempt. To not waste the spell, she decided to cast her vision toward the East and the threat emerging there. She began by looking into the past to see what the Blood King had been up to since she'd last spied on him.

He was still hard at work conquering Komshu, having destroyed a number of cities as his armies advanced. The vision disturbed her, but at least he was still occupied there. The threat to Cueldea was still in the future.

But then she noticed scouts sent further west, slinking past Komshu and into Insu in Ifran. Even before he'd conquered Komshu, the king was already preparing for his invasions beyond its borders.

She followed the first pair of scouts the Blood King sent as they crossed the border into Insu, riding on horseback. The first stretch of Insan soil was barren desert sparsely populated, and they had no encounters there. The first encounter they were likely to have was at the city of Eranshar where the Ribat of Wizards was located. They were headed straight for it.

Gwendolyn swept her Sight forward to the ribat. She could never see what happened inside it thanks to the Masking spell surrounding it, the same spell all wizards and sorceresses surrounded their domiciles with to keep prying eyes out. But from her past observations, she knew they routinely sent scouting patrols out, more for training purposes she guessed than any actual need to scout for dangers, since they were always such young men. She could see their comings and goings once they left the masked area.

She watched a number of them patrol without incident, but one pair of scouts caught her eye as they traveled east, heading directly toward the scouts of the Blood King.

They were about to encounter each other within a grove of olive trees, two wizard novitiates on foot heading right toward two Eastern warriors on horseback. When they sensed each other's presence, they readied their weapons, the novitiates their strange curved swords and the warriors their bows and arrows.

The Easterners charged, and a skirmish ensued. Gwendolyn felt a twinge of sorrow for the novitiates, expecting a bloodbath. They were mere boys against the terrorizing warriors that had swept across the Eastern continent. One of the novitiates was wounded badly and about to be slaughtered, but the other fought hard with great skill and held his own, until he tripped and dropped his sword.

Gwendolyn's blood chilled. She realized she was watching the first battle in the invasion of the West. She hadn't expected it to come so soon. Small as the skirmish was, it would be the very first defeat for Insu in a long string of defeats against the Easterners. Time was truly running out for Cueldea, and Gwendolyn had lost her secret weapon because of a lowly chambermaid that had schemed under her nose for months. She wanted to pray and retract her plea to Mother Goddess for Zenia's soul.

But wait! The boy that tripped sprang up and nearly chopped the head off the Eastern warrior. He ran to the other warrior and sliced him open. He threw his dying companion on a horse and rode back to the ribat, even though he had wounds of his own.

The two were swallowed up by the blind spot of the Masking spell. Gwendolyn kept staring at nothing in amazement. Who was that young wizard-in-training? His skill at swordfighting was high, but he was still on the verge of defeat, when he sprang up and within a moment won the battle.

She moved back to where the battle began and watched more carefully. Arrows shot at him, one of which wounded him. A strafing of the horse's shins that brought the warrior down to his level. An intense swordfight where he held his own, but slowly wearied, until he stumbled and fell to the ground.

Then he broke into tears. Into tears, like a child! The warrior smirked at him and prepared to deliver the final blow

But suddenly the boy leaped to his feet, sword magically in his hand, and struck with his curved blade, taking advantage of his opponent's haughty moment of carelessness.

He'd won the battle not only with skill, but with cunning, luring his opponent into complacency, then striking—in a battle that was probably his first.

This was a boy Gwendolyn needed to keep an eye on.

Suddenly several novitiates, including the victorious boy, emerged from the Masking spell on horseback, accompanied by a wizard with his embedded gems. They rode to the grove where the wizard directed the novitiates to clean up the battlefield. He brought the victorious boy to the downed horse and, plucking a gem from his torso, held it to his mouth. It glowed brightly, and the horse carcass vanished.

Gwendolyn gasped. She had thought those gems were only decorative, insignia that marked a wizard. Clearly they played a significant role in the magic of the Southern wizards. She had no idea what they were or where they came from or how powerful they were.

Gwendolyn moved in close and watched the scene again, listening to their conversation. The master was named Izzet and the novitiate Kasimir. The master praised the student for his victory. He also understood what needed to be done—what he made sure was done. The battle needed to be swept out of existence. The Blood King must never find out what happened to his scouts. Their mysterious disappearance in the West would give him pause, wondering what the Westerners had done to them. It would make the Westerners appear more powerful and intimidating. It would make him a little more cautious.

This ended up not to be the first victory in the Blood King's invasion of the West after all. This was a setback for him, a small one to be sure, but a setback buying a little more time. Accomplished through the quick thinking and actions of a young inexperienced man who stood against two experienced warriors.

She wanted these wizards with their gem stones on her side as allies. But would they agree? Could she trust them? She doubted it.

But perhaps there was one thing she could do. In her nights of watching them, she knew their young apprentices could be hired out for undertakings. They called them mage quests, and those seemed to be the final test to prove a novitiate worthy of becoming a wizard.

Those who hired them were always natives of Ifran. As far as Gwendolyn knew, no one from Cueldea had ever commissioned a quest. She didn't know if the wizards would allow such a thing.

But if she could harness that power from the gems, adding it her own, then adding Celeste's power to her own, she would certainly be the downfall of the Blood King.

If she commissioned a mage quest, she could bring them to Gallea, observe them, learn about them, explore their powers, test their inclinations, find their weaknesses. And she knew which one of their novitiates she wanted to hire. Kasimir, the victor in the first skirmish with the Easterners.

She had to try. She knew exactly what she wanted the mage quest to be. Find a woman and a baby hidden deep somewhere in the world. Perhaps the gems of the wizards could accomplish what her Extended Sight could not.

The next day Gwendolyn called Sighurd to her chambers. It was something she rarely did. She and he were not on the friendliest of terms, he being so passionate about serving the king. She knew her shadow rule of the kingdom rankled him, but it's what King Christian wanted, so he endured it.

She sat at a table as she waited for his knock. When he entered, she said,

"Close that door and bolt it."

He peered at her for a moment, then closed the door and slid the bolt into place. She gestured toward the other chair, and he sat.

She bore her eyes into his until he said, "How can I serve you, Mistress?"

"Who are you loyal to, Captain?"

His brow knotted. "To the crown of Gallea, of course. To the king."

"And what about me?"

"I'm loyal to you as well—as long as you serve the king."

She smiled at that and rested her hand on his. "I never doubted it. I have a mission for you, a task that's the most important task you've ever been assigned to do in the name of the king."

He flinched almost imperceptibly at those words, but said, "I swear I'll perform it faithfully."

"Take your most trusted men, three or four of them, and travel south to Insu, to the Ribat of Wizards."

He gazed at her in surprise.

"I know this is an extraordinary assignment, but the future of the kingdom depends on it."

"The future of the kingdom," he said suspiciously.

"That's right. I'm sending you down with a great deal of money, and you'll hire one of their novitiates to go on a mage quest for us."

"I don't know what that is."

"It's a quest they send their novitiates on to prove themselves worthy of becoming a wizard. The novitiate I want is named Kasimir. I want to emphasize, it's essential that Kasimir be the one selected for this, and essential that it happen as soon as possible."

She let him think about it for a moment, which he did with a frown. "And what is the quest?"

She sat back and took a deep breath. "This is why I asked you about your loyalty. I'm going to tell you things that only the king and myself know. It's about Zenia."

"The one you let the Beast kill." His tone was accusing.

"What fate would you prefer for someone who steals your queen?"

He stared back with pursed lips.

"She didn't abduct Tamara because she wanted the queen. She wanted her baby. I don't know why, but it may be to make a claim to the throne at some point. Perhaps to start a rebellion."

"That sounds awfully ambitious for a chambermaid," he said with a dark scowl.

"She was a pawn. She was acting for her stepmother, whom we believe is hiding the infant now."

"That sounds awfully ambitious for the stepmother of a chambermaid."

Gwendolyn swallowed her irritation and forced a smile. "She pretends to be a village witch in Suedeche, but in actuality she has powers comparable to a sorceress."

His expression did not look convinced. "None of this makes any sense. We have Tamara's son with us."

"Tamara's baby is a girl, a princess, and she's being hidden by the step-mother now, whose name is Eloise. We need her found."

"But...then who is the infant boy everyone says is the prince?"

"He's a substitute for the princess, until we can find her. We don't want the abduction to be known."

He smirked. "Wouldn't a baby girl have been a better substitute?"

"This is serious!" she barked at him. "We could find only one other child born last night in the outlying villages, and that was a boy."

"I mean no disrespect," he said. Gwendolyn got the feeling he meant the exact opposite. "But won't it be strange when the prince becomes a princess all of a sudden, once she's found?"

"Once she's found, we can tell everyone what happened. It won't matter then. Now listen carefully. All the wizards need to know is that our princess was abducted by a sorceress, and we want them to find her and bring her safely home."

"I understand."

"But I also want you to see what you can learn about them while you're there. Do it in a way that doesn't make them think you're spies."

"They'll probably assume we're spies anyway."

"But don't give them a reason to confirm it! Just...be careful and keep your eyes open. It's more important to arrange the quest than to gather information."

Sighurd took in a deep breath and exhaled it noisily. "And the king knows all about this?"

"Of course he knows. He commanded it. You'll tell them this is for the king of Gallea. Say nothing about me. Now who do you think you'll bring with you?"

"The ones I brought with when we found Tamara's body. Dietric and Thomas and...Hereward."

"Hereward? Wasn't he the one—"

"Yes, but didn't you say he wouldn't change for months? This journey should take only weeks."

Gwendolyn sat back in the chair and thought. Knowing nothing about the magic of the wizards, she had no idea how easily they'd detect the corruption slowly growing inside Hereward, and what they'd think if they found out. She also wasn't certain about the delay of months. The Beast was a legend, and how much information in the legend was accurate, no one really knew. She couldn't be sure when he would change.

"Does it need to be Hereward?"

"You said my most trusted men. Those are the ones whose loyalty matches my own."

"Then bring him. Keep a sharp eye on him." A thought occurred to her. "Maybe...maybe you can feel Kasimir out on the journey back, see if their magic could help him. Delicately."

"You're asking things of me a soldier has not been trained to do. I fight battles. I protect the king. Delicacy is not something I have much experience with."

"Do the best you can. The most important thing is to arrange that quest and bring Kasimir back to Luteche. Let nothing else interfere with that."

"Yes, Mistress."

"Now gather your men and prepare to leave at once. Tell no one about this before you leave. It must be kept secret."

"But if we disappear for weeks..."

"I'll make excuses for you."

He nodded and left the room.

"Gods protect you," Gwendolyn whispered, wondering if he'd return alive.

Sighurd closed the door behind him and took a moment to process what had just happened. This encounter with Gwendolyn disturbed him. It was a strange conversation, almost preposterous, and something wasn't right.

He was about to locate his three men when someone called from behind him in a harsh whisper. "Sighurd!"

He turned and found Christian hiding in the shadows of the corridor. The king beckoned him to approach.

The king slinking about in his own castle? What now?

Sighurd went to him, and Christian pulled him into his chambers, closed the door, and bolted it. He dragged Sighurd to a couple chairs and sat him down.

"Are you still loyal to me?" Christian asked.

Sighurd was instantly apprehensive. The same question Gwendolyn had asked. "I've always been loyal to you, and to your father before you."

"What did you and Gwendolyn talk about?"

"What you commanded her to talk to me about."

"Tell me what that was."

"To travel to Insu and arrange a mage quest with the wizards."

"A what?"

Sighurd's head swam. The king didn't know about this! What in the name of the Gods was Gwendolyn doing?

"To hire one of them to come here and search for the princess."

"She told you about the...princess?"

"That she was abducted, and that you found a newborn boy in a nearby village to play the prince until she can be found."

His head jerked. "Play the...she said that?"

Something was very wrong. The king didn't seem to know anything that Gwendolyn had told him. "Your Majesty, she said you knew about all this. Should I...can she be trusted?"

"Sighurd, I've played the fool since I became king. I let her run everything."

He was surprised, but pleased, to hear Christian say that.

"There's something about seeing your own son that...that..." His face became chalky. "Sighurd, do you think she really gave me an impostor for a son?"

"I don't know what to say. That's what she told me. But she said you knew."

Christian stared into space with a scowl.

"Shall I detain her and interrogate her?" Sighurd asked.

"No, no!" he said with alarm. "I've been such a fool! I've let her rule Gallea, and now...I don't know what she's up to. I don't know where her loyalties lie." He looked pleadingly at Sighurd. "I don't even know which one is my real child."

"I think...I mean, the girl is Tamera's. That much I know."

His face brightened. "So he *is* my son."

"The *boy* is your child, not the girl?" Sighurd asked. "Your Majesty, I have no idea what's going on."

"Sighurd, go on that quest of hers as if nothing was wrong. Are you bringing anyone with you?"

"Three of my most trusted men."

"Good, good. Do everything she said. Act like we never had this conversation. But watch for...anything...that might indicate what Gwendolyn is up to. We have to be very careful about this. I can't fight a sorceress."

"Yes, Your Majesty."

Sighurd walked away from the chambers in a daze. How could this day have gotten more insane? Gwendolyn plotting against the king? The queen's daughter was not the king's? Who was the boy everyone called the prince? He was glad he had a long journey ahead of him so he could think through all this, so he could figure out what he should do about it.

The only thing clear in his mind right now was, his loyalty lay with his king. Always.

Deirdre descended into the forest in the west end of Suedeche, her best estimate of where the aura had disappeared. With her Sight, she scoured the area as she flew low over it, looking for any clue she could find.

Of course she found no person. It would be the stupidest thief alive who cast a powerful spell to hide the aura, then loitered there until she was found. But there were other things that might leave a clue.

Like the faint shimmer of energy Deirdre saw near a hill in the distance.

She dropped to her feet in the midst of the shimmer. There was a boulder butted up against the hill, and behind it some freshly disturbed ground and an empty hole.

The thief had come here, retrieved something hidden in the ground—probably scrolls of spells, including *her* scrolls the thief had stolen—and cast the spell that hid the aura.

Deirdre studied the shimmer, trying to discern what the spell might have been. Every spell left characteristic fingerprints in its afterglow, but she couldn't identify anything familiar about this one.

That unsettled her more than anything else this evening. This was a spell completely unknown to her. It resembled no other spell she'd ever witnessed or cast.

Where did that Gods-cursed thief find her magic? And who is she loyal to—if anyone?

She searched around and found tracks in the dirt leading deeper into the forest toward the border with Gallea. She tried to follow them for a while, but quickly lost them. It was dark and she was no tracker.

She'd hire one first thing in the morning. She had to try, but felt little confidence it would work. After all she'd done, the thief wouldn't carelessly leave a trail to follow.

Deirdre hurried back to her tower before her Flying spell could wear out. She lay in bed devising a strategy. Brute searching would be a waste of time. It was a huge forest with Gods knew how many trappers and hunters and fugitives and bandits and recluses wandering through it. The thief would use all her power to remain hidden.

But in day-to-day living, people become careless. An ever-present danger melts into the background and becomes neglected as life is lived. Infant babies grow into impulsive girls. Spells fade and have to be recast.

Time was on Deirdre's side.

She arose and went to her worktable, gathered the materials she needed, and cast a Truth Dream tied to the emergence of that aura. Any slip of the thief or the girl that allowed it to escape its mask would trigger the Truth Dream.

In the morning she hired the tracker. After several days he returned with trepidation reporting that he'd lost the trail and he couldn't explain how. She wasn't surprised in the least, and she paid him anyway, which shocked and pleased him.

She settled back into her normal routine and waited.

Christian stiffened when Gwendolyn came to his chambers. He tried to calm himself immediately and act as if nothing was wrong.

"Am I disturbing you?" she asked.

"No, no. Come in."

She entered and went to where the baby lay sleeping and beamed down at him. "What a lovely boy! Have you named him yet?"

"Guillaume," he said, standing beside her.

She nodded. "After your father. An honorable name."

"What is it you needed?"

They went over to the chairs and sat—the same chairs he and Sighurd sat in not an hour ago. Did she know?

"I've sent Sighurd and three of his guards on a mission. They're heading to Insu."

"Insu?" He tried to act surprised.

"To commission a mage quest from their wizards."

"I...um...a what?" He remembered he wasn't supposed to know what a mage quest was.

"It's a quest they go on to prove themselves as a wizard."

"What...uh...what kind of a quest are you commissioning?"

"To find the daughter of your queen."

"*My* queen had a son," he growled, then scowled at her. "Didn't she?"

"I understand how you feel, but Tamara was officially the queen, and her daughter is still a princess. However you feel about them, we can't have the person who stole her thinking they can do that to us. It'll make us look weak."

"I thought Zenia stole her."

"Zenia was a pawn," she said. "It was Eloise, Zenia's stepmother."

"Who was she to manage that?"

She held up her hands in resignation. "She's supposed to be just a witch, living in a village in Suedeche. But she seems to be more than that."

"And you think a wizard from Insu can find her?"

"They have powers we don't have. Together I have hope we'll succeed."

Christian peered at her, suppressing the disgust he felt. This was part of her scheming, to soothe his mind over the fact that she'd commanded the Captain of the *King's* Guard to embark on a mission without consulting the king. Conveniently she left out the lie she told Sighurd, that it was the king's idea and she was following his command.

But that also indicated that she wasn't aware Sighurd had reported it to him. As far as she knew, Christian had no reason to question her loyalty. He couldn't raise suspicions now.

"It's a wise plan," he said. "I'm sure it'll succeed."

It was a *stupid* plan! Letting their enemies in on private matters, revealing to them a weakness. Did she not realize they'd send spies who cared nothing about finding a princess?

Christian didn't even want to find the girl. Good riddance to her! His heir was Guillaume, and he wanted no challenge to that. If the witch Eloise or whoever she was attempted to put forth a claim to the throne for her, he'd deny everything. Who in the world would believe such a ridiculous story, that the true queen rode off and got impregnated by some random man while the king's heir was the son of a commoner who impersonated the queen for most of a year?

Tamara was dead. In two days her body retrieved from the forest would be laid to rest before the entire kingdom. Christian would play the bereaved husband holding Tamara's *male* offspring, weeping genuine tears over her body that he really felt for his true love, the woman who should have been his queen. Tears he already shed when she was buried without ceremony in an unmarked grave, because no one was to know she ever existed.

This was Christian's revenge, to let the world think Guillaume was Tamara's child who would ascend to the throne, when in reality it was Mariam's, while the existence of Tamara's child would fade to oblivion.

He expected never to see the princess. But if this Eloise revealed her at some point, or if somehow this sinister spy from Insu found her, Christian would denounce her as a fraud.

And end the life of the princess.

As Gwendolyn rose and departed, he thought that perhaps she had the right idea after all. Perhaps it would be a good thing for the spy to find the girl, but not for whatever reason Gwendolyn wanted her. He'd assign Sighurd to accompany the spy—a wise move in any case with a *spy* roaming his kingdom—and command him to kill the child if she were ever found before anyone could learn of her existence.

He smiled to himself with satisfaction. It was the perfect plan, and he felt pleased that he had the wits to think of it. He *would* make a fine king!

He also realized he enjoyed being king. What was he thinking all that time, fooling around like a cocky youth when he could command and strategize and play the royal games of a king, games that mattered? When he could test his mettle against a sorceress?

Yes, power tasted sweet.

Chapter 9

Mage Quest

Kasimir approached the consultation hall with trepidation. He had no idea why he'd been called there. It surprised him that Faisal also waited at the door.

"You were called too?"

Faisal nodded. "All the masters are in there."

"*All* of them?"

"I saw four men arrive earlier," said Faisal. "From Cueldea, I think."

Kasimir's interest piqued. "Are they fair-skinned?"

"Fairer than the Easterners we fought."

"Were their eyes narrow?"

"No more than our own."

His excitement drove away his trepidation. He'd heard of the other two races all his life, but had never seen any. Now eleven days ago he killed two men of one race, and was about to see four men of the other race.

But why were those four men here? And why would it involve him and his brother?

The huge door swung open, and the servant beckoned to them. The two brothers looked at each other, then followed the servant in. Kasimir held his breath in anticipation.

The seven wizards of the ribat were seated around the large table with servants standing near the walls, ready to obey any command from them. The faces of the wizards sparkled with starstones from the sunlight shining through the windows.

But the sight that commanded Kasimir's attention were the four men seated together at the head of the table in a place of honor. Such colorless skin he had never seen in his life. The darkest of them had a scalp of hair as black as his own. The others had light brown, and one had hair as golden as the sun. Their faces were narrow and their noses were narrow. Except for the black-haired one, they had eyes the color of gems, green and blue.

"Thank you for coming," Izzet said, sitting next to the Northerners. He spoke in the Ruic tongue, the common tongue of the Northerners that every novitiate was taught. "Please sit down."

They took the empty chairs at the opposite end of the table from the strangers. The wizards regarded them for an uncomfortable length of time. The Northerners pierced them with their radiant eyes. Kasimir fought hard not to tremble.

"I'm sure you're wondering why we called you," Izzet continued. "These are ambassadors from the Kingdom of Gallea in the North, representing King Christian." He indicated each Northerner in turn. "This is Dietric, Thomas, Hereward. And this is Sighurd, the Captain of the King's Guard."

Hereward was the black-haired one, and Sighurd the golden-haired one.

Izzet said to the four men, "And these two novitiates are Faisal, the elder brother, and Kasimir."

"I'm honored to meet you two," Sighurd said. He also spoke in Ruic, but with an accent unfamiliar to Kasimir. "We've come by command of King Christian to hire you for a mage quest."

Kasimir and Faisal looked at each other. Kasimir could see his brother was as shocked as he was. Northerners commissioning a mage quest? That had never been done!

"Our king instructed us to request the greatest among you for the quest," the Captain said, "for which we'll pay handsomely."

Kasimir said, "My brother Faisal will be—"

"We've questioned your masters about their novitiates to learn what we could about you, and we've decided the one we want for the quest is you, Kasimir."

"But...Faisal is—"

"Master Izzet told us how you fought the scouts from the East and vanquished them, then saved the life of your brother, never having been in real combat before. Such courage and shrewdness is exactly what we want."

"Faisal is older and more experienced," Kasimir insisted. "I'd be happy to serve as his attendant on the—"

"I will be Kasimir's attendant," Faisal said, then turned to Kasimir. "You killed both of them. You saved my life. You've earned every honor they're giving you."

Kasimir peered at Faisal, conflicted with emotions. His heart swelled that his brother showed so much respect for him, but the thought of being in command of him was so foreign to him, he couldn't wrap his mind around it. Faisal had always been the one he looked up to, the one who protected him and taught him. Faisal was virtually a father to him, since their own father had died in battle. How could he command his own father?

He found the wizards and the men of Gallea peering at him with expectation. "What is the quest?" he asked.

"Our queen recently died while giving birth to a girl," Sighurd responded. "That same night, the princess was stolen and hidden away by someone with great magic at their disposal. We want your assistance in finding her."

"Don't you have sorceresses in Cueldea?" Kasimir asked. "How can I find her better than them? They know the land and the people."

"We suspect it was one of those sorceresses who stole her. We don't know who we can trust. Our own sorceress Gwendolyn is searching, but we fear for the child's safety and want to add your powers to the search." Sighurd gave Kasimir a pleading look. "Will you help us find our princess?"

Kasimir didn't know what to say. Did the wizards approve of this? Did the Northerners have some hidden purpose behind this? How dangerous would it be for him and his brother to go north into lands that might one day become their enemy?

Sighurd smiled and nodded. "I know you have many questions for your masters that you want to ask, away from our ears." He and his men stood. "We'll leave you alone with them and eagerly await your decision."

A servant led them out of the room.

The wizards regarded the two brothers, and Kasimir regarded the wizards.

"Now you know why we teach you Ruic," Izzet said with a smile, switching to their native Insan tongue.

"You'll turn them down, no?" Faisal said. "This is much too dangerous for Kasimir."

"They've offered triple what we normally require for payment," the wizard Haysiyet said.

Faisal jumped to his feet. "You'll sell my brother's life for money?"

"Sit down and be silent!" Haysiyet barked. "We care as much for his life as you do."

He sat down, scowling.

"The point," said Izzet, "is that they're extremely interested in hiring Kasimir. Almost desperate, it seems. They made a show of inquiring about everyone, but they pounced on the name of Kasimir the moment we discussed you. They came with the intention of hiring *you*."

"But...how would they even know I exist?"

Izzet responded, "We think their sorceress Gwendolyn saw you battle the Easterners and heard your name, so we also have to assume she saw me use the starstone. We suspect they're interested in that."

"We suspect they want us to send you with your forty-nine starstones," said Haysiyet, "to kill you and take them."

Faisal leaped up and cried, "No!" then sat back down at Haysiyet's withering glare.

"Please let us finish before you react," Izzet said. "We've been concerned about the North for some time. Are you familiar with how Cueldea is governed?"

Faisal shook his head. Kasimir said, "By kings, I suppose."

"They have multiple kingdoms and realms governed by other noblemen," said Izzet. "But we suspect their sorceresses, the Seven Sisters, conspire to rule the continent."

"We've employed many starstones to study them," Haysiyet said. "We fear, once they rule Cueldea, they'll turn their eyes toward us."

"You want me to be a spy," said Kasimir.

Faisal almost said something, but held himself back.

"We're considering the possibility," said Izzet. "We haven't decided."

"After your encounter with the Easterners," Haysiyet said, "we fear the East may attack us the same time the North does. We have to learn more about the North's intentions and strengths."

"Officially it would be Kasimir's quest," Izzet said, "because they insist it be him. He would wear the starstones. He would lead...officially. But in addition to attending him, Faisal, you would be his advisor and his protector."

That made Kasimir feel better. His command over his brother was for show. In reality they'd be more on equal footing.

"In effect," said Haysiyet, "this will be both your mage quests. Upon completion, you both will become wizards, and then, Faisal, you'll acquire your starstones."

"But that won't be fair to Kasimir," Faisal said. "He'll have used some of his starstones on the quest, but I'll have all of mine afterward."

"You can give to him half of the starstones he used on the quest when you receive yours," said Izzet.

Faisal nodded with a smile. "A wise plan."

"It's a dangerous plan!" Haysiyet spat. "It's essential you understand that. They'll suspect you are spies. You *will* be spies! You'll have to be careful."

"Master," said Kasimir, "all mage quests are dangerous."

"Not like this one," said Izzet. "Never have we sent our young men into the North in the service of an enemy. We're used to having the Cueldeans as our neighbors, but you must consider it as dangerous a mission as venturing among the Easterners. You must remain vigilant."

"If we're spies," Kasimir said, "do we complete the quest itself?"

"Of course," said Izzet. "It's a matter of honor. There's no harm in restoring an abducted princess to her family."

"When will you decide?" asked Faisal.

"When you decide," said Izzet. "You're the ones who'll enter into danger."

The wizard Yildiz, Artificer of Starstones, said as he hovered over Kasimir, "Now lie perfectly still, or it'll hurt all the more."

Kasimir, lying half-naked on a bed, closed his eyes as the wizard lowered his sharp instrument and pricked open the skin on his chest. Kasimir let out a grunt at the sharp pain, then felt the cold starstone pressed into the wound as Yildiz uttered incantations to seal it into place.

It was the first of forty-nine starstones the wizard would implant into his skin. Seven times seven. Twenty-nine on his chest and twenty on his face. Forty-nine stones that would be his lifetime supply of stones as a wizard.

"It's a womanly magic the witches of the North practice," Master Izzet said into his ear as he stood leaning over. "They use common substances of the earth to feed their incantations. They have an abundance of material, but their spells are weak compared to those we cast with the energy of Mabut's stars."

Kasimir winced as the artificer pricked him again to embed the second stone.

"Our starstones are powerful," Izzet continued. "We take the rarest gems of the earth, use our Ancient incantations to vitalize them with the power of the stars of Father Sky. Each stone is precious and more powerful than a dozen of their sorceress spells."

Kasimir nodded as Yildiz embedded the second stone and Master Izzet watched with intensity. He felt Master Izzet told him these things to keep his mind off the pain as much as to educate him.

"They don't even know the names of the Gods. They don't know the name of Father Sky is Mabut, and the name of Mother Goddess is Sevda. They only have a vague understanding of the children and the grandchildren of Mabut and Sevda."

"Shall I not speak the names of the Gods among them?" Kasimir asked.

"That may be wise. You must guard our secrets from the Northerners. Never let them know anything about our magic." Izzet shook his head. "I still fear this quest is too risky. But we have to know."

"I'm honored to be the one chosen," Kasimir said, "for Insu."

"This is too perfect an opportunity to spy on the Northern kingdoms before we begin the campaign to destroy the Seven Sisters."

Kasimir wrinkled his brow. "Destroy them?"

"If it comes to that. We pray to the Gods it doesn't. But it's still dangerous. And you're so young! You must be careful, my boy, and not let them discover the secrets of the starstones."

"Faisal will be there to guide me."

"You two are the most honorable students I've ever had. I was right to select you as my novitiates."

Kasimir meditated on his quest. To gather information vital to the safety of his homeland Insu. To seek out an abducted princess, stolen at birth after her mother died in labor, and to return her to her father and bring the abductor to justice. He could never have imagined such a noble mage quest to earn his place as a wizard—a *magus* in the Ancient words.

Yildiz pricked him again to embed the third stone. Kasimir was surprised to discover what a laborious process it was.

Only forty-six more to go.

Sighurd observed the two Insan youths as they sailed across the Sea of Az to Cueldea. He was particularly fascinated by Kasimir. He first met him as a boy with a clear face, but the next time he saw him, he looked all the wizard he was supposed to be. Not only was his clothing and sword exotic, but the glittering gems on his face made him look like a hero from ancient legends.

Twenty gems he counted, of varying types. Rubies, sapphires, emeralds, diamonds. If they were real—and they looked real—this youth carried around a fortune on his face. It was a wonder wizards of Insu weren't attacked on a regular basis and killed for their gems.

In fact, Sighurd had himself and his men take turns guarding the cabin where the two brothers stayed. He didn't like the look the captain of the ship gave when he saw Kasimir's face.

When asked, Kasimir explained they were ornamental, symbols of his position as a wizard. Sighurd thought that a very strange and expensive insignia for rank. His intuition told him Kasimir was hiding something.

He also wondered why Kasimir was the one chosen for the quest. Faisal was older and seemed to be more a commander than an attendant. What did Gwendolyn know about the boy?

The two young men were amazed at the view of the sea and spent hours gazing across the expanse of blue. Their city of Eranshar was well inland, and they'd never seen the sea. It thrilled and disconcerted them to be surrounded by nothing but water.

"Pray for good weather," Faisal said to his brother, looking out at distant clouds that were grey and threatening. "I hear the waves can become walls when Gimshek becomes angry, and men end up at the bottom of the sea."

Sighurd wondered who Gimshek was. One of their Gods? Did they not worship the Great Gods?

They always spoke in Ruic, which surprised Sighurd. He would have expected them to speak to each other in their native tongue, but perhaps they wanted to avoid the impression of being secretive.

Inevitably the brothers vomited over the side of the ship the first day, but their stomachs settled down by the second. When the excitement of the sea wore off, they developed a curiosity for the workings of the ship, and the crew occasionally let them do simple chores after showing them how.

That also surprised Sighurd. In Cueldea, noble born youths would never do the work of commoners. But these fellows seemed to have no concept of nobility by birth. To them everyone was an equal, and all they seemed to care about was experiencing life. To them, people had different duties and different authority, but none were above anyone else in worth, and no worthwhile task was beneath any of them. Even both youths, he learned, were addressed by the same simple title of *Master*, without distinguishing between wizard and attendant.

That appealed to him, but could be dangerous in the hierarchal system that ruled Cueldea. He felt a twinge of guilt that he envied them for it, being Captain of the King's Guard. He brushed the guilt away, knowing it was only an idle thought.

He watched for any sign of spying or subterfuge, but found none. Only reticence in divulging too much information about themselves or their country. That was to be expected. Sighurd was also guarded with information about Gallea and the king.

They arrived on the shore of Ellada, the kingdom across the Sea of Az from Insu, at the harbor city of Anthos. King Theophilos ruled there, and his sorceress of the Seven Sisters was Callista. They'd need to travel discreetly with their Insan guests. Sighurd waited until after sundown before leaving the ship and boarding a coach that the two foreigners could ride in unseen. They traveled by night.

They crossed the border into Onotria where King Lorenzo and sorceress Francesca ruled. They were allies of Gunther and Scaendelreic, so they had to be especially careful there. It was unfortunate that traveling through this country was the longest leg of their journey. They smoothed their passage from time to time with bribes along the way, especially in the ruling city of Ruo.

"This is the city where Ruic is spoken natively," Sighurd explained to the two brothers. "It's the high dialect of Onotrian, the language of this kingdom. It became the common tongue when the Seven Sisters of old first appeared here and spread out to the kingdoms in the east of Cueldea to teach women their magic."

"What's your native tongue?" Kasimir asked.

"Galleic."

"Say something in Galleic," Faisal said.

Sighurd welcomed them to Cueldea and wished them success in their quest, all in Galleic.

"I almost feel like I can understand it," Kasimir said. "It seems similar to Ruic."

"Ruo anciently ruled much of Cueldea as an empire. The languages of Gallea and Ebros to the west and Vlachia to the east are related to Ruic."

Kasimir and Faisal were fascinated with anything Sighurd told them about the cultures of Cueldea. They seemed thirsty for knowledge. He began to understand why Gwendolyn was so impressed with Kasimir.

Sighurd sighed with relief once they crossed the border into Gallea at the city of Libre. There were plains and farmland and vineyards and hill country on the highway east to Luximon. They traveled in daylight in the safety of his own country, and their moods brightened.

The last stretch of their journey was north on the South Highway to the city of Luteche. Fenweald Forest began along that road. This stretch was known for bandits hiding among the trees, watching for wealthy travelers from Luteche on their way south to the resort city of Meisson on the shore of the Sea of Az, where they could enjoy sunny beaches and high class gambling halls and high class women. Sighurd and his guards remained alert, he inside the coach, and they riding in view on top. No bandits attacked, probably because the sight of the King's Guard dissuaded them.

They arrived at the city of Luteche after dark, as Sighurd had timed it. Inside the courtyard of the castle, the sight of Kasimir caused a flurry of interest. Sighurd brought the two youths to the dining hall where they were fed, then sent word to Gwendolyn that they had arrived.

At some point, he would need to report to Christian, discreetly.

Not long after they ate, Gwendolyn received them in the Great Hall. She sat in a chair next to what Kasimir could only guess were two thrones—for a king and queen?

Kasimir felt more amused than impressed that the hall was huge and gaudy. It was decorated with statues—whether of Gods or men, he couldn't tell—and paintings of royalty and glittering chandeliers of glass and candles and huge embroidered rugs hanging on the walls. The ceiling was high and imposing and made of vaulted stone. People stood about the hall, mostly along the walls, with purposes inscrutable to Kasimir. Other kinds of royalty? Servants? Some were clearly guards. The thrones were wrought of metal ornate beyond reason, with plush cushions to comfort the royal posteriors. The rugs appeared imported from Komshu, a country of Ifran which had far greater interaction and commerce with the Northerners than Insu did.

Such ostentatious expense and effort, merely to impress.

Sighurd began the introductions. "Master Kasimir, Master Faisal, may I present Gwendolyn, the Sorceress of Luteche. Mistress Gwendolyn, may I present Kasimir, the Wizard from Eranshar of Insu, and his attendant and brother, Master Faisal."

"On behalf of King Christian, I welcome you to Luteche," Gwendolyn said officiously.

"Where is King Christian?" Faisal asked. The same thing Kasimir was wondering, but he was glad Faisal had said it. It was better for the attendant to be confrontational than the wizard.

"He's retired for the night and requests that I receive you. Tomorrow we—"

A young man no older than Faisal strode into the hall. He wore an elaborate robe, and on his head sat a crown with at least as many gems as Kasimir had on his face. Gwendolyn gaped at him as he marched with authority to one of the thrones and sat on it. Gwendolyn appeared to be hiding annoyance. Kasimir stifled a smirk.

The young man peered at Faisal briefly, but focused his gaze on Kasimir. He still wasn't used to how people in the North stared at him with his starstones.

"I am Christian, King of Gallea," the youth said. "Welcome to my kingdom. It's an honor to be visited by our neighbors across the sea."

Gwendolyn got control of her face—barely—and forced a smile onto the gathering.

"I am Kasimir, Wizard of Eranshar, and this is my attendant, Master Faisal. We are honored to be called to serve the King of Gallea."

Christian smiled with satisfaction. "Thank you, Sighurd, for guiding them safely to us. Wizard Kasimir—"

"Master is all the title I have."

The king raised his eyebrows. "Master Kasimir, has Sighurd made clear what your quest will be?"

"Briefly. He's given me no details."

Christian glanced at Gwendolyn. "Unfortunately we have few details. The queen died in childbirth, and her chambermaid—"

"Perhaps it would be better to clear the hall before discussing this," Gwendolyn said.

Christian gave her a sharp glance. "Perhaps it would." He nodded vaguely off to someone, and the superfluous people left the hall, leaving only king and sorceress, Kasimir and Faisal, and Sighurd.

Something unspoken was going on between Christian and Gwendolyn. It made Kasimir become guarded.

"As I was saying, the queen died in childbirth, and her chambermaid ran off with her—*our* daughter. We don't know why, but we know she delivered... my daughter to a witch named Eloise, who it appears may be more than a mere witch."

Gwendolyn broke in. "The chambermaid fled east. The queen was the daughter of our ally Duke Geoffrey. His duchy is Suedeche, also to the east. It's possible he may be involved."

"You think your ally betrayed you?" Faisal said.

"We're not sure. But we know the chambermaid was helped by her step-mother Eloise, a witch who lives in Suedeche, and we know they used magic no mere witch should know how to practice. We also consider the possibility that King Gunther and his sorceress Deirdre further east in Scaendelreic may have helped them." Gwendolyn added ominously, "She's one of the Seven Sisters."

"Eloise from Suedeche," Kasimir murmured to commit her name to memory.

"There's one other thing," Gwendolyn said, and she gave a quick glance to Christian and Sighurd. "I don't know where it comes from, but that child has an aura I've never seen before. A brilliant aura that rises up to the moon. Somehow Eloise has masked that aura so I can't see it with a Sight spell. But I don't know how long that mask will last."

Kasimir and Faisal looked at each other. "Did you know about this?" Faisal asked Sighurd.

He gave him a brief shake of the head.

Christian was looking down with a scowl.

Kasimir didn't know what to make of that. A newborn girl with a bright aura? That was unheard of! That was the stuff of legends and stories of jinn and changelings.

"A newborn girl," Kasimir said, "in the company of a witch named Eloise from Suedeche, with a brilliant aura that reaches to the moon, but is masked. Possibly aided by Deirdre, one of the Seven Sisters. The aura could reappear at some point." Kasimir feigned nodding thoughtfully, but felt more like shaking his head. The story sounded preposterous!

"Is there anything else you can tell us?" Faisal asked.

"That's all we know," Christian said, looking at Gwendolyn.

"The girl's name is Celeste," Gwendolyn said.

Christian said, "I'll assign some of my guards to join you, to assist you as you travel the land. They'll be under your command, Master Kasimir. I think you understand it would be...treacherous for a wizard from Insu to travel the land alone."

"Yes," Kasimir answered. "They'd also know the country and the people better than we do."

"Since you know Sighurd and his three men from your journey here, would you be comfortable with them again?"

"That would be acceptable."

Christian turned to Sighurd. "Would that be acceptable to you and your men?"

"If the king commands it, we will obey."

"I know that, but you'll travel with them away from your homes for an unknown length of time, and you'll be subject to his command."

"It would be an honor, Your Majesty."

Gwendolyn tried hard to conceal it, but Kasimir could tell she was fuming over something, as if she resented her own king being in command. Perhaps the suspicions of the Masters were right—the Northern sorceresses aspired to rule Cueldea.

"How soon can you be ready to depart?" Christian asked Sighurd.

"Give me a day to inform the King's Guard and arrange for their functioning in my absence. We can depart the day after."

"Is that acceptable to you, Master Kasimir?"

"Yes."

The king stood. "Then everything is settled. Sighurd, please escort our guests to their accommodations."

The king marched out with the same forcefulness he came in with. Gwendolyn jumped up and followed after him.

Sighurd led Kasimir and Faisal to their chambers.

Gwendolyn ordered Bernard to summon Sighurd, then stormed into her chambers and dropped into a chair.

Christian had changed, and it both infuriated and frightened her. Of all the times to grow a backbone, he had to do it in this time of crisis? It only increased her fury that she couldn't complain about anything he'd done. Of course he had every right as king to come to the Great Hall and welcome the foreigners. Of course it was essential to have men accompany the wizard, and the four men Gwendolyn sent to Insu to arrange everything were the perfect choice for that. But this marked the first time he'd ever made such command decisions without consulting her. There was no harm done—*this* time—but from this time forth she'd never know what he was thinking and scheming and might spring on her without warning. How was she to function like that?

She felt sure this would inevitably lead to the point where she'd have to consult *him* on all *her* decisions. It was only a matter of time before he began to truly act as king.

How did the Seven Sisters live this way? She was familiar with their arrogance and knew deep inside they considered themselves the rulers of their lands. But they maintained the facade of being servants to their kings.

Gwendolyn would have to learn that skill too, she realized. The alternative of staging a coup and taking over the kingdom would cause all of Cueldea to denounce her and give the Seven Sisters an excuse to openly oppose her.

The only other thing she could do was have Christian killed and replaced by the infant prince, who would need a regent ruling in his name until he came of age. She would be the obvious choice.

Before she could pursue that thought, a knock came to the door. "Enter!" she cried.

Sighurd came in and sat at the chair she indicated.

"First of all," she began, "I want to say, well done on completing your mission. It appears everything went as well as I could hope for."

"Thank you, Mistress."

"What were you able to learn about the Insan?"

"Very little. The wizards restricted where we could go and told us as little as possible."

"Were you able to learn anything from Kasimir and Faisal on the journey?"

"They are very much still boys trying to be men. I don't mean that negatively. They're clearly thoughtful and serious about their duty, and from what they told me about Kasimir, very brave. But they also show a childlike fascination with things they've never seen before, like the ocean or the workings of the ship. Inexperienced, naive in some ways, I'd call them."

She nodded as she thought. Nothing surprising in any of this. "Did you learn anything about their magic?"

"Nothing at all. They refused to say anything about it."

"What about the gems on his face?"

"I asked, and Kasimir said they were the insignia designating a wizard. Nothing more than ornamental, I gathered."

She smiled. Also not surprising they'd be tightlipped about their magic. "Let me tell you a secret, and you have to vow to keep this a secret, even from your own men unless absolutely necessary."

"I will."

"Those gems are no ornaments. They *are* the source of his magic. And he has more than what you see on his face. He also has them on his chest."

Sighurd's face showed wonder. "How do you know this?"

She resisted rolling her eyes. "I'm a sorceress. When he uses them, he plucks one from his skin and dips it in the blood that leaks out to activate it. He speaks some incantation to cast the spell with the power inside." She leaned forward as if trying to keep someone near from hearing. "I can't say where that power comes from, but I can say that they call them starstones."

He raised his eyebrows high. "They harness the power of the stars and store them in the stones?"

"My thoughts exactly. Each stone has immense power and can cast a mighty spell. But I'm not sure if they cast spells any other way. Watch carefully to see if they do. If those starstones are their only magic, that's a strategic weakness on their part. He only has so many and he'll want to use them as sparingly as possible."

"That seems almost...foolish, if it's true," he said.

"Just keep an eye out for any other use of magic."

"I'm sorry I wasn't able to learn more."

"Not at all. I expected that. You accomplished the most important part of the mission, and I'll be sure to see that you and your men are rewarded for it."

Sighurd looked down at his hands, which were fidgeting.

"What is it, Sighurd?"

"Hereward."

"Oh yes, I forgot about that."

"This new assignment will last more than weeks. He's sure to change at some point. I assume you haven't told the king."

She looked down and sighed, then looked back up at him. "It would have brought up too many questions. Do you think you can handle the situation?"

He didn't look happy at that idea. "I wouldn't know how to handle it, except to kill him before the Change."

"The legends say it happens at a full moon. Most of the time you shouldn't have to worry. But..."

"I'd have to keep a careful watch on him when a full moon comes. I wouldn't even know what to watch for. Once he changes, it's too late."

"I'll leave it up to your discretion. Consider everyone's safety. But it would be better to have him die on the quest in a way that...seems accidental."

She could see he didn't like that idea either.

"It's up to you how to handle it. But I'd prefer he go on the quest." Much better to have him change away from Luteche.

He nodded with a frown.

"The highest priority is to find Celeste and bring her back safely. Everything else is secondary. *Everything.*"

"Yes, Mistress."

He stood and left.

Gwendolyn wondered if she should approach Kasimir to see if his magic might help Hereward, but she recoiled from the idea of revealing a weakness in the King's Guard.

She set the issue aside. Sighurd would handle it wisely. Of more concern to her was Christian. She decided contemplating assassination was reckless and unjustifiable, just to avoid the nuisance of using diplomacy on him. If the Seven Sisters could handle their kings, so could she.

There was nothing left to do now but rest. Everything had been put in action. Tomorrow she'd begin afresh searching for Eloise and Celeste herself with her Extended Sight. That cursed trinket she had may negate the direct approach, but she could still search for indirect clues.

As she lay in bed, she wondered who would find Celeste first, she with her Sight, or Kasimir with his wizardly tricks. Or would neither of them find her?

That was the thought that kept her awake for a long time.

After Kasimir shut the door on their assigned chambers, Faisal immediately said, "Something's very wrong in this kingdom."

Kasimir nodded. "There's conflict between the king and the sorceress."

"Things are too unstable here. It's dangerous for you. We should return."

Kasimir scowled at him. "We've accepted a mage quest. It's our duty to fulfill it."

"What about that aura? Who ever heard of a mortal girl having an aura?"

Kasimir shook his head. "I don't know why she'd lie about that. But if it's true, there's so much more going on here than they're telling us."

"Do you even trust Sighurd? His loyalty doesn't lie with us. Who knows what instructions they gave him?"

"Like assassinate the wizard and steal his gems?" Kasimir said with a smile.

"Don't act like that's not possible."

"Wouldn't it have been simpler to kill us on the ship and toss our bodies in the sea?"

Faisal scowled.

Kasimir began removing his clothing, weary from the traveling and the formalities. "They paid us more than the gems are worth. Not much profit in that conspiracy." He paused with a thought. "Unless..."

"Unless what?"

He resumed undressing. "Unless Gwendolyn knows they're not just gems."

Faisal looked at him with alarm.

"We knew the dangers when we accepted the quest," Kasimir said. "It's our duty to fulfill it."

Faisal fell silent as he prepared for bed.

"I trust you to protect me, as you always have," Kasimir said.

"The first time you truly needed my protection," Faisal said, "it was *you* who protected *me*."

Kasimir peered at him with a sigh. "We're tired. Let's get some sleep."

Faisal pulled two sheathed daggers out of their bags and tossed one to Kasimir. "Sleep with this tonight."

The two brothers sat on their beds, palms raised to the ceiling, and spoke their prayers to Mabut, then lay down to sleep.

Kasimir stared at the dark ceiling as he dwelt on the trials ahead. Did Gwendolyn know about the starstones? Would he live through the night, or would an assassin creep into the room? Could Sighurd be trusted? How would he find a princess hidden by magic? Why did she have an aura? If they did find her and return her, would Kasimir and Faisal live to return home? Did the Northerners have any concept of honor and duty, and would it apply to foreigners?

Sleep was long coming to Kasimir this night.

Sighurd hoped he could reach his chambers and sleep before reporting to King Christian, but the summons came quickly.

Sitting together in the same chairs as before, Christian eagerly asked him, "What have you found out?"

He repeated all the things he told Gwendolyn, but said nothing about what she told him. The conflict between the two disturbed him, and he wanted to feel the king out before saying more.

"Is that all?" Christian said.

"That's...everything I found out."

"Nothing about what the wizard might really be here to do?"

"As far as I know, he's here to fulfill a quest."

Christian stood up and paced back and forth. "I'm sending you with the wizard because I have my own quest for you. I don't understand why Gwendolyn wants that baby, and I don't understand why she'd bring spies into my kingdom to search for her."

"If they are spies."

"Of course they're spies. Even if they intend to fulfill the quest, they'll still spy on us."

"I'm sure you're right."

Christian sat back down on the chair and leaned earnestly toward Sighurd. "No one's motives matter. It only matters that this is a threat to my kingdom." He sat back and took a deep breath. "I want you to help the wizard—what was his name?"

"Kasimir."

"Such strange names they have! I want you to help Kasimir find her, this... *princess*...as if nothing were wrong, and when he does, I want you to kill him and his brother. Then..." His eyes went dark. "...I want you to kill the princess."

Kill the princess echoed in Sighurd's mind. Kill an infant child. "Your Majesty, this whole situation confuses me."

Christian gazed at him in shock. "What do you mean? You obey your king, that's all."

"Gwendolyn commanded me to bring the princess safely home. You want me to kill her. What's going on between you two?"

Christian rose up in anger. "Are you loyal to me or not?"

"Of course I am," Sighurd said testily.

"Gwendolyn wants her and Gwendolyn is up to no good, otherwise why would she be secretive with me? That's all you need to know."

"We'll still have to deal with Gwendolyn."

Christian sank back into the chair. "You'll have to make sure their deaths look like an accident, or...or...happens in battle...or something."

Sighurd closed his eyes in frustration. Gwendolyn wants him to kill Hereward and hide it. Christian wants him to kill Celeste and Kasimir and Faisal and hide it. What did they think he was? A sniveling assassin working in the shadows? King Guillaume never commanded him to do such despicable things.

"Sighurd?"

He looked back up. "Yes, Your Majesty. I'll...work something out."

Christian smiled with satisfaction. "Very good. I imagine you're tired with all that traveling. Go to bed."

Sighurd nodded and left.

As he lay in bed, troubled thoughts plagued his mind. All the slayings in his career were honorable in battle or defending the king and queen and prince. Since the truce with Scaendelreic, there had been no battles, no threats, and Sighurd's duties had been peaceful.

But now things were heating up again. Kill a little girl? Kill foreign ambassadors? He was appalled to realize the honor of King Guillaume was gone. Traitorous scheming within the castle walls. The king commanding him to murder innocent souls in cold blood. It would be an act of war to kill the ambassadors from Insu. A war with them was the last thing Gallea needed.

But Sighurd was loyal to the king. Always. He knew his duty before he could admit it to himself. Obey the king. Even if an innocent baby died. Even if a war was started.

But Sighurd hadn't become Captain of the King's Guard by mindlessly obeying orders. He must obey the king, but nothing stopped him from doing his own investigations. More information could suggest other options that might satisfy the king.

Sleep evaded him for a long time as he contemplated what to do.

Chapter 10

Celeste

"Do you know what today is?" Mother said.

Celeste's ears perked up immediately. Whenever Mother said anything like that, something delightful usually followed.

"What is today, Mother?"

"Today is your birthday! You were born precisely one year ago." Mother's face beamed with a huge smile as she knelt down and gave Celeste an enormous hug. "Happy birthday, my darling!"

She had no idea what a year was, so she did what she always did when Mother mentioned something mysterious. She asked the Girl Inside. *What is a year?* she spoke inside her head.

That's how long you've been alive, said the Girl Inside.

That only seemed like forever to her. *How long have I been alive?*

Three hundred and sixty-five days.

That amount of days was just as incomprehensible to her, but it was still a number to work with. "So I was born three hundred and sixty-five days ago?" she said to Mother. It made her feel good to sound smart.

Mother shook her head with a smile, like she always did when Celeste told her things the Girl Inside taught her. "That's right. Three hundred and sixty-five days. Four seasons ago."

Season was a word she knew. That's when the world around her changed, growing warmer and warmer, and the plants and trees grew greener and greener. Mother told her the world would grow colder again one day, and the green would change to many colors. Then the leaves on the trees would fall, and something cold and white called snow would rain from the sky.

Mother said snow was cold rain, but Celeste couldn't imagine it, and she wasn't sure she could believe it. But the Girl Inside said, *Believe it! When the rain gets very cold, it turns white and fluffy.*

She couldn't wait to see the many colors and fluffy white rain fall from the sky.

"You were born late summer last year," Mother said. "You were too young to remember autumn when the leaves turn color. Do you remember winter?"

"I remember cold," Celeste said. "I think I remember white everywhere—I'm not sure."

"After winter comes spring. The days warm up, snow melts away to nothing, the trees become green, and the wildflowers grow everywhere."

"I remember those things!"

With her arms still around Celeste, Mother said, "You've grown so much since you were born." She chuckled. "*So* much!"

Celeste didn't know why that was funny, but Mother was always laughing at things she didn't understand. "What happens on my birthday?"

"Oh, your birthday is a special day! You get to do whatever you want. Then we have any kind of dinner you want. And finally, I give you a gift."

She clapped her hands and threw her arms tightly around Mother. "Thank you, Mother!"

"What would you like to do first?"

Their language for today was Ruic, which they'd been speaking. They took turns each day speaking two different languages so Celeste could learn them both. One day they'd speak Galleic, then the next Ruic. Celeste decided to test this concept of doing anything she wanted. "Today I want to speak Galleic," she said in that language.

Mother grinned and brushed her fingertip across Celeste's nose. She replied in Galleic, "You little rebel! What else do you want to do?"

"Swim in the river!"

Mother laughed. "I knew it. You're lucky you were born in the summer. If your birthday came in winter, it would be too cold."

"Can I swim right now?"

"Yes, my beautiful child. It's your birthday!"

Celeste wasted no time. She pulled her shift over her head and threw it up in the air. Mother laughed as she stood and caught it. Celeste ran naked through the forest, following the familiar smooth path to the small river that the two of them trod every day for their supply of water. She dashed into the pool just below the little waterfall that was shorter than her, and splashed around with a cry of delight.

Mother trotted up to the edge and sat on a boulder, smiling as she watched Celeste frolic. The shift lay spread out on her lap.

When she tired of dancing and jumping in the water, she sat on a smooth, submerged rock and called for a fish. It was like talking to the Girl Inside, except she reached out with her mind and spoke to the fishes. *Come, little ones. Come be my friend.*

Within seconds a tiny, sleek fish fluttered past her toes, inches away. Sunlight danced on its silver scales like it danced on the ripples of water around her legs. Carefully she reached forward and touched the fish with her finger. The fish stroked its side against her skin, then nibbled on her fingertip. It tickled.

Celeste started to feel hungry. "Can we have my dinner now?" she asked.

"Certainly, my darling. What would you like?"

She thought for a moment, feeling inside for a food craving. "Rabbit," she said finally. "Roast rabbit—no! Rabbit stew with carrots. And green beans and mushrooms."

"As you wish," said Mother, and patted most of the wetness from her with the shift as she stepped out of the water. "Now run back home and put something dry on while I prepare your stew."

Celeste dashed along the trail, stopping once to leap up and try to touch a butterfly, but it swerved away just out of reach. As she ran into the cottage and plucked another shift from the small pile of clothes near her bed, Mother pulled a couple of carrots and harvested a handful of green bean pods and mushrooms from the garden. She set a pot of water on the stove and lit the fire with some words in the strange language she sometimes spoke.

"Are you going to call the rabbit now?" Celeste said with anticipation.

"Yes, my darling."

She clapped her hands and jumped. "I love this part!"

Mother stood still and closed her eyes, then quietly spoke the words Celeste knew she would. Her eyes opened and looked about like she was searching for something, even though there was nothing around to see. Celeste used to think she was looking for the animal she was about to call, but over time noticed that Mother always had a worried look on her face while she did this part.

Mother sighed and muttered more to herself than Celeste, "It's safe." It wasn't the first time she said that either, but Celeste didn't know what she meant.

Safe from what? she once asked the Girl Inside.

I don't know, said the Girl.

Mother smiled and went outside. She followed, staying several feet behind so as not to disturb her. Mother dropped to her knees and leaned forward on her elbows. She held her hands forward and cupped them as if she were trying to catch something, then spoke more of the other words that Celeste couldn't understand.

They're the words to a magic spell, the Girl Inside once told her. *In the language of Mother Goddess.*

Celeste knew who Mother Goddess was—Mother had taught her. She was the mother of all female humans, giving birth to the first woman. She was one of the Great Gods—the powerful beings that created everything and ruled over the whole world. Some people worshipped all the Great Gods, some people only specific Gods. Many women, especially village witches, worshipped Mother Goddess.

A village witch is a woman who works magic for the people she lives among, said the Girl Inside in answer to her question. That answer made her wonder again about the "other people" that both Mother and the Girl Inside talked about from time to time, but she'd never seen.

She knew from previous experience that Mother's magic would take a few minutes to call a rabbit, and she was hungry. She didn't want to wait that long. So she ever so carefully reached out her own mind to call a rabbit, hoping Mother wouldn't notice. Her ability to call a small animal was much faster than Mother's.

But as soon as she reached out, Mother cried in a harsh whisper, "Celeste, what are you doing?"

She quickly pulled her mind back. "Nothing, Mother."

But the rabbit appeared from the trees anyway and crept its way toward Mother's cupped hands. It was brownish grey and large, with pink skin on the inside of the ears. Mother returned her attention to the rabbit, cooing more words that Celeste didn't understand, until the rabbit hopped toward her and nestled within her cupped hands.

She struggled to her feet while hanging on to the squirming rabbit. "Please, you have to be careful with that."

"With what?"

"I saw it," Mother said with a scowl. "I can see when you reach out. It looks like a shining light coming from inside you."

Celeste knew that wasn't entirely true, because she'd reached out lots of times to call creatures, like the little fish in the river, and Mother never said a word. Yet this time she did see, and Celeste figured it must be because of the spell Mother cast.

"It's too dangerous for you to use your special powers," Mother said as she walked into the cottage.

"Because of other people?"

"Yes." Mother sat in a chair by the table and stroked the rabbit on the back of its neck. "Now fetch me my knife, please."

Celeste did so and, as Mother killed and cleaned the rabbit—a messy business with all that blood—said, "When can I see other people?"

"I don't know. Not for a while." She sighed and looked at Celeste. "I don't want you to be afraid of other people, sweetheart. Most of them are nice and friendly. But there are some who are evil and might harm you. Some of them are very dangerous."

She nodded. She couldn't understand why anyone would want to do such a thing, but she trusted Mother.

"If you ever see another person, run home immediately and tell me. Then we can decide together if they're the nice kind or the dangerous kind."

"If they're the dangerous kind, what do we do?"

Mother smiled. "You leave that to me, child. I have some powers that can protect us."

She brought the prepared rabbit to the pot and sliced it and the vegetables up. She dumped all the pieces into the boiling water and added some meal and seasonings.

"While that cooks," Mother said, "I want to give you something."

"My gift?" she said eagerly.

Mother smiled and went to her bed and reached under the pillow, pulling out a small object wrapped in a handkerchief. She brought it to her and placed it in her hands.

Celeste unfolded the handkerchief and found a glittering trinket inside, a golden crescent moon with a dainty chain attached to it.

"It's beautiful!" She clutched it to her breast and grinned. "It's like yours."

Mother pulled the necklace from underneath her dress. It too had a crescent moon, but dull and silver. "Mine is old and worn. Yours is shiny and new."

Mother took the necklace from the handkerchief and slid the chain around Celeste's neck. "It's an enchanted necklace. I placed the most powerful spells I know on it, spells of Protection for you."

Celeste plucked the trinket by her finger and thumb and held it out to look at it. "Is it gold?"

"Yes, it's gold." Mother leaned forward and kissed her on the cheek. "I've spent the last month making it for you."

"When? I never saw you."

Mother grinned. "While you were sleeping. Please, wear it always—even when you swim naked in the river. Wear it always so it can protect you from danger."

"Thank you, Mother!" Celeste threw her arms around her.

"Happy birthday, my beautiful girl." She looked her up and down. "You're one year old, and yet you look more like...four years old."

"I'm four years old?"

"Well..." Mother became thoughtful. "According to time, you're one year old. But according to how you've grown, you're more like four years old. You've grown up fast!"

Celeste beamed with pride.

"Yes, if anyone asks you, tell them you're four years old."

"Other people, you mean?"

Mother's happy expression disappeared. "Yes...well, never mind."

When the rabbit stew was ready, the two of them ate eagerly. It was the most delicious rabbit stew Celeste had ever eaten, because it was her birthday stew.

And when night came, she fell asleep in her bed, dreaming of the day she could see other people, and clutching the golden moon that hung around her neck.

On her second birthday, Celeste woke up early, a couple hours before dawn, while Mother snored away. It was her birthday, and that meant she could do whatever she wanted. But a part of her knew that Mother wouldn't like her sneaking off to swim in the river alone—birthday or not.

Mother never let her be off on her own for very long, and Celeste was starting to feel smothered because of it. She was growing up—very fast, Mother kept saying—and she was too old to have Mother watching over her every minute.

Mother always talked about danger, but Celeste had never seen any in her two years of life. She'd never seen any dangerous animals—not a bear, not a wildcat, not a wolf—and she certainly hadn't seen any "other people"—dangerous or otherwise.

And besides, she wore the golden moon around her neck that Mother had given her on her first birthday. It would protect her, Mother promised.

She went to the door, touching the trinket that hung on it, a silver oval with a ruby in the middle, hanging by a chain. Once she asked Mother what it was for. "Just some decoration," she answered. "Don't you think it's pretty?"

She did think that.

It was going to be another hot day. She could tell as she walked the short trail to the river. But the early morning air was still cool. Halfway to the river, she turned off the trail and climbed her favorite hill, the one with a clearing in the trees where she could lay back on the meadow grass and gaze at the sky. She'd been coming here more and more in the evening, especially during a full moon, and there had been a full moon for the past three nights.

She lay in the grass, feeling the dew seep into her nightgown, listening to the gentle rustling of leaves in the breeze. The birds started their early morning chirping. The stars blazed in the sky, and the Mistress Moon, one of the Great Gods, hung low in the west.

"Mistress Moon, why do I feel so good when you shine on me?" Celeste murmured out loud.

She knew there must be some kind of connection between herself and the moon. How many times Mother had said, "Your eyes sparkle with the silvery light of Mistress Moon," or, "How bright your hair is, like the glory of Mistress Moon."

When the moon disappeared below the trees and the fingers of Master Sun—another of the Great Gods—rose in the east, Celeste continued to the river. The splashing of the waterfall was like laughter, and the chirping of the birds like Mother singing. She pulled her nightgown off and touched a toe into the pool and jumped back with a squeal at its chill. Maybe she should wait until the sun's face appeared.

She sat on the submerged rock, the coldness of the water nipping her buttocks. A breeze made her shiver. Yet it felt so good to sit among the trees and let the sensations of nature wash all over her skin. She felt connected to the pulses of the forest and the hidden life that dwelt among the trees—like she was as much a part of it as any rabbit or deer or bird. As sunrise peeked above the treetops with its rosy glow, her heart leaped at the beauty of it, and its heat warmed her.

She stood and braced herself—she was determined to go into the water, chilly or not. She stepped in gingerly. The cold didn't bother her feet much, nor her legs to her knees, but when she tried to sit in the pool, the chill on her body above her legs made her jump back up with a cry.

What was that? Did she hear something in the forest, a noise on the other side of the river while she cried out?

She stood in the pool, trembling, and listened hard against the noisy waterfall, her hand grasping the golden moon.

A definite crack of wood, a definite rustling in the leaves of the bushes, and something appeared out of the trees. Celeste gasped.

It was tall—taller than Mother—and rugged. A person, but like no person she'd ever imagined. Its hair was black as ashes and scraggly, reaching down past its shoulders, and hair grew from its face like a coat of fur. The creature was naked from the waist up, smudged with dirt and glistening with sweat, and from the waist down wore a ragged piece of clothing that hugged both its legs tightly—not like the shifts and gowns that Celeste and Mother wore. Its feet were covered with tough-looking shoes.

It carried a strange thing in its hand, a curved piece of wood with a string attached at both ends. Across its shoulder hung a long container that had sticks poking out from the top with feathers attached to the ends. It made Celeste sad to think that birds might have died to provide those feathers.

The creature stopped when it saw her and stared with piercing eyes. Celeste's trembling turned into an uncontrollable shiver, and she held up the moon before her, pulling the chain tight against her nape. The creature tilted its head to one side, its eyebrows raised, and it spoke.

"Hello."

"Are—are you other people?" she struggled to say.

It smiled beneath that facial fur and said, "Yes, I suppose so."

Her grasp on the moon tightened. "Are you evil or nice?"

He laughed a booming laugh. "That's a very good question. But I won't hurt you. I just came here to bathe." He looked her body up and down. "Like you, I guess. I hope you don't mind."

Is this other people? she asked the Girl Inside.

Yes. He's a man.

She nodded and let the moon drop back to her chest. Mother had talked about men before. They seemed like magical creatures to Celeste, never having seen one. Now that she had, he still seemed like a magical creature.

The man must have thought her silence was agreement, because he sat on a fallen log, laid his curved stick and container on the ground, and pulled his enormous shoes off.

He's as grown up as Mother, but his breasts are as flat as mine.

A man's breasts never grow out, the Girl Inside said, then giggled. *Unless he's fat.*

The man stood and untied a rope around his waist. He dropped the clothing hugging his legs and stepped out of them. There was an ugly scar on his leg.

Her eyes widened as she looked where his legs joined his body. *What is that thing hanging there?*

That's his penis. All men have them instead of a vagina.

The man strode into the pool, and she backed away to the shore. He looked down where she was staring and laughed. "You've never seen a man before, have you, child?"

What's it for? she asked the Girl.

He pisses from it, and he uses it to love a woman in a way that creates babies.

The man walked up to the waterfall and knelt into the pool. He leaned forward and drenched his hair in the fall, whooping—probably from the cold.

Celeste stared as he splashed water over his chest and back, working off the grime and the sweat. *Uses it how?*

Best to ask Mother about that, said the Girl.

She gazed with fascination. The man pulled out of the waterfall and turned to sit in the pool. "Oh, that's cold!" he shouted.

Impulsively she blurted out, "Can you piss for me?"

The man's head jerked toward her, and shock showed in his face.

"I—I was wondering how you do it."

He frowned as he gazed back. "I already did a few moments ago. I have nothing left now. Sorry."

"Well..." She crept forward a few steps into the pool. "Then could you show me how you love a woman with your penis?"

His eyes shot wide open. "How old are you, little girl?"

"Um...I'm...eight years old."

The man's eyes studied her nude body slowly, from head to foot. It made Celeste feel uneasy. She began fondling her moon with her fingers.

"There's something about you," he murmured. "I can't...quite..."

Celeste became apprehensive. She'd been curious, but now Mother's warning came back to her.

"What's your name?" he said.

Mother had told her to run if she ever saw other people.

"Do you live out here in the woods?" he said. "Do you live alone?"

Celeste turned and ran, then realized she had forgotten her nightgown. She rushed back, grabbed it, and fled as fast as she could, terrified that the man was chasing after her. Why did there have to be a trail leading right to their cottage?

She reached the cottage and flung the door open, then closed it behind her except for a crack. The trinket rattled against it as she peered through the crack, watching the trail.

"What are you doing?" Mother said from her bed. "And with your nightgown off?"

She jumped and turned. "Oh, I..." If she told her about the man, Mother would know she'd snuck out. "...have to piss." She opened the door and stepped out, closing it behind her, then stood next to it, ready to rush back in if the man appeared. If he didn't, there was no reason to tell her what happened, and Mother wouldn't be upset.

The man didn't appear.

She realized she really did have to piss and headed for the pit, never taking her eyes off the forest trail.

Maybe her necklace kept him away.

"Mother, it's started!" Celeste shouted as she held the skirt of her shift out. A spot of blood colored it down by her crotch.

Mother turned from her cooking and looked. "Oh, Goddess, it has!"

"This means I'm a woman now?"

Mother came over and crouched down, holding the hems of the shift out herself. "Yes, yes, you're becoming a woman. Just a month after your third birthday." She shook her head. "You're growing so fast. Too fast!"

As she kept an eye on the food cooking on the stove, Mother showed her how she needed to wear undergarments to hold in place the rag that would catch the blood. She didn't have to explain much, since Celeste had seen Mother do it.

When the rag and undergarments were in place and a clean shift draped over her, they sat down to eat. "You're growing too fast," Mother said again, a somber look on her face. "This can't go on forever. I've stolen too much life from you already."

That had to be the strangest thing Mother ever said, and she said a lot of strange things. What in the world could it mean, stealing life from her? *I don't know*, the Girl Inside said. *But you are growing up very fast.*

They ate their meal in silence, Mother deep in thought. When the meal was over, Mother still didn't move. Suddenly she looked down at her plate as if she were surprised it was empty.

"Celeste," she said in a tone that she'd never used before—a quiet, serious tone, touched with sadness. "It's time for me to tell you your story. I need to start teaching you things so you can protect yourself."

Protection again. What was this terrible danger that Celeste needed protection from? Other than that one strange encounter with the man last year, she'd never run into anything dangerous. And nothing had come of the man.

Mother began to speak. She told her about Zenia, a girl whose parents had died at the hands of burglars that had invaded her home. Mother raised her as her own daughter and taught her to work magic.

Zenia gave birth to a baby who did not survive, and a few days later the wife of the duke who ruled the land died in childbirth. Zenia became the wet nurse and raised the duke's daughter as her own, like Mother had been to Zenia.

The daughter's name was Tamara.

Something inside Celeste glowed with a warm feeling at the sound of that name. She couldn't tell if it was coming from herself or from the Girl Inside.

When Tamara grew, the young king of the land took her as his wife, but not out of love. He loved another who became his mistress, and except for their first night together, Tamara never slept with the king. One day she ran away and loved a man in the forest. From that love came a baby.

Mother explained how the baby had a curse on it, how the sorceress of the land wanted to kill the mother and take the baby so she could use its dark magic to make her the most powerful sorceress in the land, how Zenia helped Tamara escape and give birth to the baby, and how Tamara sacrificed her life to make the dark power in the baby pure and good.

"Celeste," Mother said, "that baby was you."

She nodded. As Mother told the story, she knew inside somehow that the baby was herself. "My true mother is Tamara," she said thoughtfully.

"Zenia gave you to me to raise as I raised her, as she raised your mother. She knew I had power to protect you."

"This is why I can call the animals."

Mother nodded.

This is why the Mistress Moon fills me with delight when I lay on the hillside.

I suppose so, said the Girl Inside.

Is this power who you are? Are you the child of Mistress Moon?

I don't know. Maybe.

"But, Celeste," Mother continued, "this power is dangerous for you to use. You have a bright aura of magic inside you that any sorceress or witch can see when they use the Sight. I've seen that aura. Whenever you use your power, that brilliant light flows out from inside you for any witch to see."

Celeste looked at herself. She could see nothing but a girl in a pale white shift. "I want to see it."

"It's too dangerous."

"Please, just a little? What chance is there that a witch is looking at us right now?"

"More chance than you might think," Mother said somberly. But she gazed at Celeste with eyes that glowed with affection. "I suppose a small glimpse here inside the cottage won't do any harm." She stood up and said, "Come with me. Time to start your lessons."

Curiosity overwhelmed her as she followed Mother out the door and down the trail to her hill. What lessons?

Mother didn't climb the hill. Instead she circled around until they came to a huge, gnarled stump with a gaping, rotting hole in its base. The tree that had once grown from it lay toppled on the ground, worms crawling on it. The rot of the dead tree filled Celeste's nostrils.

Mother knelt before the hole and reached into the neck of her dress. She pulled out the necklace with the worn silver moon. Celeste had seen it many times before, but in this place under these circumstances, the trinket took on a mysterious charm for her. She wondered what Mother would do with it.

Mother smiled. "Never just reach into the hole. I've placed a trap on it."

She extended the trinket into the hole. Celeste thought she saw—or did she just imagine it?—a faint sparkling flow from the trinket to the hole and fade away.

"Your golden moon will do the same thing," Mother said, "if you ever need to get in here. For a short while we can reach in."

"What does the trap do?"

"Nasty things to an intruder," Mother replied with a twinkle in her eye.

Celeste grimaced as Mother stuck both hands into the dark hole, disturbing several cobwebs and the ugly spiders perched on them. She pulled her hands back, and within their grasp was a wooden chest. "Every so often I come and check to make sure it's safe."

"When? I've never seen you leave."

"Always when you're napping. You nap a lot, you know, just like you eat a lot. Because you're growing so fast, I suppose."

No, she didn't know. She napped when she was tired and ate when she was hungry, and it never seemed like anything more than normal to her.

"Why haven't you told me about this chest before?" she asked with a hint of resentment.

Mother lifted the lid of the chest. "That is your first lesson, my sweet girl," she answered. "This is the most important lesson I'll give you. Listen very carefully!"

She resolved to listen.

"I can't emphasize too much how important this lesson is. Your life depends on it—and my life—and possibly the fate of the whole world."

"I promise!" Celeste said with wonder. She'd never seen Mother so earnest before. The whole world?

"Inside this chest is all the magic I know. Books, notes, scrolls, some rare plants and seeds, and—a special artifact. I've not dared use them these three years because we *must stay hidden*."

"Hidden from who?"

"There are two sorceresses who know of your existence. Gwendolyn is the one who threw your mother in a dungeon so she could take you when you were born. The other is Deirdre, the sorceress in the next kingdom over. Both of them want you so they can use your power."

She became disturbed. Two sorceresses wanted to take her? She was vague on what a sorceress was, but she understood they were powerful and could be evil. "Are we safe?"

Mother smiled. "Yes, for now. If we weren't, they'd have already come. Often I've wished to use my magic to see what's going on in the world, but that would only endanger us."

Celeste peered at the chest as if it were a fairy treasure—a magical thing like in the stories Mother had told her to amuse her in the night. And she realized, that's exactly what it was! She couldn't wait to see what was inside it.

"I know you're a sweet, innocent thing that has never experienced the outside world. I know you have no idea what evil and cruelty is. But you have to trust me, Celeste, trust me like you've never trusted me before. *You can't let Gwendolyn or Deirdre get hold of you!*"

The way she said it frightened Celeste. Her tone sounded like a mixture of fear and anger. It was a tone she'd never heard from Mother.

"They'd use you in ways that would hurt you like you've never been hurt before. They may even kill you."

Fear swept over Celeste. She fell to her knees and reached out to hold Mother's hand. Mother took it and gripped tightly.

"But that's only the beginning, dear Celeste. They'd use your amazing power to hurt others, to rule the world and bring sorrow and pain to everyone in it."

"Why, Mother?" she pleaded as tears fell from her eyes. "Why would anyone do that?"

Mother shook her head slowly. "I don't know. I don't understand how people can be so cruel. But I know they can be. I've seen it. I lived through a terrible war where I saw cruelty you wouldn't believe."

Celeste's tears flowed, and Mother hugged her. "I'm sorry, sweetheart. I wish I didn't have to frighten you like this, but you have to understand. This is your first, most important lesson. You are a princess, born to a queen. You have special powers that your mother gave her life to give you. A more special girl does not exist in the whole world. You *must not* let anyone capture you!"

She lifted Celeste's face up by her chin and looked into her streaming eyes. "Do you understand?"

She nodded as she said, "Yes, Mother."

She smiled comfortingly and wiped the tears from Celeste's face with her sleeve. "That's the end of lesson one, sweet girl. Now we can have some fun!"

The fear within her gave way almost at once to excitement as Mother positioned the chest so she could see inside.

Mother pulled out a small book bound with a cloth cover. "This is the book of spells my teacher gave me. Inside are all the secrets of a village witch." She handed it to Celeste. "Be very careful with it. The pages are old and easily damaged."

With as much care as she could muster, she examined page after page. The handwritten words inside were nothing Celeste had seen before.

"I'll have to teach you to read them," Mother said.

"This is the Ancient Tongue?"

Mother shook her head. "How did...I know you know things I've never taught you. Is it your power?"

"It's like a voice inside my heart—a girl's voice. I call it the Girl Inside."

Mother perked up. "Does this Girl have a name?"

"She thinks she has one, but she doesn't know what it is."

Mother nodded with a strange, wistful half-smile on her face, then laid her hand on a page of the book. "Are you ready to learn another language?"

She nodded enthusiastically.

"You don't *have* to know what the words mean to make the spells work, but it's better if you do."

Next Mother showed her the scraps of parchment that she'd written notes on as she expanded her knowledge of the magic arts, then several scrolls rolled up, made of lambskin, with more of the exotic writing on them.

"These are spells from the Ancient Magic—from the days of the original Seven Sisters. This magic came directly from the Great Gods themselves. No village witch has anything like these!"

Celeste gazed at them, and her heart almost burst with the thrill of having such magnificent treasures before her eyes.

"But this!" Mother lifted a black bundle from the box, something heavier than the other things by the way she lifted it. "This is the most valuable thing in my possession."

"What is it?"

"It's a scrying globe, and even the sorceresses have no such thing. You can look in it and see anything anywhere in the world. It's tucked away inside a concealing sack to hide it from prying eyes."

"Where did you get it?"

Mother tilted her head as she lifted her eyebrows and giggled. "Maybe it's best if I don't tell you just yet."

The wonder of this treasure was so amazing that Celeste felt little disappointment at not knowing where it came from—for now.

"I don't dare take it out, because..." Mother glanced about as if she were afraid someone was in the woods watching. "Well, I can open the sack just a bit so you can peek at it."

Trembling, Celeste gazed into the sack as Mother pulled back its lip. Inside was a shiny ball that looked like glass. Celeste thought she could see a faint otherworldly sparkle inside it, but maybe that was just her imagination.

"We're finished here," Mother said as she snapped the sack closed, placed everything back in the box, and closed the lid. "Let's go back now."

They returned to the cottage with the chest, Mother constantly peering about with apprehension. More than any of her words, Mother's behavior drove home the first lesson. She had to be as careful as she possibly could. She vowed to Mother Goddess and to Mistress Moon that she'd never allow the two terrible sorceresses, Gwendolyn and Deirdre, to find her and capture her.

"Now!" Mother said with glee as they settled in. She retrieved the book of spells from the chest. "Your second lesson!"

She opened the book to the first page. "This is the first spell any witch learns—a spell of Sight. See these words in the title? In the Ancient Tongue they read, *Thou shalt see*."

"That's the name of the spell?"

"In the Ancient Tongue. We just call it a Sight spell. Now see this list at the end?" She slid her finger across the words. "Magic requires sources of energy to work, and that energy comes from physical materials. The materials can be just about anything, but certain materials work best for certain spells. The materials for the Sight spell are listed here."

"But I've never seen you use materials."

"Using the materials casts a stronger spell, but you can also just say the words. The air from your own breath as you speak is the material that provides the energy. It's the easiest way to cast a spell, but it's also the weakest form of the spell. As long as you can speak, you can cast a breath spell."

Mother led her through the words of the Sight spell, helping her to recognize the strange letters and pronounce them correctly. When she had each individual word down well enough, Mother said, "Now read the whole thing straight through, and you will give yourself Sight!"

She did so, trembling with excitement, and with the last word she spoke, she felt a tingling sensation spread from her mouth and wrap around her body. The physical images of the cottage around her dimmed, and wild flashes of color filled her vision. Garbled noises filled her ears. Unbelievable sensations washed over her body. The experience alarmed her.

"Look at me, Celeste." Mother's voice came as a distant shout through the noise. "Look at my eyes and concentrate."

Celeste did so, and slowly Mother's face appeared before her.

"This is the hardest part, separating out all the noise and focusing on what you want to see. Keep looking at my face and listening to my voice, and you'll learn how."

It took some time, but she was finally able to control her focus enough to push all the random sensations aside and see and hear and feel what she wanted to see and hear and feel. She looked around and saw all the nearby trees in the forest—right through the walls of the cottage—and all the scurrying little creatures within it. She heard every bird singing within a hundred feet. She could smell the aromas of every wildflower and feel the wind feathering the treetops. "This is wonderful!" she cried.

"Now look at yourself," Mother said. "Look at yourself and reach out to call an animal."

Celeste focused on her own body with her Sight, and with her mind called to a squirrel she saw leaping from one branch to another. As she did so, a blinding glow formed near her heart and stretched out toward the door of the cottage. "Oh Mother Goddess!" she cried, and the shock broke her concentration. The glowing finger dissolved.

Celeste sat for a moment panting, her head swimming. "It was so bright, so bright and beautiful."

"Yes, it is beautiful—the most beautiful thing I've ever seen. That's the magical aura of your power." Mother placed her hand on Celeste's arm. "But, my sweet girl, any witch within miles can see it if they look this way with Sight. You're like a fire in the night when you use your power."

She understood, having seen how brilliant her aura was. "I won't use my powers again," she promised.

"Not for now, anyway, darling. You'll need to practice using them eventually, but we need to be very careful about how you do it."

Celeste worked hard to master the spells in Mother's book. She instructed her to cast a Sight spell before casting any other spell and look around to make sure no one was near. "Almost all magic gives off an aura that can be seen with Sight, except Sight itself. Make sure no one is watching."

Celeste never found anyone watching. Occasionally she'd see someone moving through the forest or on the road in the distance, but they always went about their business, never paying attention to the cottage. She was surprised to see how many "other people" came and went, yet Celeste had never encountered them—except for the one man two years ago.

When she asked Mother about that, she pointed to the trinket on the door and said, "A special Warding spell. That's the nice thing about amulets. The Ancients cast permanent spells on them, and they don't give off an aura. It's better than the Masking spell sorceresses use. That hides them, but it leaves a blank spot so every witch knows something's going on there. This amulet just...distracts them from us."

Autumn came with its fiery colors, then winter with its frozen white rain called snow, then spring with its fresh greens and joyful wildflowers.

She found out that learning magic was more than memorizing spells or collecting the right herbs and flowers and insects and weeds and minerals to crush or burn. The greatest effort was in learning to control the energy she released, to focus or to aim or to concentrate on a precise location to fix the spell. Any slight wandering of her mind would alter the results significantly, sometimes even diffuse the spell into a useless burst of magical sparks.

Concentration was not a strong point for Celeste. She'd spent her life wandering from wonder to wonder in the forest, indulging her whims. Sometimes she became grumpy with the effort. Mother had to scold her, then console her.

But as the seasons changed, she learned and she improved, and come an evening in midsummer as both she and Mother lay in the grass on Celeste's hill, watching the stars appear and the full moon rise as they rested from a particularly grueling session, Mother declared, "You've learned enough that you could be a village witch now. You could use lots more practice, but you'd manage."

Celeste beamed with pride as she absorbed the vitalizing glow of the moon. Maybe she was overly tired, but the moon seemed to invigorate her more than usual tonight.

A nightingale fluttered down from above and landed squarely on her chest, right between her dainty breasts. "Mother, look!" Celeste whispered, barely breathing.

"That's amazing!" Mother whispered back.

The nightingale cocked one eye, then the other, toward Celeste's face. She reached out her finger and stroked the reddish brown feathers on its back.

Something rubbed against Celeste's bare foot, tickling it. She pulled away with a squeal. The nightingale leaped into the air and flew off.

"What was that for?" Mother asked.

"Something tickled me." She sat up and looked. "A hedgehog."

The hedgehog ambled toward Celeste and nuzzled her knee.

"How odd," Mother murmured, looking around.

Leaves rustled off to the left, and a deer popped out from the forest. It glanced around the top of the hill, then strode directly toward Celeste.

"Are you calling these animals?" Mother said harshly.

"No!"

The deer crept up to Celeste and nudged its nose against her arm. Mother muttered a quick breath spell, then cried, "Oh Goddess, no!"

"What is it?"

Mother jumped to her feet. The deer scampered away and the hedgehog waddled as fast as it could. "Your aura—it's coming out!"

Celeste uttered her own spell and instantly saw a thin shell of brightness surrounding her entire body. A narrow strand of brilliance rose from her heart toward the face of the moon.

"We've got to go—now!"

Mother tugged Celeste to her feet and pulled her along by a hand. "That shaft rising up to the moon—that's a beacon to anyone looking for you."

The two females raced down the path back to the cottage. "Do you have your necklace on?" Mother shouted back.

"Yes," she said, clasping the moon with her free hand.

"What a fool I was! What a fool I was!" Mother chanted. "I should have paid more attention. I never thought it would seep out by itself."

Celeste gazed around with her Sight as they ran, trying to see if anything or anyone strange were in the woods around them. She thought she could make out some fleeting images in the distance behind them, but it was hard to focus while running through the woods.

"Oh Goddess, dear Goddess, they're coming!" Mother cried as she peered about with her own Sight. "We're too late!"

Chapter 11

Hereward

Hereward took up the rear as the six of them began their quest down the East Highway to Suedeche. Sighurd took the lead with Kasimir and Faisal. Immediately behind them were Dietric and Thomas. The king had provided horses for the wizard and his attendant.

Kasimir and Faisal gaped at Fenweald Forest, tall, ancient, thick, and wild. "Is this forest haunted?" Faisal asked.

Sighurd chuckled. "Some say it is."

"How big is it?"

"It covers thousands of square miles," Sighurd answered. "It stretches from Gallea into Suedeche and Scaendelreic and Cithania to the northeast and the Duchy of Brebannia in the northwest."

"It's massive," said Kasimir. "I've never seen trees so tall, growth so thick."

Faisal laughed as he looked at Kasimir. "The closest we've seen is that grove of olive trees."

Hereward didn't blame the foreigners for being in awe of the forest. He felt its oppressiveness himself whenever traveling this road, especially after being attacked by the Beast. As they passed into Suedeche and the trees thinned out and villages and fields popped up, he felt as if he'd escaped a prison.

The inhabitants of the villages gaped at the travelers. To see an entourage of the King's Guard was a rare enough sight, but to see two Insan men with their strange clothing and swords and dark skin must have been as exciting and terrifying to them as if a magical being from children's fantasy stories had materialized before them.

Then there were the gems on Kasimir's face, the thing the villagers stared at with the greatest fascination. Hereward had spent the entire time on the Sea of Az staring at them. He still wasn't used to them.

It was a good thing he and his companions accompanied the foreigners. He could only imagine how Kasimir and Faisal traveling alone would have fared. They could have been perceived as invaders. They could have been murdered in their sleep for the gems.

Because Eloise was from Suedeche and because of Gwendolyn's suspicion that Deirdre helped her with the abduction, they decided to search Suedeche first, then Scaendelreic. They presented themselves to Duke Geoffrey in the city of Suedeche. The man was middle-aged, but looked old and haggard since the death of his daughter. Sighurd explained to him their mission was to find the abducted newborn daughter of one of their noblemen, whom they had reason to believe may have been brought to Suedeche.

He carefully avoided mentioning she was the duke's own granddaughter. The duke thought his grandchild was a prince, not a princess, alive and well in Luteche. Hereward didn't understand exactly what was going on, but Sighurd seemed fine with it, and it wasn't his place to question such things.

Duke Geoffrey granted them full liberty to search his duchy. Search they did for the next several months. Kasimir kept muttering things wherever they went. He explained they were breath spells of Sight he used to look for anything out of the ordinary. Hereward never saw him practice any other magic. He began to wonder if this wizard had any magic more powerful than a witch.

In each village they visited, they interrogated the inhabitants. But after several months, they found nothing unusual, other than discovering the village where the traitors Zenia and Eloise had lived, a quaint community called Vilnetal. Hereward gathered Eloise had been beloved before she disappeared. Some said she deserted them and resented that she left them with no witch for a month. Others worried that something terrible had happened to her. Sighurd never told them what he knew about Eloise.

Eventually the village convinced an apprentice from the city of Suedeche named Cosette to come be their witch.

Throughout their journey, Hereward slept fitfully. Weighing constantly on his mind was the dread of his impending Change. Privately he told Sighurd they should kill him now. He was too much of a danger to everyone. Sighurd refused, saying Hereward was too valuable and deserved to live as much life as he had left. He assured him that he'd keep a careful eye on him for any change. They would deal with it when the time came.

The night before they were to leave Suedeche, Hereward lay sleepless in his bedding. The sky was cloudy, but the full moon shone through as a vague glow of light. Every night a full moon appeared, he struggled to sleep, plagued with dreams of the Change as soon as he dozed.

As he lay in his bedding, he heard a rustling behind him. He turned and found Kasimir rising quietly as the others slept. He crept away from the dying embers of their fire into the shadows of the night. Hereward assumed he was heading for the pit they'd dug as a latrine, but he went a different direction and stopped with his back facing the camp, a shadow in the night. Kasimir looked down and seemed to fiddle with something, then muttered words that Hereward couldn't make out. A brilliant light flared up where his hands were. Kasimir was a silhouette before it.

The brilliance flowed up to Kasimir's face and faded away. He stood motionless for a moment, them slowly rotated, his face gazing off into the distance. Hereward squinted his eyes to a slit, pretending to sleep, as the wizard faced him.

He kept rotating until his back was turned to Hereward again, then stopped. His shoulders seem to droop, as if disappointed. He returned to his bedding.

Hereward closed his eyes and pondered. His best guess was a Sight spell to scan the area for any hint of the princess. But that was no breath spell. Where had its glowing power come from?

Immediately Hereward's mind went to the gems.

This couldn't be the first time Kasimir had done that while everyone slept. He must have searched the countryside this way many times. Yet none of the gems on his face were missing. How did they work? Did he have other gems, hidden away under his clothing?

In the morning, Hereward brought Sighurd aside. "I saw something last night. Kasimir—"

"I know," Sighurd said. "He does that every time we leave an area."

"I think I might know where his power comes from."

"The gems. I know. Gwendolyn knows."

"He has more of them under his clothing."

"I know. But we're not supposed to know, so..."

Hereward nodded. "Understood."

But he understood more than just to keep quiet. He understood that the wizard had great power at his disposal, a power secretive enough that they weren't supposed to know about it. A power that...perhaps...might help Hereward with his curse.

That evening they crossed the border into the kingdom of Scaendelreic. Unlike Suedeche, this was no ally. They'd fought a nasty war with Gallea and nearly won. Crossing that border was dangerous, and that fact troubled Hereward as much as his impending Change. They slunk in under cover of darkness and took advantage of the thick forest to hide in during the day. Kasimir kept uttering a breath spell to make sure they avoided anyone.

The search here was more arduous. Officially interrogating citizens was not possible. Dietric posed as a traveler and asked the sort of questions curious travelers would ask, to see if anyone knew of anything unusual. Because his family originated from Scaendelreic, he knew the language. Because he was born natively in Gallea, he had an accent that none of the natives of Scaendelreic could quite place, enhancing the illusion that he was a traveler. When they asked him, he always said he was from somewhere else in Scaendelreic that was far away.

The Insan wizard and his attendant had to remain in the forest.

A month after entering Scaendelreic, the six of them sat around a fire. A full moon was about to rise, and its glow shone above the horizon. Hereward became agitated. This was nothing like his usual apprehension. He physically felt an agitation throughout his body. He beckoned for Sighurd to come near.

"I think it's happening," he said quietly.

Sighurd studied him. "Are you sure?"

"I don't know! I only know a full moon is coming, and I feel wrong."

Thomas came over carrying his sword. "He's changing, isn't he?" He looked at Hereward with compassionate eyes. "I promise it'll be quick."

Now that the moment was upon him, Hereward didn't want to die. "Sighurd." He nodded toward Kasimir. "The gems?"

Thomas said to Sighurd, "If we wait until he changes, it'll be too late."

Hereward grunted as a tingling shot through his body. "Please, Sighurd!"

Sighurd looked at Kasimir, who sat peering at them somberly.

"Captain!" Thomas hissed. "Give me the order!"

As the others conversed casually, Kasimir kept his eyes on Hereward. Something was troubling him, as if a fever were overcoming him. In countless breath spells of Sight, Kasimir had noticed a strange sense of darkness about him, as if a shadow constantly clung to him. It troubled him ever since their quest began. But Hereward had never done anything suspicious or sinister, so Kasimir kept quiet about it. And watchful.

But tonight something was different. While away from the others, he spoke a Sight spell and watched Hereward. The darkness seemed to be intensifying. His countenance was grim, and his eyes glared from under his brows with a savage gaze. Like a predator.

Hereward called Sighurd and Thomas over, and they spoke in hushes. Thomas prominently carried his sword. Kasimir felt it—something dangerous was about to happen.

He stood and called, "Sighurd, is something wrong?"

He turned to him. "Uh...we have a...problem."

"What problem?" he said as he approached them.

Sighurd hesitated before answering. "Hereward was attacked many months ago and wounded by a...a wolf."

"The scar on his shoulder?"

Sighurd nodded.

"Has it become infected?"

Sighurd took a deep breath. "It was no ordinary wolf. It was a legendary creature, a cursed creature. We call it the Beast."

Anger welled up in him. Cursed beasts were a part of the lore in Insu, and attacks by them were always serious business. Why wasn't he informed of this before they began their quest? "We have our own legends...about changelings."

"He hasn't changed before," Sighurd said, then looked at Hereward. "I think this may be the night."

Hereward's breathing became gruff and heavy, almost like a steady growl.

"He needs to be destroyed before it's too late," Thomas said.

Kasimir gazed at the man, feeling pity for him. But the danger was too great for the rest of them. Reluctantly he said, "Then...I guess you'd better. I'm sorry, Hereward."

"Can you...do anything?" Sighurd asked as his eyes focused on Kasimir's face.

He had no idea what he could do about it. Such curses were ancient things, coming from a power very different than the magic of the wizards. Was this a thing the power of a starstone could purify?

He looked out at the glow on the horizon. Evren—the Mistress Moon—was on the verge of showing her face. He should pull out his scimitar and lop the man's head off himself. Their very survival was at stake.

But with the time he'd spent traveling with Hereward, he was as reticent to do it as Sighurd.

"Such curses are more ancient than our magic," he said, but as he said it, he knew he couldn't slay Hereward, nor could he command others to do what he couldn't do. It went against his training to waste a starstone on something when he had no idea it would even work. But for the sake of the group and Hereward himself, he had to try.

He turned to walk into the shadows, but Sighurd stopped him with a hand on his arm. "We know about your gems."

Kasimir studied him in disbelief. How had they found out?

Hereward let out a definite growl. A faint reddish glow loomed in his eyes.

With a grunt of resignation, Kasimir opened his garment, revealing the starstones. The others stared at them. He plucked one and dipped it in the blood, held it in his hands and spoke incantations. The stone flared into brilliance.

The first sliver of moon appeared. Hereward snarled, and the red in his eyes intensified. His gaze was no longer at the ground, but upon Kasimir standing before him. A luminescent fog formed around him. He jumped up and leaped into the air with a roar. Kasimir balked and threw the brilliance at him. It burst into a blinding flash that burned an image in his eyes of a half-man, half-beast suspended in the air in mid-pounce, dark hair layered on his face, fangs bared and dripping saliva, claws extended toward him.

Kasimir shut his eyes, waiting for the creature to tear him to shreds. The night became suddenly silent. When nothing happened, he opened them. The afterimage of the blinding glow took a moment to clear. When he could see again, he found the partially changed Hereward lying on his stomach on the ground convulsing, with his claws still extended as if in attack.

Everyone rushed toward Hereward.

"Stay back!" Kasimir ordered. "I'm not sure what's happening."

He watched as Hereward's convulsions quieted. The low growl returned, and his clawed hands began twitching in a grasp. He lifted his head, revealing glowing red eyes.

"I think you'd better restrain him," Kasimir said. "Get your ropes."

Dietric, Thomas, and Faisal scrambled in their saddlebags for rope.

"Hurry up!" Sighurd called as Hereward struggled to rise up on hands and knees. He placed his foot on Hereward's back and held him down.

"Tie his hands behind his back," said Faisal as they came with the rope. "Then tie him to a tree."

"Use lots of rope," Kasimir said. "I have no idea how strong he'll be."

Dietric and Thomas went for each arm. Kasimir said, "Don't let him scratch you or bite you. He's probably still...infectious, or...whatever."

Dietric and Thomas pulled each arm behind Hereward's back and tied them together as Sighurd's foot pressed hard on his rump and Faisal's foot held him in place just below his neck against his increasingly violent struggles.

It took all five of them to pull him to a tree and four of them to hold him in place as Kasimir secured him to the trunk with four ropes. They stepped back and watched him somberly as he struggled, growled, and howled.

Kasimir shot smoldering eyes at Sighurd. "You should have told me from the beginning."

Sighurd lowered his head and nodded.

As they watched, Thomas said, "I don't think it cured him."

Kasimir shook his head. "I think it only arrested his Change."

"Permanently?" Sighurd asked.

Kasimir had no answer.

When it appeared the ropes would hold, they returned to their fire, but kept a steady eye on Hereward.

"We should try to get some sleep," Kasimir said.

"I'm not sleeping!" Thomas said.

"I suppose I'm not either."

After a while, Hereward calmed down. His head rested back against the tree, his growls stopped, and the red in his eyes gradually faded. In time, only the man Hereward remained tied to the tree, drenched in sweat and eyes closed.

"Is he cured now?" Dietric said.

"No," Hereward said with a hoarse voice. "I still feel the urge to change."

"How did you come back?" asked Faisal.

"I fought...I fought. I didn't want to be a Beast. I pictured myself being a man... I'm a man... I'm the King's Guard. Not a wolf."

Sighurd said, "Your stone may not have cured him, but it looks like it softened the curse."

"But for how long?" said Thomas.

Kasimir stood and walked over to Hereward. "I'm sorry my starstone couldn't remove your curse."

He chuckled as he closed his eyes and rested his head back. "At least I'm not a Beast all night."

"We'll have to keep you tied up until the moon sets."

He nodded. "Please do. I'm still fighting it."

They stood guard two at a time through the night. Hereward remained quiet with his eyes closed, perhaps sleeping, but at one point woke them all as he chanted loudly without opening his eyes, "I am a man. I am a man. I am a man. I am the King's Guard."

Everyone expressed relief as the sun rose with Hereward still being Hereward. As they untied him, Sighurd said, "We may have to tie you up every night there's a full moon."

He smiled wearily. "Better than slaying me."

The next night they tied him before the moon rose. Kasimir said, "Tonight we'll see how powerful my stone is."

"Will you cast another spell if he needs it?" Sighurd said.

A starstone each night of a full moon? For how many years? He didn't have enough of them to last more than a few. "I pray to Mabut it won't be necessary."

Hereward did turn into the partial beast again, but the ropes held again, and he fought back to humanity in a shorter time. "I think I'm getting the hang of this," he said.

"I'm sorry you have to go through it," Kasimir said, "but thank the Great Gods it's manageable."

Hereward whispered wearily, "Thank you."

He chanted again once that night, but otherwise remained calm.

On the third night, the glow came, and he became the half-beast for a moment, then reverted quickly back to a man. He slept throughout the night.

A month passed. The first night of another full moon came, then the second. He showed no signs of changing while tied to a tree. He only seemed more irascible during the day. On the third night, they let him sleep unrestrained in his bedding, keeping watch by twos.

They all survived until morning.

King Christian received word that Duke Geoffrey would travel to Luteche to meet his grandson, now that the prince was old enough to understand who he was. At first Christian panicked, afraid the duke might find out, but after a while he realized this was a golden opportunity.

Gwendolyn pulled him aside with a warning. "We have to keep him believing Guillaume is his grandchild. He can never know about Celeste."

He glared at her. She still treated him like a child. "Do you think I'm stupid?"

Her eyes seemed to say *yes*, but she responded, "No, of course not."

Christian watched as Geoffrey met two-year-old Guillaume, talked with him, and even got down on the floor and played with his toy soldiers with him. He felt a pang of guilt, seeing such affection when the boy wasn't who the Duke thought he was, but Christian shook it off and thought, *Yes, Duke, love your grandchild. Cement it into everyone's mind that he is your grandchild.*

Almost two years in Scaendelreic, Hereward thought gloomily, *and we've found nothing here either.*

The kingdom consisted mostly of the towering Hocberc Mountains to the south and Fenweald Forest to the north. Almost nobody lived in the mountains, which made them prime territory for someone to hide in. It didn't help that winter was on its way.

They searched the mountains that resided in Scaendelreic. The rest spilled over into Onotrea, a kingdom just as hostile to Gallea. Between that and the deep mountain snow, Kasimir decided to move on to the forest in the north.

Forest snow was not mountain snow, but it was still months of misery trudging through it. They barely covered a fourth of the forest before spring finally came, to their relief.

By the time they'd searched all of it, spring, summer, and autumn had passed. Hereward kept his urge to change under control.

Before leaving Scaendelreic, they passed through Scaendel once more. That night there was no moon. Long after the city fell quiet, Kasimir used a starstone to cast a Sight spell and ventured into the city where Gunther's castle resided and where Deirdre's tower rose high above everything else. Hereward accompanied him. They wore cloaks with hoods.

Kasimir scanned the city as they went. He stood before the castle, peering intently at it. "I see nothing suspicious there," he said.

He stood silently before Deirdre's tower. "There's a mask surrounding it."

"Can you see nothing?" Hereward asked.

"This close, the starstone can just barely penetrate it. I see only shadows. But I also see no human figures but one. I assume that's Deirdre."

"No servants or anything?"

Kasimir shook his head.

"She's a solitary bitch," Hereward said with a chuckle.

To his relief, they left Scaendelreic the day after. Next they'd search Fenweald Forest back in Gallea. Another winter in the forest.

"We should have searched there first," Thomas grumbled, "closer to home."

Hereward nurtured his own silent grudge, but it was against magic itself. He was grateful for Kasimir's effort to soften his curse, but he'd always imagined sorceresses and wizards being able to wave their hands and speak exotic words and accomplish anything they wanted. That's why it was called magic.

But after two years of dreary wandering in the villages and cities and mountains and forests of Cueldea, he realized magic was as tedious as any other profession. Workers of magic had abilities no regular mortals had, but they had to wield them as painstakingly as a craftsman with his tools.

They first combed the area of Fenweald Forest south of the East Highway. At least winter was milder there than in the forest in Scaendelreic further to the north. By the end of winter they'd returned to their starting point at the city of Luteche, but not to the end of their quest. There was still the forest to the north of the East Highway, and that was nearly as huge as the forest in Scaendelreic.

At least they'd be searching without snow for the next three seasons.

Kasimir didn't want to take a rest in Luteche. Hereward had never seen such a driven man at such a young age. They rode in the night past the south side of the castle along the East Highway as it veered into the North Highway to Sicana Harbor. The view of the castle from this direction was breathtaking. It was built on a promontory cliff that jutted into a curve of the River Sicana. A waterfall tumbled from the high ground on the east side of the castle, and another, narrower fall tumbled down on the west side from the artificial moat of diverted river water.

Kasimir stopped at the point of the curve and admired the view. Hereward understood that Insu was an arid land and figured, with the awe in Kasimir and Faisal's eyes, this must be a view they'd never seen before.

The highway followed the river northward past a ferry located at a point where it widened and slowed on its journey to the sea. In the morning they crossed on the ferry, then continued searching eastward into the forest.

Another year went by as they scoured the west end of the forest, and another winter. All they ever found were denizens of the forest. How many hunters and trappers had they detained for information? How many bandits had they routed? A good thing for the countryside, but it didn't bring them one day closer to finding Celeste.

With each passing month, Hereward became more and more certain they were on a fool's errand. That princess was well hidden and would never be found, even with this celebrated wizard with all his glittering gems.

A thunderous noise came from ahead as Hereward and the others rode.

"What is that?" asked Kasimir. By now, he and Faisal had become conversant in Galleic, so they spoke in that language exclusively instead of Ruic.

"The Falls of Eircana," Sighurd answered.

"We should turn away," said Hereward. "They're haunted."

"Haunted?" said Faisal.

"The Seven Sisters of old said so. They warned us to stay away."

Kasimir and Faisal looked at each other and smiled. "I want to see these haunted falls," Faisal said.

The two of them galloped ahead. Hereward looked at Sighurd with distress.

"Afraid of ghosts?" Sighurd asked.

Yes, he was. After the attack from the Beast, he took supernatural things very seriously.

The sun kissed the spray with a golden hue as it hung low in the sky. The thunderous noise of the falls drowned out all other sounds in the forest. The River Sicana was wide here as it cut through the thick forest to reach a gash in the land where it plummeted down both sides to a narrow ribbon of water flowing through the chasm until the walls around it gradually sloped down for about a mile to meet the level of the river. The Falls of Eircana consisted of many falls that overflowed at various points along either side of the gash.

Mist cooled Hereward's sweating face, dirty from a day of riding and searching. He marveled at the view before him. Such breathtaking beauty! But its magnificent oppressive size in the waning daylight made it feel all the more haunted.

Kasimir rode to the edge of the cliff with his brother Faisal, two majestic figures against the red background of sunset. If they gazed with awe upon the falls in Luteche, they must be positively enraptured with this view.

Sighurd and Hereward rode up next to them.

"This is the most beautiful place in the world," Faisal said with reverence.

Kasimir said, "See how the mist sparkles in the sun like the stars of the heavens."

"You should see what the sun does to your own face," Sighurd said.

Kasimir smiled. "I *have* seen it, on the faces of the wizards of Eranshar."

"What makes it haunted?" Faisal asked.

"The Seven Sisters told the story," said Thomas. "When Father Sky commanded his children to mate, Master Fire refused to mate with Mistress Earth. He'd fallen in love with a mortal woman. It angered Father Sky, and he chased that woman to kill her, but she fled down the River Sicana on a raft. Mistress Earth opened up a gash in the earth before her to swallow her up." He gestured at the chasm. "She fell over the falls, and legend says she's still falling to this day."

"Do you believe that story?" Faisal asked.

"Most people believe it enough to avoid the falls," Sighurd answered.

"There are other stories of lovers whose families forbade their love," Hereward said. "They came here to leap and join that woman in death. Some say the Throat of Mistress Earth is full of the souls of lovers who have died."

"Is that what you call this chasm?" Kasimir said.

"That's its popular name," Sighurd said.

"Sicana, Eircana—very similar words," said Faisal. "Do they have a special meaning?"

"We're told Sicana means forbidden water, and Eircana means forbidden falls," Sighurd replied. "They say it's the Ancient Tongue of the Seven Sisters." He smiled. "The only words of the Ancient Tongue we men are allowed to know."

Hereward peered down with them into the chasm. The mist rose in the twilight like the ghosts of the fallen lovers.

Admiring the chasm, Kasimir said, "I don't believe Father Sky or Mistress Earth are so vindictive."

"You believe in the Great Gods," Sighurd said, "yet when we sailed the Sea of Az, you mentioned Gimshek."

"We do believe in the Great Gods," Faisal said, and looked at Kasimir pointedly. "But we also know their names."

"Who is Gimshek?"

"Grandson of Storms, offspring of Master Air and Mistress Water."

"And what are *their* names?"

"Havi and Sushezad."

"And Father Sky is Mabut," said Kasimir, "and Mother Goddess is Sevda."

"How did your people learn their names?" Dietric asked.

"They're the names from *our* Ancient Tongue, handed down from wizard to wizard throughout time."

"Let's find a dry place away from this drenching mist of the souls that haunt this chasm," Sighurd said and grinned at Hereward.

They scouted out a flat, dry clearing away from the waterfall, but where its soothing thunder could still be heard. They unpacked their gear and laid out their bedding. Dietric and Thomas took off into the trees to hunt down a meal while Hereward and Sighurd gathered wood for the fire. Kasimir and Faisal pulled the cooking gear from its sack—something that took a long time for Hereward to get used to. These two masters and royal guests pitched in with the daily chores right along with everyone else, never waiting to be served.

Dietric and Thomas returned with two rabbits and two squirrels. Sighurd pulled some cheese and bread from a pouch. "We'll need more supplies soon," he murmured.

"I'll go fetch some water," Hereward said while Sighurd lit the fire and the hunters began skinning the animals.

When the meat was roasted and the cheese and bread passed around, the five men ate in silence, weary from the day's travel. But Hereward knew their weariness, like his own, was from more than a day's physical effort.

The sun set and the stars popped out. The glow of a full moon about to rise broke above the eastern horizon. Hereward felt the agitation of the Change trying to come, but he was used to enduring it by now. The wind picked up, rustling the leaves and cooling the men as they downed the last of their meal.

"We're never going to find her," said Thomas.

"We'll find her," Dietric said, but without conviction.

"We've been at this for over three years," Thomas growled. "Where else is there to look?"

"We've still got more forest to search," Hereward said.

"Why can't Kasimir use his gems and...just locate her?" Thomas said.

"Starstones," Kasimir said. "They're called starstones."

"Why?" Dietric asked, but Kasimir didn't answer.

"How many more years before we can end this tedious quest and go home?" said Thomas.

"I can never go home until I find Celeste," Kasimir said.

"What if she's dead?" Dietric asked.

"Then I must find that out. Someone with powerful magic has hidden her, but I *will* find her."

Thomas scoffed in derision.

"If I must, I'll cast a Spell of Power."

"Haven't you already cast a spell of power with Hereward?" Sighurd asked.

"A Spell of Power is seven times more powerful."

"Then cast one now, so we can go home," Thomas said.

"A Spell of Power is nothing to trifle with!" Faisal said angrily.

"Who's trifling? We've been searching for *over three years!*"

"Most wizards never cast a Spell of Power in their lifetime," Kasimir said. "It releases immense power."

Thomas sneered. "I don't believe such a thing exists. That's why you won't cast it."

Hereward's agitation grew as Thomas spoke his rebellious words. He jumped to his feet, grabbing his sword. A fog began to form around him. The other men recoiled in horror. Thomas drew his sword.

"You *will* be silent!" Hereward bellowed. "You are in the service of the king, and you'll perform your duties without complaint."

Kasimir reached out and gently pushed the sword down. "It's alright, Hereward. His doubt is understandable."

His words calmed Hereward, and the fog dissipated. But he continued scowling at Thomas. To Sighurd he said, "What do you say?"

Sighurd gazed into the fire for a moment, then said, "I say we fulfill the mission that King Christian gave us, and trust in the commander he ordered us to serve."

Thomas pointed at Hereward with his sword. "It's dangerous to keep that man alive."

"Thomas, we're all weary," Sighurd said as he continued to stare at the fire.

Thomas grunted in disgust and stormed to his bedding.

———

One day at sunset, a month before their fourth year had passed, Kasimir stopped their riding through the forest with his hand raised. He'd cast one of his endless breath spells of Sight and seemed to be listening for something.

"What is it?" Sighurd said quietly.

"There's something ahead...someone."

There'd been lots of someones ahead of them over the years, but Hereward had never seen him react like this to any of them. Did he dare hope...?

He felt agitation creeping up inside him. A throbbing began in his scarred shoulder.

Kasimir eased his horse forward as quietly as he could. The others followed. After a couple hundred yards, Kasimir stopped again and dismounted. The others dismounted too.

Hereward came up beside him, massaging his shoulder, and peered deep into the trees to see what he might be detecting.

Kasimir looked at him, then at his shoulder, then ahead again. "Someone's ahead," he repeated. "Someone...unusual."

They crept forward another couple hundred feet, until they could see a cabin through the trees. Kasimir stopped and renewed his Sight spell.

"Cast your Spell of Power!" Thomas hissed in a harsh whisper.

Faisal and Sighurd turned and glared at him.

"Stay here," Kasimir said, then started forward again. The rest of them drew their swords and followed anyway.

"What do you see?" Sighurd asked.

"An aura."

"Celeste's?"

Without answering, Kasimir entered the clearing where the cabin was. There was a small garden filled with ripe produce soon to be picked. There was a large stack of chopped wood against the wall. Dark smoke billowed from the chimney.

Kasimir crept to the front of the cabin and stood before the closed door. Faisal stood on one side of him and Sighurd on the other, swords raised. The others stood behind them.

Hereward's heart pounded. Something filled him with edginess, and he began to tremble.

"It's not in here," Kasimir said. "It's..." He looked toward the corner of the cabin where the wood pile was.

A man stood there. He was tall with strong muscles. His hair was long and black. He had a full, black beard. He had no shirt on, but wore trousers and shoes. He was deeply tanned. He stood in a defensive stance with an axe held ready to swing.

"Are you here to slay me?" he said.

"Who are you?" asked Kasimir.

"My name is Edmund."

"*What* are you?"

"What are *you*?"

"I'm a wizard from Insu."

"I'm a woodsman from Gallea."

"I can see your darkness," Kasimir said with a scowl.

"You're a lot darker than I am."

Rubbing his throbbing shoulder, Hereward said, "Are you the one who did this to me?"

"Did what?"

"Are you...the Beast?"

Edmund broke out in a hearty laugh, startling everyone. "You're not the first person to accuse me of that."

"Is it true?" Kasimir said.

"When was the last time the Beast appeared?" Edmund said as an irritated look spread across his face. "Four years ago I heard him howling in the forest. How many full moons have there been since then? Have you heard any reports of him during those years?"

"Then why do you have a dark aura about you?"

"I don't know what you're talking about."

They bore their eyes into each other.

"I'm not the Beast. If you don't believe me..." Edmund nodded to the darkening east. "There's a full moon tonight. Wait around and see if I change."

"So you can attack us when we can't defend ourselves," Thomas said.

Without taking his eyes off Edmund, Kasimir said, "Hereward, do you sense anything unusual?"

"My shoulder aches."

Edmund peered at Hereward intensely. "It seems to me *I* should be the one worrying about *him*."

Kasimir looked at Hereward and noticed his trembling, which was becoming worse. "Hereward?"

"There's something about being here," he said. "I...I'm having a harder time controlling it."

Thomas backed off with his sword raised and shouted, "Are we going to stand here while the moon rises and be surrounded by two Beasts?"

"Everyone back away," Sighurd said. The group backed off from Hereward.

"Kasimir," Faisal said, readying his scimitar, "I think we'd better—"

"I'm still controlling it," Hereward said with irritation.

"The moon's rising," said Dietric.

The tingling and sickness Hereward felt with each full moon hit him hard this time. He chanted gruffly, "I am a man. I am a man. I am the King's Guard."

He peered at Edmund, who watched him intensely with a grim look. The others watched both men with weapons ready.

"I can see both your auras deepening...darkening," Kasimir said.

"Can't you see that *he's* the Beast?" Edmund said, axe poised.

They waited in fierce silence as the moon slid up above the horizon.

"They're not changing," Dietric said.

But Kasimir didn't seem to hear. He stared at the moon hanging just above the trees.

"The aura!" he cried.

"So he is changing!" Thomas said.

"Celeste's aura!" Kasimir dashed toward the forest and the horses. "Hurry, before it disappears again!"

They rushed to mount their horses, then galloped east past the cottage. With something to focus on, Hereward felt his agitation easing. He glared at Edmund as he passed, who stood with his axe raised and his face scowling as he watched them go by.

Kasimir rode in the lead as the horses plummeted through the forest, following the thin strand of light rising from the trees to the moon. He goaded his horse as fast as he could, not worrying if his men were keeping up with him.

As the moon rose, the column of light arced with it and grew more intense. It looked like a thick vapor flowing from the earth to the sky. Kasimir shot his Sight ahead, following the column to its source. He immediately found a woman and a girl lying on a hill.

He nearly lost his grip on the reins. The aura emanated from the girl, but the girl should be four years old. This girl was practically a woman of fifteen or sixteen years.

How could Celeste be so old?

And why, after all these years, did her aura suddenly appear?

No matter. He charged through the trees, fearing the aura would disappear. He could sort the rest out later.

He came upon a creek with a tiny waterfall. It almost amused him how quaint it was after the sight of the River Sicana with its thundering falls. Ahead the column of light had grown, a stream of brilliance stretching from the moon to the earth. It ended in a sphere of aura surrounding the girl. The sphere was on the move, running further away.

There was a path through the forest in that direction. "We've got her!" he shouted back to the others, not bothering to see if they were close enough to hear, and spurred his horse forward, splashing through the pool beneath the waterfall. He charged down the path. The aura looked like a streak of daylight against the dark sky.

The woman and the girl fled toward a cabin. *So that's where you've been all this time*, Kasimir thought.

With his Sight, he could hear the woman cry, "Oh Goddess, dear Goddess, they're coming! We're too late!"

"Indeed you are," Kasimir said with fervor.

Chapter 12

Falls of Eircana

Deirdre woke with a gasp. For a few seconds she was disoriented, then she recognized the tingling of the Truth Dream.

She rushed to the balcony, uttering a breath spell as she went, and peered out. There it was! A thin strand of that amazing aura reaching from the earth to the moon.

Everything was ready—she'd kept everything ready for four years. Her Flying spell and her robe to cast it on, a pack of materials for spells she might need to cast. In moments she launched herself from her balcony and swept through the air toward the stream of light, never bothering to change out of her sleepwear.

The aura looked to be located well within Fenweald Forest in Gallea. She pushed the Flying spell to its limits with the force of her will. The wind blasted her face, fluttered her eyelashes, caused her to squint. She choked on an insect that flew into her mouth and swallowed it, but she didn't care. She'd waited four years for this.

That nasty witch-thief had been clever. She ensconced herself and the child where no one could find them. Never a sign, never a hint of magic. Not once in those four years did she use the scrying globe again, not even for a few seconds. It must have driven her crazy to never peer into its crystal sphere and see what was going on in the world. It *had* driven Deirdre crazy not to have it.

But tonight she'd get it back. And the girl, now four years old. And the thief. And her revenge.

The ribbon of aura was moving swiftly. Dear Gods, someone must be pursuing her! Considering where the aura was, it was probably Gwendolyn or her minions. Deirdre groaned, trying to squeeze more power into the Flying spell, but it wouldn't move any faster.

The movement of the aura sped up. This was no longer a person fleeing on foot. This was the speed of a horse. Deirdre was close enough now to get a sense of direction in the movement. The aura was moving irregularly, rushing through the forest. It moved in a deliberate zigzag pattern—trying to avoid the pursuers. *It won't do you any good!* thought Deirdre. *Your aura continually points the way.*

The aura shrank and closed in on itself. She gasped in alarm. Did the thief cast the spell again? Would she have to wait four more years for it to reappear?

She sighed with relief when the aura stopped shrinking just before it disappeared. It was a thin shell around the girl, but still glowed enough to be visible from this distance.

The zigzagging continued. It seemed to be heading for the River Sicana. A foolish move. That huge river would be an impasse for her.

The aura flashed into brilliance again, shooting its column back up to the moon. Any village witch who looked could see it now. Deirdre gave the girl high marks for trying, but the aura must have been too much for her to contain.

She flew with all her might, her colorful robe fluttering madly in the wind.

"Quick, Celeste," Mother said as they dashed into the clearing where the cottage was. "Call my horse."

"What horse?"

"I've kept a horse out in the woods all this time. You can call her faster than I can."

"But they'll see my—" She stopped short, gazing at the finger of light that stretched from her chest up to the moon, and realized it didn't matter anymore. She reached out with her Sight and her inner power. Another column of brilliance flared through the forest, combing the surrounding landscape for a horse.

There, some distance from the cottage in a meadow where she'd never been, a mare grazed. As her column of power touched the horse, its head perked up, looked around, and the animal started walking in the direction of Celeste. She called for it to hurry, and the mare broke into a gallop, dashing through the trees.

The pounding of horse hooves reverberated from the forest trail behind them.

"Is the horse coming?" Mother cried.

"Yes."

Mother grabbed her hand and pulled her behind the cottage out of sight of the path. The mare bounded from the trees ahead of them, a ghostly shadow in the night, and trotted up to Celeste while Mother peered around the corner.

"Does your Girl Inside know how to ride?" Mother said.

The Girl responded yes before Celeste could ask.

"She does."

"We were supposed to ride together when this happened, but it's too late."

The pursuing horses thundered into the clearing.

Mother pushed Celeste onto the mare. "Flee, my child! Flee! Remember your golden moon, and whatever you do, *don't let them capture you!*"

"Yes, Mother," she said.

Mother slapped the horse into action.

"I love you," Celeste called over her shoulder.

"I love you, my sweet princess," Eloise murmured, then rushed out from behind the cottage in the opposite direction, hoping to distract the pursuers from Celeste.

It seemed to work. Six men on horseback reined their horses in her direction.

Four of the men wore uniforms of the King's Guard, but the other two were dressed in the colorful garb of the continent of Ifran and had skin as black as the night. Gems glittered in the moonlight on the face of one of them.

Eloise had never seen such a man, but she'd heard tales. This was a wizard from Insu!

And as a wizard, he must surely see Celeste's aura as easily as Gwendolyn.

"Oh, dear child, flee!" Eloise wept as she ran.

"Sighurd, capture her," the wizard cried, pointing at Eloise. "Bring her back to the castle. The rest of you, follow me."

Eloise ran for the forest, but the one named Sighurd caught up quickly, leapt to the ground, and fell upon her. He slid a cloth out and aimed for her mouth.

She uttered a Flash breath spell as fast as she could, barely getting it out before the guard shoved the gag into her mouth.

Sparks burst before his face. The man cried out and slapped his hands against his eyes. Eloise tried to push him aside, but he leaned hard on her, shoving his knee into her back. She grunted through the gag.

"Nice try," he said as he wiped the tears from his eyes and blinked until he could see again. In a moment he had her hands tied behind her back.

As Sighurd manhandled her onto the horse, she prayed to Mother Goddess, *Protect her!* Then she cried out to Celeste in her mind, *Flee child! Don't let them capture you!*

The Girl Inside whispered to Celeste, telling her exactly what to do to ride the horse. Celeste clung tightly to its mane and dug her heels into its side to keep it running as fast as it could. She spoke into its ear with her mouth and into its mind with her power, "Please, dear horse, please run fast and take me away from those evil men."

Mother's words rang in her ears over and over: *Don't let them capture you!*

"No, Mother, I won't. No matter what."

It was hard to concentrate her Sight bouncing up and down on a horse, but she could still see the vague images of the four men pursuing her. She was some distance ahead of them, but they rode powerful horses.

"Dear Mother Goddess, save me," Celeste prayed. She looked down at the golden moon hanging from her neck and wondered how much power it had against evil men.

Maybe she should stop and gather up materials to cast a powerful Protection spell. But no, surely Mother had already cast the most powerful Protection spell she knew on the necklace, and stopping would only waste time. If the necklace couldn't save her, no spell Celeste cast would.

"What should I do?" she asked the Girl Inside.

Maybe you can travel in a confused path so it's harder for them to track you in the night.

She did so, zigzagging back and forth. After some time she looked back again with her Sight. The soldiers still came directly at her, closing the distance.

"Can they see my aura?"

If she only knew how to hide it like Mother had done when she was born. It was her aura that gave her away. Without it, she might be able to hide from them.

But a thought occurred to her. If she can send her aura out at will, maybe she can pull it back in.

She tried. Instead of thinking her aura out, she thought it within her. The finger of light broke from Mistress Moon and glided down to earth. Her mind gathered the aura up and pressed with all her might, until most of it was inside her. There was still a glow immediately around her, but no matter how hard she pressed, she couldn't get it all inside.

"I hope that's enough."

Celeste came upon a little river. It must be the same river she'd played in all her life, but a part of it she'd never seen before. The Girl Inside said, *Ride in the water. That can hide your tracks.*

Celeste steered the horse into the water and galloped downstream. Her pursuers never wavered from following. She knew it wouldn't be long before they caught up with her. She clutched her golden moon in one hand and whispered, "You're my last hope, Mother."

The trees ended, and Celeste came out into a clear area. There was a dark expanse ahead with ripples glistening in the moonlight. She realized it was a large body of water. The ripples all moved in one direction. It was a river, but a river the size of which she had never dreamed! The creek her horse sloshed in was a tiny finger that flowed into it.

She could never cross that! Celeste veered to the left away from where her pursuers were and rode out of the water back onto dry land. Without the thick trees of the forest, her mare could run much faster. She urged it to its limits, hoping it wouldn't collapse from exhaustion.

Her Sight showed the pursuing men veer directly toward her and continue to close the gap between them. Was there nothing she could do to shake them from her path?

Don't run from me, Kasimir thought. *I'm trying to save you.*

But she must know nothing about her real family. She thinks the witch that stole her is her mother. She thinks *we're* trying to steal her from her family.

It would be a tough thing to explain. Would she even believe him? What a shock it would be to learn your beloved mother was your kidnapper.

There was no point trying to explain it to her. He'd have to act like the enemy she thought he was. Only after she was safely in his care could he try to explain things.

Kasimir rode steadily toward the aura. The girl zigzagged about, trying to lose him in the forest. Of course it didn't work. Her aura blazed everywhere she went. She must have no idea he could see it.

Suddenly the column of light broke from the moon and descended to earth. Kasimir's heart leaped with fear. It was disappearing again! He'd lose Celeste just as he was on the verge of finding her.

He switched the focus of his Sight to the girl herself while he could still see her. It would be difficult to follow her that way, especially riding hard on a horse. But if her aura disappeared, he could lose her altogether.

The column of brilliance withdrew into a sphere surrounding the girl, then that sphere began to shrink. She was drawing it inside herself where he wouldn't be able to see it. Kasimir grit his teeth. If she started zigzagging again, she might still escape him.

But the aura never quite disappeared. It became a glimmer surrounding her skin, and in his Sight she looked like a being of light, easy to track.

He admired her noble effort to escape. It was fortunate for her that she failed, but he felt sorry for the fear she must be experiencing.

Her glimmering figure slowed, hesitated, then dashed off to the left. She must have reached the River Sicana.

Celeste must not know the terrain, otherwise she'd have turned right. That would have led her into Suedeche with a chance to find help—if her horse could maintain that speed for so long. Instead she headed for the cliffs and the Falls of Eircana.

And a perfect opportunity for Kasimir and his men to trap her.

Kasimir veered his horse directly toward the cliffs. The three guards and Faisal followed. The horses huffed noisily as they ran.

The pursuit wouldn't last much longer. He could sense her horse growing weary, slowing its pace. The king's horses breathed and sweated heavily, but there was still strength in them. They should reach the cliffs nearly the same time she did.

What was this? Far off to the left, Kasimir's Sight detected movement dashing through the forest with great speed. It had a dark aura like Hereward's. Keeping one eye of Sight on Celeste's glimmering form, he studied the dark aura, trying to identify it.

There was a powerful animal within it. A huge wolf.

The Beast!

His first thought was Edmund, but the woodsman hadn't changed with the rising of the moon, and Kasimir had not used a starstone on him.

Whoever the Beast was as a man, it was coming—this night of all nights, this moment of all moments, in this location of all locations—heading as fast as it could straight for Celeste.

Why?

Little time remained before the three parties would converge together at the cliffs—Kasimir and his men, Celeste, and the Beast. He pushed his horse to its limit. He *had* to be there first—before Celeste, before the wolf—or he could lose control of the whole situation.

Suddenly Celeste's aura burst from her and filled the space around her. The column of light leaped up to the moon once again. She was near the cliffs—close enough that she could probably hear the thundering of the waterfall. He realized that he could hear it himself through the swirling sensations of Sight.

He also realized, the Beast was moments away from devouring her.

Deirdre reached the river and sailed over its reflected moonlight. Only a short distance remained to the aura. She'd have to land discreetly and prepare a spell to deal with whoever was in pursuit.

The aura came to a stop at the edge of the river, then turned to the left and continued along its banks. Deirdre wasn't familiar with the terrain around here, but she knew the Falls of Eircana were not far ahead. Indeed, as she approached, she could hear their thundering, first through her Sight, then through her ears.

In hot pursuit of the aura were five men on horses. And further away a black aura flew toward the girl with the speed of a swift animal. She knotted her brow and studied it, then gasped as she realized it was the Beast. She couldn't tell whether men or beast would reach the girl first.

The aura came to a stop by the cliffs of the falls. Deirdre was nearly there. Everything was converging at a clearing near the falls. She dove for the edge of the forest, grateful that the Flying spell made no more noise than the wind.

Her feet lit on the ground just within the edge of the trees. At once she heard a dreadful howl.

The effort to contain her aura drained Celeste. Its energy fought to burst from her body, and she knew she couldn't hold it in much longer.

The men behind her never wavered. They cut across the forest in an attempt to catch up to her. They could still see her. Holding in her aura did no good.

With a gasp of relief she let it go. Her aura flooded out and shot up to the moon. She felt an invigoration as the power of the moon filled her soul. If only she could share that invigoration with her tired mare.

Could she? She reached her aura out to encompass the horse. It did seem to liven up, hold its head higher, dash a little faster.

But it wouldn't be enough. The men and their horses were nearly upon her. No matter what she did, she would soon face them.

A noise thundered before her. She looked up in the sky for a storm, but the sky was clear with stars. The thunder came from ahead, not above.

She saw where the river ended—a sudden nonexistence at the edge of the world. Desperately she reined her horse to a stop, looked forward, and gasped.

Mist caressed her face. The thunder pounded from below. She saw the flood of the river washing over the edge of a cliff, disappearing in the moonlight-shrouded mist.

The edge of the cliff was a few paces ahead of the mare's hooves. If the thunder of the waterfall hadn't caught her attention, she'd have ridden herself and the horse right over the edge!

Something crashed through the forest brush. Celeste twisted the mare around to face the noise. Five men on horses shot from the trees. They reared to a stop as they saw Celeste.

Three of them looked like soldiers as Mother had described them in her stories. The other two men in front were dressed in red and blue and gold. Their skin was shockingly black, and the face of one of them was covered with glittering stars of many colors.

Other people indeed! Such people she had never imagined.

The colorful man reached inside his clothes and yanked. He winced as he did so. More noise came from the forest in another direction. An enormous creature burst into view, thick with fur, shoulders high enough to reach Celeste's head were she standing before it. Its snout stretched out from its head with fierce, jagged teeth. Glowing red eyes blazed in the night.

"The Beast!" one of the men shrieked, grabbing his shoulder. A glowing mist formed around him, hiding him. His horse turned to face the Beast. The glow disappeared, and another huge Beast leaped from the horse onto the ground and charged.

"Hereward!" the glittering man shouted as he pulled a glowing ball of light from his clothes.

The two monsters collided in a fury of black hair and glinting fangs and hellish howls. They bit and clawed in a frenzy of rage.

The glittering man's hands flared up as he spoke words that must have been magic words, but in a language different from the spells Mother had taught her. A globe of shimmering burst from the flaring object. It surrounded the glittering man, his companions, and Celeste. The two wolves, caught within the globe, leaped in the air with a yelp and pranced backward until they crossed outside its boundary.

"Grab her!" the glittering man shouted to the other men.

"But the Beasts!" one of them cried, gaping at the creatures who returned to attacking each other.

Celeste kicked the mare into action and fled in the direction she had come. The glittering man chased after her and blocked her way, brandishing a long, curved blade. The globe of shimmering moved with him, but it was large enough to keep everyone within its sphere.

"By the heart of Mabut, I'll slit your throats if you don't capture her!" said the glittering man.

"Not while the Beasts are here!" the other man spat, his sword raised ready to defend himself.

The creatures growled and gnashed around the edge of the sphere, glaring their fiery red eyes at each other. One of them bit deeply into the belly of the other. It yelped with agony as it fell back and writhed on the ground.

"I cast a Protection spell," the glittering man shouted. "Stay close to me and you'll be safe."

Celeste tried to flee in another direction, but the other black man moved faster on his horse and blocked her path again. The chasm gaped behind her, blocking her way.

The shimmering bubble faded from Celeste's view as her Sight spell died. The other men scrambled their horses closer to the glittering man. She uttered another breath spell of Sight, and the shimmering popped into view again.

The one creature tore at the wounded one until it lay silent and lifeless, a mass of flesh and blood. The creature turned toward the men and charged, but was repelled by the bubble. It pranced and raged along its edge.

Celeste's horse stood between the four men and the cliffs.

"Celeste, please," the glittering man said. "Come with us. We're here to protect you."

"Never."

"Take her," he said to the others.

The other black man moved toward Celeste. "Make it easy, child. Come with us. We won't hurt you."

Celeste held the golden moon out before her. The man stopped with a grunt and a surprised look on his face.

"Never," Celeste hissed. "You want to bring me to Gwendolyn."

"Yes," said the glittering man, smiling, "and your family. Your father, King Christian, sent us to find you and bring you home."

"He's not my father!" Celeste cried, keeping the moon raised.

"Enough of this!" The glittering man spurred his horse forward. It took several steps, then stopped with a yelp. The glittering man's eyes went wide as he let out an "Oof!"

"It's that necklace," said the other black man. "It has a warding on it."

The glittering man pulled his shirt open, revealing more gems on his chest. Celeste gasped as he tore one from his skin, grimacing as he did so. Blood trickled down. He rubbed it in the blood, then held it in his open palm before him and spoke his strange language.

The gem glowed fiercely, then exploded.

At the same time, the moon in her hand exploded. She screamed with shock.

Oh Goddess, no! The last protection she had—gone!

Deirdre peered out from the trees and saw the men and the young woman on horseback with a great bubble of Protection surrounding them. She gaped as she saw, raging like demons outside the bubble, *two* Beasts in ferocious conflict. Where had the other Beast come from? The men kept glancing back at them in dread. One creature tore into the other, downing it, and ravaged it until it lay still. It then charged the men, but jumped back when it hit the sphere.

But one man—one amazing man—ignored the Beasts completely. He faced the young woman directly. He wore colorful clothing, and his skin was as black as the night. Most amazing of all were the colorful stones twinkling on his face.

Deirdre knew at once who the man was, a wizard of Insu. She'd met one before, long ago, when she traveled the northeastern shores of the Sea of Az, down where the Elladans and Vlachians and Arazim dwelt.

Gwendolyn must have hired him to search for the girl. For here he was, trapping the girl against the cliff. Except the girl was no girl of four years. She was a young woman. Yet there was no kind of Illusion spell on her. How could she be so old?

Deirdre considered her next move. If she negated the spell of Protection, the men would have to forget the girl and deal with the Beast. Deirdre could cast a Warding spell to protect herself, then rush in and grab the girl and jump over the cliff to fly back to her tower. She'd have to move fast before the Beast could attack the girl.

Deirdre dropped her pack and rummaged through it for the ingredients she'd need for the two spells. The Warding would be easy. The Negation would be tricky, because meddling with the spells of an unknown magic was unpredictable. Especially the spell of a wizard of Insu, with which she had no experience.

"Now, child," said the glittering man, "will you come with us peacefully?"

Celeste gaped at him, at the creature that raged helplessly outside the protective sphere, at the torn body of the wolf who before her eyes returned to being a man lying on the ground, at the other three men on either side of the glittering man, blocking any chance of fleeing.

She couldn't let Gwendolyn capture her. She knew now from experience how other people could do evil things. These men chased her, frightening her. They drew long, vicious blades and threatened her. The Beast tore their friend apart, and they didn't shed a tear.

Mother was right. There was evil in the world of "other people"—and they were it.

Can you think of anything else to do? she asked the Girl Inside.

I'm sorry, Celeste, I can't.

Then I'll join my mother. I won't let Gwendolyn have me.

Kasimir was relieved when Celeste slowly dismounted her horse, not taking her eyes off him. She must have finally realized she couldn't escape. He continued to smile at her with as much friendliness as he could muster as he climbed down from his horse. At last, at last he could fulfill his quest! Her captor was now captured, the princess was safe, and soon both of them would be back in Luteche.

Celeste stood beside her horse, eyes piercing Kasimir. He grew uneasy. Something in her gaze disturbed him. A determination, an intensity, a grimness that didn't belong in the eyes of a defeated girl.

He approached her, reaching his hand toward her. "Come. I'll protect you."

"Never," she whispered, turned, and dashed for the cliffs.

"*Great Mabut, no!*" he shrieked as he ran after her.

She leaped, arms outstretched. He skidded to a stop, barely avoiding the cliff himself. The Beast howled and barked and raged.

Her dark silhouette dropped into the mist of the thundering waterfall. The brilliant aura around her shone through the gloom, then flashed with a blinding burst of light.

Kasimir lifted his head and bellowed, "Great Mabut, no! Great Gods, no! By the stars, how can this happen?"

The flash of aura dissipated until darkness returned. Kasimir stood by the precipice, hearing nothing but the thundering of the mighty river plummeting over the edge, just as Celeste had plummeted.

"By the stars," he wept, "how can this happen?"

Chapter 13

Deirdre's Treasure

The girl dismounted from her horse. Deirdre knew she had to act now or it would be too late. As she cast the spell of Warding, she played out in her mind how she'd rush in and grab the girl, then leap over the cliff.

Suddenly the girl dashed for the cliff and flew out into the night, her arms stretched out to the side. For an instant Deirdre thought she'd cast a Flight spell of her own. But the girl plummeted.

Deirdre raced to the cliff, dodging trees, and flung herself out with her own arms outstretched. She willed herself down the cliff as fast as she could, knowing as she dropped that she wouldn't reach the girl in time.

Indeed, that aura reaching up to the moon flashed away into oblivion before Deirdre had dropped more than a couple feet. She cried out in frustration.

Plunging swiftly, Deirdre barely swooped back up before her body dashed itself against the rocks. She swept back and forth, searching for the girl's body. The air was thick with roiling mist. The moisture in the air clung to her robe, seeping into it. The robe grew heavy. She'd never flown into such wet air before and had no idea how it would affect the spell.

She sailed along the cliff away from the waterfall, trying to will herself back up, but the heaviness of her robe fought against it, and she could only maintain her altitude. Finally the cliffs veered away from the river, giving her space to land on dry ground away from the river bank.

She pulled her robe off and held it out to flutter in the wind. She spoke a spell to dry it. In a couple of moments she was able to put it on again and launch herself back into the air. She flew up along the cliff onto high ground. She could still hear faint cries from the men off in the distance, but she didn't care what happened to them. The girl was lost, and now Deirdre had to retrieve her pack of materials from where she left them, then try to retrace the girl's path to see if she could find the thief and her stolen treasure.

She flew carefully out of sight of the men and landed where her pack was. She attached it to her waist and launched into the air again. She flew over the area the girl had zigzagged through as best as she could remember, then made her best guess where the whole chase might have started. Deirdre searched in a crisscross pattern for anything unusual in the forest.

She had to land and cast the Flying spell once more. As she did so, she realized she was well away from where she thought she was. How had she gotten so turned around?

She cast the spell and launched back into the sky, returning to the zigzagging part of the chase. She followed it again and found herself a good mile away from where she intended to be before realizing it.

She landed with exasperation and thought. This was not carelessness. Something was distracting her, deflecting her, from where she intended to go.

Renewing her Sight spell, she lifted back into the sky and perused the landscape for some aura, some glimmer, even a faint shimmer of a spell at work, and found nothing.

Of course there would be no shimmer. The thief couldn't hide for four years with a shimmer surrounding her. But a spell with that much power had to give off a shimmer.

Unless it emanated from an amulet. That cursed thief had been prepared!

Deirdre thought hard about what kind of spell it could be. It was essentially a Warding, keeping unwanted creatures away. But no typical Warding that merely pushed them away. Something subtle that merely deflected their attention away so gently, they didn't notice they were being deflected.

No wonder she couldn't trace the thief's tracks four years ago. No wonder the tracker she hired could never follow them.

But the Insan wizard had found the girl. He had her brilliant aura to focus on, and a subtle spell couldn't deflect his attention away from something that blatant. That's what Deirdre needed to do to find the location.

As she flew, she noticed a creek weaving through the forest that emptied into the river. Two people dwelling four years isolated in the forest needed a water source. That creek came from the same direction the girl had fled.

Deirdre could stay on track by focusing on that and hopefully get close to where they'd dwelt those four years.

She flew to the creek and followed it. Before long she realized she lost it and couldn't remember when it happened.

A curse on that cursed amulet! Subtle, maybe, but powerful. She'd have to get her feet wet to follow it.

She flew back to the creek and landed in the middle of it. She waded along against the current. When she realized she'd stepped several paces out of the water into the forest without noticing, she halted with a cry of irritation. She returned to the middle of the creek with a grim determination and waded upstream, keeping her head down and focusing on the water.

She came to a pool and a waterfall. The waterfall was small, but just a bit too high to jump up to the top. She didn't dare step out of the creek to go around it. She might not come back.

She looked around for inspiration and noticed a trail stretching from the left bank into the forest. She grinned widely.

Keeping her head down with her eyes locked to the path, she walked. Many horse prints littered the path—fresh ones. They must be from the horses of the men who pursued the girl. She smiled with satisfaction.

The path gave way to a clearing. Raising her head, she saw the cottage before her. "I've got you now, thief!" she said quietly and triumphantly.

Deirdre studied the horse prints surrounding the cottage, how they pranced around in the clearing, then raced off into the forest. She found another set of prints—a single horse—that galloped to the side of the cottage, then raced off in the direction of the East Highway. She stooped over and studied the ground carefully in the dim light and found human footprints all over the ground in this spot. A skirmish on foot had taken place here.

This was definitely where the pursuit began. Most of the horses chased after the girl. Deirdre had no doubt the other rode off to Luteche with a captive. That captive was probably the thief. Now in the hands of Gwendolyn, she thought angrily.

She sighed. Perhaps her thirst for vengeance could be satisfied with whatever torture Gwendolyn put her through. But Deirdre still wanted her treasure back, and she needed the thief for that. Where were her scrolls? Her concealing sack?

Where was her globe?

With the thief in her possession, Gwendolyn would eventually find out—if the treasure hadn't already fallen into her hands. Had that happened, there was little Deirdre could do now, and she'd know soon enough when Gwendolyn started using the globe. But if Gwendolyn didn't have the treasure yet—and Deirdre thought that likely, since this careful thief would have carefully concealed it—Deirdre needed to start looking.

The obvious place to start was the cottage—which of course meant it wouldn't be in the cottage. However much she loathed the thief, she respected her intelligence. But she searched the cottage anyway, just in case. She wanted to rummage, scattering everything about with glee, but she didn't want the thief to know she'd been there. Petty revenge, she admitted to herself, but she wanted the satisfaction of the thief going for her treasure and finding it gone. If Gwendolyn let her live to come looking for it.

She found two sets of clothes for two different-sized females, some food, simple furnishings, various trinkets sitting out in the open, so probably weren't amulets, and a little book. She opened it and found spells and notes written in a dainty scrawl. The spells were nothing special—the sort of things a village witch would practice.

The notes had to be the girl's. The thief had been teaching her magic. Deirdre was hardly surprised. She'd have done the same thing under the same circumstances.

She set the book back down and searched harder, trying to find something that was the thief's—some book of notes or scraps of parchment—anything to hint where the real treasure might be.

To her frustration, she found nothing. Angrily she kicked a chair over, then carefully righted it back in place.

As she turned to leave, she noticed a chain and trinket hanging on the inside of the door with a ruby embedded in it. She took it down and held it up. "What have we hear, thief?"

Enchanted amulets had simple commands to activate and deactivate them. She tried a number of deactivation commands, until suddenly she felt a slight pressure in her brain dissipate. Subtle indeed! The pressure must build up slowly as a person approaches. Deirdre never noticed it was there until she stumbled on the word to deactivate it.

This was something she couldn't leave behind. She kissed it and said, "I'm going to call you my Amulet of Deflection," then dropped it in her pack, feeling pleased. Her first act of revenge, stealing one of the thief's treasures.

But it didn't make up for her missing treasure. She walked outside and peered about indecisively. Where would Deirdre have hidden it if she were the thief?

Two possibilities. Somewhere near enough to have quick access to it. Somewhere far away where it couldn't be traced, even if this cottage was discovered.

She sighed as she gazed off into the forest. She had the sinking feeling that she might be no closer to her treasure than when she started.

Sighurd pulled his horse into the clearing where Queen Tamara's body had been found. It felt as terribly dark and haunting as that night four years ago.

He dismounted and tied the horse to a tree. He helped Eloise off, drew his sword, pulled her to a fallen tree, and sat her down on it. Sitting next to her several feet away, he pulled the gag down.

Immediately she started speaking unknown words.

He flicked the tip of his sword up and pressed it against her neck, drawing a drop of blood. "Casting spells will open up your throat."

She nodded carefully, and he lowered the sword, gazing at her fiercely, then looked off into the trees. What should he do with her?

His duty was to obey Kasimir's command. Return her to the castle.

But his duty was also to obey the king's command. Kill her quietly and dispose of her.

Out of the corner of his eye, he saw her study him, then glance toward the trees. "You wouldn't get two steps," he said.

She let out a small chuckle. "Am I a prisoner of the king or the sorceress?"

"The king wants me to kill you. Which would you prefer?"

"That's a hard choice. Quick death, or slowly tortured to death."

He chuckled somberly.

"Who was that man with the sparkling face?" she asked.

"The reason I haven't killed you yet. Who was that young woman who rode into the forest?"

"My granddaughter."

"Your granddaughter." So she wants to play games with him? "Then where's Celeste?"

"Celeste?"

He tapped the tip of his sword on the ground. "That sparkling man is a wizard of Insu. Gwendolyn hired him to find Celeste. He saw Celeste's aura. The young woman is the one he chased after." He bore her with his eyes. "Why is four-year-old Celeste a young woman?"

She paused just a fraction of a second too long. "I don't understand anything you're talking about."

"He *will* capture her and return her to Luteche. King Christian will try to have her killed. Gwendolyn will try to stop it. Why does Gwendolyn want her?"

She looked down at the ground and remained silent.

"Who are you?"

She took a deep breath. "Just an old witch from Suedeche."

"Old Witch from Suedeche, I may be your only chance. I may be Celeste's only chance."

"Aren't you the Captain of the King's Guard? The right hand man of the king? The king who wants us dead?"

"I *am* the Captain of the Guard." He touched the tip of his sword to her chin and made her lift her head until she looked at him. "I'm also not a butcher. I might be able to bring myself to slay you, but the thought of killing a child causes me anguish."

"It should," she said softly.

"But my first loyalty is to the king, and he commanded me to kill you both." He jabbed his sword into the ground and turned to face her, saying earnestly, "I need to know what's going on. Help me find a way to not kill you two."

She stared at him for some time with strong emotions playing across her face. "What's your name?"

"Sighurd."

"I know you're right, Sighurd. The wizard will capture Celeste. We'll both end up in Luteche at the mercy of Gwendolyn and King Christian, which is no mercy at all."

"Then tell me, why does Gwendolyn want Celeste so much?"

She seemed on the verge of opening up, but ended up saying, "After all you've done in her service, how can I trust you?"

He exhaled in exasperation and pulled her back to the horse. They continued on to Luteche.

There was nothing for Deirdre to do but hope the witch hid the treasure nearby. The whole point of having such a treasure was to use it when needed. The thief would avoid using it as long as she dared, but she must have known the day would come when she'd need it.

Deirdre went back inside the cottage and placed her pack on the table. She sat and pondered—how would the thief hide the treasure?

Somewhere deep in the forest of course, where no one would likely pass, guarded by a trap spell that would spring if anyone happened to find the hiding place. There were hundreds of different trap spells known to sorceresses, and with everything this thief had done, Deirdre had to treat her as a sorceress.

She rummaged in her pack for the necessary things to cast her modified Sight spell. Because traps, like amulets, were static things, set and left in equilibrium until triggered, the magical aura they gave off was faint. The tumult of sensations in Sight could drown out perception of them. Deirdre had adapted the words of Sight to suppress sensations from the real world and enhance the detection of magical energy. With materials to maximize its power, her ability to detect magical traps was boosted. She'd still have to take great care searching for it, and once finding it, she'd have to study it to see how it worked and come up with a negating spell.

She had no doubt the thief included a Truth Dream that would trigger when the trap was sprung. However the trap incapacitated the intruder—injury or unconsciousness or death—the thief would want to come and deal with them as soon as possible. Deirdre wanted to get her treasure back without triggering the Truth Dream. Not only did she not want to spring the trap, she wanted the satisfaction of the thief finding an empty hiding place.

Assuming Gwendolyn let her live.

It took many minutes to cast the Sight spell, using many different materials mixed just so. The modified spell felt very different than the usual Sight spell. No rush of overwhelming sensations to sift through and focus on what she wanted to see. It was a whisper, barely perceptible, that hardly altered her normal vision at all. Just a faint intensity in the images around her.

For two hours she stumbled through the trees around the cottage in the dark. Normally searching in the dark would be a huge disadvantage, but it acted as a further suppressor of natural sensations so the energy of the trap would be more noticeable. Then she followed the trail to the creek and waterfall. Nothing tried to deflect her away as she returned, verifying the trinket she deactivated was the source of that spell. She climbed the hill with the open meadow on top. She walked entirely around the hill. She haunted endless nondescript stretches of woods, and nearly got lost once. By the time the sun began to rise, she still hadn't found the trap.

Maybe there was no trap around there to find.

Deirdre cursed generously when her Sight spell faded away. She'd have to cast it again! It bothered her to still be here, exposed in the glare of day, but at least she could move faster through the forest.

Hunger gnawed at her, so she scavenged a handful of things from the garden and munched on them while she sat in the cottage preparing the spell again. This was her last chance. She didn't have the materials for a third casting.

She cast the spell. The faint intensity returned, and she headed out quickly. She wasn't quite sure where else to look. She'd been pretty thorough so far. Perhaps she should cover the same area again, but from different directions to give her a new perspective. She may catch something she missed the first time through.

She started down the path first so she could drink generously from the creek to quench her thirst. As she returned to the hill, she decided to circle it in the opposite direction from before. After two-thirds of the way around it, she came to a rotting stump she'd passed before. From this direction, she could see directly into a gaping hole on its side that she hadn't noticed before.

And there it was!

Within that hole, a subtle shimmering. Deirdre cursed subtle spells as she marched up to it and studied it. The shimmering was a sheet of energy a few inches inside the hole. From almost every direction, a person could walk past the stump and notice nothing. This witch was clever indeed!

But finding it was only half the battle. Now she had to decipher the trap. She studied the patterns of shimmering. With the hundreds of possible traps, it could take days for her to work out the specifics of a particularly intricate one. She hoped this witch, as clever as she was, would only know a simple trap spell.

And that's exactly what it was. The trigger was easy to detect. She could see the slight bulge outward in the sheet of shimmering from a slightly greater pressure inside. All it would take to spring this trap was to break the surface of shimmering, then the pressure behind it would blast out, spewing...something.

She didn't care what the trap spewed. Something incapacitating, to be sure. All she cared about was negating it.

The thief had chosen wisely. All traps were finicky things—intentionally. What good was a stable trap difficult to spring? But the pressure trap—a simple one to set—was particularly challenging to counteract.

A Negation spell wouldn't do. That would just dissolve the sheet holding the nastiness in, and it would be free to come pouring out.

A quick method would be to trigger the trap while standing behind it, reaching around and poking it with a stick to avoid the spray of whatever spewed out. But that was too risky because trap setters expected that, so traps were mostly filled with noxious vapors that would spread too wide too fast and catch any person within dozens of feet from it in any direction.

And Deirdre still didn't want to trigger the Truth Dream.

But there was a way to deal with it. She returned to the cottage to gather up the materials she'd need. Each type of trap required its own type of deactivation. Had the witch set a trap that Deirdre wasn't prepared to deactivate, that would have caused more delay as she searched for the necessary materials.

But the Gods smiled upon her this time. The pressure trap, being simple to set but difficult to counteract, was a favorite, and Deirdre had the right materials on hand. She brought them back to the stump and went to work on the spell, preparing the materials and speaking the words.

The energy of the spell flowed out from the burning materials and coalesced into a shimmering sphere between her cupped hands, similar to the sheet of energy with its own pressure inside, but more resilient so slowly penetrating it wouldn't make it burst.

Casting the spell was the easy part. Now all she could rely on was her own gentle and meticulous manipulation of the sphere of energy. Carefully she positioned it against the shimmering sheet of the trap until its surface appeared perfectly flat instead of slightly bulging outward, equalizing the pressure outside with the pressure inside. It was exacting work. The slightest twitch and the pressure would cease to be equal. She'd spring the trap on herself.

She let go, and the sphere remained in place. She studied the surface to satisfy herself that the placement was sound, then slowly inserted her hands through the skins of energy into the hole, cringing as she did so.

She breathed a sigh of relief as her hands closed over a chest inside. It was larger than she'd have preferred, but not too large. She should be able to pull it back out.

Holding her breath the entire time, Deirdre slid the chest out as slowly and evenly as she could. It was hard to resist the temptation to just yank the chest out and be done with it, but that would break the surface of the sheet and the sphere.

After what seemed like an eternity, the chest was free of the trap. Deirdre lowered it to the ground and sat back, shaking her stiff hands and breathing freely. Then she gently grasped the counteracting sphere of energy between her hands and pulled it back. She stood—a difficult thing to do with her stiff legs and hands full of energy—and tossed the sphere against a tree. It dissipated with a satisfying pop and spray of sparks.

Deirdre knelt back down before the chest and opened it, trembling with anticipation. There they were—all her stolen treasures! The scrolls, the concealing sack, and—she pulled back a lip of the sack's opening—the glimmer of the scrying globe.

She gave out a whoop of delight. "Thank you, Mistress Earth!"

But there were also scrolls that had never been part of her treasure. This thief had accumulated more than what she'd stolen from Deirdre. A part of her was distressed, wondering how she'd gotten them, but most of her was elated that the thief had graciously made Deirdre more powerful than before.

She wanted to pull the other items out and see what they were. She wanted to unmask the globe and see what was going on in the world. But daylight was growing and she'd been there too long already. It would be wiser to leave immediately.

Deirdre brought the chest back to the cottage. She had to think a moment how she would carry it while flying. It was too big to fit in her pack. She'd have to leave the chest itself behind.

First she removed the ingredients she'd need to recast her Flying spell, which had long worn off. Then she tried stuffing the scrolls and the sack with the globe into her pack. She had to discard some of the more mundane materials she brought with her, and even then it was a tight fit, but she managed it.

Deirdre took the chest holding her discarded materials outside to the edge of the forest and tossed it deep into the trees. It landed where it was easily seen from the clearing, so she walked into the trees and tossed it further in. This time it landed behind some brush where it was concealed.

She paused a moment, gazing at the brush and contemplating what had happened that night. The girl was dead and permanently out of her reach, but that meant she was also permanently out of the reach of Gwendolyn. Deirdre might not be able to exact revenge on the thief personally, but she felt confident Gwendolyn would handle that for her. The rise of another rogue sorceress had been aborted.

And Deirdre had her stolen treasure back, plus more.

She nearly giggled at the satisfaction. This was a great day!

Deirdre attached her pack, cast the Flying spell, then leaped with joy into the air, never coming back down until she reached the balcony of her tower.

Chapter 14

The White Dragon

Wind filling its wings. A rush of air splashing its face. It glides and glides through the air, timelessly.

A ghostly ball of light above. The blackness it floats in is full of twinkling dots of light. It moves toward the glowing ball, not knowing why. Something draws it toward that bright circle. A warmth in the cold darkness. Strength in its weariness. A sense of belonging, of rightness.

It must ascend to the light.

What am I? it thinks, not in words.

I'm not sure, something replies.

Where am I? it asks.

In the sky gliding through the air, comes the reply.

I like how this feels.

So do I.

It continues to fly, gently flapping its enormous wings as it goes, not understanding why that feels right, but its forward movement continues. There are lights above. There are lights below. What are all those lights?

The lights above are stars, the something answers. The lights below are reflections of the stars in the sea.

What is the sea?

A great expanse of water. Deep, cold, dangerous. It frightens me.

The sensation of fear disturbs it—an unpleasant sensation. I do not like "frightens," it says.

Neither do I.

Then we must leave the sea.

Yes, return from where we came. There was land there.

With a flap of its wings, with a whip of its tail, it arcs around until it faces where it came from. Ahead there is a change in the surface of the sea. It froths. It leaps and dances. It crashes against the hard land.

The glowing ball in the sky (the moon, says the something) sheds light on everything below. The land begins where the crashing waves end, a dull smoothness. The water tumbles onto the smoothness, then flees back.

After the dull smoothness comes another sea of rippling waves, lighter in color. Is this another sea? it says in alarm.

No, this is a field. Those are tall grasses, and they bend as the wind blows.
Wind?

The air flying past them, like it flies past us.

The feeling of the wind is pleasurable, and its apprehension melts away.

Ahead are tall, dark objects. The wind ruffles them in a different way. They make another endless sea unto themselves.

What are they? it asks.

Those are trees, the something inside answers.

This is a sea of trees?

It's called a forest. It's hard to see now because of the darkness. But the sun will come up. That's a ball of light many, many times brighter than the moon. It will fill the whole land with light and color and life.

Life?

Other creatures, like you and me, that move and breathe and think. Many different kinds of creatures.

What am I? it asks again.

Let me study you, the something says.

It feels the something exploring inside, touching here and there without touching.

You have great wings that extend far. An enormous body of grace and power. Your skin is scaly and white. Your head has piercing eyes that see far, and your snout is filled with razor teeth. Your tail is long and balances you as you fly. I believe you are a dragon!

A dragon, it says, testing the word. Is that good?

A dragon is a rare and magnificent creature, beautiful and frightening at the same time. A dragon fills other creatures with awe and dread. Some say there is magic in a dragon—great power that few can withstand. Some say that dragons are the children of the Gods.

What magical power do I have?

I don't know. The legends say that each dragon has a unique power all its own. But I don't know how much the legends are true. I have never known a dragon.

Yet you are inside me. How can you have never known a dragon?

I don't know! It's a mystery.

What are you?

I am the Voice inside you that knows. But I don't know what I am.

Another mystery?

The Voice giggles. Yes, another mystery.

For one who knows, you have many mysteries.

I know more than you!

The white dragon frowns at this. Why do I know so little? If I am so big and majestic and powerful, why am I so helpless?

I don't know.

What is my name?

I don't know.

Which God am I a child of?

I don't know.

The dragon smirks. You are the Voice inside me that knows nothing!

The Voice emanates an unpleasant feeling. It says, What is that glistening ribbon that stretches into the forest from the sea?

I don't know, the dragon says.

It's a river, a ribbon of water flowing from the land to the sea. Where does that water come from?

I don't know, the dragon says with a scowl.

It falls from the sky. When the season is warm, it falls as drops of water and is called rain. When the season is cold, it falls as little flakes of ice and is called snow. How many seasons are there and what are they like?

Fine, the dragon pouts. You are the Voice inside me that knows little, but knows more than me.

The Voice laughs.

What is *that* ribbon through the forest? It cuts like the river, but is much narrower, and there is no water.

That ribbon is a highway where the men and women of the world travel.

Men and women?

People. Creatures of the world that have thinking minds like you and me. Other creatures have simpler minds and think simpler thoughts. They exist to live, not to understand.

We exist to understand?

Among other things.

I understand nothing!

You've already learned much, and you will learn more.

Look what the river does! the dragon cries as it swerves toward the ribbon of water. It catches the light of the moon and sparkles with it. How beautiful that is!

There is much beauty in the world, says the Voice. Wait until day. You will see even more beauty as the light of the sun brings the colors out.

I can't wait to see day! the dragon cries as it beats its wings and rises far above the world. I want to see everything. I want to understand everything.

The dragon instinctively rises toward the moon. Energy seeps through its scales from the light of the glowing ball. The dragon looks down, sees the strip of highway through the forest, and follows it with its eyes, until it comes to a distant clearing where many strange objects cover the land. There is one magnificent object rising from tall rocks where the river falls over the edge beside it.

What is that? the dragon cries as it swoops toward the objects.

That, says the Voice, is a city. The largest object is a castle. A king lives there.

What is a king?

The man who rules the land, telling others what they must do.

The castle grows as the dragon zooms toward it.

Will he tell me what to do?

He'll probably be afraid of you.

Why?

Because you're big and powerful and could kill him if you wanted to.

What is kill?

Make him stop living, so he can never do or think anything again.

The dragon ponders that a moment, then asks, Why would I want to do that?

You probably wouldn't. Killing is usually a bad thing to do.

If I don't want to kill him, why is he afraid of me?

He doesn't know you don't want to kill him.

I see movement on the highway, the dragon says. Strange creatures. What are they?

They are people—two of them sitting on another creature. A horse, which they use to travel fast and far, much faster and much farther than people could travel on their own feet.

Is one of them the king?

I don't know. I can't see them. They're too far away, too small.

We will have a look at them. I want to ask the king some questions. Maybe he will know what you do not.

The king is probably in the castle.

Then I will go to the castle. I will speak to the king.

How will you ask him? the Voice says.

I will speak to him.

You can't.

I speak to you. I will speak to him as I speak to you.

I am inside you. You can't speak to him as you speak to me.

I will! the dragon says stubbornly. I have to know. I have to understand.

The white dragon swoops down.

I am doomed! Kasimir wept as he knelt before the cliff. *Celeste is dead!*

His quest was a failure. Not an aborted quest because the princess had been dead all along. That would have been embarrassing, but no black mark against him. He could return and await another quest.

Not a quest where he had a temporary setback, where she slipped through his grasp, but he could pick up her trail later.

This was a quest that had succeeded—almost! He had her in his grasp, and lost her. Permanently, irretrievably lost her. He had *failed*. He had failed *forever*, through his own incompetence.

Celeste was so indoctrinated by the witch that she willingly gave her life rather than be captured and returned to her family. He should have anticipated that possibility.

I am doomed! he wept.

And that poor, sweet, innocent girl. It tore his heart to think of her running over the edge of that cliff, plummeting through the mist, her bones shattering on the rocks below, knowing exactly what would befall her when she made the choice. It anguished him with the anguish of the accursed to think of that pure, dazzling, powerful aura dissipating in a flash of light into the mist of the waterfall. All because of a lie the witch had told her, and because of his own accursed carelessness!

He wanted to rush over the cliff after her. He wanted to flee to strange lands and never face those who hired him or Master Izzet who chose him and trained him. He was a loathsome failure.

But he couldn't bring himself to commit such acts of cowardice in the face of the girl's courage. The only way he could honor her now was to exercise as much courage as she had shown, to face those who had trusted him and take full responsibility for her death.

In his own land, he would be shamed beyond hope of redemption. If he ever reached his own land. Perhaps someone in Luteche would assassinate him for his failure. Kasimir almost wished for that, to purge his soul of the shame before he stood before Mabut.

If anything could ever purge such shame.

Faisal tried to console him, but he brushed his brother away. "I am doomed!" he cried.

When he was able to get himself under control, Kasimir stood up and looked at his men. There was one missing. "Where's Hereward?"

They went over to the body, wondering which of the two Beasts had died. They found the decimated body of Hereward.

They buried him where he fell, honoring him with their words. "Now you can haunt these falls with the lovers," Kasimir said solemnly, and in his despair meant it as a blessing.

Kasimir rode ahead of Faisal and Dietric and Thomas, leading the way down the East Highway, keeping his head high even as he fought back the tears of self-loathing. Sighurd would already have arrived with the witch, would already have excited everyone with the announcement that they'd found the princess. When

Kasimir and his men rode in, everyone would be ready to praise him, would look for the princess, would not see her, would start asking questions.

He disconnected his feelings and let his heart go numb, so he could endure the impending shame.

Gwendolyn, Christian, and four-year-old Guillaume sat at the dining table in the Great Hall eating a late evening meal when cries of terror rang from the courtyard. The three of them perked up and looked at each other.

A voice shouted, "Dragon!" More screams rang out.

"By the Gods, what..." Gwendolyn leaped to her feet and rushed out of the keep, followed by Christian and Guillaume and the servants.

In the courtyard a few of the King's Guard stared into the sky while everyone else fled into various buildings. Gwendolyn looked up.

Descending out of the dark was a monstrous creature, striking white in color, huge wings extended. A terrifying head at the end of a long neck peered down with a snout filled with fangs. A long tail undulated behind it, terminating in a flat diamond fin.

Christian and Guillaume came up beside her, gaping at the dragon.

"What are you doing out here?" Gwendolyn cried. "Guards, protect the king and prince!"

Guards surrounded the three of them, facing the dragon, swords raised.

The dragon hovered above them, peering down at them, each beat of its enormous wings blasting wind as if from a storm. It descended until it stood on its legs, filling half the courtyard, and wrapped its wings behind itself. The serpentine neck arched as the snout came within a few feet of Gwendolyn.

The creature stared. Gwendolyn stared back, terrified but mesmerized. Those silvery eyes pierced into her, and the head cocked back and forth as it studied her.

Everyone held their breath in silence.

Quietly, Gwendolyn uttered a breath spell of Sight. A brilliant aura erupted around the dragon.

What by the Gods is going on here?

The dragon's snout drew closer to her, inches away. The breath from its nostrils blasted her, cold and smelling of musk. The huge nostrils sniffed, sucking her hair towards them.

She broke out with sweat. *We are about to die!* But what could she do? Frozen here like this, all she could do was cast breath spells. Breath spells against a dragon?

The dragon's eyes squinted, and the head rose up and coiled back.

No time left! She shouted the most powerful breath spell of Entrapment she knew. Instinctively the guards grouped tighter around her and the king and prince.

Gwendolyn felt the spell flow up and surround the monster. Its eyes widened in dismay. Its wings opened wide and thrashed. Its body shuddered violently. The spell broke into a shower of sparks and dissipated into the night.

"*Run!*" Gwendolyn shouted. The guards grabbed Christian and Guillaume and pulled them into the castle.

Gwendolyn cried a spell of Protection as the dragon head shot forward with its jaw open wide. A blast of white vapor shot from its mouth. It hit the globe of Protection surrounding her and spread out across the courtyard, flooding over the remaining people still standing and gaping.

They cried out as they glowed with an eerie light—eerie like the full moon in the night sky. Their bodies glowed brighter and brighter until they were too dazzling to look at, then dissolved into a white mist that swirled about. The swirls of mist shot up into the sky. Their feathery wisps merged with the light of the moon and disappeared.

The dragon arched its neck back, raised its head to the sky, and gave off a deafening shriek. It flapped its wings, nearly blowing Gwendolyn back, and launched into the air. It made a circle around the castle, turning its head toward Gwendolyn and shrieked once more, then shot up into the sky and disappeared into the night.

Gwendolyn dropped to her knees, trembling with shock.

The white dragon flew to the castle, swooped down, and landed on the ground, studying the people before it. They stood without motion, as if they were made of rock. The mouth of the person in front moved. Quiet sounds came out. The dragon noticed a new power glimmering around the person. It didn't understand the power, but it made the dragon feel exposed, vulnerable.

What is that power? the dragon asked.

I don't know, the Voice answered.

Again you don't know.

It leaned forward and concentrated on the person in front. The eyes of the person looked cold, harsh. Something felt wrong.

Why do I feel frightened? the dragon asked.

I'm the one that's afraid, the Voice said. That woman frightens me.

The dragon squinted at the woman. The fear bothered it, and it wanted the feeling to go away. If that woman frightens the Voice, then perhaps that woman needs to go away.

The woman made more noises, and suddenly the dragon felt a tightness surrounding it, squeezing its scaly skin. It was an awful feeling. It tried to shake the tightness loose, and it broke into pieces.

A deep urge came over the dragon, a deep churning in its gut, driven by instinctual fear. The woman made a loud noise, and some of the other people scrambled away. She made another bunch of noises. A bubble of power surrounded her.

A reflexive urge forced the dragon's head forward. A pressure squeezed its insides, and a strange white smoke whooshed from its mouth.

The smoke blasted past the bubble of power and caught the others in the area. They disappeared in a stream of white smoke that fled up to the moon. The dragon felt a rush of energy when the smoke hit the moon.

The dragon panicked. This was too strange a place with frightening things happening. It leaped up in the air with a cry, flapped its wings, circled around, cried out again, then fled away into the dark.

As Sighurd and Eloise approached the castle, he heard cries from the courtyard. A word stood out: *Dragon!*

He looked up as a giant white dragon descended from the sky and hovered above the court.

"Great Gods above!" He reared the horse to a stop and jumped to the ground, stepping forward as he gaped. He was beyond shocked. Dragons were even more of a mythical legend than the Beast. He couldn't believe there was one before his eyes.

Eloise began muttering under her breath.

"No spells!" he shouted.

"I'm casting a Sight spell so I can study the dragon."

He turned away, and she began the spell again.

The dragon lowered itself to the castle courtyard, but still towered above its walls. It arched its neck and dropped its head down out of sight.

He glanced at Eloise. She gazed ahead with glassy eyes. "Can you see anything?" he asked.

"I...I..."

The dragon's head arched up, shook itself, pulled back and recoiled forward with a blast of white mist spewing out of its mouth. The mist flowed out when it hit the walls. Small patches of mist coiled up to Mistress Moon and disappeared into her face.

The dragon spread its wings and shrieked, then launched into the sky and flew a circle around the castle. It looked down and shrieked once more, then flew into the night.

"*Did you see anything?*"

"No," she said breathlessly. "Just a dragon and an aura of magic around it."

He looked at her with accusing eyes. She looked down at him and pursed her lips.

He mounted up and kicked the horse into movement. "Where did a dragon come from?" he shouted back to her.

"How could I know?"

"Why tonight of all nights?"

She said nothing. He urged the horse into a gallop and rode to the castle.

The dragon flew aimlessly, wandering above the forest. It feared to go anywhere else. The sea of trees at least was familiar.

What happened at the castle? it demanded of the Voice. I don't understand any of it.

The woman is a caster of spells. She frightens me.

What are spells?

They are magical things that give people power they don't normally have.

Why does that woman frighten you?

I don't know. When I saw her, I got a feeling of danger. She must be evil.

What is evil?

Evil is when people hurt other people.

She tried to hurt us. I felt it.

Yes. We should stay away from her.

It flew on, soaring high above the trees, then swooping down low to skim over them. The moon climbed high in the sky, and the higher it climbed, the more exhilarated the dragon felt.

It noticed a disruption in the ribbon of water, a deep gash in the land were the water fell in a thunderous roar to the chasm below.

I know this place! it cried.

It swooped down and followed the river until it reached the gash. It dove into the mist that rose up from the chasm. The sensation was cool and wet.

It flew along the river until the walls of the chasm wore away. It continued along the river until it saw the water was leading back to the castle where the king was.

I will not go there again! it cried and zoomed up in an arc to go back the way it came.

It flew over the sea of trees until it came to a clear place in the midst of the forest where no trees grew. There was something moving in that place. A creature running straight for the dragon. The dragon hovered above, and the creature stopped below it, leaping and making loud noises.

What is it? the dragon asked.

It's a wolf. A huge wolf.

Is it evil?

It's a dangerous animal. But...

A feeling grew within the dragon, a feeling of familiarity, of warmth, of reassurance, of desire.

There's something about that wolf, said the Voice. Something that makes me want to be with it. Please, dragon, land there by that wolf.

The dragon felt the same feelings, so it dropped to the ground and lowered its head to the wolf. Unlike the evil magic woman, it felt only warm feelings from the creature.

The wolf nuzzled the dragon's snout with its snout and made playful noises. It frolicked back and forth, delighting the dragon. It raised its snout and cried triumphantly to the sky.

I love this wolf, said the dragon.

It's I who loves this wolf, said the Voice.

Why do we love it?

I don't know.

I think it loves us. I want to stay with it forever.

So do I.

Suddenly the wolf perked up and crept toward the direction the dragon had come from, the direction of the castle. It growled, then gave off a loud howl.

What's the matter, wolf? the dragon said.

The wolf broke into a dash for the edge of the clear place and disappeared into the trees.

Don't leave! cried the dragon as it beat its wings and lifted into the air. It flew above the trees, following the wolf.

Before long the dragon could tell the wolf was heading toward the castle. Don't go there! the dragon cried, and regretted that the wolf couldn't hear it like the Voice could.

The dragon shrieked and flew ahead, stalling before the wolf with its wings beating, hoping it would understand not to go there. The wolf pranced around, then veered past the dragon and continued to run.

The dragon feared the evil woman, but it feared losing the wolf more. It climbed back into the sky and followed it back to the castle.

Chapter 15

Blood Queen

Sighurd and Eloise rode through the outer gatehouse. He trotted the horse across the courtyard, its hooves clacking on the cobblestone. "Decide now, Witch," he said. "Are you prisoner of the king or the sorceress?"

"I guess I'll choose Gwendolyn," she said. "Maybe she won't kill me, and maybe Christian will kill *you* for not killing me."

He urged the horse into a gallop.

They crossed the drawbridge, dismounted at the inner gatehouse, and he handed the reins to a guard.

She decided to make one more attempt. As quietly as she could, she began the words to the Flash spell she'd thrown at Sighurd when he first captured her.

With blinding speed his sword flew out and pressed against the side of her neck. He slid it down, cutting a shallow slice along her skin. The blood flowed in a curtain.

His flaming eyes convinced her to make no more attempts.

The guard led the horse to the stables, and Sighurd led Eloise into the guardhouse and handed her over to his guards.

"Aren't you concerned the king will execute you?" she said softly.

"If Gwendolyn kills you, that will fulfill my duty." He looked at her with a smug smile. "Do you think Gwendolyn will kill you?"

Of course she'll kill me, she said to herself, irritated at his taunting. He scoffed when she didn't answer.

She could learn to despise this captain.

Sighurd marched away and flopped down onto a chair in the Great Hall, ignoring the buzz around him as the servants and parasites of the court prattled on about the dragon. He should report to Christian right away, especially while

Gwendolyn was distracted with Eloise right now, but he was too preoccupied with the dilemmas seething in his mind. He needed time to compose himself.

But the king found him and called "Sighurd!" as he came into the hall in an excited state. Sighurd stood for him. Christian said, "Did you see the—"

"Yes, I saw it."

"Where did it come from? How can it exist?"

"I have no idea, Your Majesty. I didn't think they were real." Sighurd had no desire to get caught up in the excitement over the dragon. That was one shock too many.

Christian's demeanor suddenly changed. "Why are you here?" He looked around conspiratorially then whispered, "Did you finish the job?"

Sighurd struck an official stance. "We found Celeste and the witch who hid her. Kasimir ordered me to bring the witch back before he rode off in pursuit of Celeste."

Christian, looking apprehensive, pulled Sighurd out of the Great Hall into an empty corridor. "Where's the witch now?"

"I delivered her to Gwendolyn."

"In the name of the Gods, why? You were supposed to kill her."

Sighurd wanted to snarl at him, but he forced a knowing smile. "What do you think Gwendolyn will do to her?"

"But I ordered you—"

"—to make sure she died in a way that couldn't be traced to you, and you gave me discretion on how to do it. If Gwendolyn kills her..."

Realization spread across Christian's face, and he grinned. "Very clever. But what about the girl?"

"Kasimir should have her by now. He should be on his way back with her."

Christian scowled angrily. "I don't want *her* in the hands of Gwendolyn."

"I'll command my guards to meet him in the courtyard and escort him and the girl to your chambers."

"Gwendolyn will be watching."

"Not with the witch commanding her attention."

Christian grinned. "Good, good! After you instruct your guards, wait with me in my chambers." He turned and walked away.

Sighurd watched him with a deep weariness as Christian climbed the staircase. The situation gnawed at him, and he needed time to rest and think. How could he maintain his integrity and still serve his king?

Gwendolyn's chambers. Eloise knew the instant Sighurd's guards led her in and chained her to the wall. There was nothing more identifiable than a sorceress' chambers.

But chains on the wall—that was something she wouldn't expect. Yet with

Gwendolyn, it didn't surprise her.

Before long a man came in, walked up to her, and leered at her with a smirk. He looked more a servant than a guard, but his demeanor shouted privilege. Gwendolyn's personal servant?

With his nose literally up in the air because of his short stature, he gloated, "You are going to suffer!" and walked out.

Of that I'm sure, Eloise thought.

It didn't matter. She was certain Zenia wore these very chains four years ago and suffered tremendously. Eloise could only feel honored to follow in her courageous footsteps.

A long time passed before Gwendolyn entered. She paused at the door to peer at Eloise with a grim face. "Bernard!" she shouted.

The man of short stature appeared, looking vastly less cocky than before.

"Why isn't she gagged?"

"I'm not going to cast any spells," Eloise said. "I'm not stupid enough to take on a sorceress." Not with breath spells, anyway.

"Very wise," Gwendolyn said. She waved Bernard away and shut the door, then walked up to her and peered into her eyes. "Hello...*Eloise.*"

She barely suppressed flinching at the sound of her name. Her heart sank. Zenia must have told her, and Zenia would only tell her if...

Gwendolyn gazed at the slit Sighurd had put on her neck and dipped her finger in the blood. "Gave Sighurd some trouble, eh?"

"Not enough."

"Who by the Gods *are* you?" She wiped the blood onto Eloise's clothes and began to pace slowly. "You've caused more trouble than you could possibly be worth a dozen times over." She whirled to pierce her with her gaze. "Yet you're nothing more than a pathetic old village witch, aren't you?"

Eloise peered at her defiantly.

Gwendolyn strode toward Eloise until she was inches away. "Or are you? You've done things no mere witch could do. Where did you get your power?"

She glared at Eloise as if expecting an answer. Surely she knew Eloise would remain silent as long as she could hold out.

In a moment, Gwendolyn's glare relaxed, and she returned to pacing. "At first, I thought the sorceress Deirdre helped Zenia. It made sense. If Duke Geoffrey heard about how we...treated his daughter, he'd have wanted to rescue her. Scaendelreic lies on his border and is our enemy. I'm sure King Gunther would be delighted to lend his sorceress to the cause, and I'm sure Deirdre would have been more than happy to cooperate."

Her pacing brought her close to Eloise again. "But after an extensive period of...compelling persuasion...Zenia admitted she never met Deirdre."

Eloise steeled herself against the heartache she felt for Zenia. She refused to let the sorceress get to her.

Gwendolyn stopped inches away again. "I have nothing but admiration for Zenia. I honor her courage. You should be proud of how well she withstood my efforts."

Eloise kept a stone face, but inside her heart was breaking.

"Who was she to you anyway?"

"She was my stepdaughter and my apprentice."

Gwendolyn began her pacing again. "A witch and her apprentice. That's what I assumed. Until a certain Purification spell...and a certain aura illusion... and four years of hiding a little girl whose aura couldn't be hidden from any witch in Cueldea with a breath spell."

She glared at Eloise once more. "So I ask again, who are you?"

"A village witch from Suedeche."

"Who performs magic worthy of a sorceress."

Eloise looked at her with a defiant smugness and remained silent.

"No answer?" Her eyes squinted a fleeting instant. "I'll tell you what I think. I think you *are* a pathetic witch who could do none of those things on her own. I think *you* helped Zenia, and Deirdre helped *you*."

Eloise acted like she didn't care, but inside she was delighted. Gwendolyn still had the story wrong.

"Do you want to hear how Zenia died?"

She did not, because she knew it must have been terrible. But she remained silent.

"I tied her naked to one of the posts in the execution field, then I called the Beast. Do you know what the Beast is, witch of Suedeche?"

Eloise couldn't hold back her reaction to this. The Beast killed Zenia?

Gwendolyn smiled at the reaction. "Of course you do. I'm sure the legends have spread to Suedeche. I called the Beast that night, and it devoured Zenia, one ripping bite at a time."

Eloise let a tear streak down her face. It didn't matter—it's what Gwendolyn would expect

"Do you know what the legends say about the soul of a person who dies by the Beast?"

"Mother Goddess, bless the soul of Zenia. Purify her of the corruption." Another trickle escaped her eye.

Gwendolyn nodded. "Tonight the moon will be full again. What do you think, witch of Suedeche? Do you think perhaps the Beast will be out tonight? Shall we find out?"

"You think I'd tell you where Celeste is, even with that threat?"

Gwendolyn crept up to Eloise and caressed her cheek. "No, I don't. It didn't break Zenia either. It wasn't until I brought out the children."

She couldn't keep the shock from showing on her face.

"Orphans with no one to miss them. Tender Zenia couldn't bear to see the

Beast rip them apart. That's what broke her, and she told me about you...and Celeste."

Eloise let the tears fall, for Zenia and for the children. "Which is why I never told her about *my* plans."

Gwendolyn's face became dark with smoldering anger. "Enough of this! We've wasted too much time already." She advanced on Eloise as if she were the Beast. "You're condemning Cueldea to destruction. We need that girl now!"

"What on earth are you talking about?"

"I've seen the Blood King in the East. The greatest, the most brutal tyrant the world has known. He cut a swath of destruction across the Eastern continent with his armies and his magic. At this very moment he stands at the borders of Komshu, battling them to destruction."

"Are you mad?"

"They're months away from victory, and when they've destroyed Komshu, they'll come here."

"How can you know all this?"

"With my Extended Sight—a powerful spell a pathetic witch like you could never dream of. I showed Zenia. She knew."

"Then show me."

Gwendolyn scoffed. "It didn't sway Zenia. It won't sway you."

"Of course it didn't sway us! There must be another way besides murdering an innocent child."

"There's not enough time to find another way."

"That's not it," Eloise sneered. "You lust for power, and you love to kill."

"I'm not killing. I'm saving lives."

"I know, I know," Eloise smirked. "Saving the people of Cueldea from some imaginary threat from the East that might someday come."

"I get no joy out of killing. But I will sacrifice the life of one girl to save millions from brutal slaughter. Celeste was a gift from the Gods to protect us."

"You're a monster," Eloise whispered harshly.

"It takes a monster to stop the monster in the East. Bernard!" The door swung open as she moved to her work table and gathered things up. "Get Ismael and Audric to bring the children out."

Bernard nodded and closed the door.

Children? Oh Goddess, she was going to do the same thing again, and Eloise couldn't let that happen any more than Zenia could. She hurriedly began a spell of Entrapment.

Gwendolyn whirled around and threw something from her skirt pocket. It crushed against the wall near Eloise's head. A bluish vapor flowed out.

"So you *are* stupid enough to take on a sorceress," Gwendolyn leered as she marched to her. As Eloise's eyes drooped, Gwendolyn's gloating words filtered through. "And yet I stopped you with the same silly witch's vapor Zenia used."

———

Eloise woke to find herself gagged and strapped to an execution post outside the castle walls. She was naked. It was dark. The full moon shone high above. Gwendolyn was laying out a circle around her with materials and oil.

"Welcome back, Witch," she said. "Since you're not *stupid*, you must know what's about to happen."

Two guards brought out a group of naked and crying children tied into a line by their wrists. They staked them into place where Eloise could get a good view of them.

"How could you?" Eloise cried, but it came out muffled and garbled.

Gwendolyn stood before her and held a thin stick up. "Last chance. You know how this plays out."

What could she do? What could she do? What could she do? She thought desperately. She couldn't let the Beast devour those children. She couldn't betray Celeste.

What could she do?

Gwendolyn shrugged and spoke the words that ignited the stick. "Maybe you'll get lucky. Maybe the Beast won't be out tonight." She dropped it into the oil, and flames encircled Eloise.

"What are you fools doing!" came a fierce shout.

Eloise looked up and Gwendolyn whirled around. Sighurd ran toward the two guards. They shrank back in fear. "Mistress Gwendolyn commanded us," one of them said.

"You are the King's Guard," Sighurd bellowed, bearing down on them like the wrath of the Gods. "Did the king command you to do this atrocity?"

They cowered before him.

"Did I command it?"

"No," the guard said weakly.

"Then get these children out of here!"

The guards scrambled to yank the stakes out and return the children as Sighurd turned to shoot the darkest glare at Gwendolyn that Eloise had ever seen. He marched toward her. Eloise watched with dread as Gwendolyn walked toward him with a dark expression and began the words to a Paralyzing spell.

The howl of the Beast reverberated from the forest. Sighurd and Gwendolyn turned to look.

A screech rang out from above. Everyone looked up to see a shadowy figure flying across the sky, blocking out the stars. Its silhouette stood out clearly as it crossed the moon.

The dragon!

Gwendolyn began the spell again. Sighurd ran toward her and slugged her on the jaw, knocking her to the ground.

The Beast leaped from the trees, leered at them, and began stalking toward them with a low, threatening growl.

Sighurd rushed to Eloise and started undoing the straps from her arms and legs. Gwendolyn tried to sit up, but was too woozy.

The dragon shrieked as it made another pass overhead, then dove.

Sighurd pulled the straps off and held Eloise by the arm as they ran for the castle gate.

Gwendolyn managed to get to her hands and knees.

The Beast roared and charged. The dragon swooped down.

Gwendolyn gaped as the Beast lunged toward her and the dragon zoomed down on her. She fumbled in her pocket and pulled out the globe of Warding vapor and slammed it into the ground in front of the Beast.

The vapor swirled up. The Beast recoiled with a yelp. The dragon swooped back up. Gwendolyn struggled to her feet, knowing the vapor wouldn't hold back the Beast for long, and the dragon—probably only seconds. She dashed back, catching a glimpse of Sighurd and Eloise ahead running for the castle.

Gwendolyn didn't have a chance of fleeing that far before the monsters attacked. She dove behind the post as the dragon circled around for another dive and the Beast pranced back and forth with his red eyes burning at her, waiting for the vapor to dissipate. She felt as naked as Eloise with nothing but a large wooden post between her and the monsters.

She studied that post and thought. Ideally, specific materials worked best for specific spells, but theoretically any material could be used to empower any spell. Improvising could lead to unpredictable, even dangerous results, but Gwendolyn had no choice. As the dragon dove straight for her and the Beast advanced again, she held her arm up to protect her eyes and spoke a spell of Protection, incorporating for its material the wood the post was made of.

It exploded with a deafening crash and pummeled her with slivers of wood. Some of them bit into the exposed skin of her arm.

The sphere of Protection engulfed Gwendolyn just as the dragon blasted its white breath at her. The mist flooded around the sphere, but didn't penetrate. The dragon whooshed back up and circled around for another approach.

The Beast lunged for her. It rebounded back as it hit the sphere. The creature jumped around in rage and attacked again. Again it was repelled.

The dragon plunged as the Beast backed away. Its serpentine neck coiled back and whipped forward, gasping a torrent of thick white vapor that fumed around the sphere.

Gwendolyn huddled down, painfully picking chunks of wood from her arm and clothing. Blood trickled from multiple wounds. She thanked the Great Gods her spell worked, but she wondered how long the attacks would last. The amount of wood in the post should cause the Protection spell to last a long time, but having improvised, she couldn't guess how long.

Long enough to last until morning, when the Beast would have to leave? She looked at the moon. Well past midnight, but still hours to go before it set.

But the dragon? She had no idea how long it would persist. Well into daylight?

Gwendolyn peered toward the castle. She could see people on the ramparts gazing at her while the monsters attacked again and again. None of them dared come help her, of course. They'd be fools to. She'd just have to ride this out in her protective bubble and hope it lasted long enough.

She realized she needed to piss. She cursed as she went to the far side of the sphere, lifted her dress, and squatted for the guards to see. Then she had to sit in that confined space and endure the stench.

Where did you come from? she thought as the dragon blasted her once more. She cast a Sight spell and studied it. Its aura was a bright, gleaming aura, as bright as...

"Celeste's," she said out loud.

Why would a dragon have Celeste's aura?

She looked at the Beast, glaring at her as he made another attempt. *And you... Why did you appear the night Celeste was born, after an absence of centuries?*

She watched them, the dragon circling and swooping and blasting with its breath, the Beast prancing and howling and leaping against the sphere. A majestic dragon and an accursed wolf. Two mystical creatures working in concert to attack her. A dragon that was a mythical monster from the past that should not exist, but soared above her with the aura of a young girl. A changeling wolf who emerged from a man at night when the moon was full. A man who would have a dark aura surrounding him when viewed with Sight, as the Beast had a dark aura. A girl who had a bright aura, but had been born with a dark aura, just like the Beast.

Just like the Beast.

Things clicked in her brain. She looked at the Beast—a wolf that was a man who probably dwelt somewhere in the haunting expanse of Fenweald Forest.

A woodsman.

She looked up at the dragon—a dragon with the aura of a girl from a mother who fled one night into that same forest and came back pregnant with an infant whose aura was as dark as the Beast. A girl that would probably be a wolf right now instead of a dragon without the purifying power of Mistress Moon.

Gwendolyn crept to the edge of the sphere on hands and knees as if *she* were a wolf. She peered into the Beast's burning red eyes, and it peered back, almost nose to nose, with snarling lips and a drooling mouth and a low growl.

"I'm going to find your daughter," she said with a wicked smile, "and I'm going to drink her blood."

With those words, a thought hit her like a bolt of lightning. What powers she'd possess when she drank the blood of a changeling dragon! Perhaps she'd become a changeling too. And if she could drink the blood of one changeling...

She wondered what kind of monster she'd turn into after drinking the blood of a dragon *and* a wolf. A thrill swept through her as she thought of the immense power she'd have.

She met the Beast's feral glare with her own solid gaze. "And then, I'm going to find you, and I'm going to drink *your* blood."

Gwendolyn awoke in a panic. She let herself fall asleep! She jerked up and peered around in dread.

The moon was gone. The sky was rosy with a rising sun. She spoke a breath spell. Her sphere of Protection was gone. Birds in the trees sang. A cool morning breeze rustled the leaves. The ground sparkled with dew. No wolf or dragon loomed over her.

It was a beautiful morning!

She prayed thanks to the Gods that her spell had lasted long enough. The Beast was gone at daylight, and so was the dragon—another indication it was a changeling.

Guards from the castle came to her. They asked her if she were alright and expressed their amazement at what had happened and how she survived. They helped her to her feet and escorted her back to the castle.

Gwendolyn was in a better mood than she could remember for a long time. Life seemed vivid again after nearly losing it. Her path was clear now. She had two astonishing sources of power that she only had to find and capture and sacrifice. She'd have the power to overwhelm the Seven Sisters, to rule over all of Cueldea, to unite the countries of Ifran with her, to vanquish the Blood King.

By the Gods, she could even conquer his whole sweeping empire!

She laughed as a thought came to her. Because she'd obtain all that power through the drinking of blood, she could call herself the Blood Queen.

But for the opposite reason from the Blood King. She'd unite the world into one vast empire of peace and prosperity, free of the terror and wastefulness of war. And with all that power from the blood of two changelings, if the legends were right, she'd live a long, long life—longer even than the Seven Sisters with their longevity spells—and rule over a worldwide golden age for centuries to come.

The world would thank her for it.

Chapter 16

Failed Quest

Kasimir, Faisal, Dietric, and Thomas entered the outer gatehouse and rode across the cobblestone to the keep. Kasimir sat straight and stoic in his saddle, suppressing the turmoil inside him. They were met by other of the King's Guard.

"Master Kasimir," one of them said, "the king requires us to escort you to his chambers immediately." He looked at the group as if searching. "There was supposed to be a girl..."

The four of them dismounted, but the guards stopped them. "Kasimir only, by order of the king."

"I'm his attendant!" Faisal roared.

"By order of—"

"He will accompany me," Kasimir said forcefully. "It's his duty."

The guards hesitated, but stepped aside so Faisal could pass.

"Where's the girl?" the guard demanded.

"There is no girl," Kasimir growled.

Sullenly, the guard led them up to the king's chambers, knocked, and entered. "Master Kasimir, and...his attendant," he announced, then closed the door as he left.

Christian and Sighurd sat at a table with other empty chairs. Christian said, "Your brother, but no princess?"

Kasimir knelt down and prostrated himself before the king. The shame burned within him. "I have failed my quest. Celeste is dead."

Sighurd rose to his feet. "You killed her?"

"We had her trapped against the cliffs at the Falls of Eircana. Rather than be captured, she leaped to her death."

Christian gaped at Sighurd, then broke into a grin. "Then all is accomplished! The girl is dead, and Gwendolyn will take care of the witch."

Kasimir wanted to jump up and strangle the king, but he only rose back up on his knees. "It was my quest to find the princess and return her safely."

"That was Gwendolyn's quest. I commanded their deaths."

"That was the quest Sighurd hired me for. I failed."

Christian strode over to Kasimir and grabbed his arm. "Stand up, man! You've accomplished what we wanted."

Kasimir stood, resisting the urge to wrench his arm in disgust from the king's grip. He tried to suppress his emotions to keep from shaking.

"I'll reward you with a bonus," Christian said. "You have my permission to stay in Gallea for as long as you wish. Enjoy the whorehouses in town! Visit the resorts in Meisson!"

"My quest was to rescue the princess. If you deceived me when you offered it, then I'm no longer obligated to fulfill it."

"Don't you understand? You *have* fulfilled it!"

"Not in my eyes!" Kasimir said, and he began trembling in spite of his efforts. "Not in the eyes of my masters."

Christian shook his head in puzzlement. "Suit yourself. Go home to Insu. Your masters have been well paid." He turned his back on him and returned to the table.

"If you'd like," Sighurd said, "you can retire to the chambers we assigned you when you first came and rest before you leave."

Kasimir peered at him, still shaking, then turned and walked out with Faisal following.

They strode to their chambers. Faisal sat, but Kasimir paced back and forth in frustration. "Is there no person with honor in this country?"

"Do you think Sighurd deceived us?" Faisal asked.

Kasimir stopped to think, then shook his head. "He and his Guard may be the only honorable ones in Luteche. I think he was deceived when they sent him to Insu."

"What do you want to do?"

"I want to leave at once! I don't want to stay one more night in this castle."

"Where should we go?"

"We can stay at an inn in the city."

"With our strange clothing and your starstones?"

Kasimir pressed his hands against his head. "This accursed kingdom! We'll hire a coach and leave tonight. Night will be better anyway."

"Alone through all the kingdoms even Sighurd was anxious to bring us through?"

Kasimir spread his arms out. "What would you have us do? Stay in the city's whorehouses?"

"I would have us stay one more night in this accursed castle and make secure arrangements for travel."

"Great Mabut in the sky!" Kasimir cried in anguish. "Why has this happened to us? Four years of our life wasted trying to rescue a princess who killed herself rather than let us help her."

"It's not your fault. You fulfilled your duty. It's no stain on your honor that they deceived you."

"Four years, Faisal. We'll return as novitiates, older than any novitiate there. I wish Mabut had let the Eastern barbarians kill us that day."

Faisal stood and hugged his brother. "You are still the man who vanquished them, who saved us both so we could report the threat to the masters. You're the one the masters trusted to fulfill this quest in the North."

"The *Northerners* chose me, not Master Izzet."

"He could have turned them down."

"He couldn't. They needed spies here, and I was the only one the Northerners would accept."

Faisal grabbed his arms and peered into his face. "Kasimir! I've watched you for four years as you fulfilled your duty and remained true to your quest. You commanded four of the king's most seasoned men with authority, even when they became weary of the quest. You faced dangers no other novitiate has faced on a mage quest. And you succeeded!"

"She died!"

"You found her and you had her. You had no way of knowing a young woman would jump off a cliff."

"I should have anticipated it."

"No one could anticipate that!" He kissed Kasimir on the cheek. "You are the most honorable and courageous man I know. I love you, Brother."

A knock came to the door, and Sighurd stepped in.

"May I talk with you?" he asked.

Faisal marched over to him with cold eyes. "Yes, you may talk with us! You can start by explaining why Kasimir's quest switched from rescuing a princess to killing a princess."

Sighurd glanced out into the corridor, then closed the door behind him. "That's what I came to talk about."

Kasimir approached them. "Were you part of the deception when you came to Insu?"

"If I were to answer your questions, it could be considered treason."

"You said you were here to discuss it," Faisal growled.

"I am! But first I wanted you to understand the serious position I'm in."

"You were already in a serious position when they sent you to deceive the Ribat of Wizards. That's an act of war—"

"Faisal," Kasimir said, taking hold of his arm. "Let's sit down."

They sat around a table, and Sighurd said, "Christian's father, King Guillaume, appointed me Captain of the Guard during the war with Scaendelreic. He was a king of honor and integrity, and I proudly took the oath swearing loyalty to him with my life. I've never broken that oath. When he died, my oath transferred to his son."

"I understand loyalty and honor," Kasimir said.

"But Christian was very young then, several years younger than he is now. Guillaume talked with me often about what kind of king he wanted to raise Christian to be, but the war came, and the priority became to protect the kingdom. Guillaume had no time to see to his son's upbringing while engaging in the war."

Faisal said, "What does any of this have—"

"Let him finish," Kasimir said.

"Guillaume relied heavily on Gwendolyn, since we were fighting King Gunther's sorceress as much as his army. When Guillaume and queen Delphine were killed, Gwendolyn naturally continued to conduct the war."

"I take it she did well enough to avoid defeat," said Kasimir.

"She and Deirdre worked out a truce. Neither of them could subdue the other, and the war became too taxing on both countries. But when the war ended, Christian was still young and had no interest in ruling, so Gwendolyn just kept ruling...as unofficial regent."

"Is *she* a ruler of honor and integrity?" Faisal asked.

Sighurd smirked. "She certainly has her own style. I can't point to any truly questionable thing she's done." He frowned. "Except one. But I also have no feel for her motives."

"This is disturbing," Kasimir said. "Who really rules Gallea?"

"Christian is king—officially. I won't say he has no character. I've never seen any love of malice in him. But he *is* youthful and impetuous and unprepared to be king, and his interests have been the interests of youth. Hunting, jousting, women..."

"So the reality is, Gwendolyn rules Gallea," Kasimir said.

"Until Prince Guillaume was born. It seems holding his son and heir inspired Christian to become a king."

"What does all this have to do with your deception?" Faisal said.

"What I'm trying to say is, no one here intended to deceive you. Gwendolyn conceived the quest, but when we returned from Insu, Christian wanted to turn it into his quest."

"Explain that," Kasimir said.

"Gwendolyn was the one who sent me to you, but she said it was by the command of the king. Before I left, I talked with Christian, and he knew nothing of the quest. His command to me was to do what Gwendolyn ordered me to do, but to also...well..."

"Spy on us," Kasimir said, "like I was instructed to spy on you."

Sighurd smiled. "Not only on you, but to see if I could figure out why Gwendolyn wanted Celeste back."

"Did he tell you his intent was to kill the princess?" Faisal asked.

"I don't think that was his intent, until after we returned from Insu."

"Wanting a little girl murdered sounds like malice to me," Faisal smirked.

"Faisal, please!" Kasimir said.

"I think he's just afraid," Sighurd said. "He doesn't know what to do about Gwendolyn."

"No one seems to know," said Faisal.

"And that's my point." Sighurd leaned forward on the table. "Knowing all this, you tell me, who actually authorized the quest?"

Kasimir sat back, contemplating. Gwendolyn was the one who wanted the quest, therefore the quest was to find the princess and bring her safely home. And that meant he'd failed.

But Christian had assented to it, and the quest was paid for by the king's treasury. That made it his quest, therefore the quest was to find the princess and quietly see to her death. And that meant he succeeded.

But that intent was never communicated to Kasimir, and if it had been, he never would have accepted the quest.

"Sighurd," he said, "I see why telling me all this could be considered treason, and I'm grateful you trusted me."

"I've traveled four years with you. I know you're a man of honor."

"But the fact is, it doesn't matter to me who authorized the quest. I was only told it was to rescue the princess. To secretly turn it into an assassination was an act of deception. Your king used me, and I consider the quest nullified. I know you're an honorable man, but you serve a dishonorable kingdom, and I'm going home. Please arrange for our—"

"Master Kasimir, perhaps I'm in no position to ask, but before you leave, I'd like to make one request."

"What is it?"

"The witch Eloise. It's too late for Celeste, but wasn't it part of your quest to bring her safely here as well? I assure you, she's not safe."

"I did. What happens after that is not part of my quest."

Sighurd leaned in close. "Christian told me that he fears Gwendolyn, that he can't fight a sorceress. The truth of the matter is, I fear her too. He's right. We could never take control of Gallea back from her if she refuses to relinquish it."

Kasimir sighed with weariness. "Sighurd, you have my condolences for the plight of your country, but this is not my concern." He stood up to escort Sighurd out. "I'm going home."

"But you failed."

Kasimir glared at him with a dark scowl. "My quest is invalid. I haven't—"

"Your quest was always to return Celeste home, regardless of what scheming Christian might have done." Sighurd stared him down. "You failed. And not because she was assassinated."

"How dare you..." Faisal snarled.

"But what if you could replace your invalid quest with a new one, a legitimate one, an honorable one?"

"What do you mean?" said Kasimir.

"Gallea paid for a quest. I assume that payment is not refundable."

"It most certainly is *not*," Faisal said.

"We paid for a quest, and you failed us. But with a new quest, you can redeem yourself."

"I do not like being manipulated," Kasimir said angrily.

"I'm not trying to manipulate you. I'm pleading with you. I know Christian would make a good king with the guidance of honorable men. But I have no faith that Gwendolyn will cooperate. We cannot fight her alone. But you, a wizard of Insu—"

"He can't become embroiled in the politics of your country," Faisal said. "You're the enemy!"

"Potential enemy," Kasimir said.

Sighurd pierced Kasimir with his gaze. "What if our quest could keep us from becoming enemies? What if we never became a threat to Insu? Would that serve your country? Would that fulfill your duty?"

The suggestion shocked Kasimir. "Is that something you could possibly guarantee?"

"An inexperienced and frightened king wanting to grow up, afraid of a powerful woman who usurped his rule. How much influence do you think men he respects and trusts would have over him? How much influence do you think a wizard who could protect him from Gwendolyn could have over him?"

"Kasimir..." Faisal said anxiously.

The door burst open with Dietric excited and breathing heavily. "Sighurd, come quickly! Gwendolyn, she's..." He looked at Kasimir and Faisal. "She's doing again what she did with Zenia."

Sighurd's eyes gleamed with rage. To Kasimir he said, "Decide now! I'm about to defy Gwendolyn." He flew out the door.

"What's going on?" Kasimir asked.

Dietric hesitated to answer.

"Dietric!"

"Gwendolyn's calling the Beast."

"What in the name of Mabut for?"

"To get Eloise to talk."

"Where can I see?"

"You can see from the rampart."

Kasimir followed Dietric out. Faisal groaned and went after them.

————

Kasimir leaned over the wall of the rampart, peering at the appalling sight in the distance. Dietric, Faisal, and the guards stationed there watched beside him.

The witch Eloise was strapped naked to one of several posts in what looked like an execution field. A circle of materials surrounded her. Gwendolyn stood before her holding up a stick. Some distance behind her was a string of naked children tied together by their wrists and staked to the ground, with two of the King's Guard standing watch.

Kasimir couldn't believe what he saw. This was the woman he'd been serving all these years?

The end of the stick flamed up. Gwendolyn dropped it onto the circle of materials, and flames swept around the circle.

"What are you fools doing!" came a fierce bellow as Sighurd ran toward the guards. They cowered before him. "You are the King's Guard. Did the king command you to do this atrocity? Did I command it? Then get these children out of here!"

The guards pulled the stakes out and herded the children back toward the castle as Gwendolyn strode toward Sighurd with a fierce expression and her lips moving, speaking words.

She's casting some terrible spell on him!

He reached for a starstone to stop her. But before he could, a bloodcurdling howl reverberated from the forest and a screech rang out from the sky.

Kasimir looked up and saw a huge silhouette fly across the face of the moon. Did he see what he thought he saw? No, it was impossible!

Gwendolyn began speaking again. Sighurd ran to her and slugged her, then rushed to the witch.

From out of the forest lunged the Beast, growling and slavering, and stalked toward them.

"Sighurd!" Kasimir called out reflexively, even though Sighurd was too far away to hear.

Sighurd stopped at the witch and began to undo her bonds. Gwendolyn lolled woozily on the ground. The Beast continued to advance toward her.

The giant thing in the sky screeched again, then swooped down. "Great Mabut and Sevda!" he cried as he saw clearly the monstrous white dragon, wings spread wide, long neck stretched down with a head and vicious snout full of teeth aimed right for Gwendolyn.

Kasimir watched with horror. Even with the Beast and a dragon attacking, Sighurd stood his ground and kept working at the straps to free the witch—his enemy!

Gwendolyn managed to get up on her hands and knees seconds before the two monsters reached her. She threw something at the creatures that burst open and released a dark vapor. The Beast yelped and recoiled, and the dragon veered back into the sky.

That vapor couldn't possibly hold those creatures back for long. He looked back at Sighurd, who had finished releasing the witch and ran with her back to the castle.

Gwendolyn scrambled to the post and hid behind it. As if that would help! But she spoke some words, and the post exploded into a shower of slivers.

The dragon swooped down again, coiled its neck, and struck like a cobra with a white blast of breath that flowed around Gwendolyn. This would kill her for sure.

But when the blast ended, Gwendolyn remained unscathed.

The Beast attacked, but was repelled by an invisible force.

Quickly he spoke a Sight spell and saw the bubble of protection around her. She'd used the matter in the post to power a protective spell, powerful enough to save her from a dragon and a cursed wolf.

He knew she was a powerful sorceress, but this vividly drove into him just how powerful she was, worthy of the fear of Christian and Sighurd. He and his fellow novitiates and even his masters had scoffed at the power of the witches of the North, calling their magic womanly.

At that moment, Kasimir learned that womanly did not mean weak.

He sought out Sighurd and Eloise, who were about to enter the gatehouse.

"That's the man I should be serving," he said with conviction.

Eloise was glad Sighurd still held on to her as they entered the gatehouse. Her head was reeling from the shock of being saved from the Beast when she'd resigned herself to a gory death.

It wasn't until inside the walls of the castle when people stared at her that she remembered she was naked. Immediately she felt embarrassed, then laughed at herself for caring about such a trivial thing after being given her life back. Sighurd called for some clothing for her, which was provided by the time she reached the inner gatehouse.

The movements of putting on the clothes helped calm her and gave her the time to think clearly. "Thank you for saving me, Sighurd."

He nodded and said, "Would you like to see how Gwendolyn's faring?"

"May Mother Goddess forgive me, I do," she told Sighurd with a smile.

He brought her up to the rampart. The first thing she saw was the white dragon circling around and making a dive with its jaw wide, ready to deliver another blast. She looked down and saw Gwendolyn still there, still in one piece, crouched down.

How was that possible? She should be dead by now.

The white blast flowed around her, hiding her. The dragon soared back up. The blast dissipated, and Gwendolyn remained unscathed.

The Beast pounced, but was repelled back. Clearly Gwendolyn had cast a

Protection spell. Eloise uttered a Sight spell and saw the protective bubble she knew had to be there. But what a powerful bubble! That was no breath spell. How had she cast it at a moment's notice?

She looked around and realized Gwendolyn was crouched right where Eloise had been tied to the post, but the post was gone.

"Clever girl," she murmured.

She turned her attention to the dragon and saw the same blazing aura she'd seen the first time the dragon appeared. An aura with the same signature as Celeste's aura. She couldn't understand it.

She looked at the Beast with its dark aura fuming around it like a black smoke. She studied dragon and Beast as they continually bombarded Gwendolyn. It was almost as if they orchestrated the attack together. What could be the connection between the two of them?

She thought of a time before when the Beast, after a centuries-long absence, suddenly appeared on a momentous night, at the very time and place Celeste was born.

What was the connection?

She turned to Sighurd and asked, "Have you heard from any of your men about Celeste?"

He became somber at the mention of her name and pointed.

A hundred feet away along the rampart in the dark of the night and in the midst of several other guards, she saw the star-spangled face she'd caught a glimpse of at her cottage as he galloped into the forest after Celeste. The wizard of the South with the black skin, his face twinkling each time the bright white breath of the dragon flared.

"What's his name?"

"Master Kasimir."

She walked over to him. His companion, the other black man from the South, stood next to him. Their eyes were fixated on the battle. Eloise leaned on the edge next to him and said, "What did you do with Celeste...Kasimir?"

Startled, he jerked his head toward her. "Isn't she supposed to be a prisoner?" he asked Sighurd as he walked up.

"I've released her," Sighurd said. "Hello, Dietric, Faisal."

"Captain," Dietric said.

Kasimir stared at her with an unsettled look, then looked down. "I couldn't capture her."

Eloise frowned. "Then where is she?"

"I caught her at the Falls of Eircana. Rather than submit, she jumped off the cliff."

"*What?*" She gaped at him in shock, then looked up at the dragon and whispered, "Oh sweet Mother Goddess!"

"What is it?" Kasimir said.

"Do you wizards of the South know how to cast a Sight spell?"

He scowled at her. "I already have."

"Then look at that dragon. What do you see?"

He looked up, his brow knotting, and his jaw fell open. "That aura..."

"She has even greater power than I imagined," she said with wonder as she looked up at the dragon. "Now look at the Beast."

He nodded. "I've seen this aura too. The same one Hereward had. The same one as..." He looked at Sighurd. Together they said, "Edmund."

"Who's Edmund?" she asked.

Sighurd said, "We know where the Beast lives."

Chapter 17

The Forest Girl

The girl felt a chill throughout her body. She shivered, and her eyes opened to daylight.

The first thing she saw through her hazy vision was a man—a naked man, eyes closed, black hair and beard flowing from his head. She blinked multiple times and rubbed her eyes, but the man was still there.

The wind blew across her, and she shivered again. She looked down and realized she was naked also. No wonder she was cold!

The man stirred, then moaned softly. The girl sat up alert, thinking she should be frightened, alone and naked with a strange man. But there was something about him, something soothing, something familiar.

The man opened his eyes. He saw her at once, and at once sat up straight. He stared at her until it made her uncomfortable. She looked away and saw that she was in a meadow surrounded by a thick forest of trees. Through the meadow cut a small creek, gurgling pleasantly. She and the man sat at the edge of the meadow, near where the creek flowed into the trees.

She looked back at the man, who continued to stare.

"Who are you?" the man said.

She thought about it, but nothing came to her. "I don't know."

"Where did you come from?"

She thought again. "From...here? I don't remember being anywhere else."

His brow knotted with an intense expression on his face, then a smile formed at the corner of his mouth. He looked her up and down. "Are you a child of the forest?"

The girl glanced at the trees, at herself. "Maybe I am."

The man's smile filled his face. "A girl who roams the forest and sleeps naked in the meadow."

The girl scowled, feeling self-conscious at his teasing. "I don't know how I came to be here."

His eyes unfocused and drifted off into space. "I knew another woman, once, almost a girl herself. I found her wandering in the forest."

His words made something inside her stir, as if awakening.

"But she rode a horse." His eyes focused back on the girl. "And she wasn't naked."

The girl's first impulse was to respond with her own teasing, but the feelings that stirred within her distracted her too much to think of anything clever to say.

The man stood and offered his hand to her. She took it, and he lifted her to her feet, then gazed at her warmly. "My name is Edmund."

"If I have a name, I don't know what it is."

He nodded as if knowing something unspoken. "That's alright, Forest Girl. Maybe you'll remember later."

The sun flashed its first rays above the trees. The Forest Girl shuddered at its sudden warmth. "That feels good."

"We should get you to my cabin." He gazed about the meadow. "We're about a two hour walk from it. Are you strong enough to make it?"

She scowled at him and replied obstinately, "Of course I am."

He laughed.

"But..." she added softly. "...I'm very hungry."

He nodded as if he already knew. "So am I, but I've often made a journey like this on an empty stomach."

"Often?"

He smiled. "But it's been a while." They followed the creek into the forest. He kept making furtive glances at her body. It made her uncomfortable. "Why do you keep looking at me?"

"I'm sorry. It's just that...your skin, it's so perfect and without blemish, or... scars." He looked her up and down as he said it, then realized what he was doing and looked into her eyes. "I mean, it's beautiful skin. You're very beautiful."

She blushed with her conflicting feelings. She felt wary, but his words warmed her. She decided to give him the same treatment and studied his body.

"You do have a scar," she said as she gestured at his thigh. "A nasty one."

He looked down, then smiled. "A very old one."

"Do you always walk two hours into the forest to sleep naked in the meadow?" she said, glad she thought of a way to tease him.

Edmund stopped before a bush with deep blue, almost black, berries hanging from its branches and began plucking them into one hand. "Here's something to ease the gnawing until we reach my cabin. Then I can offer you a real meal."

The Forest Girl stood next to him and began plucking. "You eat those. I can get my own."

He chuckled as she stuffed berries in her mouth until it was full, then continued picking more into her hand while she chewed. Edmund ate the berries he held, but didn't pick any more.

The berries tasted exquisite, so moist and sweet and strong with flavor. When her hand was full, she pushed more berries into her mouth and chewed. Her body seemed to crave them so much.

She plucked enough berries from the bush to fill her hand, then stepped away and gave Edmund an expectant look. He began walking. She followed him deeper into the forest.

"My cabin is along this creek. Any time you get lost in the forest, find the creek and follow it, and you'll find me." He looked back at her with a smile. "If you can figure out whether to go upstream or down."

"How will I know?"

He shrugged. "I know this forest, but I don't know how to explain how I know. I can only say, if you come to a large river, you went the wrong way."

The memory of a small river flowing into a large river brushed her mind.

His gaze moved down her body. "I'm afraid I don't have any girl's clothing. But I'm sure one of my shirts will cover you well enough, like a shift."

The Forest Girl nodded as she placed berries into her mouth, one by one.

His gaze ended on her feet. "The forest is not kind to bare feet. Be careful where you step." His teasing smile reappeared. "But I suppose you're used to it, since you're a Forest Girl who wanders through the wilderness naked."

She scowled. "You never answered. Why do you often make this journey?"

"I have reasons," he said, looking ahead. "Personal reasons." He looked at her body and smirked. "At least I *know* why I'm out in a forest meadow naked."

The Girl glared at him.

They reached a part of the creek where a small waterfall babbled over a short drop, forming a pool in the creek.

The Forest Girl stopped with her eyes wide, gazing around. "I know this place." She jumped in the water and laughed as she splashed around.

Edmund peered at her in amazement.

She saw a flat boulder submerged in the pool near the far edge. She went over and sat on it, letting her feet soak in the water. The water and boulder were familiarly cold on her buttocks. She saw little fish swimming in the pool and wished one would come close to her.

One did come close, swimming up to her feet and nibbling on a toe. It tickled, and she giggled.

Edmund seemed frozen in place as he watched her. "But that was only two years ago," he murmured.

As he spoke, standing naked by the pool, she looked at him, and a strong sense of familiarity flooded over her. She studied the scar on his leg, then peered at the one thing no woman had.

"What is that?" she whispered as if reliving a dream.

Something inside her said, *It's his penis*. But she already knew that answer.

He noticed where she was staring and looked down himself. "You wanted me to show you how I piss." They locked eyes. "But...you...you can't...you're too old."

She looked around and noticed a trail leading into the forest. "I grew fast," she murmured without thinking. She knew that trail would be there. "Where does that go?"

"I've never been down it."

She jumped up and ran down the trail. He jogged after her.

She reached a hill on the right and stopped, gazing at it with wonder. "My hill," she whispered. She turned to Edmund as he trotted up. "That's my hill!" she exclaimed, pointing, then looked down the trail.

"You know what's down there, don't you?" he said.

"Mother." She continued to run.

She came to a clearing that she knew would be there and paused as the cottage came into view. "Mother!" she called and ran to the door.

She flung it opened and stepped inside, eager to see Mother again. But no one was there.

Edmund stood in the doorway. "This is your home?"

"It is," she spoke softly, gazing about.

"Where's your mother?"

"I don't know," she said, feeling dismay at her absence.

"Well, I guess you can put your clothes on now," he said, looking at a stack of shifts sitting on a small table near the smaller of two beds.

"What about you? I have nothing for you." She studied his large physique. "Maybe you could wear one of Mother's gowns."

He laughed. "I'd look pretty silly."

Gazing at him, she felt a hodgepodge of strange feelings welling up inside her. Fascination, apprehension, familiarity, excitement, desire...

Desire for what?

He peered back at her with the same intensity. "I...uh...noticed a garden out there. Maybe we can eat here."

"Yes," she said enthusiastically, feeling her stomach gnawing.

He went out to the garden. She stood inside watching him through the open door as he bent over to pull vegetables. She remembered there was something hanging on the door and swung it closed to look. But the something was not there. Only a peg that once held it up.

She went over and picked up a shift. She stared at it, thinking how strange it would be to walk around clothed while he remained naked.

She tossed it back on the stack and stepped outside.

He was on his way back with a handful of carrots. "Is this okay?"

A thrill shot through her. "Why carrots?"

"They just seem right for you."

Carrots did seem right, and it unsettled her that she had no idea why. "And green beans and mushrooms."

He gazed at her with a perplexed look.

"And a rabbit...for stew?" she added.

He gazed at her with amazement. "What's happening here?"

"I can call a rabbit."

"You can...*call*...a rabbit?"

She stiffened with dread. What was she doing? She wasn't supposed to let any other people know—

Other people!

She gaped at him, wondering if she should flee. Flee to Mother. But where was Mother?

"Is something wrong?"

She peered at him and tried to calm down. Surely he couldn't be the evil kind of other people. He'd been nothing but kind to her.

"Yes, I can call a rabbit."

"You must really be a Forest Girl, if you can do that."

Almost at once a rabbit hopped up to them. Had she already called it with the mere thought of calling it? She knelt down and let it crawl into her hands. "I'll get this ready," she said and went back inside.

She skinned the rabbit and sliced its meat into strips, working with the proficiency of much practice. He dropped the carrots on the table and went outside, returning with green beans and mushrooms. In a basin of water, he rinsed the dirt from his hands and the vegetables he'd harvested. He found a pot and filled it with water from the drinking bucket, placed it on the stove and studied it. "Do you have something to light it with?"

Without thinking, she spoke some words in a different language that ignited the flame. He gaped at her. "So you're a witch."

Thinking consciously about it caused the memory to flee. "I guess I am."

He sliced the vegetables in and added the strips of rabbit she cut and handed to him.

"It's not a very fancy stew," he said, "but I'm sure you're starving."

"More than I can remember. Although...maybe I really can't remember."

He smiled at her. "I just wish I could offer something worthy of your beauty."

She blushed again. "You really think I'm beautiful?"

Edmund gazed at her intensely. "More than any woman I can remember, and I *can* remember. Your hair glows with the light of the heavens. Your eyes flash like quicksilver. Even your..." He glanced down at her loins. "...lower hair is gentle gold."

She looked down at her loins and wondered, if her patch was so different, what other girls looked like.

When it was ready, they sat across from each other at the table and ate. It was a strange thing to her, eating with a man in her own home, and eating with him naked. She'd never done that with Mother.

Where was Mother?

"This is the same meal I gave to that other woman I found," Edmund said with a wistful look in his eyes. "What was that? Four...five years ago? She was beautiful too. Almost as beautiful as you."

His eyes locked on hers. His gaze pierced into her. Those thrilling, frightening feelings came back to her, spread like lightning through her. Her breathing became quick and shallow.

"You look like..." he said quietly. "If your hair were a little darker..."

His gaze frightened her, but she couldn't look away. Her heart pounded so hard, it felt as if it would break through her chest.

"And that little girl... You look... Did you play naked in that stream when you were younger...much younger?"

She could hardly breathe, her feelings were so intense. His gaze had a grip on her that she thought she could never break free from.

"Who are you?" he whispered intensely.

She knew him. Not only from the creek when she was young, but...somewhere else. A different place, a different time. And yet a place and time not unlike this here and now.

"Did you love her...that woman?" she asked.

"Very much."

"Did she stay with you?"

"For one day."

"You didn't want her to stay?"

A tear formed in the corner of his eye. "More than anything I wanted her to stay. But I couldn't let her."

"Why not?"

Edmund slid away from the table and stood up, facing away from her. "I can never let anyone stay. I don't dare."

She stood slowly and crept up to him, touching him on the arm. "Will you send me away too?"

He gazed at her with a wild look in his eyes. "I'm...not sure. Somehow I know you. Somehow...I...love..."

His voice trailed off. Gazing up into his face, she felt the familiarity burn within her, a passionate familiarity. "I know you too...somehow. Somehow...I love..."

They fell into an embrace and kissed. His lips, his scent, all of it familiar and welcome. All of it satisfying a hunger that she felt had been there all along, even though she never noticed until this moment.

Somehow they lay on the bed with him on top of her. Her body pulsed with a fierce sensual pressure, building, building.

Somehow she survived the explosion, so new, so exotic, so exhilarating and so frightening—yet so comforting and...so familiar.

When the Forest Girl awoke, she found herself lying next to Edmund, her head resting on his arm, her arm on his chest. He lay awake staring at the ceiling.

She leaned over and kissed him on the cheek. "I love you," she murmured in his ear.

He pulled her closer. "I love you."

"Will you really send me away?"

Tears trickled from his eyes, and he chuckled through them. "I won't have to." He jostled onto his side and faced her. "I'm sure now. I could sense it while we made love."

"What do you mean?"

"You're a changeling."

"A what?"

"Like me. You change."

"I don't remember anything about...changing."

The man nodded with a smile. "That's how it is in the beginning. It takes a while to remember who you are after your first time."

"I don't understand any of this."

"And your hunger. It's always intense after the Change. Every time."

The Forest Girl sat up, almost in tears with frustration. "Edmund, you're making no sense."

He gazed at her with compassion, then pulled her into an embrace. "They call me the Beast around here. There was a time, whenever the moon was full, I changed into a wolf."

She pulled back to look into his face. "Are you teasing me again?"

"I'm deadly serious. I'm cursed with an ancient curse, more ancient than the—well, you wouldn't remember the Seven Sisters. I turn into a wolf, and in my mindless state, I attack people." Tears flowed from his eyes unself-consciously as he swung his legs to the floor and sat up. "They say that those I kill are cursed for eternity. I pray to the Gods that isn't true."

She stared at him in shock, barely able to make sense of his words.

"And when I wound them, the corruption seeps into them, until they're plagued with the same curse as I."

"You change into a wolf?" was all she could think to say.

He nodded. "I was attacked—hundreds of years ago. I was a young man with a wife and three children. Someone chased the creature away before it killed me. I..." He rested his face in his hands as his elbows rested on his knees. A shudder passed through him. "In my rage, I tracked the man down and killed him for doing that to me."

Her head swam as she tried to make sense of what he was saying.

"For several months after the attack, nothing happened. Then on a night of a full moon, I felt...wrong. I felt something happening, then I remembered nothing—until I woke up naked in the woods with a...with a..." A sob kept him from continuing. "I went home and—" A horror seeped into his eyes as he remembered. "Oh Gods, I pray it's not true!"

Comprehension slowly seeped through her dazed mind. A changeling—a person who changed into a wolf and attacked people.

"I'm going to change into a wolf?" she said.

"You must have already, last night, because you didn't remember anything when you woke up."

"No," she moaned. "I can't be a wolf. I don't kill people." Her tears slid down. "I'm not evil."

He thought, then stood and pulled her to her feet and spun her around, examining every part of her nude body. "You have no scars. But you couldn't heal so perfectly from a wolf attack." He pointed to his own ugly scar.

"Because I was never attacked. I'm not a wolf."

He peered at her as he thought hard. "You *are* a changeling. I felt it."

"Please, I don't want to change," she said through her tears.

He bundled her up in his arms. "You can learn to control it. In time, you can resist the Change."

"I can?"

"I'll help you. I've learned to control it. I can go...many, many years without changing. I can resist the moon."

"But didn't you change last night?"

He let go of her and sat on the bed. "I did. And four years ago."

"Why? You could hurt people."

He shook his head. "I've gone two hundred years without changing. But four years ago I felt a powerful urge to change. I fought it as hard as I could, but I couldn't resist."

"Why four years ago?"

"I don't know. For two nights I couldn't resist changing. Then I could resist again for four years." He looked up at her. "Last night, I couldn't resist again. And I woke up next to you."

A chill ran through her.

His eyes widened as he gazed at her. "How long ago were you born?"

She took a step back. "I...I'm sixteen years old."

"Two years ago you were half that age." He stood and took her hand. "Were you born four years ago?"

Her eyes welled up. She blinked, and the tears slid down.

"I think...somehow...you called the Beast out when you were born...and again when you had your first Change."

She wept profusely as she shook her head. "No...no..."

He embraced her fiercely. "I can help you. Together we can resist changing."

"Send me away! I don't want to be responsible for...for making you..."

"No matter where you go, we'll both still change. Together we can stop it."

She tried to stop crying, but it took a while before she could say, "Do you promise?"

"I promise."

She looked in his eyes, his deep compassionate eyes that seemed filled with centuries of pain, and her feelings for him overwhelmed her. In his compassionate gaze she could see a ferocity of soul that made him feel dangerous—and thrilling. She kissed him with all the passion she felt. "Edmund, love me again. Love me like we're wolves *now*."

The sky glowed red with sunset through the windows. Edmund climbed out of bed and took a deep drink of water from the bucket.

The Forest Girl stood and walked over to the window, dreading what was coming. "The moon will be full again tonight?"

"For three nights it's full."

Her face grimaced deeply. "Do you think I killed anyone last night?"

He came up behind her and put his arms around her. "I have no way of knowing."

"No!" She broke away from him and went over to her shift lying crumpled on the stack.

"It'll just tear apart when you change."

She grabbed it and tugged it over her head. "I refuse to change. You said you'd help me."

"I *will* help you. But you can't learn it in a few minutes."

"No!" In defiance she slid it down her body. "You promised."

He looked at her with affection and sadness. She gazed at him with pleading eyes. "Please, Edmund. I don't want to kill anyone."

He sighed as he looked down at the floor, then walked over to her. "Soon you'll feel a tingling in your gut, almost like you need to vomit. The feeling will grow more insistent until it overwhelms you. If you can hold an image in your mind of yourself as a human, hold tight and unwavering no matter how sick you get, then you can resist the change until the feeling passes."

"How long before it passes?"

"Too long. Mere moments—but an eternity."

She felt the tingling begin, ever so faint. "Will you resist it with me?"

"Certainly—if you can. If not, I'll join you."

The tingling grew. "Are you feeling it too?"

"Yes, my love."

Her stomach felt strange, then giddy, then queasy. She pictured herself standing tall and defiant and human. She scrunched her face with the effort.

"It's hard!" she cried.

Edmund embraced her, her head against his chest. "Hold on, hold on."

The image wavered. She concentrated with ferocity to keep it steady. The queasiness grew, feeling like a terrible pressure inside her.

"Just a moment or two longer," he comforted. "You are a woman. A beautiful woman. The most beautiful woman in the world."

She felt as if her skin would burst and her innards ooze out. "Edmund!" she cried.

"Hold on!"

Her head grew dizzy. She felt like she'd pass out. "Edmund, I can't..."

He broke the embrace and gently pulled the shift over her head. He nudged her shoulders until she faced the door. "It's better if the Change happens outside. A wolf makes such a mess of a cottage."

Together they walked naked through the door into the twilight and stood in the wide clearing, facing each other.

"I feel sick!" the Forest Girl cried.

"It's because you're fighting it. Just look at me and let it happen. It will be over in no time."

She peered into his eyes, his loving eyes, and with a sigh of relief, let go. The pressure washed over her, spinning her head. She sensed a grey fog creeping into her vision from the edges. His compassionate eyes widened with shock, and the last thing she heard before she succumbed to dizzying blackness was Edmund crying out, "Great Gods! You're not a wolf at all!"

The white dragon spread its wings wide and launched into the air. The great wolf leaped about as if celebrating the dragon's flight.

The dragon circled around the wolf, swooping playfully back and forth. The wolf pranced, pawed the ground, and barked with delight.

With a flourish, the dragon swept forward and glided over the tree tops. The wolf did one last dance and plunged into the forest, chasing after the dragon.

Together they chased unerringly toward the full moon as it rose above the horizon.

Chapter 18

New Quest

Sighurd closed the door to Kasimir's chambers and leaned against it. He perused the group before him, the ones who'd stood on the rampart and watched as the Beast and the dragon pummeled Gwendolyn with attack after attack. Kasimir, Faisal, Dietric—and Eloise, the one he rescued from death. The one who shouldn't be in this sensitive gathering. The one who shouldn't be alive.

And neither Gwendolyn nor Christian would be happy about that.

"I've committed treason," he said, looking at each of them in turn. Dietric was the only one who looked troubled.

"I thank Mother Goddess you did," Eloise said. "I may have to stop disliking you."

"How did you commit treason?" Dietric asked.

He gestured to Eloise. "The king commanded me to make sure she died."

Dietric took a moment to think about it. "Did he say when and how?"

"He left it to my discretion."

Dietric looked at her and took a deep breath. "To save her from a savage death isn't treason. You can still give her a merciful—"

"She will not die," Kasimir said forcefully.

"No, she will not die," Sighurd said. "I *have* committed treason."

"Why?" Dietric seemed as troubled as Sighurd felt.

He took a long time to respond as his conflicting emotions battled within him. When he did respond, he spoke deliberately as he sorted out his own logic.

"I chose to serve King Guillaume because he was honorable. I think Christian can become as honorable as his father. He's never been taught how."

"It may be too late," Eloise said. "His character was molded in his youth."

"That's what I'm counting on. As obstinate as he could be, he always respected his father. I pray to the Gods that's what molded his character."

"But the king's command is the king's command," Dietric said.

"Is it?" Sighurd said. "Is loyalty only mindless obedience? If I let him do this thing, then his character *will* be set. He'll learn to be a brutal king."

"It won't be treason if you persuade him to rescind his command," Kasimir said.

"Is that true?" Dietric said. "Can we be so loose with our interpretations of duty?"

"I have the same dilemma," Kasimir said. "What is duty? Is it mindless obedience?" He gazed at Faisal. "Didn't Master Izzet teach us that a true disciple must be wise and resourceful in carrying out his duties?"

Faisal's expression was grim, but he remained silent.

Kasimir walked over and stood next to Sighurd. "This man came to Insu and offered me a quest in the name of King Christian. But it really came from Gwendolyn. Christian wanted a different quest that was kept hidden from me. Where is my duty? To Sighurd? Gwendolyn? Christian? To my honor that demands the quest be nullified because they deceived me?"

He gestured to Dietric and Faisal. "Like Sighurd, I have an attendant who wants me to follow the strict interpretation of duty. Faisal is my older brother, and his task was to guide and protect me on this quest. This would have *been* his quest if Gallea hadn't insisted it be mine."

He marched up to Faisal and looked him directly in the eyes. "But it *is* my quest and my decision on how to fulfill it."

"It's my quest too," Faisal said somberly.

Kasimir peered at him, embraced him, and kissed him, then returned to Sighurd. "I officially declare my quest invalid due to the deceit of King Christian. I now have discretion to do what I think is wise as I return to Insu." To Faisal he said, "And so do you, Brother. If you choose to return at once, I'll have no ill feelings."

"What in your wise discretion will you do on your way back to Insu?" Faisal said with a touch of sarcasm.

Kasimir looked at Sighurd. "Tonight I witnessed the one man in all of Cueldea who displayed the kind of honor and courage that deserves my loyalty. You offered me a new quest, Sighurd. I accept it, and...on my way back to Insu...I'll fulfill *that* quest."

"That sounds like a long journey home," Faisal growled.

"It's my choice," said Kasimir.

"We have another matter, more immediate," Sighurd said as he looked at Eloise. "I saved the witch...for now. But her life is still in danger."

"And Celeste's," Eloise said.

"Can it truly be possible that was Celeste?" Kasimir asked.

"Is it possible for a dragon to appear at all?" she said. "Is it possible for a man to become a wolf?"

"Is the life of a girl who can turn into a dragon truly in danger?" Faisal said.

"On the nights with a full moon, perhaps not," she said. "What about the rest of the time?"

Sighurd stepped over and sat at the table. "The new quest I proposed was to join together to regain power from Gwendolyn, to help Christian become the king he can be, and to form an alliance between Gallea and Insu to—"

"To oppose the Seven Sisters, I hope," Eloise said.

That took Sighurd by surprise. "Don't you think Gwendolyn will be enough of a challenge?"

She slowly shook her head. "You men are so oblivious. You think all your wars and political scheming matter. The Seven Sisters orchestrate all that in the shadows." She looked pointedly at Sighurd. "You'd think Gallea would have figured that out by now. Not only with Gwendolyn's intrigue, but the whole war with Scaendelreic. You think King Gunther dreamed that up? He was manipulated by the Seven Sisters to attack."

She turned to Kasimir and Faisal. "And you two, flaunting your wizardly glory with your exuberant clothes and intimidating curved swords and face gems. Once the Seven Sisters have cemented their power in Cueldea, they'll turn their sights on Ifran. They want the entire West."

Faisal and Kasimir peered at each other with intense expressions.

"Take *that* spy report back to your masters," she added, "courtesy of Eloise the humble witch of Suedeche."

She stood and walked over to face Sighurd. "My daughter Zenia was murdered by Gwendolyn. Her daughter Tamara died while fleeing from Gwendolyn so she wouldn't be murdered. *Her* daughter, my great granddaughter Celeste, has had to live four years in isolation, fearing that Gwendolyn would find us and murder us—and she still may succeed."

She leaned forward on the table and looked at each one of them. "I have more reason to hate Gwendolyn than any other person alive, I'd wager. But without Gwendolyn, Luteche would already be under the control of Scaendelreic and Deirdre. Without Gwendolyn, the Sisters would already be planning their move against Ifran. In a sick sort of way, she's been a blessing to us."

She sat back down and rested her hand on Sighurd's. "I'm forever grateful that you saved me, and I think your new quest is an inspiring thing. But it's too shortsighted. Wrest power from Gwendolyn, yes. Help Christian grow up and become a great king. Make an alliance with Insu. But be aware, that leaves us all vulnerable to the Seven Sisters."

"It's as our masters thought," Faisal said darkly. "We *are* threatened by the North."

"You make it sound like fighting Gwendolyn is the wrong move," Sighurd said.

"Not at all," she answered with a grin. "You've already allied with a wizard of Insu. He's accepted your quest. And I...well, I've managed to pick up an Ancient spell or two over the years, by hook or by crook."

"So you're saying," Kasimir said, "that we need a different quest, a bigger quest?"

"I think your current quest is fine. Just be aware that, after Gwendolyn, the task is not complete. Be aware, the Seven Sisters are the true enemies." She scanned everyone. "*All* our enemies."

Sighurd peered at each of them. "With Kasimir and Eloise, we may be enough to take on Gwendolyn, but against seven sorceresses?"

Her eyes gleamed. "When we find Celeste, we'll have a dragon on our side."

"If you're right about Celeste," Faisal said.

"And perhaps a Beast," Eloise said.

"You expect to have any influence over the Beast?" Dietric said.

"Not me. Celeste. You saw how they attacked Gwendolyn together."

"No, no, no!" Faisal said, standing up and walking away. "Too much depends on your assumptions about the dragon." He turned to Kasimir. "You've nullified our quest and we need to return to Insu."

"With your spy report," said Eloise.

Faisal glared at her. "And what will stop you after you've defeated the Seven Sisters from bringing your dragon and Beast to Insu to defeat *us*?"

"One witch, one dragon, and one Beast against all the wizards of Insu?"

"One witch, one wizard, and *maybe* one dragon and Beast against seven sorceresses?" Faisal growled.

Kasimir jumped to his feet. "Enough! Eloise brings up important considerations. But right now there is only one quest, a quest that fulfills the spirit of our original quest. We accomplish that, *then* we can talk about other matters and make other plans. By then we should have settled the question of the dragon and the Beast." He turned to Sighurd. "Do you still offer your quest?"

"I do."

"I accept your quest." He turned to Eloise. "It sounds like you want to join us. Is that true?"

"I most certainly do."

He turned to Dietric.

The man deliberated, then said to Sighurd, "I serve Sighurd, Captain of the Guard—as long as he remains loyal to the king. Will you vow to assure Eloise and Celeste's death at some point...unless King Christian rescinds his command before that happens?"

Sighurd had no desire to make such a vow, since he had no conviction he could carry it out. But the intense look on Dietric's face caused him to realize that, yes, he must make it. Without it, his actions would be perceived as treasonous by the King's Guard, and he'd lose all his influence to make the changes he wanted to make.

"I vow, Dietric."

"Then I'll go on this quest."

"I dearly hope you persuade the king," Eloise said sharply. "I'd hate to have to become the enemy of the man who saved me from the Beast."

"My sentiments exactly," said Sighurd.

Kasimir turned to Faisal. "Brother, can you join me on this quest? We *will* protect Celeste and Eloise, and we *will* work to protect Insu from...whatever enemies of the North we have, just as our original quest demanded of us."

Faisal gazed at him with a tight expression for a long moment, then took a deep breath and sighed it out. "I am your attendant, Master Kasimir."

"What of Thomas?" Dietric asked. "Do we keep all this from him?"

"Do you think he'd join us?" Sighurd said.

"I think he'd see it as treason...at first. I also think he could cause a lot of trouble if we exclude him."

"Will we do anything so different from what you've already been doing?" Eloise said.

"Only bringing you along," Sighurd said.

She smiled. "Is it necessary to discuss all the...intricate details with him?"

"He's not stupid," said Dietrich.

"I'll handle Thomas," said Sighurd.

"Then it's settled," said Eloise. "Gentlemen, our path is clear. The first steps we need to take are finding Celeste and returning to my cottage so I can retrieve my chest of magic secrets, otherwise I am of no use to this quest."

Faisal said, "It took us four years to find her the first time."

"That was when I hid her from you. Now I'm helping you. Perhaps that's how you can explain me to Thomas."

"I'll handle Thomas," Sighurd emphasized. "But right now, I have to handle two other guards."

He looked at Dietric, and the two of them marched out the door.

Sighurd waited in his captain's quarters for the two guards he summoned, pacing back and forth trying to stay calm as he fumed.

Ismael and Audric finally arrived, escorted by Dietric and Thomas. By their nervousness, they had to know why they were here.

Sighurd said, "Four years ago you gathered up orphan children and delivered them to Gwendolyn."

"We didn't know what she wanted them for," Ismael said plaintively, angering Sighurd all the more.

"But you found out, and when you did, what did you do?"

Fear was written all over their faces.

"I should have had you executed back then. But the children were not harmed, and I understood how Gwendolyn ruled in those days. I understood you believed you were doing your duty."

"Yes!" they eagerly agreed.

"But what did I tell you, four years ago?"

"She still rules Gallea," Audric said.

"And I still command you! This time you did it with full knowledge of what she'd do. I should have you executed now. But I weary of all this bloodlust surrounding me. You are banished from the Guard."

He turned to Dietric and Thomas. "Take them to the dungeon until I can decide what to do with them."

They escorted them away.

Sighurd flopped into a chair and breathed heavily to calm his rage. Once he did, he realized he needed to be more careful. He was no more match for a sorceress than Christian, and if he pushed too far too fast, the new quest could end before it began.

But he couldn't get the image of those naked children shrieking in terror out of his head.

Gwendolyn marched down to the dungeon with indignation. The euphoria she felt after surviving the night was dashed when Bernard came with the report that Sighurd had imprisoned the guards who helped her.

All these years since she commissioned the quest and Christian showed some backbone for the first time, he'd been pushing here and there, testing his boundaries, and she'd been able to handle him well enough. But this defiance from the Captain of the Guard was a new level of pushing.

First he interfered with her handling of Eloise, nearly getting Gwendolyn killed in the process, and now he'd thrown the guards she could most rely on in the dungeon. This was too much. She had to exert her authority again.

She arrived at the entry chamber to the dungeon and demanded to see the imprisoned men. The two dungeon guards let her pass, of course, although they insisted on escorting her to the cell, which peeved her.

"Thank you," she said when she stood before Ismael and Audric, but the guards didn't leave. "I will speak to them in private."

They looked at each other, then left and shut the door. Through its small window, she could see they remained firmly in front of it.

"What happened?" she said.

"Captain Sighurd is punishing us for helping you with the orphans," said Audric.

"But you obeyed my orders."

"You're not the king."

As she feared. Sighurd was escalating the effort to recover Christian's authority. "What's he planning to do with you?"

"He banished us from the Guard," Ismael said, "and left us here until he decides whether to execute us."

"So he's passed no sentence yet," she said with satisfaction. "Since you're free of your duty to the King's Guard, I want to take you into my employ. Will you accept?"

They looked at each other in surprise. "Yes, Mistress," Ismael said.

"You understand that makes you loyal to me. Now that you're banished, your vows with the Guard are no more."

Their expressions said they understood. It was a better outcome than they could have hope for.

"Guards!" she called, and the door opened. "I'm taking them. They work for me now."

The guards stood obstinately in the way. "Orders from Captain Sighurd."

"I'm countermanding those orders."

"He specifically mentioned you."

The last of her patience evaporated away. She began to speak the words of a spell. Their eyes widened in alarm, and they stepped aside for her.

It was only a Sight spell, but they wouldn't know that. As she left the dungeon with Ismael and Audric, she knew the four years of quiet posturing back and forth with Christian and his men were over. They'd both made their first confrontational moves.

The battle had begun.

Chapter 19

The Pilgrim

The light surrounded her, blinding her. She couldn't make out anything through the brilliance.

But soon it faded away. Before her stretched an expanse of highway cutting through a thick forest. The distant sky glowed with the red of a sun just below the horizon. Sunrise or sunset?

Her head was in a daze. Where am I? she thought. Who am I? She shook her head to clear it and tried to remember something, anything.

She'd come to this place for a reason. What place, she didn't know. What reason, she couldn't recall. But it was an important reason, a critical reason. She could feel it.

She had to find somebody—that much she remembered. She had to find somebody and tell them what she knew. Except she didn't know what she knew.

She looked at herself and found her body clothed in a flowing white robe with a hood raised over her head, made of a delicate and shining fabric. There was a word for this fabric. It took a moment to coax the word from the mist in her mind: silk. The robe meant something—again, she couldn't remember what.

A sliver of sun appeared above the horizon. Sunrise. That meant she faced east. Peering around revealed nothing but the highway stretching east and west and endless trees on either side. There was nothing to do but head down the highway until she found something that might clear her mind. East was as good a direction as any, since she already faced that way. More than that, it felt right. It felt familiar.

Her footsteps mingled with the morning chirping of the forest birds. The air was crisp and cool and smelled of pine. She marveled that no one else traveled a highway that was maintained so well, but that may be due to the early hour.

It wasn't long before someone did appear. First she heard the thumping of the horse hooves and the rattling of the wheels, then she saw the horse-drawn wagon appear around a bend in the road.

A man and a woman rode in the wagon. They spoke to one another, but they weren't close enough for her to make out any words. Almost at once the two of them noticed her, and their conversation ceased immediately. The horse slowed to a stop as they stared at her with what looked like shock.

She moved to the side of the road to give them room to pass. They only stared. She gestured for them to pass. The man came to his senses and steered the wagon to hug the other side of the road as far as he could. As they passed, they nodded deeply and silently. She returned the bow, not knowing what else to do.

Once past, their conversation started up again, hushed and animated. She look behind her. They quickly turned their heads away from staring at her.

Who *am* I? she wondered. Why did I have such an effect on them?

She tried to think. What had she been doing before the blinding light? What was that light? It didn't come from the sun, which hadn't cleared the horizon yet. She could think of no natural source for such a light while standing alone in a forest.

A memory of sorts came to her. A sense of descending a great distance. She remembered nothing about the descent, no distinct images as she floated down. Only brilliant light.

Before that, nothing at all.

At another turn in the road, the forest gave way on the left, opening up to a field. A creek flowed across it, emptying into a great river in the distance. Next to the creek stood a cottage, quaint and homey. A large portion of the field was cultivated with green crops.

Three children knelt at the creek, dipping buckets into the water. The oldest, a girl, stood first and headed back to the cottage, holding the bucket handle with two hands and letting it flop against her thighs as she walked. The other two boys were still in the process of filling their buckets. The smaller boy grunted to lift his up and pour it over the back of the taller boy, who yelped and swung his bucket up to drench the shorter boy.

They broke into a free-for-all, filling their buckets and drowning each other. The girl set her bucket down and ran back to scold them. She was rewarded with two simultaneous drenchings, which evoked a squeal from her. She dashed for her bucket and stormed after the nearest boy—the younger one who started it all—and deposited its contents over his head.

A woman charged out of the cottage and shouted motherly curses upon them, which sent the children scampering for more water in their buckets. As they turned to carry the buckets to the cottage, they saw her. They stopped, buckets hanging from their hands, and stared. The mother followed their gaze and froze when she saw her.

The family never moved and never took their eyes off of her until she passed out of sight.

Another cottage appeared, and another, growing in frequency as the trees thinned out more. Everyone outside the cottages stopped what they were doing and stared. Many of them bowed.

The woman plodded on, becoming more and more uncomfortable. She ceased bowing back as the people became more numerous. Before long she was in a full-fledged village that the highway passed through. Shops, peddlers, grocers bedecked the road. The entire community came to a halt as she entered, staring at her.

One wizened old man scampered up to her and dropped to his knees. "Good Lady, may I be of service?"

She gaped at his bald scalp, confused. Why were these people treating her this way? As the pause lengthened, the man turned his head to peer up at her with one eye. "My Lady?"

She didn't know what to say to him, until she realized hunger and thirst gnawed at her. "Some drink and some food would be nice," she said.

"This way, Good Lady," he said as he rose and gestured toward an inn. He led the way, and each person she passed bowed.

What am I? she wondered desperately. Some kind of royalty?

The inn was boisterous with patrons consuming their morning meals, but when she entered, they all fell silent and gaped. It was more than she could stand. "Please, all of you, don't mind me. Carry on."

The innkeeper rushed forward, and the old man took that as his cue to leave with one more great bow. The patrons returned to their meals, but in a subdued manner, speaking quietly and continually glancing at her.

"How may I help you, my Lady?" the innkeeper said. A serving girl came up behind him and waited.

"What village am I in?"

"Premveille, my Lady," he said.

"I just need a little to eat and drink. I've been traveling since sunrise."

"My pleasure," he said as he led her to a table and pulled the chair out.

"But...I'm afraid I have no money."

The innkeeper gave her a puzzled look. "It's an honor and a blessing to serve you." He waved the serving girl to the kitchen and beckoned for her to sit.

She sat and lowered the hood from her head. "Why do you say that?"

His confusion grew. "Don't you know who you are?"

"I'm sorry," she said as she looked down with embarrassment. "I can't remember anything."

The nearest patrons stopped their conversations to look at her, then glanced at each other.

"You're a Pilgrim of the Mother Goddess," said the innkeeper, "as were the Seven Sisters of old."

The words sent her head swimming. She could almost picture herself kneeling in supplication before Mother Goddess sitting on her magnificent throne, surrounded by that blinding light.

"How...how do you know I'm a Pilgrim?"

"Your robe...the white silk robe of a Pilgrim," he said as his eyes shone. "The legends describe it. They say one day another would come."

She shook her head in bewilderment. "What does all this mean, a Pilgrim? The Seven Sisters?"

His confusion made him speechless. He searched for words. "How can you not know who you are?"

She mulled over what the innkeeper said. A Pilgrim of the Mother Goddess. The Seven Sisters. Her soul seemed to radiate at the words, but she could find no meaning for them in her memory.

"Are there more of us in the world?" she asked.

"In all my life," he replied, "I've never heard of a Pilgrim upon the land, not since the—"

"Seven Sisters of old. What were they?"

"Demigods sent to minister to us, to teach our women the Ancient Magic."

"What am I supposed to be able to do with this...Ancient Magic?"

A low drone of conversation broke out. Some of it sounded like grumbling.

He shook his head in disbelief. "Bless people. Heal the sick. Protect people from danger. Prophesy of things to come."

She contemplated what he said as he stood silently by. The serving girl returned with food and water. The Pilgrim took the plate and mug and gulped at the drink immediately, quenching her searing thirst.

The guests of the inn ate in silence, watching her, many with grim faces.

After taking a few bites of her meal, she said to the innkeeper, "I don't know if I have any power to heal. I don't know how I'd protect people. I don't know any prophesy. I don't know why I'm here."

"She's a fraud!" someone spat quietly.

The innkeeper glared in the direction of the speaker. A part of her felt like the comment was true.

"It will come to you eventually, my Lady, I'm sure." He bowed low and added, "If you need anything else, don't hesitate to tell me." The man and the girl headed off to serve other patrons.

She continued to eat in silence, pondering what she'd learned. She wracked her brain for memories. Almost she thought she saw fleeting images, felt fleeting emotions, heard fleeting instructions. Her sense that she had a purpose was great. She felt an urgency in that sense. Whatever she was sent to do, she needed to begin as soon as possible.

But how could she begin when she had no idea what her purpose was?

She gazed around the room, wishing something would trigger a memory. The people around her expended great effort to appear as if they were ignoring her, some more successfully than others. The inn felt familiar, as if she'd been there before. But the sense of rightness she'd felt earlier as she headed east was absent. This village must not be her destination.

The thing for her to do then was to continue traveling eastward on the highway as soon as she finished her meal. That much she felt confident about.

A short, plump woman walked up to her, bowing profusely. "I'm terribly sorry to bother you, noble Pilgrim, but my daughter is crippled from an injury to her legs. Please, could you heal her?"

The patrons perked up at the words and stared unabashedly to see what would happen.

The Pilgrim stared at the woman, feeling surprised and disturbed. What by Mother Goddess was she supposed to do to heal the daughter—even if she did have the power to heal? What words would she speak? What gestures or rituals would she perform?

Why would Mother Goddess send her here with a purpose, but steal her memory away so she couldn't accomplish it?

If it were true that she was a Pilgrim, and Pilgrims were sent to bless people, she should at least try to heal the daughter. Maybe if she acted, it would simply come to her what to do.

"I don't know if I can heal her," she said to the woman. "But if you fetch her, I'll try."

Gratitude flashed across the woman's face as she bowed and hurried out of the inn. The entire room was silent as people peered at her. She tried to ignore them as she finished her meal.

Still the woman had not returned, and the Pilgrim sat motionlessly staring at the empty plate, her hands in her lap. The serving girl came and took the plate and mug, saying, "Is there anything else I can do for you, Good Lady?"

She looked up and shook her head. "No, thank you."

The girl bowed briefly and departed.

She went back to staring at the empty table. The rest of the patrons returned to their business. It was some time before the woman returned.

The daughter was barely a woman herself, pleasant in appearance with pitch black hair. She struggled in on wooden crutches. Her legs were thin and frail and twisted grotesquely. It looked as if the injury had crushed her bones, and they had never healed properly.

The woman brought her daughter to the Pilgrim, who stood to meet them. The attention of everyone was drawn to her once again. The silence was palpable. She could see in some of their eyes hope, expectation, and she knew if she could heal the daughter, others would fetch friends and kinsmen for her to heal.

She returned her gaze to the daughter, who peered at her with awed eyes. "Hello, sweet girl," she said.

The daughter replied with a trembling voice, "Will you heal me?"

"What's your name?"

"Ilsa."

The Pilgrim took her hand. "Ilsa, I don't know if I have that power. I'll try, but you must understand, I don't know if I can."

Ilsa nodded. The silence in the room became more intense, if that were possible. The Pilgrim knelt down before her and gently cupped her hands around the calf of each leg. She waited to see if any knowledge of healing came to her, but nothing happened. All she could do was lift her eyes heavenward and pray.

"Dear Mother Goddess, please bless this girl with health in her legs. Heal the injuries and restore them whole so she can cast her crutches away and walk normally. As your...Pilgrim, I beg this of you."

She closed her eyes for an instant, then opened them and looked down. The legs looked no different. She suppressed a sigh of disappointment and stood up.

Maybe if the girl put weight on her legs, strength would flow into them.

Supporting Ilsa with both hands under her arms, the Pilgrim said, "Let your mother take the crutches and see if you can stand without them."

The mother reached for the crutches, hands trembling, and carefully slid them out from under her daughter's arms. Immediately the Pilgrim felt her weight drop heavily onto her hands. She had to lurch to hold her up.

Ilsa's legs wobbled and nearly buckled. They would have if the Pilgrim hadn't supported her. Tears came to the Pilgrim's eyes. "Give her back her crutches," she said softly.

A few derisive chuckles peppered the room. Patrons turned away with unsympathetic expressions.

With tears forming in her eyes, the mother returned Ilsa's crutches. A look of bitter disappointment permeated their faces.

"I'm so sorry!" the Pilgrim said, hugging her. Her heart ached for the young woman, and she wished with all her being she could heal her. Her desire burned so passionately, she felt her own body couldn't contain it. It seemed as if the desire flowed out of her into Ilsa

With wide eyes, Ilsa looked down. Her legs straightened out, developed a healthier color, and appeared to strengthen.

The Pilgrim dropped back into her chair, feeling dazed from a loss of vitality and the shock of the change in the girl's legs.

Ilsa tried putting more weight on her legs and broke out in a grin. Her mother watched in amazement. She threw her crutches to the floor and almost lost her balance. The mother grabbed her and steadied her.

The entire room held its breath as she took a careful step, then another, and another. She leaped up with a cry of joy and embraced the Pilgrim fiercely.

A cheer erupted throughout the inn.

Her mother dropped to her knees and hugged the Pilgrim's legs. "Thank you, thank you, Good Lady. Praise be to you! Praise be to Mother Goddess!"

The Pilgrim tried to stand up, a struggle with her weariness and two woman clinging to her. They pulled away from her in deference so she could rise to her feet.

Many patrons rushed out through the door. She knew where they were heading. "I think I need to go outside. There'll be more room."

The patrons parted as she walked to the door. Outside in the street was a buzz of excitement as word spread. People flocked around her.

Two children guided a blind man to her. The children gave her an exaggerated bow, mimicking what they'd seen the adults do. "Please, Lady Pilgrim," one of them said, "will you heal our father?"

She gazed at the man and his fogged eyes and felt compassion for him. She touched his eyes and let the compassion flow out.

His eyes cleared, and he gazed about with astonishment. The children hugged her and the man dropped to the ground and praised her.

She healed another, then another, then collapsed to the ground exhausted.

A woman and a girl rushed up to her. "Move away! Move away!" the woman scolded the crowd. "Can't you see you've drained the life out of her?"

She and the girl crouched before her. "I'm Joycelin, the witch of Premveille, and this is my apprentice. Please let us help you."

They took hold of her and raised her up. Ilsa came beside her. "Let me help *you* now." She looked down with a grin at her legs. "See, I *can* help you now!"

Her mother joined them, and as the four of them led her away, the innkeeper shooed the crowd back. "Leave her be! Let her rest."

They brought her to Joycelin's hut and laid her on a bed. "Never in my life did I dream I'd one day minister to a Pilgrim of Mother Goddess," Joycelin said.

"Please don't worship me like the others."

Joycelin grinned. "You'll kill yourself if you try to heal a whole village at once." To the apprentice she said, "Take care of her." She pushed the rest of them out the door and closed it behind her as she went outside.

"Is there anything you need?" the apprentice asked.

"Just to sleep."

The girl smiled, stroked her hair, and began singing a lullaby in a voice sweet as a bell.

"Go home!" Joycelin's voice called out. "She's not going to heal every snuffle and bruise you have. Only those with serious ailments."

The crowd shouted out their maladies, calling for help.

"You—come back in a hour. You—the next hour after that. You, then you, then you, then you, then you—each come back one hour after the previous one. That's all!"

The voices of the innkeeper and Ilsa and her mother joined her in admonishing the crowd to disperse. The noise slowly died away. Joycelin returned inside, shut the door, and slid the bolt closed.

The Pilgrim could barely keep her eyes open as the lullaby ended. "What's your name?"

"Ninette," the apprentice said as the Pilgrim drifted into sleep.

The hour of sleep refreshed her. Ninette gave her food and drink while the first supplicant waited outside to be healed. Joycelin brought each one in, spaced an hour apart, each with a serious malady. The Pilgrim healed every one of them, and the hour wait between kept her from exhausting herself. Ninette granted her every request whenever she needed anything.

After seven healings, Joycelin said, "That's all of them. The rest are not so serious. I can handle them myself."

A crowd still buzzed outside the hut. "Get more sleep," Joycelin said, glancing at the door with irritation. She opened it and called, "The Pilgrim is sleeping now. Come back tomorrow." She shut the door decisively.

"I can't stay another day," the Pilgrim said. "I need to move on."

Joycelin smiled slyly at her. "I only told them to come back tomorrow. I didn't say you'd be here to help them."

"That girl, Ilsa. What happened to her legs?"

"She was run over by a wagon."

"Couldn't you heal her then?"

"I wasn't the witch here when it happened. I'm told the village witch was traveling at the time, and her apprentice was the one who tried to heal her. She wasn't very experienced yet, and she didn't understand that bones need to be set before casting a Healing spell, or they'll just heal where they are." She shrugged with a sad expression. "You saw the results."

"Couldn't you, well, break them again and let them heal properly?"

"I considered that, but they were such a mess, I'd have had to break them in all sorts of places. I didn't think there'd be much improvement. I'm not sure the other witch could have healed her completely anyway, had she been here." She smiled and patted the Pilgrim's arm. "I'm so glad you came along."

The Pilgrim slept until dark, then devoured a late meal that Ninette had prepared to still her ravenous hunger.

"It would be best if you left while everyone sleeps," Joycelin said, "but will you be safe traveling in the night?"

"I don't know. But if I have the power to protect, I suppose I should be able to protect myself."

"Well, there's no forest to the east, so there aren't likely to be any bandits about, at least until you reach the city."

"Which city is that?"

"Suedeche. My Lady, you're in the Duchy of Suedeche, ruled by Duke Geoffrey."

Those names rang familiar. She knew she'd been here before.

When she was ready to leave, Joycelin grabbed the door handle, but paused to say, "There are some people here to see you."

She became anxious. She had no desire to exhaust herself with more healings right before traveling. But if there were people in need...

"Very well."

Joycelin opened the door for her, and she walked out.

In the dark and silent night, three people stood waiting for her with wide smiles—the innkeeper, Ilsa, and her mother. Ilsa had a pack slung over her shoulder. She knelt on one knee and bowed her head. "My Lady, I'd be honored to be your servant in all your travels."

The Pilgrim was astonished. "No, no, you have your life to live."

She looked up. "I had no life until you came. I want to repay you, and...I want to see the world."

"Please get up." She gave Ilsa her hand and helped her up, studying her face, then her mother's. The mother nodded.

"I've packed all my needs," Ilsa said as she hefted the pack on her shoulder, "and brought provisions for us. And..." She slid an impressive dagger from a sheath on the side of the pack and held it up. "...this for protection. I couldn't use my legs, but I learned how to use this!"

The Pilgrim laughed. "I pray you'll never need it. Are you sure about this?"

Ilsa nodded enthusiastically.

She looked at the mother. "Are you sure?"

With tears forming in her eyes, she nodded. "Take care of her."

Ilsa hugged and kissed her mother, then hugged the innkeeper, then Joycelin, and finally hugged and kissed Ninette. A warm sense of familiarity swept over the Pilgrim. She remembered that about village life, how everyone knew everyone else, and either loved one another or despised one another.

"I'm ready," Ilsa said, wiping at her eyes.

The Pilgrim hugged everyone in turn. "Thank you for all you've done for me today."

"Thank you for all *you've* done," said Joycelin. "Remember to be more discreet when you heal people, so you're not overwhelmed."

She laughed. "I've learned my lesson."

The mother said a quiet and heartfelt, "Thank you."

"You've blessed my establishment today," the innkeeper said.

The Pilgrim lifted her hood over her head, and she and Ilsa headed east down the deserted road. She looked back at the ones remaining behind, still watching them go, and felt like she was leaving a family, even though it had only been one day.

———

The forest was gone. Meadows and rolling fields and cultivated land surrounded the highway with the river running parallel in the distance. The occasional cottage dotted the landscape. No bandits assaulted them. No wild animals attacked. Ilsa's dagger remained safely ensconced in its sheath.

Before long they came to a fork in the highway. Ahead the main road continued east. The smaller road headed northeast toward the river.

"What lies ahead of us?" the Pilgrim asked Ilsa.

"The city of Suedeche."

"What lies that way?"

"I don't know. Probably another village."

She sensed the familiar tugging, but not down the main road. She realized she knew the northeast fork. She'd traveled it often. Her sense of urgency intensified as she faced that direction.

Without realizing it, her feet had already started down the path. A sense of warmth and comfort possessed her. The sight of the rolling lands and the river ahead stirred memories. It felt like home.

The first faint light of day glowed on the horizon by the time they reached a village. It was much smaller than Ilsa's, less organized and more like a random collection of scattered cottages. But it filled her with delight to see it. There was no activity in this predawn hour.

"Ilsa," she murmured, "this is my home. I remember."

"You lived as a human before?" Ilsa asked with wonder.

"I must have."

They crept into the center of the village. The Pilgrim swept her gaze around, taking it all in, savoring the joy of coming home. She stopped as she faced one cottage.

"There," she said, pointing. "That's where I lived."

They headed for it, but before they arrived, the door of a nearby cottage flew open, and a woman rushed out. She stopped several feet away, gaping at the Pilgrim, then dropped to her knees

"My Lady, I am your servant."

"Please get up," she said as she flung back her hood. "*I'm* here to serve, not to be worshipped."

The woman stood up uncertainly. "What can I do for you?"

"What's your name?"

"Roslina."

"Roslina, who lives in that cottage?" she said, pointing to the one that felt like home.

"Cosette, the village witch."

They walked to the cottage and looked it over. "This was once my home." She turned to Roslina. "Do I look familiar to you?"

"No, my Lady! How could you? You're sent from Mother Goddess."

"I'd like to visit Cosette."

Roslina knocked, and after a short wait the door opened. A woman with dark hair stood there, her eyes puffy slits from sleeping.

But the eyes didn't stay slits for long. She gaped at the Pilgrim, then at Roslina, then dropped to her knees.

"Pilgrim," said Roslina, "this is Cosette."

"My Lady," Cosette said, "I'm honored."

"May I come in?"

Cosette jumped to her feet and stepped aside in invitation. The Pilgrim entered, feeling uneasy. The furnishings and their arrangement were unfamiliar, but the place itself was familiar. Ilsa and Roslina came in behind her.

"This was once my home," she said.

"My Lady, I've lived here for four years. The witch before me was here even longer. Are you sure this was once your home?"

The Pilgrim wandered about, looking at and touching things. "I can feel it."

A rush of memories flooded in. A terrible night when bandits attacked her family as she lay sleeping. She was just a child, beaten and left for dead while her parents were killed. The village witch took her in to this very cottage, nursed her back to health, and treated her as her own daughter. She taught her to be a witch herself.

She turned to Ilsa, her heart beating with emotion. "I remember. My name is Zenia."

"You're Zenia?" Roslina said in shock. "We heard you were dead." She examined the white silk robe, then looked up at her again. "Were you?"

Chapter 20

A Cottage and a Cabin

Gwendolyn pulled together the materials she needed to cast the Extended Sight spell. Because it was so powerful, its materials were costly, and it took exacting effort to cast it. She reserved it for important uses. Over the last four years she'd cast it now and then to make another attempt at following Eloise from the moment she disappeared. Every time, that strange spell deflected her Sight.

But now she had a new starting point to work from. With the attack of the dragon last night and the realization that the dragon was Celeste, she could begin there and follow it to see where Celeste ended up after changing back to a girl.

It was unsettling to watch herself cowering under the attack of the dragon and the Beast, knowing how close she'd come to dying. She saw herself fall asleep, saw the moon drop low to the horizon, and watched the dragon and Beast finally break off their attack to flee eastward into the forest.

This is the moment she needed!

The dragon flew in arcs and loops to allow the Beast to keep up. It was almost a playful ballet the way they interacted with each other. Clearly they had a connection, an affection for one another. Not surprising, if they were father and daughter. Everything about their behavior seemed to confirm that supposition.

They traveled deep into the forest until they reached a meadow. The moon was all but gone, and they settled onto the ground.

The Change took place. A glowing fog around them that hid them from sight as the transition unfolded. When the glow disappeared, two naked humans lay there with their eyes closed, a man with black hair and beard and muscles developed from many years of hard work, and a young woman.

What by the Gods is this? This isn't Celeste! She should be four years old now, not a young woman.

Yet as she studied them through Sight, she could see the shell of aura surrounding them, the man with a dark aura and the woman with the same bright aura as Celeste. But unlike Celeste's, hers did not rise into the sky.

No, not to the sky. To the moon. She realized the only time she'd seen Celeste's aura was at night when the moon stood high in the sky. Then it rose like a column to connect to the face of Mistress Moon. It must be that when the moon was gone, the aura broke from it and slid back down to the girl.

But why is the girl a woman? Had Eloise been able to accelerate her growth? How much magic did that witch know?

Or maybe, she thought with a shiver, this wasn't Celeste after all.

No, it had to be. Too many of the puzzle pieces fit together. More likely Eloise simply knew a spell to accelerate her growth as part of her strategy to hide the infant.

The two figures awoke from their sleep. They acted sheepish toward each other, as if they didn't know each other. Or perhaps it was only because they found themselves naked together. They spent a great deal of time talking, but Gwendolyn wasn't interested in that. She only wanted to see where they went so she'd know where to capture them. Rather than let time play out normally, she rushed her Sight forward and followed them as they sped through the forest along a creek.

They came to a small pool and waterfall and remained there a moment. Suddenly the woman raced down a path until she came to a clearing where a cottage stood.

Gwendolyn felt a thrill shoot through her at the sight. A hidden cottage deep in the forest near a creek for a water supply and a garden for food. Just the sort of place a witch might bring a child to hide from the world. This must be where they were all these years.

But if this were the place, why didn't the Deflection spell deflect her Sight this time?

Perhaps because Eloise was no longer there. No matter. Now she knew where Celeste and the Beast went in daylight, remaining conveniently together so she could capture them together. It was time to act before anyone else interested in the girl found her, like Deirdre, or Eloise, that Gods-cursed witch that should be dead now if it weren't for Christian's Captain of the Guard.

She broke her Sight with a Negation spell and rushed to the door, opened it, and shouted, "Bernard!"

He appeared and said, "Yes, Mistress?"

"Tell Ismael and Audric we have to leave *now!*"

He nodded and left. She closed the door and hurriedly prepared for their journey. By tomorrow, she should have her two sources of power safely in her hands.

If she could get there first.

———

Sighurd went to meet Thomas in his quarters.

"I hear Gwendolyn's furious with you for saving that witch," Thomas said.

"I serve the king, not her," Sighurd said. "That's what I came to talk about. We're continuing with the quest."

"But we have the witch, and Celeste is dead."

"The witch doesn't think so. She thinks Celeste is a changeling...that becomes a dragon."

Thomas scoffed. "That tiny little woman is the dragon?"

"It would explain why Gwendolyn wants her so much."

"Do you believe it?"

"I think we need to be sure. If Celeste is still alive, we haven't completed our quest."

Thomas shook his head and walked away, then turned back. "Four more years of trudging through the snow because the witch thinks that dragon is a woman?"

"Not this time. We're bringing the witch with us to help us find her."

"She'll help us find the girl she hid from us all this time?"

"She was hiding her from Gwendolyn, not the king. The king wants her back personally. She'll help us if I assure the girl's safety."

"Does the king assure her safety?"

"The king will do what he will. I promised to keep the girl safe from Gwendolyn."

Thomas laughed with a smirk. "This sounds insane!"

Sighurd looked him pointedly in the eye. "Will you come with us?"

His face became somber. "I'm the King's Guard. If you order me, I'll go."

"We're still under the same orders from four years ago, until we verify that Celeste is really dead."

"How soon do we leave?"

"Immediately."

Sighurd left and headed for his own quarters to prepare for the journey. Eloise intercepted him on the way.

"I need to get my chest of scrolls," she said. "or I'm just a useless village witch again."

"That's the plan," he said.

"That means I need my necklace back."

"I assume Gwendolyn has it," he said. "I'm not going to confront her over a piece of jewelry."

"I need it to deactivate the trap I set, or I can't get to my chest."

"This is bad timing, Eloise. I defied her to save you, and she defied me by releasing those two guards from the dungeon. Things are pretty fragile between us right now."

"If I don't deactivate it with my necklace, it'll poison us."

"Can't you cast a spell to make it go away? Or do you always leave poisonous traps lying around after you're done with them?"

"Yes, I can cast a spell to make it go away," she snarled. "Right after I use the necklace to get the scroll out and read it. I don't memorize every spell."

He shook his head and sighed. "Wait here."

Sighurd stood before Gwendolyn's door, glancing at Bernard as he sat ubiquitously in his chair in the hallway so he could jump whenever she shouted for him. The man disgusted him with how fawning he was toward her.

Bernard gave him a cold look. "You don't want to talk to her now."

Sighurd cast a dark glare at him and knocked.

"Come!" she shouted from inside.

He opened it and found her bustling about, throwing things into a pack. A sword in a scabbard lay on her table. When she saw who it was, her eyes narrowed. "Have you come to apologize for stealing my prisoner and almost getting me killed?"

"Eloise had a necklace. She wants it back. I assume, since you stripped her naked, you have it."

"I don't have time for this."

He walked further in. "She wants it back."

"Why?"

"It's a...it has sentimental value."

"Either she's a bad liar or you are. She wants it because it's not a necklace. It's an amulet." She paused her activity to look at him. "Now why should I hand over a magical amulet to my enemy without knowing what she can do to me with it?"

He didn't bother with another feeble lie. "She needs to open a magical trap."

She froze for a moment, deliberating, then returned to her bustling. "It's over on my worktable. A silver chain with a crescent moon."

He paused to slide his fingers across the scabbard. Where was she going? And what by all the demons did she need a sword for? And why was it so easy to get the necklace?

"Give her my regards," she said without looking at him.

He grabbed the necklace and walked out the door feeling uneasy. What was she up to?

Curse that man! Gwendolyn thought as he marched out of her chamber with the necklace.

A part of her worried what Eloise had stashed behind a magical trap. Any other time she'd be keenly interested in finding out. But there was no time to deal with that now. All that mattered now was getting to Celeste and Edmund before anyone else.

After that, Eloise could do whatever she wanted, for all the good it would do her.

Sighurd found Christian out in the courtyard practicing his archery. The king had excellent grouping that veered only slightly from the bullseye. He waited until Christian shot the arrow already nocked in his bow. "You sent for me?"

Christian pulled another arrow out and nocked it. "Who are you loyal to, Sighurd?"

That question again? "To you, Your Majesty."

He shot the arrow dead center. "Why is it that I seem to be the only one who doesn't know what's going on in my kingdom?" He dropped the bow on the ground and pulled Sighurd away from the servants around him.

"I hear shocking stories of Gwendolyn calling the Beast, feeding children to it, hiding in a magical shell while it and the dragon attack her all night. I hear you stole her prisoner from her so she wouldn't be killed—after you promised me Gwendolyn would take care of that for us. I hear you banished your own guardsmen to the dungeon, but she released them and hired them as her servants. I hear she's heading off somewhere on some Gods-cursed chase, and that you're about to leave the city with your own men, those spies from Insu, *and* the prisoner I wanted dead."

He glared into Sighurd's eyes. "I learned all this while enjoying a pleasant meal after a good night's sleep because I thought all was well. What in the name of the Gods is going on in my castle?"

"My apologies, Your Majesty. I intended to tell you, but things have been happening quickly this morning." The first lie he'd ever told his king.

"What things?"

"It appears reports of Celeste's death may have been premature. I convinced the witch to help us find her. I promised to keep her and the girl safe."

"Keep them safe?"

"From Gwendolyn. I said nothing about your wishes." Another lie. "Also, the witch claims to have a stash of magic hidden away. She promised, if we retrieve it, she'll help us against Gwendolyn."

Christian knotted his brow. "You believe all this?"

"I think we need to verify if it's true. That's why *we're* leaving. I can't speak for Gwendolyn. I have no idea what she's doing."

Christian glanced around. "Listen to me, Sighurd. If you find the girl, I want her dead. If you find this stash of magic is a lie, I want the witch dead. If she does anything to betray us, I want her dead. Do it yourself—immediately. I want this over and done with!"

"As you command," Sighurd said with a bow and left, counting three lies he'd told his king for the first time in his life. His only consolation was that the lies were the mildest of his treasonous acts.

He couldn't wait to get out of the city.

Each of them rode horses from the royal stables, Sighurd, Kasimir, Faisal, Eloise, Dietric, and Thomas. They talked about visiting Edmund's cabin first, since it was more or less on the way to Eloise's cottage. "Maybe he knows where Celeste is," Dietric said. "If they're connected as changelings, maybe they're together."

Eloise was anxious to get to her chest before someone else stumbled upon it, but she had to agree that was a possibility.

Thomas said, "By the time we get there, it'll be after sunset. There's a full moon again tonight."

"We'll need to camp overnight," said Sighurd. "I want to find the man, not the Beast."

They camped several miles away from the cabin along the creek that flowed past it. They were somber that evening before they went to sleep, huddled in the oppressive forest with the moon looking ominously down from above. Their conversation focused on what the Beast and the dragon might be doing right now, where they might be, how close they might be. For the first time in her life, the face of Mistress Moon looked foreboding to Eloise rather than comforting. She expected to hear a howl or see a massive silhouette fly above them.

In the night Eloise awoke, having to relieve herself. Thomas stood watch, or at least sat watch by the fire. The rest of the men slept soundly.

"Eloise?" Thomas said.

"Have you seen anything?"

He shook his head. "I feel like the night Hereward first changed."

"I'm sorry about what happened to him."

He nodded. "Why are you awake?"

She smiled as she looked at the sleeping men. "I hate how you young people can sleep through the night without visiting the trees."

He smiled back. "Be careful."

She headed for the creek and picked her way along the bank until she found an open spot that was sufficiently secluded from the camp. As she arranged her clothing, she thought she heard a rustling in the forest. She spoke a breath spell of Protection and prayed to Mother Goddess that it was nothing more threatening than a deer.

She squatted, the hair on her skin prickling the whole time. She cast a Sight spell and looked around. To her horror she saw a dark aura in the trees creeping silently toward her. She stopped her flow prematurely and stood to adjust her clothing back into place.

A bright glow above caught her Sight's eye, nowhere near the moon. She looked up and gasped. The dragon slid silently through the sky as a luminous being. It circled around and gazed at her, then descended and lit on the ground on the other side of the creek, facing her.

Eloise froze in dread as its neck reached over the creek. Its snout came within a couple feet of her face, and its eyes studied her as it cocked its head back and forth.

But the dragon showed no sign of menace. Eloise looked deep into its silvery eyes. "Celeste?" she said softly.

The dragon's eyes flinched.

She carefully extended her hand and brushed the side of its snout—*her* snout. "Sweet Celeste," she murmured. "What a magnificent creature you are."

The dragon closed her eyes and nuzzled her snout into the hand.

The Beast crept out of the trees, its head low and its eyes burning. Eloise suppressed her fear as much as she could and stood perfectly still.

The dragon's head swung over to the wolf and nuzzled its snout. The burning red glow in the Beast's eyes softened to a warmth as it nuzzled back. The dragon returned to Eloise and let her stroke her head. The Beast watched, then crept up to Eloise and lowered its head. She gingerly reached her other hand out and scratched it behind the ears. "Edmund?"

The Beast's tongue lolled happily as it panted.

"Why, you're just a little puppy dog," she said softly, "when you're not enraged."

The dragon raised her head and gave off an exultant cry, then flapped her wings and rose into the air. The Beast yelped gleefully and scampered off after her. The horses in the camp whinnied with alarm.

Eloise fell back onto the ground, propping herself up with one arm, panting to catch her breath and calm her spinning head. Thomas rushed along the creek to her with sword raised. "What was that?" The rest of the men followed behind him. Thomas helped her to her feet.

"It's nothing," she said. "I saw the dragon fly by and the Beast running after her. They didn't seem to notice me."

"Her?" said Faisal.

"Celeste," she said. "She and the Beast *do* stay together."

Kasimir uttered a spell and looked in the sky. "I see her." The dragon glow sailed north, getting further away. "I think the incident has passed. Let's get back to sleep."

They returned to their bedding. Dietric took over guard duty. He sat at the fire, but kept his sword stuck in the ground, ready to grab.

Eloise settled in, lying on her back and gazing at the moon. "See you in the morning, Celeste," she whispered.

At daybreak they ate a hasty breakfast and quickly packed. Kasimir said a simple, "Let's go."

They approached the cabin carefully. Eloise expected to see Celeste and Edmund there, having seen them together in their changeling state so near. She approached with excitement. The others were more apprehensive.

The cabin looked eerily familiar, just as Zenia had described it from Tamara's story. The garden, the unusually large pile of chopped wood for one man, especially for the summer, the axe propped up against it, the creek babbling nearby. It was as if a dream had come to life.

They dismounted. Kasimir knocked, but no one responded. He looked at the rest of them.

"Mother Goddess, just open it!" Eloise said. Her nerves couldn't take any more waiting.

He creaked the door open and peered in. "Edmund?"

He turned back. "No one's there."

Eloise let out a sigh of frustration and pushed past him. The cabin was empty.

"There's no telling where they may have changed back," Sighurd said. "They may have a long walk ahead of them."

"We wait here," Eloise said.

She and Kasimir sat in the only two chairs, Dietric and Thomas on the bed, and Sighurd and Faisal on the floor leaning against a wall. They waited, with little to say to each other.

They waited, perking up at any forest noise that might be someone or something approaching.

They waited as Eloise became more and more agitated. "It's been at least two hours," she said. "Maybe they went to my cottage."

Sighurd stood. "We'll go there. We can return here on the way back."

"Before dark, I hope," said Thomas.

Chapter 21

Edmund

The Forest Girl awoke with her stomach growling. There was a thunderous noise behind her and the sight of Edmund lying naked before her. His eyes were still closed. He was beautiful to her with his severe black hair and beard and his powerful muscles.

She scooted across the grass of the clearing and lay next to him, then began gently caressing his arm with the tips of her fingers.

Why do I love you so much? she thought.

It's I who loves him, said the voice inside her.

Who are you?

You call me the Girl Inside.

Memories came to her of the voice teaching her things. Why did she have a girl inside? *Do you remember my name?*

I don't remember my own name.

Edmund stirred, opened his eyes, and smiled. Suddenly he jerked to a sitting position. "I saw it. You're not a wolf."

She remembered him saying that right before she changed. "What am I?"

"Well..." He seemed hesitant to say. "I only had an instant to see, but you became something large with huge wings and sharp teeth and white scales for skin."

She peered at him in shock.

"I swear you looked like...a dragon."

"*What?*"

"A beautiful white dragon."

She was speechless. "Are you mocking me again?" she finally said.

"Gods, why would I do that? I swear it's true."

"But why a dragon? Was I attacked by a dragon once?"

"You don't have scars from any kind of attack."

She remembered Mother talking about dragons, but only in stories of fanciful creatures and monsters. Mother's stories of gigantic dragons with deadly weapons of breath frightened her, and she'd cried, "Will a dragon come and destroy us?"

"No, Celeste," Mother had laughed. "Dragons are no more real than the fairies and goblins in the stories."

She looked at Edmund in surprise. "My name is Celeste," she whispered.

Yes, that's your name! the Girl Inside said.

"What did you say?" Edmund said.

"My name is Celeste," she answered loudly and grabbed him in a fierce embrace. "My name is Celeste, and I love you."

They kissed passionately. He lay back down and drew her onto him. It was strange and thrilling to love him in the open where someone could see them, feeling the moist wind waft over her naked back and buttocks. It enhanced the intensity of her experience.

Mother had always given her warm and affectionate love. Edmund gave her a love that burned with fire and caused her to cry out with its ferocity. It seemed absurd to call those two things by the same word.

They lay pressed together with the sun warming their skin, Celeste rubbing her fingers through the hair on his chest. She tried to imagine her dainty hand as a great dragon appendage with vicious claws. "How many people do you think I've killed?"

He squeezed her tight. "It's not your fault. You never asked for this any more than I did."

"Do you think we killed last night?"

"The reason I live in the forest is to avoid people I might end up killing."

"Edmund, I need to know."

"It does no good. There's nothing you can do."

She gave him a long and luxurious kiss, then peered deeply into his eyes. "We could kill ourselves."

He shook his head. "There was a time I thought of doing that."

"Why didn't you?"

His eyes unfocused as he gazed off into the distance. His face seemed wistful, but sad. "Someone asked me not to." His attention returned to her. "And anyway, I learned to control it, and...I'm afraid of what might happen to me if I did kill myself."

"Won't you kneel before Mother Goddess?"

"Well, Father Sky for men, but..." His face clouded and dropped. "I'm afraid the Gods will condemn me for the people I've killed."

"You told me it wasn't our fault."

He grinned wide, obviously forced. "Yes, you're right. It's not."

"Wouldn't the Gods bless us for doing it to spare the lives of others?"

"I don't know," he said softly.

She studied his face. His eyes were filled with a deep sadness. "Edmund," she spoke gently, "if I'm killing people, I don't want to live."

His forced smile returned. "Somehow, my love, I don't think you've killed anyone."

"How can you say that?"

"You're too sweet and innocent. I can't imagine you killing anyone."

"I can't imagine *you* killing anyone! You're not an evil man. But you say you have."

"Out here in the forest, we probably never found anyone to kill last night."

"Don't treat me like a child. I know you're trying to make me feel better, but I don't want to feel better. I want to know the truth."

"And if you learn you've killed someone?"

"Then I want to die."

"But Celeste," he said as he stroked her hair, "*I* don't want you to die."

His touch was soothing and pleasant. His words warmed her heart as the breeze cooled her body. The thunderous noise soothed her soul.

"Celeste," he said contemplatively. "That's a beautiful name. Even more beautiful than Tamara."

That's my name! cried the Girl Inside, startling her.

"What?" she said.

"I said your name is—"

"Not you." *Your name is Tamara?*

Yes!

Tamara—that's my real mother's name.

Yes, and Mother's name who raised you is Eloise. I remember.

Are you my real mother?

The Girl Inside didn't respond at first. Finally she said, *I was a mother, before I died. A woman cut me, and I bled to death as my baby suckled.*

The story Mother had told her! *You* are *my mother, and that woman was named Zenia.*

Yes, Zenia. Beloved Zenia, said the Girl.

"Celeste?" Edmund asked with concern.

Her eyes focused on him. "Who is Tamara to you?"

"She was the one who came to me, the one I loved, but had to send away."

"You were the woodsman she found when she fled into the forest."

"I suppose so."

"Tamara was my real mother."

His eyes widened in shock.

"You're my father," she said as her head spun with emotion.

He leaped to his feet. "Your my... Great Gods!" He studied her. "No wonder you look so much like..."

Her emotions thundered in her ears. But no, it was the thunderous noise she kept hearing since she woke. "What is that?" She stood up and peered around.

Behind her she saw a wide river coming to a gash in the ground and rushing over it with a thunderous roar. "I know this place!" She marched to the edge and gazed at the massive flood of water pouring into the chasm, at the thick mist rising up from below.

Edmund came up beside her. Images flooded into her brain like the water flooding into the chasm.

"I jumped over this cliff," she said breathlessly. "I jumped over it, and...the next thing I knew, I woke up next to you."

"This must be where it happened. The stress caused your first Change." He gazed at her with concern. "Thank the Gods you *weren't* a wolf. You'd have died."

"I tried to die." She walked over to the spot where she once stood. "Gwendolyn's soldiers had me trapped over here against the cliff." She pointed. "They stood *here*...and *here*...and..." The images of that night overwhelmed her. The glittering black man dismounted his horse and stood before her, coaxing her to come with him.

"Two of them were black," she said, "and one of them had gems on his face."

"I've seen these men!" he cried. "They came to my cabin not two days ago."

"They wanted to bring me to the sorceress Gwendolyn, but I wouldn't let them. I jumped." The night played vividly before her. "There were three others, and one of them... Oh dear Goddess!"

She turned to where the one man had been and saw a fresh mound of earth. Next to it was a huge dark stain of brown. She gasped with her hand to her mouth. "Oh, my dear Mother Goddess, that's his blood!"

Edmund looked where she was facing. "What is that?" he said ominously.

"They must...they must have...buried..." She could hardly breathe. "That's the man the Beast..."

She saw again the enormous monster charge the man, its eyes blazing a devilish red, its fangs bared with saliva dripping. The man turned into another Beast. The two battled until one of them killed the other.

The man must be the one buried there, because Edmund was still alive. She looked at him, panting heavily. "The Beast...the Beast killed... *You*...you killed..."

As she stared at his face, it seemed to transform into the face of the Beast, mouth extended into a threatening snout with deadly fangs, eyes burning hellishly red.

Terror gripped her. She shrieked and bolted.

"Celeste!" Edmund cried after her.

She ran feverishly until she reached a creek...*the* creek she played in all her life, that she followed to the river on the mare that night—just two nights ago. She ran along its bank, ignoring her gnawing stomach, ignoring the burning in her bare and vulnerable feet as they pounded on the forest floor.

She ran and ran and ran. Her energy drained from her, but she had to keep going. All she could think of was home. *I must get home!*

She forced her feet forward when all her body wanted to do was lie down and sleep for an eternity. Her feet left prints of blood on the forest floor. Her naked body was covered with scratches from clawing branches as she fled.

After an endless time, she was about ready to collapse from exhaustion. She came to the pool and waterfall. The sight of it reassured her. She plunged through the pool. Its cold water soothed her stinging soles and washed the grit from her wounds. She pushed all her remaining energy into running down the trail. The dirt stung her feet all over again.

She exhausted her last ounce of energy as she reached the cottage and flung herself against the door with a loud thud. Her feet ached and her lungs pumped with a searing pain for air.

When she recovered enough to move, she flung the door open to dash in, but froze in place with a scream.

"Hello, Celeste."

The woman planted a hand over her mouth and dragged her inside.

Edmund ran after Celeste as fast as he could, but she was light and swift. His muscles were powerful after all the wood chopping and hunting he'd done over the centuries, but his bulk slowed him down. He could see her as she ran along the river to the creek and dashed along its bank until she plunged into the forest.

He feared he'd lose her. But he realized he could still sense her, as he had been able to sense other changelings in his past. But never before at such a great distance. She was like no changeling he'd encountered before. Perhaps because she was his...

No! He couldn't think about that right now.

He considered becoming the wolf who could catch up to her quickly, but in that changed state he'd have no control over his behavior, and he feared what he might do. She'd be no dragon then, but a helpless, fragile girl.

He noticed faint footprints of blood on the ground, which confirmed that his sense of her location was real, but pained him that she was tearing up her feet.

Why did she flee? She remembered the night of her first Change and said she saw the Beast kill a man. But she must know he'd never harm her as a man. Her vivid memories of the Beast attacking that soldier must have traumatized her. Abstractly she already understood he was that monster, but when her memories returned and she relived that moment, then looked at him—what terror must she have felt? It made him wish all the more he could catch up to her and hold her in a comforting embrace. Yet he was probably the last person she wanted comfort from right now.

He tried hard to push away the thought that he'd made love to his own daughter. Never in his life had he done such a depraved thing. But how could he have known? The only woman he'd loved for ages was five years ago when Tamara appeared in the woods, almost as if a gift from the Gods. Any child from that union couldn't possibly be as old as Celeste.

The bloody footprints continued all the way to the little waterfall, becoming more pronounced as she ran. They headed into the pool and disappeared. He thanked the Gods she had gone where he hoped. His arrival might only traumatize her more, but he had to make sure she was alright.

He rushed down the path to the clearing and bellowed, "Celeste!" He ran around the cottage and checked the perimeter of the trees to make sure she wasn't hiding outside. "Celeste! Where are you?"

He ran to the cottage door and swung it open. "Celeste!"

He was greeted with two sword points inches from his chest. He backed off, and two soldierly men advanced on him.

"Where's Celeste?" he snarled.

"Lie down on your stomach!" one of them ordered.

Centuries of turmoil, anguish, and wrath welled up inside him. His body tingled all over, and the all too familiar sickness in his stomach throbbed. He felt his eyes burning. For two hundred years he fought these sensations each sundown of a full moon night, but this time he let the feelings flow through him.

A fog of illumination formed around him, and just before he blacked out, he saw the two men fall back in horror.

Eloise led the way through the forest along the banks of the creek that flowed past Edmund's cabin. She was almost certain it was the same creek she and Celeste visited practically every day, and following it would be faster than picking their way through the trees to her cottage.

They reached the waterfall, and she led them down the path, past the hill, and around it to the stump. Standing before it, she pulled the chain of her crescent moon amulet over her head and said with a grin, "Now, Sighurd, you'll be glad I made you get this."

She stooped down before the hole in the stump and inserted the moon into the darkness, then put the chain back over her head. She reached into the hole, eager to feel her chest once again and know her Ancient Magic was safe in her hands.

The hole was empty.

She fell back onto the ground in a daze. "Oh dear Goddess, no!" Tears formed in her eyes.

"Eloise?" Kasimir took her hand and lifted her to her feet.

"How can it be gone? The Truth Dream didn't trigger." She swung her eyes about in a desperate attempt to find an answer. "I'm afraid I'm of no use to the quest. I'm nothing more than a village witch again."

"Who took it?" Sighurd said indignantly.

"Only one person beside Celeste knew I had it." Her eyes squinted with a cold anger. "Deirdre. I pray she didn't find Celeste too."

"Could Celeste have taken the chest?" Kasimir asked.

"Not without her moon necklace."

Kasimir cringed as he said, "I'm afraid that was destroyed."

She shot a grim scowl at him.

"You're still essential to the quest. You'll help us find Celeste."

"You don't understand what I had in that chest."

"I understand what *I* have!" he said forcefully and touched a gem on his face.

She peered at them, studying the reflections in their facets. "Alright, Wizard, tell us. What *do* you have?"

Kasimir glanced at Faisal, who watched gloomily. "We call them starstones. Our master wizards infuse them with the power of the stars of Mabut—of Father Sky. I can cast powerful spells with them."

The power of the stars? For a moment she forgot her despair as her professional curiosity got hold of her. She lifted a finger. "May I?"

He nodded. She touched one. It only felt like a gem. "Do you recite specific words for each spell?"

"I tell the stone what I want it to do, in the ancient language of the wizards."

"It'll do anything you ask it to do?"

"If it has the power to do so."

"How do you know if it doesn't have the power?"

"The spell fails, and I've wasted a starstone."

What a fascinating concept, she thought. She wondered if their own Ancient Tongue could be so versatile with spells. She'd pieced together portions from different spells to design variations on them. She wondered if she could create her own spell whole cloth, then wondered how dangerous experimenting like that would be.

"Thank the Goddess you decided to join with us," she said. "Without you, we'd stand little chance against Gwendolyn."

"Is your cottage nearby?" Sighurd said.

"There's food and water too," Eloise said. "We can refresh ourselves. Just a little further down the trail."

Kasimir went ahead with the rest following.

Edmund sat on the ground in a daze with his back to the decimated remains scattered between him and the cottage. Movement caught his eye, and he looked toward the forest where the trail exited. His head cleared as he saw the black man with the gems emerge from the trees. Behind him came the rest of the men that had recently visited him.

All but one. The one he must have killed as the wolf.

"You!" he growled. The anger arose in him again. He stood up, feeling the sensations of the wolf coming. "I should have killed you when I met you."

The men stopped warily and drew their swords. Edmund crept toward them as his body tingled.

"Edmund, we come in peace," Kasimir said.

The glow began to form around him.

A woman ran out from behind the men, waving her arms and shouting, "Wait! Wait!"

The interruption broke his concentration. The glow faded, and the sensations of Change ebbed.

"They're here to help me get Celeste back."

That inflamed his anger more. "They tried to capture her and bring her to Gwendolyn!"

"They understand now that she deceived them."

"Celeste tried to kill herself because of them."

"I know, I know," she said soothingly as she approached. "But she survived... thanks to you being her father."

Her tone and her words calmed him against his will. "You know about that?"

"I had a strong suspicion."

"Who are you?"

"I'm Eloise...Celeste's mother." She pointed to the cottage. "I raised her here."

He looked back, saw the remains again, and felt regret return. "They tried to take me prisoner."

"Who were they?" said Sighurd.

"I don't know."

Sighurd walked over to the remains and examined them. "You did a thorough job. I can't recognize them. I don't see any official markings on the clothing either."

"Any guesses?" Eloise said.

"They could be from Scaendelreic," Sighurd said. "They could be from Luteche. They could have been here for Celeste. They could have been here for the Beast. They could have been opportunistic renegades holing up in an empty cottage."

"Edmund," Eloise said, "do you know where Celeste is?"

"She ran from me. I thought she'd come here, but all I found were *them*." He pointed to the remains.

Sighurd said, "I don't understand. You came here in the night as the Beast?"

Edmund studied Sighurd, hesitating to tell them. He knew from experience how they'd react. But he shook his head and said, "They pointed their swords at me and provoked the Change."

"You can change into the Beast in daylight?" Thomas cried, holding up his sword.

"I can change whenever I want, day or night." Seeing their concerned expressions, he added more gently, "But I never want to."

Thomas pointed at the remains with his sword. "You must have wanted to *this* time."

That was too much for him. "I will not stand here and be interrogated! You're the ones who tried to capture Celeste."

"He's too dangerous," Thomas said. "We should slay him now."

"And provoke the Change again?" Sighurd said.

"Kasimir can use a starstone to soften *his* curse," Dietric said, "then he can control it."

"I can control it just fine," Edmund said gruffly and locked eyes with Thomas. "Unless I'm provoked too much."

Eloise shook her head. "No wonder the Seven Sisters wouldn't share their magic with men. The issue right now is finding Celeste."

Kasimir sighed. "I'd hoped we would find her and you together and save a starstone. Let me search." He walked a few steps away, then opened his shirt to reveal more gems on his chest. He twisted one until it came loose. Blood oozed out, and he dipped the gem into it.

Edmund watched with amazement as the gem glowed as if a tiny sun were inside it. Kasimir spoke incomprehensible words. The shining star seemed to encompass him, then flash away. He gazed out with wide and glassy eyes and slowly rotated in a circle as if examining the eternities. Only the Gods knew what he could see.

When he faced east, he stopped and stared. "I see something."

Eloise spoke other unknown words and looked, but she seemed disappointed. "What do you see?"

"A glow, just above the horizon, barely noticeable. A glow like Celeste's glow. Like the dragon's."

"Can you tell where?"

"Somewhere in Suedeche, I believe."

Her face lit up with hope. "Suedeche? Deirdre wouldn't take her there."

"Would Celeste have a reason to go there?" Sighurd asked.

She grinned wide. "Her mother's home. Both her mothers' home, Tamara and I." She turned to the others, her face alight with excitement. "Pull all you want out of the garden. Fill your bellies and your packs. Take all you want. I won't be coming back here anymore."

She took several steps eastward, gazing out with affection. "We're coming, Celeste. We're coming home to Suedeche."

———

The moment Deirdre arrived at her tower, she set the scrying globe back on its perch and caressed it warmly. After all these years, it was back where it belonged. But she only spent a moment indulging her emotions. She was tired of being blind, and she wanted to look out into the world.

Of immediate concern was Gwendolyn and the wizard from Insu, now that the girl was dead. They were the things that threatened the precarious peace the Seven Sisters had preserved in the North—discounting the minor wars they instigated. Their plans were ambitious—creating a peaceful empire throughout the continent of Cueldea, grander than the Onotrian Empire, free of conflict under the rule of female sorceresses. It's what the original Seven Sisters had hoped to accomplish.

And she and her sisters were well on their way to achieving it. They were in the process of making their first move with the war on Gallea, one of the largest kingdoms without a sorceress of the Seven Sisters, when Gwendolyn came on the scene and disrupted the balance of power.

Now the Southern Wizards had come to Cueldea, disrupting the balance even more. Perhaps they came under the pretense of helping Gwendolyn, but Deirdre knew what their ulterior agenda had to be.

She stood before the perch of the globe, intentionally high so she couldn't sit while using it for hours and become drowsy. She gazed into the globe and searched for the wizard.

She wasn't sure she'd find him. If he were in Luteche reporting his failure to Gwendolyn, the Masking spell surrounding the castle would hide him. Perhaps Gwendolyn would be angry enough to kill him, although it was unlikely she'd be so careless as to cause such a serious diplomatic incident.

Or maybe Deirdre would find him traveling back to Insu after being banished for his failure.

Instead she found him traveling on the East Highway accompanied by his black companion and the three men that were with him when Celeste died.

And—to her disbelief and irritation—the thief accompanied him.

But her irritation quickly dissolved into a malevolent satisfaction as she realized they probably brought the thief with them to retrieve Deirdre's treasure. "I can't wait to see the look on your face, Thief," she murmured. They wouldn't reach the trap until well after dark, so Deirdre decided to return to them later.

She looked next for Gwendolyn, also unlikely to find since she was probably ensconced in her chambers behind the Masking spell. To her surprise, she found her riding east also, and well ahead of the wizard, accompanied by two men she didn't recognize.

What was so compelling about heading east, that everyone was traveling there? Deirdre traced the East Highway all the way to the border of Suedeche, searching for any reason, and found nothing.

But across the border in a little village along the outskirts of Suedeche, she spotted a glow of aura that looked very much like the dead girl's aura.

How could she have survived that fall?

In the daylight, her aura didn't reach to the moon like a beacon for all to see. It huddled around her on the ground where it was harder to notice. She focused in on the aura. It radiated from within a simple cottage. She slipped inside and found the recognizable trappings of a village witch and three women conversing. Two of them looked like normal peasants. But the third one was dressed in a white silk robe with a hood pulled back—the exact description of the clothing of the Seven Sisters of old, who promised they'd send one of their own back one day. She was the one who radiated the aura.

A Pilgrim of the Mother Goddess.

As Deirdre gazed into the globe with astonishment, the Pilgrim's head jerked up as if startled. She turned her face toward Deirdre and gazed directly into her eyes.

Deirdre jumped back from the globe, a chill running down her spine. The Pilgrim had caught her spying on her.

But even more shocking, Deirdre recognized the face. Her wrinkles of age were smoothed out. Her hair was a vibrant color with none of the streaks of grey. But Deirdre still recognized her.

It was Queen Tamara's servant. The one who had spirited her out of the castle, who had delivered her baby and sacrificed her to purify the baby. The one who had fallen in a meadow and been captured by Gwendolyn, presumably to be tortured to death.

Now sitting very much alive in a witch's cottage in a village in Suedeche, wearing the robe and emanating the aura of a Pilgrim of Mother Goddess.

Deirdre sat back on a chair breathlessly, needing to think. What did it all mean? The servant must have died and returned as a Pilgrim—but why? Is this why everyone traveled east? A pilgrimage to meet the new incarnation of one of the original Seven Sisters?

She cursed the thief once more for having stolen her globe and keeping her blind to so much going on in the world.

This was something she had to monitor carefully. The current Seven Sisters relied on their claim of being successors to the original demigods to maintain their authority, but in reality they were glad no demigods were around today to interfere with their plans. Deep down all of them knew they were a kind of usurper, pretending they were successors to the real ones when their only true power was to possess remnants of the Ancient Magic the Seven Sisters of old had taken from the world. Deirdre wasn't sure what it could mean to her and her Sisters to have one of their kind back on earth. This was a vastly greater wild card than Gwendolyn could ever be.

This was also something she should inform the Seven Sisters about. But not just yet. She needed to find out why the Pilgrim was here and why the others traveled to meet her.

And she was in no hurry to relinquish her advantage to those other six hags.

Chapter 22

The Great Hall

The loud thud on the door startled Ismael and Audric, but Gwendolyn had been watching with Sight and knew it was Celeste falling against it in exhaustion. She leaped up from her chair and waited, facing the door. She could hear Celeste's heavy breathing.

When the door opened, Gwendolyn said, "Hello, Celeste," with a deep satisfaction and planted her hand across her mouth. She dragged Celeste inside and flung her to the floor. The girl immediately began a Flash spell, but Gwendolyn threw a globe on the floor next to her. The vapor put her to sleep before she could finish it.

She peered down at Celeste lying naked and wrinkled her nose in disgust. "Get one of those shifts over there," she commanded Audric.

She noticed her scratches and bloody feet and spoke a Healing spell. As it worked to close her wounds, Audric returned with the shift. Gwendolyn slid it over Celeste's head and worked it down her body. There was little chance of waking her. Gwendolyn used a sleep vapor more powerful than any village witch knew how to concoct.

"Tie her and gag her," she ordered. Audric and Ismael bound her hands behind her back and tightened a gag around her head.

With her Sight, Gwendolyn could see Celeste's father rushing toward them in his slower gait. To see him running through the forest with his manhood flopping about as if he were still a wild beast disgusted her even more than Celeste's nakedness. His eyes burned with as much ferocity as the Beast's eyes staring at her through her protective bubble. It disturbed her. She wanted to be gone before he arrived.

She ordered Ismael and Audric to wait for him and capture him, emphasizing once more that she needed him alive at all costs, then immediately left with Celeste. Let the men trained for combat handle him.

She mounted her horse and rode through the forest to the East Highway, clinging to unconscious Celeste sitting in front of her. The ride back to Luteche was the most vulnerable part of this journey. She'd tried to bring some of the King's Guard with her for protection, but that accursed Sighurd had forbidden them to obey her orders without his approval, so she had to rely on breath spells and the sword she brought to neutralize any threats. She was no swordmaster, but she'd handled one enough times in her youth to be able to whack someone a time or two. She'd never win a swordfight, but she only needed to deflect a threat long enough to dash past it and flee for the castle.

Bernard had suggested hiring ruffians from the city as bodyguards. She smirked at that. There was no time to recruit them, she didn't want word getting out what she was doing, plus those unsavory types could pose a greater danger than any threats on the road. Her best defense was to drive the horse swiftly to the castle without anyone knowing she was out there.

They reached the highway where the horse could break into a full gallop. She kept a sharp lookout ahead with her Sight, scouring for any encounter best avoided, ready to duck into the cover of trees if necessary.

Celeste's sleep was deep, but after miles of a pounding gallop along the highway, she began to rouse. Gwendolyn thought of casting a breath spell of Sleep on her, but that wouldn't last more than a few seconds with their bouncing ride, and it didn't matter anyway. The girl was bound and gagged and could muster no more power than any young woman.

Celeste looked around groggily, gathering her bearings, then began to squirm. She was surprisingly tenacious for such a petite woman. Gwendolyn had to grip tight to keep her from falling off. "If you fall, you could die," she warned her.

That seemed to calm her, thank the Gods. Gwendolyn's arm would have been aching by the time they reached Luteche if she had to clamp down on her the whole time.

Suddenly the horse slowed to a stop and wandered over to the edge of the highway where it began to munch on grass. What in the name of the Gods? This was a steed of the king, trained to obey its rider under the pandemonium of battle, yet no matter how hard Gwendolyn tugged at the reins and kicked it in its sides, it refused to go, and merely circled around in place, whinnying in protest.

Something crashed through the forest. A huge moose charged out of the trees and headed down the middle of the highway directly for them. Gwendolyn yanked and yanked on the reins, but the horse only pranced in place and waited for the moose to butt them in spite of its agitation.

Gwendolyn struggled to pull the sword out of the scabbard, digging her heels deep into the sides of the horse for support and clinging tightly to Celeste. The moose landed a partial blow on the horse's flank. The horse neighed in fear. When the moose charged again, Gwendolyn swung the blade down on its head. The moose bellowed and stumbled, then rushed back into the forest with blood seeping from its scalp.

A flock of birds swarmed down from above and swept into Gwendolyn's face, one after another. She tried to bat them away with the sword and connected with a few of them. The horse complained and pranced in place as her control on the reins faltered. To keep from being thrown, she squeezed the sides of the horse with all the might in her legs and squeezed Celeste around her waist so tightly she could hear a faint grunt from her mouth through the gag.

After she bloodied enough birds, they flew off in a chorus of cackles. But she barely got a chance to catch her breath before large figures dashed through the trees toward them. A herd of deer pranced onto the highway in front of them and, one after another, lifted up on their hind feet and flailed with their forehooves before dropping back on all fours.

She pelted their legs with her sword, sometimes hitting them with the flat of the blade, sometimes gashing their flesh. Finally the deer backed off, then turned and fled.

Several foxes shot out onto the rode and nipped at the horse's legs. The poor creature broke into a panic and ran in the wrong direction on the highway. Gwendolyn clung tightly to its shanks and to Celeste with no hands available to grab the rein.

A hawk soared in from far above, claws outstretched, aiming right for her eyes. She barely managed to duck in time and nearly dropped the sword. The hawk circled around. She held the sword up high, ready to strike. The hawk dove down, and she slashed the blade into it. The blow vibrated through her arm. The hawk spun off the blade and plummeted to the ground in a heap of twitching feathers.

"How are you doing this?" she shouted to Celeste.

A black bear lunged into the road before them. The horse halted and reared high, winnowing loudly. She had to drop the sword and hang on to keep herself and Celeste from falling to the ground. The bear stood on its hind legs and roared with its sharp teeth glistening in the sunlight and its claws spread out menacingly.

Gwendolyn slid off the horse clutching Celeste. Once on the ground, the girl struggled hard to break free, but she clung tightly to her as she reached down and grabbed the sword. The bear dropped to its feet and charged them. She brandished the blade high above and gave out a threatening cry. The bear stopped and reared on its hind legs again, answering the cry with his own roar.

"Send him away, or I'll let him kill you!" she hissed into Celeste's ear. Even through the gag, Gwendolyn could make out the loud "*Ha!*" she said in response.

Celeste kicked her in the shins and squirmed her way free. Gwendolyn cried out and tried to grab her, knowing she'd flee deep into the forest while Gwendolyn fought off this animal, and she would lose her.

But Celeste ran for the bear and stood near its side, looking back at Gwendolyn. For an instant her heart jumped into her throat. The bear could swipe the life out of Celeste in one instant before she could do anything to save her.

But the bear kept roaring at Gwendolyn while the girl stood next to it with smug eyes.

In desperation Gwendolyn shouted a Flash spell, roared her own battle cry, and charged the bear, blade outstretched, as the bear batted at the sparks in his eyes. Celeste's eyes grew wide, and the bear dropped to attack.

Gwendolyn manage a stab in the bear's chest as it raked its claws across her arm. The bear bellowed and she cried out in pain. Its other paw slashed down, catching her face. The side near her right eye burned.

She drove the sword deep into the bear's abdomen. The creature howled with its snout raised to the sky, then toppled over, moaning and twitching while blood pooled on the highway.

Celeste gaped at the bear, then at Gwendolyn, then dashed toward the forest, hands still tied behind her back. Gwendolyn leaped into motion, chasing after her. The girl ran clumsily, not having her arms for balance. Not far into the forest, she stumbled and fell hard with no hands to break her fall. Gwendolyn rushed to her side and turned her over, hoping she wasn't badly injured. Her face was scraped with bits of grit embedded in her skin. Tears formed in her eyes.

Something flapped down from above, landed on Gwendolyn's head, and batted at her scalp with a sharp point. A Gods-cursed woodpecker! She swung the blade over her head, catching the body and dropping the bird to the ground. It screeched its agony as a wide gash on its wing oozed blood.

The shrill cry of a lynx came from above. Gwendolyn turned and found it perched in a low branch twenty feet away, glaring at her with its light brown eyes.

"Celeste, stop this!" she shouted as she readied her sword. "I'm bringing you back and nothing will stop me."

The lynx cried out and crept forward toward the edge of the branch.

"You're only forcing me to kill these poor animals."

A touch of sorrow formed in Celeste's eyes, but also grim resolve. She was as determined to escape as Gwendolyn was to keep her. "Gods curse you!" Gwendolyn said. "You brought me to this!"

She hesitated only an instant. The hilt of the sword came down on Celeste's head, knocking her out. The wound trickled blood.

The lynx pounced from its perch, hitting the ground and creeping forward as if stalking prey. Gwendolyn stood tall and flailed her arms, shouting, "Scat! Get out of here!"

The lynx backed up a step. She poked at it with the sword. It pranced back and forth, then scampered away with a cry.

Gwendolyn sheathed her sword and gently picked Celeste up. She carried her to the horse, which had not wandered much with its training finally kicking back in. She lay her down on the ground and wet a cloth from her water skin, then daubed at the trickle of blood on her head and the scratches on her face. "I'm sorry, little princess, but you gave me no choice." She wanted to cast a Healing spell, but was afraid that might bring her back to consciousness.

She lifted her up and placed her on the horse, then climbed up while keeping her from tipping over. It took some effort. Finally they were situated, and she spurred the horse down the highway.

Eyeing the sun low in the sky, Gwendolyn rode through the courtyard to the inner gatehouse and handed off the horse to the guards there. She didn't have much time before the girl would cease to be a girl.

The guards stared at her with concern. "Mistress, your face!"

In her haste, she'd ignored the stinging of her clawed arm and face until she forgot about it. With his words, the stinging returned full force. She touched her face and felt ragged flesh. Her hand came away bloody.

"I'll see to it," she said, and with Celeste flung over her shoulder, hurried inside, across the Great Hall, up the staircase, and into her chambers. She tied Celeste to a chair, tossed the sword and the empty scabbard on the bed, and began pulling things off the shelves she'd need for two spells.

Celeste stirred and moaned and opened her eyes. They remained unfocused for a moment, then peered up into Gwendolyn's face. She grimaced and looked about the room.

"I admire your determination," Gwendolyn said, "but it'll do you no good to summon any wild animals here. The guards will fight them off at the castle gate."

Tears pooled in her eyes.

"It pains me to do what I have to do, but I'm running out of time."

Celeste's brow knotted.

"I'm not going to explain why. It did no good explaining to Zenia or Eloise. I'll only say that I need your power to protect Cueldea from destruction."

Celeste said something hateful through the gag, but it was incomprehensible.

"I don't need your cooperation," Gwendolyn said as she crushed the materials for her first spell and poured oil on them. "I'll slit your throat and drink your blood as you die. Your power will seep into me as your mother's vitality seeped into you while she died. I only wish I could thank Zenia for purifying your power. I'll much prefer changing into a dragon than a wolf."

Celeste gave out an angry sob.

Gwendolyn cast the Healing spell while sitting at the table, then closed her eyes. The stinging magic spread across her arm and face and knitted the claw wounds together. She gazed at herself in a mirror and scowled at the lines of scars running down her temple and cheek, coming precariously close to her eye. She nearly lost that eye!

A black-and-red striped spider dropped down on a strand of web before her face. Gwendolyn gaped at it and reached for an empty jar. It was a rare kind useful for various spells. She brought the open jar up to capture it, but it dropped on the table, scampered to the edge, and leaped. She let out a cry as she brushed it off her clothes. Immediately a cockroach skittered across her table.

"What is this?" she said as she flicked it off.

She felt a pressure on her feet and tickling on her legs. She looked down and saw rats crawling over her shoes and more cockroaches climbing up under her clothing. She cried more forcefully and kicked the rats away and stomped her legs, trying to shake the cockroaches off.

Beetles, cockroaches, centipedes, ants swarmed up her body and over her clothes. Flies and gnats buzzed around her face. Bees and birds flew in through the window. The bees stung and the birds pecked.

Gwendolyn glared at Celeste, who glared back with shining eyes. Suddenly the rope on her hands dropped to the floor as two rats scurried down off the back of the chair.

Gwendolyn tried to shout a Flash spell, but a centipede crawled into her mouth, and she coughed and spat it out. Celeste yanked the gag from her mouth and shouted the Flash spell Gwendolyn couldn't finish. A burst of sparks sprayed around her face, blinding her. She moaned at the stinging pain and wiped at her eyes until she could open them.

Celeste stood in the middle of the room in the midst of an empty space untouched by bugs and rats with a triumphant look, holding the sword in both hands.

Gwendolyn twitched at the stings and bites that plagued her all over her body. The flood of insects and spiders nearly covered her as they scampered up to her neck. She began a Warding spell, but a beetle and spider invaded her mouth. She gagged and involuntarily swallowed them.

The door burst open. Bernard rushed in shouting, "Mistress, there are vermin all over—"

Celeste charged him with the sword pointed at him. It sunk deep into his belly. He cried out in anguish and fell back against the wall. "I'm sorry," she said as he slid to the floor, then put her foot against his chest and pulled the sword out. She rushed out the door.

Gwendolyn wiped the little monsters from her face and covered it with her hands as she spoke a spell of Warding around her. The vermin scrambled away, leaving a wide circle of empty space around her. She gathered up the materials for the Healing spell, then quickly headed to Bernard and cast it. The empty space stayed with her as bugs scurried away from the Warding.

He looked at her with eyes of pain and gratitude through his hard breathing as his wound healed. "Mistress," he said, "you're puffing up."

"I know." She ran to a flask of potion that counteracted the stings and poisons of small creatures. She took a deep draught and stoppered it and returned to Bernard. "Are you okay?"

He nodded. "There's still pain."

"There will be for a while." She kissed him on the forehead. "Dear, loyal Bernard." She helped him to his feet. "Celeste is free somewhere in the castle, and it's nearly moonrise."

The alarm in his eyes showed he understood.

As Celeste stood with the sword pointed at Gwendolyn, a rage welled up in her that she never felt before. She was about to charge the sorceress and start hacking when the door flew open and a man stood there. Celeste saw an opportunity and reflexively dashed with her sword out. The eyes of the man popped wide as he saw its point coming at him.

Before she could stop, before she could think, she drove the point into his belly. She instantly regretted it. "I'm sorry," she said as he slumped to the floor.

But he took the sword with him. Her survival instincts kicked back in, and she pushed on him with her foot so she could yank the sword out.

She bolted out of the room and found mayhem in the corridor as people tried to beat the creatures away she'd called from the dark recesses of the castle. They were beginning to thin, since she'd stopped calling them after the rats gnawed the rope off and freed her.

She looked left and right, wondering which way to go. Most of the people and mayhem was to the left, so she ran right. She rounded a couple turns, holding the sword out threateningly as she passed stray people, none of them soldiers, who fell back against the wall with alarm.

After the second turn, she came to the end of the corridor where a giant double door stood. She looked behind her and found no one pursuing her, but she didn't want to wait around until someone did. She tried the door, and the lever moved. Carefully she pushed the door open, cringing at its creaking, and peaked inside, ready to bolt if something threatening was inside.

A little boy sat on the floor playing with toy soldiers. He looked up at her in surprise.

She stepped in, closed the door, and slid the bolt into place.

"Who are you?" he said.

"I'm Celeste. Who are you?"

"I'm Guillaume, the prince."

She took a few tentative steps toward him and smiled. "I'm the princess."

His scowl said he didn't like that. "There's no princess. There's only me." He stood up and marched toward her. "My father is King Christian and my mother is Queen Tamara."

She crouched before him. "My mother's also Queen Tamara. We must be brother and sister."

His face lit up at that.

He's no son of mine, the Girl Inside growled. The Mother Inside, she reminded herself—her mother Tamara.

Shush! To Guillaume she said, "How old are you?"

"Four years old."

A chill shot through her. This child was as old as she was—in years. To think she could have been like him right now, small, innocent, naive, ignorant of the ways of adults. If Gwendolyn had found her like this, she'd be completely vulnerable and probably dead right now with Gwendolyn drinking her blood.

"People want to kill me. Is there somewhere safe I can hide?"

He nodded enthusiastically, took her hand, and brought her to a full-size mirror on the wall. "Father said I should hide here if there's ever any danger." His small fingers pulled on the edge of the mirror. It swung open, revealing a passageway.

"Thank you, Guillaume."

She stepped into the passageway and turned to wave, but he stepped in with her and closed the mirror door. Small openings in the walls of the corridor let barely enough sunlight in to see with.

"No, you need to stay here," she said. "It's too dangerous."

"Then I'm supposed to be here."

"No, *I'm* the danger."

He eyed her sword with blood on it. "You going to kill me?"

She looked at the sword, then held it behind her back. "I would never kill my brother. That's only to protect myself."

A woman's voice came from the other side of the mirror door. "Guillaume, I think I've killed all the bugs and...Guillaume?"

He grabbed her hand and pulled her running down the passageway. They turned a corner, and he stopped.

"Who's that?" Celeste whispered.

"That's Henrietta, my nurse."

"Guillaume!" the voice called faintly.

"She knows about this place."

The mirror door creaked. "Guillaume?" the voice echoed down the passageway, much louder. They waited, then the door creaked closed.

He took her hand and led her further down the passageway.

"Who wants to kill you?" he asked.

"The sorceress Gwendolyn."

His face went dark. "I hate her! Father hates her."

She smiled. "Then we'll be good friends. I hate her too."

They passed a few junctions with other passageways, but Guillaume kept leading her straight ahead. At the end was a door. She walked toward it.

"No, not there," he said as he pulled her to the side wall. "That's just to trick people in case they find this place." He spoke the word that meant *open* in the

Ancient Tongue. A rectangle of stone blocks in the wall slid back, creating a door-sized opening. He crawled past the blocks and disappeared into the dark.

With wonder, Celeste followed him in. The space was pitch dark, with barely a trickle of illumination coming from the passageway.

To her shock, Guillaume spoke more Ancient words, a Fire spell that ignited the lamps in the room. He told the blocks to *close*. As they slid back in place, he sat in a chair and beamed proudly at her.

She gazed around the large room. It was furnished with chairs and tables and beds, pantry shelves of food and supplies, a hearth to cook on, and a constant stream of water flowing into a basin.

"Guillaume," she said as she sat next to him, "who taught you those words?"

"Gwendolyn."

A dread ran through her. That meant Gwendolyn knew about this place. This might be a safe place for Guillaume, but not for her.

"Did she teach you any other spells?"

He brightened up. "She taught me how to throw sparks in people's faces." He made staccato noises with his mouth as his fingers fluttered before his eyes. "And she taught me how to make a wall of protection around me." His mouth made an explosive noise, and he waved his hands out to indicate the wall forming around him. "I can also say words that make me see things." His lips and voice made a warbling sound as he swung his head back and forth with his index fingers pointing out from his eyes.

Sight! It reminded her that she had no idea what time of day it was, and tonight would be another full moon. "I know that spell too." She cast the spell and gazed out. The sun was already setting, and to the east the first signs of moon-glow appeared on the horizon.

She jumped up. "Guillaume, I have to go—*now!*"

"It's dangerous for you."

She rushed to the sliding blocks. "It's dangerous for us if I stay here."

"Why?"

"Have you heard about the dragon?"

"I saw it!" he said with pride.

She uttered the word that slid the blocks out."That was me, and I'm going to change into one any moment now."

"That's stupid! You're not a dragon."

She looked around at the room. "If I change in here, I might break this room, or I might die. But you *will* die." She squeezed into the passageway.

"But you said you'd never kill me," he called.

"Stay here! You'll be safe here." She spoke the word that slid the blocks back into the wall and ran down the passageway to Guillaume's chambers.

———

Relieved that the insects avoided her with the Warding spell, Gwendolyn pulled the materials together to cast a stronger Sight spell. Bernard, holding his belly with one hand, stood near her to remain in the Warding spell's protective bubble. Through the window she could see she had maybe five minutes before the moon rose.

The spell took effect. She immediately turned and scanned the castle. With her aura, Celeste should be easy to locate.

In seconds she found the glow off in the royal living areas, somewhere around Guillaume's chambers. Possibly in that secret passageway. She looked closer and saw Celeste in the secret room with Guillaume. Celeste slid the stone blocks open and squeezed out, then closed them behind her, keeping Guillaume inside.

Good! Gwendolyn wanted that boy alive. She ran out into the corridor and nearly collided with Christian rushing toward her with his sword drawn.

"There you are!" he cried. "What are all these bugs and vermin about?"

She ignored him and ran down the corridor.

He ran after her. "I command you to tell me!"

"Celeste summoned them," she said as she turned a corner.

"Celeste? She's in the castle?" He caught up with her and pushed her against the wall. "Where is she?"

"I don't have time for this!"

A murderous glare filled his eyes. "Where is she?"

"She's in Guillaume's chambers."

His eyes went wide, and he dashed off.

Gwendolyn hurried after him. "Don't kill her! I need her."

"For what?" he called.

"To protect Gallea from the Blood King."

He turned and shoved his hand against her, stopping her. "What by the demons is the Blood King?"

"There's no time! She's about to become the dragon."

"Have you gone mad?"

She pushed him aside and ran to Guillaume's chambers. His footstomps were close behind her. She flung the door open and found Celeste holding Henrietta off with the sword. The mirror was swung open, revealing the passageway.

Celeste looked at her and cried, "I'm about to change!"

"I know," Gwendolyn said.

Christian came up beside her. "I need to kill her now before she changes."

Gwendolyn cast a Flash spell on him and rushed toward Celeste as he cried out and batted at the sparks burning his face.

Celeste threw the sword at her and went for the window. Gwendolyn batted it away with her arm. It sliced her across the claw scars on her arm before it clattered on the floor.

Celeste climbed up on the window sill, ready to jump.

Guillaume appeared from the passageway and gaped at everything going on.

Gwendolyn cried, "Oh no, you don't!" and cast another Flash spell.

The sparks in Celeste's face caused her to fall back. Before she hit the ground, Gwendolyn caught her and clamped her hand over her mouth.

"By the Gods, you will let me kill her!" Christian roared.

Guillaume ran out to intercept him. "No, Father! She's my sister."

Gwendolyn cast a third Flash spell on Christian as she dragged Celeste past him and out the door.

"By Father Sky, I will kill both of you!" Christian howled.

Gwendolyn heard Guillaume shout a Flash spell, and Christian howled in rage again. *Good boy!* she thought.

Guillaume chased after her, crying, "Don't kill her! She's my sister. She's the princess."

Curse Celeste! She'd been talking too much to Guillaume. "I'm not going to kill her," she called back. "I'm trying to save her."

When she reached the top of the staircase, Celeste seemed delirious. Gwendolyn removed her hand from her mouth to test if she would speak, but she didn't. Thank the Gods! It'd be hard enough to drag her down the stairs without having to waste one hand on her mouth.

As she took careful steps down the stairs clinging to Celeste with one hand and to the rail with the other, Celeste began to glow. It wasn't the glow of her aura that Gwendolyn saw with her Sight. It was a very different glow that formed around her, opaque like a thick mist.

Great Gods, she's going to change in my arms!

Gwendolyn could barely see the steps as the glow widened and encompassed her. Celeste grew heavier, and when they reached the bottom, it was all Gwendolyn could do to drag her onto the floor of the Great Hall. She dropped her and ran.

Guillaume rushed down the stairs. Gwendolyn grabbed him as she passed. Christian charged down the stairs behind them.

A shrill roar trumpeted from behind her, hurting her ears in the enclosed space. She dashed out of the hall and paused to glance back.

The dragon's head was high, near the top of the vaulted ceiling. The eye's glared straight at Gwendolyn. The head shot down, mouth gaping.

Gwendolyn dove with Guillaume away from the opening as a blast of dragon breath flooded from the hall. She huddled against the wall with him weeping in her arms. Wisps of the breath feathered her arm, stinging it.

Christian gave out a terrified cry from the hall. She heard something metallic clang onto the floor.

The dragon shrieked again. There was a thud that reverberated throughout the castle.

Gwendolyn set Guillaume down. "Wait here," she whispered and crept toward the opening to peer into the Great Hall.

Christian's sword lay at the bottom of the staircase. His clothes lay in a pile on the stairs. There was no sign of the king.

The dragon flapped its wings, hitting the walls of the hall. It bashed its head against the ceiling. The stone cracked, and bits of gravel dropped to the floor.

Great Gods, would that ceiling hold?

The dragon saw her and arched its neck again. Gwendolyn scrambled away, barely evading the blast of vapor. She crawled to Guillaume and took him in her arms.

"Will she kill us?" he said with tears glistening on his cheeks.

"She's trying to."

"She said she wouldn't kill me."

"Maybe she lied. Maybe a lot of things she said were a lie."

The dragon shrieked again. Its snout jutted from the Great Hall into the corridor and sniffed loudly. Gwendolyn stood up and ran with Guillaume down to the next corner. She looked back. The dragon head appeared and turned toward them, eyes piercing them. She ducked around the corner.

The blast was weaker without the coiled strike of the neck. A smattering of billows reached the junction they had just fled from.

She moved on to the main corridor reaching from the Great Hall to the inner gatehouse. The guards stationed there huddled near the gate as far away from the rampaging dragon as they could without leaving their posts.

Gwendolyn ran to them and handed Guillaume over to Lucien, a lieutenant of the Guard. "Get him to the safe room! He's the king now."

He looked at her in shock. "Christian?"

"Dragon breath."

He took Guillaume and scrambled up the gatehouse stairs to the network of secret passages. She looked at the inner gate with its portcullis raised, then out through the courtyard to the outer gate with its portcullis down. "Open the outer gate, in case we need to abandon the castle."

A guard immediately turned and passed the order on.

Gwendolyn crept toward the Great Hall. The dragon continued to shriek and rage and blast its vapor in all directions. Some of it billowed partway into the corridor.

When she went as far as she dared, she pressed herself against the wall and gazed into the wide entry to the hall. Another crash and larger bits of stone crumbled from above. Ceiling debris littered the floor around the creature.

Another crash and another large chunk of ceiling stone crashed into pieces on the floor.

She prayed to the Great Gods, "Let the walls hold. Let the ceiling hold. Oh Gods, please let that ceiling hold." She cast a breath spell to strengthen the ceiling, but had little hope it would matter, remembering how the dragon shattered the Entrapment spell she'd cast the first time it appeared.

She needed to get to her chamber and cast a stronger spell.

She returned to the gatehouse and went up the stairs, opened the disguised door and entered the secret passageway. It passed on the right of the upper part of the Great Hall on its way to her chambers. With each thrashing of the dragon, its walls rattled. Gods, if the dragon battered the wall instead of the ceiling, it could break through and swallow Gwendolyn in one bite.

She reached the door to her room and entered. She prepared the spell and cast it, then returned through the passageway to the gatehouse where she ascended to the rampart.

The moon hung low in the east, probably no more than an hour after rising. A rectangular opening in the roof from a stone block that had fallen gleamed light from the Great Hall. A blast of dragon breath shot through into the air. With a crash, the roof near the opening vibrated. "Please Mistress Earth, please Father Sky, don't let her break through."

The pounding went on relentlessly. The ceiling shook with each crash. She renewed her Sight spell and saw the reassuring shimmer of magic from her Strengthening spell envelope the roof. But this was a dragon. Could it hold through the night?

Another block fell, and after an hour or so, another. The dragon snout poked out, and white vapor blasted from its nostrils.

The snout disappeared, and another crash rattled the roof. For another hour the pounding continued, then another block fell. Gwendolyn eyed the moon, creeping across the sky at an unnervingly slow pace. Another crash caused another block to loosen and fall.

The dragon's head lifted out and shrieked. It looked around and, spotting the people on the rampart, blasted them with its breath. Gwendolyn ducked behind a merlot and uttered a quick Protection spell, hoping the guards along the rampart had been able to hide.

After endless rampaging and three more blocks tumbling down, the moon was perhaps an hour from setting. She heard commotion from the outer gatehouse. Someone shouted, "The Beast!"

She ran to the other side of the rampart and watched as the Beast bounded through the outer gate. Guards in the courtyard scattered, but the Beast ignored them. It ran straight for the inner gate.

Great Gods, what is the Beast doing here, running free? What happened to Ismael and Audric? They should have had him in the dungeon before nightfall.

The wolf disappeared into the keep. She could hear it howling inside. She looked with her Sight and saw what she expected to see, the Beast prancing and howling around the dragon, and the dragon reaching its head down to nuzzle it.

Good! Maybe the dragon would stop battering the ceiling.

But barely a moment passed before the dragon lifted its head and shrieked as it battered again. So much for that hope.

She collared a guard and said, "Close the inner gate. We'll trap the Beast inside and deal with him when he's a man."

The guard nodded and left. Gwendolyn returned to the other side of the rampart and watched. There was a rhythmic thud. The dragon head bobbed up and down in the hole, and the roof vibrated with each thud. It was trying to fly through the roof!

The Beast responded with a howl.

Three more blocks fell, and that began a cascade along a line of blocks, creating a long, narrow opening.

The dragon trumpeted and the wolf howled. Memories of being trapped in a bubble as they attacked her haunted Gwendolyn. She shook them off, reminding herself she was not the one trapped this time. She had them trapped, and in a short time she'd be stealing their life vitality.

If the roof held.

It didn't. More pieces fell crashing to the floor. The hole widened. "Gods, no!" She could see the shoulders of the wings as they made one great flap to take off, and she saw her plans flying away with that dragon. But the wings struck the sides of the hole, and the dragon fell back, crying out furiously.

She checked the moon. It was halfway closer to the horizon than before. "Please, Gods, hold that roof, just a little longer."

The sky slowly brightened as the moon sunk. In the last few moments of night, the raging wolf and the frustrated dragon protested with a terrifying cacophony. A couple more blocks broke away, but the hole must have reached the supportive beams on either side, keeping it from growing large enough for the wings to fly through.

At last the moon set with the dragon and Beast still within the walls of the castle. Gwendolyn's relief was immense. She rushed back down, gathering guards with her as she went. They stood at the end of the corridor by the gatehouse, waiting for the noise to subside. When the monsters became silent, she led the guards into the hall.

On the floor in the midst of stone blocks and massive rubble lay Celeste and her father, both naked and asleep. A glow around them faded away. The hall was in shambles. Statues toppled and broken, paintings torn and on the floor, rugs fallen from the walls, one of the thrones askew, the chandelier in pieces on the floor.

"Bind him and gag him and bring him to my chambers," she said quietly as she crept to Celeste. She kicked ripped pieces of cloth aside, all that was left of her shift.

Gwendolyn crouched down beside her and lifted a strand of hair away from her face. Looking at that sleeping, angelic face, Gwendolyn felt a twinge of regret.

"Dear, sweet girl," she murmured. "You're as noble and brave as Zenia. But I have to...I have to."

She picked her up and carried her to the stairs, uttering a sleep spell to keep her from waking.

"Celeste!" cried her father.

Gwendolyn turned and looked. He lay there bound with ropes, glaring at her. She smiled at him in triumph. Soon she and Gallea would be rid of the Beast for good.

The glow formed around him. She gaped in shock. But the moon was gone!

The guards cried out in terror. Bits of rope fell from the glowing sphere to the floor. "It's the Beast!" The guards scattered.

Gwendolyn hurried up the stairs as fast as she could manage. By the time she reached the top, the Beast bounded to the base of the stairs and locked its red eyes on her.

She ran.

The Beast howled. Its claws clicked against the stone of the steps.

The door to her chambers was the first door down the corridor. She had no idea if she'd make it. "Bernard!" she shouted.

The second door down opened. Bernard leaned out, saw Gwendolyn, saw what was behind her, and his face drained blood.

"Open my door now!"

He ran for it and pushed it open just as she got there. They both rushed in, and Bernard slammed it closed.

A half second later the Beast crashed against it. Bernard jabbed the bolt closed.

"Bernard, tie her to the chair."

The wolf kept pounding on the door as Bernard took Celeste and secured her. Gwendolyn hurried to her worktable. "How in the name of the Gods did the Beast come out in daylight?" So much for those accursed legends! She finished gathering up the materials for her spell. A couple cockroaches skittered across the table.

Bernard gave out a shocked cry. Gwendolyn looked up. Celeste was still slumped over with her eyes closed, but with a faint smile on her lips. Two rats had climbed up the chair and were chewing at her ropes, with Bernard a few steps away staring at them in disgust.

"Not this time, girl," Gwendolyn said and grabbed a vial of sleep vapor waiting to be infused into a globe. She rushed over and unstoppered it under Celeste's nose.

The vapor rose and swirled around, but none of it went up her nostrils. Gods, she was holding her breath. Gwendolyn needed to hold her own breath as the vapor swirled toward her face.

Great Gods, how had she come to this? In a breath-holding competition with a belligerent girl!

Rats and insects and spiders started swarming around her. "Breathe, curse you!" she shouted and slapped the back of her head. Celeste gasped from the shock and sucked the vapor in. Her head immediately drooped in sleep.

Gwendolyn inhaled a little of the fumes. Her legs were rubbery as she headed back for the table and the invading creatures scattered and disappeared. She completed the preparations for the spell. The Beast pummeled relentlessly on the door. It made a loud crack.

"Great Gods above, why are you making this so hard?" She threw the spell materials into a sack, then went to a bare part of the wall and spoke a command. Four blocks slid back, creating an opening. She reached inside for the chest she kept there—all her magic secrets she'd scavenged from the hidden place behind the Falls of Eircana. She only needed the scroll with the spell, but she didn't have time to rummage. That door wouldn't hold.

She placed the chest in the sack and said, "Bernard, grab her. We can't stay here."

She noticed the empty scabbard on her bed. Curse the netherworld, her sword was still on the floor of Guillaume's chambers. She grabbed the scabbard.

The door shuddered and cracked at the upper hinge. Gwendolyn hurried to the mirror and pulled it open, held it so Bernard could carry Celeste through, then closed it just as the door crashed to the floor.

They ran down the passageway. The Beast howled with rage. Its cries seemed to shadow them as they fled. It must be tracking Celeste's movements and paralleling them through the corridors of the castle. No matter. To be a threat now, the Beast would have to figure out the entrance was disguised as a mirror and paw it open, then speak the word that opened the entry to the safe room.

When they reached the fork to Guillaume's room, she dropped her sack and said, "Wait here." She hurried down it, uttering a Sight spell to make sure the Beast wasn't there, and carefully eased the mirror door open. The sword lay in the middle of the floor.

She dashed and grabbed it just as the Beast thudded against the door. She dashed back to the mirror and swung it shut behind her.

She slid the sword into the scabbard, and they rushed down the passageway until they came to the end. Gwendolyn spoke the word and opened the entrance to the safe room. She dropped her sack through the opening and squeezed through.

When she looked around, she was struck with surprise as she saw Guillaume and Lucien inside staring back at her. She'd forgotten about them.

"Mistress...Celeste!" Bernard called.

Gwendolyn turned and pulled Celeste through. Bernard followed. She laid Celeste on a bed, then sat on it and turned to Lucien. He gaped at Celeste lying naked.

"Turn your eyes away, you brute!" she cried. "Bernard, is there anything here we can put on her?"

He found a blanket, and Gwendolyn covered Celeste with it. "The Beast is at large in the castle," she told the lieutenant.

"In daylight?"

"Yes! Go out and take care of him."

"Yes, Mistress," he said with a quaver in his voice and wedged himself through the opening.

Gwendolyn closed the entry with a word, then gazed at the featureless wall. She felt awful for sending him out there when it was obvious Ismael and Audric together couldn't handle the Beast, but she couldn't have him in here when she slit Celeste's throat.

Guillaume came over to Celeste and peered at her. "She was the dragon?" he said incredulously.

"She changes, like the man who becomes the Beast."

His face went dark. "She killed my father."

Celeste stirred. Gwendolyn held her breath. The last thing she needed was for her to wake up. But she remained asleep.

"Bind her legs before she awakens," she told Bernard, then looked at Guillaume. She didn't want him around any more than Lucien, but she didn't want to send him out there with the Beast haunting the corridors.

If the prince despised Celeste for killing his father, maybe she *could* cast the spell in front of him. "I'll make sure she won't kill anyone ever again. Would you like that?"

He nodded, then looked up in alarm as the cry of the wolf filtered through the thick stone walls. It sounded near. It could definitely sense and track Celeste.

"There'll be blood," she said to Guillaume.

"Will she die?"

"Yes."

He nodded.

"If you become frightened, turn your head away."

The wolf howled again. Gwendolyn expected to hear Lucien cry out as it attacked him, but he never did. Perhaps he had the sense to ignore her command and flee the castle.

She emptied the contents of her sack on the table near the bed, then opened the chest. It contained multiple scrolls, each tied into a roll with a string, several pieces of jewelry, a bag full of gold coins for an emergency, and her most prized possession, the Magic Eater amulet, a gold locket on a chain.

She sought out the scroll she needed and set the chest aside. She prepared the materials to strengthen her Sight spell in one bowl, then the materials for the vitality stealing spell in another, and poured oil over both of them. She lay out the scroll and held it open with four stone weights, each on a corner.

Finally she lay a knife and two sticks out.

She took a moment to gaze at the things that were about to bring her the power she sought for so many years, trying to ignore the howls of the Beast. Listening to them and looking around the hidden room she had to flee to, she realized, if the man could change into the Beast at any time, even in daylight, he was much too dangerous to deal with. She'd have to settle for Celeste's power alone. It seemed as if the Gods kept giving her gifts, then taking them away.

But it was only a mild disappointment. Celeste lay before her, ready to give up her magnificent power. Nothing could stop Gwendolyn now. Not the Beast who howled helplessly behind thick stone walls. Not Christian who was fool enough to be blasted into nonexistence by dragon breath. Not Sighurd who was off on some fool's errand trying to help a ridiculous witch retrieve some treasure she thought was so important. There was no other enemy who knew about the existence of this room.

All she had to do was cast the spell, slit Celeste's throat, and drink the blood that oozed out.

She ignited one stick and cast the Sight spell so she could monitor the flow of Celeste's vitality as she drank her blood. Celeste's aura blazed brightly, a sphere that surrounded her. It was even more magnificent seen through a powerful Sight spell at such close range.

She knelt before the bed and stroked Celeste's hair. "Such a beautiful girl. Such a beautiful aura." Her sympathy for the girl was diminished by her anticipation over having that aura emanate from herself.

She froze as she noticed a slight aberration in the aura around her abdomen. "Great Gods, what is that?" she whispered. She leaned over within inches of Celeste's belly and studied it.

The aberration was a flutter, subtle almost beyond detection. A discontinuation in the natural flow of her aura. So subtle, she could easily have missed it.

But it was something she'd seen before. A tiny pinprick of aura with the same dark signature she'd discovered in Tamara's womb four years and nine months ago. The same dark signature as the Beast.

She shook her head in amazement, a smile forming on her lips. "What have you been doing, you feisty girl?"

Gwendolyn was elated. How foolish of her to mistrust the Gods! Just as they snatched the power of the Beast from her, they replaced it with his powerful child. A power conceived by *two* changelings, not one! She'd be conjuring up a lot of sleep vapor and charm potions to keep Celeste acquiescent, but it would be worth it.

"Congratulations, little princess," she murmured, stroking Celeste's hair. "You get to live another nine months."

Chapter 23

The Great Gods

"I don't understand," Edmund said. "I don't sense her in that direction. Earlier today I could sense where she was."

"Do you sense her in any other direction?" Eloise said.

He stood silently for a moment. "No. But I suppose I can't sense her if she's too far away."

"What about the wolf?" Dietric said.

"No!" Thomas barked, "You're not turning into the wolf."

"I have no idea what the wolf can sense," Edmund said.

"Does this matter?" Eloise said. "We see her aura. Who else could it be?"

"I don't see why *he* needs to come at all," said Thomas.

"She's my daughter."

"Didn't you already agree to have him be part of the quest?" Eloise said.

"That was before we knew he could change into the Beast any time he wants. How can we protect ourselves from that?"

"I'll just follow you to Suedeche anyway," Edmund said.

Sighurd added with a smirk, "You want the Beast in front of you where you can watch him, or do you want him following behind you where he can sneak up on you?"

"He has no horse," Thomas said desperately.

Sighurd turned to Edmund. "Couldn't the Beast keep up with our horses?"

"Certainly."

"No!" Thomas barked. "You stay a man!"

Sighurd tried to suppress a smile, with limited success.

Thomas resentfully let Edmund wear the spare clothing he had in his pack. He was the only one whose size compared to the bulky woodsman.

"You can ride with me," Eloise said to Edmund. "I'm a wizened old lady who doesn't take up much space."

Thomas insisted Edmund and Eloise ride at the head of the group where he could keep an eye on them. As they rode, Eloise said quietly so only Edmund could hear, "I saw you last night, you and Celeste."

"What do you mean?"

"In the night while the others slept, you came to me, dragon and wolf."

He tensed up. "I don't under—how did you survive?"

She patted his hand on the reins. "You both were quite affectionate to me."

"I don't see how that's possible."

"You may have more control as the Beast than you think. The dragon recognized me and let me touch her snout. You recognized her affection and let me scratch you behind the ears."

He pondered in silence a moment, then nodded. "I believe you."

"You may not remember anything from being the wolf, but the wolf remembers something, or senses something, of who you are, and who Celeste is. The wolf retains your basic goodness."

"The wolf tears people apart like the cursed monster he is."

"All I know is, you didn't tear me apart last night."

Master Sun hung low in the sky as they entered Suedeche. They paused while Eloise and Kasimir cast Sight spells to find the precise location of the glow.

A warm feeling came over her. "I think she's in Vilnetal. Dear Celeste, you really did find your way home."

"I agree," said Kasimir. "Perhaps I should warn you, some of the villagers are upset you abandoned them."

"You've been there?"

"Over the last four years I've been everywhere."

As they traveled on, Eloise became more certain the aura was in Vilnetal. They passed fields and farms and cottages and came to Premveille, the first village of Suedeche. As they passed through, they stirred excitement as the people gawked at the extraordinary procession of the King's Guard and black men of the South. An innkeeper stood outside his establishment and said, "Such strange visitors we've had lately!" before inviting them to stay.

"Thank you," Eloise said, "but we need to reach our destination."

At sunset they came to the fork that led to Vilnetal. The aura clearly lay down that path. Eloise could hardly contain herself with the excitement of seeing Celeste again, alive and safe within her home village. She hoped the people of Vilnetal had welcomed her and were treating her well.

The sun began to set as they entered the village. Thomas spurred his horse to catch up with Edmund and said, "Can you also choose not to become the Beast when the moon compels you?"

"You already know I can. You saw it when you first met me."

Thomas gave him an unconvinced look. "You mean back when you lied to us?" He fell back with the others.

Eloise ignored them both. She was immersed in the joy of seeing her home again. Few people were about during this time when most of them had their evening meal, but those few gave them the same amazed stares as everyone else. Three of them, old friends, came up to her. "Eloise, you've come back!" and "Where have you been?" and "Why did you leave us?"

"The stories can wait," she said as she passed. "I want to see my cottage."

"Your cottage belongs to Cosette now," one said. "She's our village witch."

Eloise nodded and rode on. Cosette was unknown to her. She hoped she'd served her village well while she was gone.

By the time they reached the cottage, both her and Kasimir's Sight was fading. But she could still tell Celeste's aura came from within. She slid down before Edmund had fully stopped the horse and ran to the door, eager to hold Celeste in her arms.

She knocked and gazed at the cottage with a warm feeling. Roslina opened the door, took one look at her, and grabbed her in a fierce embrace. "Eloise, you're home."

"My dear friend."

Roslina's eyes glowed. "Come in, Eloise. You'll never believe who's here."

Eloise remained silent with a smile. She didn't want to spoil her surprise. The first person she saw as they came in was a woman she didn't recognize. Next to her was another woman, much younger, she also didn't recognize. But there was time for introductions later. She immediately turned toward Celeste's glow.

But it wasn't Celeste. The shock made her head spin, and a dread ran through her. It was a fully grown woman, dressed in a white robe with a hood pulled back. In her shock, it took her a moment to recognize the face.

"Zenia!" She rushed to her and gave her the embrace she'd intended for Celeste. "Dear Goddess, it *is* you. How are you here?"

"She's a Pilgrim of Mother Goddess," the unknown woman said as she walked up. "I'm so happy to meet you, Eloise. My name is Cosette."

Eloise couldn't think what to say. Her mind was stunned with the appearance of Zenia and the absence of Celeste. She wanted to shout for joy and drop to her knees in anguish.

Instead she turned to Kasimir with an accusing look.

"I'm so sorry," he said. "I should have kept looking. I just assumed—"

"So did I," she said, softening with the realization. "But where could she be?" She looked at Zenia. "We thought your aura was Celeste's."

Zenia hugged her again. "I'm sorry to disappoint you."

"Oh Zenia, you haven't disappointed me. You're back from the dead!"

Edmund came forward. "In moments the moon will rise and the dragon will fly again. It should be easy for Kasimir to find her then."

Kasimir nodded and walked out the door. The others followed. Zenia took

Eloise's arm as they went. "Now I know why I was led here. To wait for you."

The sun had just set, and the face of Mistress Moon began to peak over the horizon. Thomas eyed Edmund suspiciously, but there was no sign of Change.

Kasimir looked around at the scattering of people in the area who stopped and stared as he and Zenia came out. He turned to Faisal with a questioning look.

"Sorceresses and soldiers know about the starstones," Faisal said. "Some villagers won't matter."

He opened his clothes and plucked a starstone, dipped it in the blood, and brought the shining gem to his mouth where he spoke the words. The observers gasped as the stone flashed, and the brilliance seemed to flow into his eyes.

"Look east first," Eloise said, "toward Dierdre's castle."

He did and said, "I don't see anything, but she does have that Masking spell."

Eloise let out a troubled sigh. "Would that be powerful enough to hide her aura from you?"

"I don't know. When I was close to the tower, my starstone let me see faint shapes inside. It's possible I could see that bright aura through the mask." He continued to scan the horizon in a circle as everyone watched in silence. Everyone but Edmund, Eloise noticed, who seemed to become agitated. Thomas backed away a few steps and put his hand on the hilt of his sword.

"I see something!" Kasimir said as he faced west. "Low to the ground. I think it's somewhere near Luteche."

"Could she be attacking the castle again?" Eloise asked. "Please tell me Gwendolyn doesn't have her."

"I can't tell from this distance. But...yes...it's the aura of the dragon. I don't think Gwendolyn could contain a dragon."

Edmund stepped toward the west, gazing as if he could see the aura. A glow formed around him. Thomas cried, "The Beast!" and drew his sword.

From the glow leaped the Beast, eyes burning. The villagers screamed and scattered. Thomas pushed past everyone and charged after him. But the Beast ran down the road heading out of the village and disappeared.

Thomas pointed his sword and shouted, "See? He *can't* control it!"

"He didn't attack you," Eloise said with disdain, "nor anybody else." She looked down the road where the Beast had disappeared into the dark, feeling relief. "The dragon called him." She took a few steps forward, gazing where the Beast had disappeared. "He'll protect her, if Celeste needs protecting."

"Come inside," Zenia said. "There's nothing more you can do now."

Thomas stared down at the clothing he'd donated to Edmund, now on the ground in tatters. "Gods curse changelings!" he muttered.

"Celeste is a changeling," Eloise said with a sharp look.

He looked at her frowning, then marched inside.

Before Eloise went back in, she gazed once more down the road. "If you run into Gwendolyn," she murmured, "I pray you tear her throat out."

———

"Who is this beautiful girl?" Eloise said after they settled in the cottage.

The girl blushed. "My name is Ilsa. I serve the Pilgrim."

Eloise broke out in a huge grin. "How wonderful! Take good care of her. She's my daughter."

A look of surprise broke out on Ilsa's face. She dropped to one knee in a bow.

"Oh no no no, there'll be none of that!" Eloise said as she lifted the girl back up by her hand. "I'm just an old witch."

"We need to regroup," Sighurd said. "Celeste should be somewhere with Edmund by morning, so she should be safe. Eloise, on the other hand, has none of her stronger magic." He looked at Zenia with an unsure expression. "But we have a...Pilgrim of the Mother Goddess with us now. If you *are* with us."

"I'm here for Eloise and Celeste," she said.

Eloise smiled and patted her hand. She still couldn't believe Zenia was back.

"What does it mean to be a Pilgrim?" asked Sighurd.

"Do you mean what powers do I have?"

He shrugged.

"Yesterday morning I found myself walking along the East Highway with no memory of who I was. Since then I've been learning and remembering, bit by bit. I don't know what all my powers are yet. I do know I can heal the sick and injured."

"A Pilgrim," Cosette said, "is an emissary from the Mother Goddess. A demigod, as the Seven Sisters of old were."

"I'm just a soldier," said Sighurd. "I don't know much about them. Didn't they provide the magic the Seven Sisters use today?"

"That and much more," Eloise said. "They first appeared in Ruo of Onotria. They came to share their powers with select women of character who could use them to bless humanity. They spread out to kingdoms in the south and east— Onotria, Ellada, Vlachia, Scaendelreic, Lechici, Cithania, and Rothenia."

"Each country that has one of the Seven Sisters today," Cosette said.

"They each taught magic to one woman in the kingdom they went to, both Life Magic and Death Magic. They provided them many more spells and many more amulets than the Sisters today have."

"What happened to them?" Dietric asked.

"Wars happened," Zenia said. "The terrible wars you hear about in history. In the hands of humans, the power of the Seven Sisters was corrupted."

"They regretted ever giving that power," Cosette said. "They took most of it back. Some say they took the magic from the earth. Others say they hid it away in places no one would ever find. They left the witches of Cueldea with nothing but basic Life Magic to serve the people, and allowed the seven women they'd chosen to keep only a few of the more powerful spells and amulets they had."

Eloise said, "Today the Seven Sisters guard their magic treasures fiercely, from each other and from any rogue sorceress that might arise, like Gwendolyn."

"Where did Gwendolyn get her magic?" Dietric said.

Eloise chuckled. "That's what the rest of us would like to know. She seems to have arisen out of nowhere."

"Where did you get *your* special magic?" Thomas asked accusingly.

"Does it matter now? I no longer have it."

He gave out a *hmph*.

"Do you bring the magic of the Seven Sisters back with you?" Sighurd asked Zenia.

"I'm still trying to figure that out myself," she answered. "I don't remember everything yet."

"If you do, keep it to yourself. We humans inflict war on ourselves well enough without it."

She smiled at him.

He took a deep breath and shifted in his seat. "That still leaves us with the question, what do we do next? Do we need to explain our quest to you, Pilgrim?"

"Does it include helping Celeste and Eloise?"

"It does, and forming an alliance between Gallea and Insu. And removing Gwendolyn from power."

Zenia raised her eyebrows. "You don't dream small."

"I've been thinking," Dietric said. "What will Suedeche do when Gwendolyn's gone?"

"What do you mean?" asked Sighurd.

"Geoffrey aligned with us to protect his duchy from Scaendelreic. He aligned with us because of Gwendolyn. If she's gone..."

"Is Suedeche so powerful, we need to concern ourselves with them?" Thomas said.

"We'll have Kasimir and whatever the Pilgrim brings," Sighurd said. "These things we can still offer Geoffrey."

"Will Geoffrey trust a wizard of Insu?" Dietric said. "Will Kasimir and the Pilgrim stay around indefinitely to protect both of us, Gallea and Suedeche?"

"There'll also be Celeste," said Eloise.

"A dragon? Will Geoffrey be comfortable putting his trust in a dragon?"

"Are you driving at something?" Sighurd said.

"We should go to Geoffrey now and inform him. Explain everything, from what happened to his daughter to our quest. We should form an alliance between him and *us*, not between him and Gallea." He turned to Thomas. "And yes, Suedeche *is* that important. They've maintained a standing army on the border with Scaendelreic to watch our backs."

This talk disturbed Eloise. "Geoffrey is further east. Celeste is out west."

Dietric gazed at her with tenderness. "You did a masterful job protecting her from Gwendolyn. But she has another protector now. He'll look after her."

She felt anger welling up. "She's also *my* daughter."

"Geoffrey's our ally," Sighurd said. "We have a duty to inform him about our quest. To do otherwise could seem like a betrayal. We don't need another enemy."

"Considering what Gwendolyn did to his daughter," Zenia said, "he might be happy to join our quest."

Sighurd said, "I take it that means *you're* with us?"

She smiled broadly and squeezed Eloise's hand. "How can I not stand by my own mother?"

Zenia's brow knotted. She seemed to falter, then her face changed dramatically. Its features became fluid and seemed almost to take on more manlike features.

"How can I not stand by my captain?" she said in a different voice.

"Hereward?" Sighurd whispered in astonishment.

They all gaped at her in amazed silence as her face returned to normal. It was Sighurd who first came to himself enough to speak. "Why is Hereward inside you?"

She looked around at them as if perplexed. "Who is Hereward?"

"He was one of us who searched for Celeste. He died protecting Celeste and all of us from the Beast."

Her expression became empathetic. "I'm sorry for your loss. I honor his sacrifice."

"You don't know what just happened?" Thomas said.

"I'm sorry. I'm still trying to understand things."

Another silence, broken by Cosette. "It sounds like you're traveling again, heading to Geoffrey's castle tomorrow. You could use a good night's sleep."

Between Cosette and Roslina's cottages, they managed to bunk everyone for the night. Cosette insisted that Zenia and Eloise take her sleeping quarters. "You two need some private time together."

"Thank you," said Eloise.

They sat together on the bed. Eloise's eyes misted as she gazed at Zenia fondly, remembering the young woman trying to master the intricacies of magic in this very cottage. She'd been a more fearful child than Celeste with the terrible things that happened to her and her family. Fearful, yet with a quiet strength that came out when things mattered to her. And the things that mattered to her were the people she loved.

Now Zenia was a Pilgrim, calm and self-assured as Eloise had never seen her. She'd made the ultimate sacrifice to protect those she loved, and instead of enjoying her well-earned bliss in the presence of Mother Goddess, she chose to return to this troublesome world to continue the fight.

"Zenia, you are the most caring, self-sacrificing person I know. Have I ever told you I love you?"

"Many times, Mother," she said with a smile. "And everything I am, I learned from you."

"Not everything," Eloise corrected with a grin. "I never taught you how to be a Pilgrim."

"I think you did. Any qualities I have that make me a good Pilgrim, I learned from you."

They fell into an embrace and held it for some time. This was the first chance she'd had to enjoy Zenia's presence without interruption.

"I'm so sorry I failed you," Eloise said.

Zenia pulled away from her. "Whatever do you mean?"

"You trusted me to protect Celeste." Tears formed in her eyes. "But we still don't have her, in spite of all my efforts."

Zenia smiled lovingly at her. "Oh, Mother. You protected her for four years, long enough for her to become a woman herself."

"But now everyone has to put themselves in danger for this quest. And what if Celeste is on the ground in Luteche because Gwendolyn..." She couldn't finish the sentence. "If I'd been more careful..." Tears pooled in her eyes and started to slide down her face.

Zenia held her again. "Gwendolyn capture a dragon? Don't torture yourself over this. You did wonderfully. Everything will turn out well."

"Do you know something?" Eloise said hopefully.

Zenia smiled. "I have a feeling."

"What *is* the mission Mother Goddess sent you for? Do you remember yet?"

Zenia smiled mischievously. "I may not have been entirely forthcoming in the presence of others."

Eloise grinned. "You little demon! You take after me too much."

"I remember a great deal now. But when I first came, I learned what happens if people find out about my powers. It nearly overwhelmed me. It's better if I don't reveal everything."

"Even to me?"

"Oh Mother, you're the one grand exception."

Eloise said with her own impish tone, "Then tell me everything!"

That night years ago when Zenia stood bound to the post, staring with horror as the Beast approached her, despair filled her soul. She betrayed Eloise, she betrayed Celeste, and would now lose her life and maybe even her soul for all her effort. She uttered prayer after prayer to Mother Goddess—for Celeste, for Eloise, for Cueldea, and for her own soul.

The pain was overwhelming as the Beast bit into her. Her mind went into shock. The body being torn apart was no longer hers as she watched as if from a distance. Her head swam in a fog of meaningless sensations.

She thought she saw a beam of light shining into her face. It reminded her of Celeste's aura ascending to the moon. She wanted to reach out to it, reach out as if she could bundle up Celeste in her arms again. Her desire seemed to fill her with hope and joy, seemed to draw the pain away—or was it the beam of light filling her?

She did reach out. It felt like unseen hands grasped hers and pulled her into the light. She was encompassed by light. She became light. A warm feeling of love surrounded her.

She found herself kneeling before a throne of light. She looked up and saw a face that was unknown to her, but sublimely familiar to her. In that moment she learned that the legends about her cursed soul were wrong.

"Welcome, my daughter," said the woman with the familiar face.

She bowed deeply on her knees and said, "Praise you, Mother Goddess."

"Praise *you*, my daughter. Your sacrifices for the ones you love have sancti-fied you."

"But I'm just a poor old witch who's not very smart."

"Arise and sit with me." Her hand extended to Zenia and lifted her up. She found a seat underneath her and gazed into the eyes of Mother Goddess, eyes that could forgive anything and love everything.

"You have a request to make of me," said Mother Goddess.

"Protect Celeste," she said simply.

"Eloise is protecting her now."

"Will you let her know about the Blood King?"

"No," said Mother Goddess. "You will."

Her head swam. Would Mother Goddess send her back?

"The time is not yet," Mother Goddess said as if she heard Zenia's thoughts. "Celeste is still young. The souls are not ready. The Blood King is still preoc-cupied in the East."

"When?"

"When the time is right."

Many times Zenia sat in the arms of Mother Goddess and watched Celeste grow with astonishing speed. She could see the essence of Tamara living inside her, speaking to her and educating her, and rejoiced that mother and daughter could know each other. She watched with joy as Eloise loved her as completely as she'd loved Zenia. She saw how Celeste met her father as a child splashing in the pool. Her heart cried out with anguish as she watched Celeste leap from the cliff, but instantly clapped her hands with joy as she watched her transform into a majestic white dragon who soared away from death. She felt a guilty satisfac-tion as the dragon confronted Gwendolyn, but then a tragic sorrow as her breath dissolved the bodies of innocent people standing by while Gwendolyn remained unscathed.

"It is time," said Mother Goddess. "The souls are ready."

Zenia didn't understand what that meant, but suddenly a group of souls stood before them. One of them was Hereward, the man who'd been killed by the Beast while defending Celeste and the others the night she became a dragon. The other souls were those that had streamed up in twisting swirls to Mistress Moon when the dragon breathed on Gwendolyn.

"As I sent the Seven Sisters," said Mother Goddess, "so will I send all of you as my Pilgrim. Your vitalities will be joined. Together your life forces will have the power of a demigod."

"Why these souls?" asked Zenia.

"Each of you have been touched by Celeste. Hereward was present the night of her birth and the night of her transformation. The others were sent to Mistress Moon by Celeste's breath. But you, Zenia, will be the face of the Pilgrim because you are the one who made the request."

Zenia asked to see Mistress Moon before she left. Mistress Moon greeted her warmly, with a face pale and fair as the moon itself.

"Thank you for helping me purify Celeste," Zenia said.

"Thank you for your courage," said Mistress Moon. "Thank you for saving my Celeste from the sorceress."

Mother Goddess joined Zenia and the souls together. She still felt like Zenia, but sensed the others with her. As the light that once brought her to kneel before Mother Goddess surrounded her and pulled her away, she forgot everything.

Eloise sat speechless, taking it all in. "You make it sound more glorious than I ever imagined," she finally said.

"It's even more glorious than I can explain."

"Is that what the original Seven Sisters were? Mortal souls joined together?"

"Yes," Zenia said, smiling, "but many more than are within me. As souls develop, they're joined together to form demigods, yet live as their own individual selves in an existence of bliss apart from each other, as the organs of our bodies live their private lives, unaware of the lives the person they're a part of live."

"What happens to demigods? What happens to you after you accomplish your mission?"

"As demigods develop, they're joined together to become Gods themselves."

"And the Great Gods?"

"The Great Gods were created by the Ultimate One, who is to them as the Great Gods are to us, and just as mysterious."

Eloise took a deep breath and shook her head, trying to wrap her mind around it. "It's breathtaking to contemplate."

"Even for me, and I've been there."

"So you're here to warn Celeste about the Blood King?"

"It's what I pleaded to Mother Goddess to do."

"Gwendolyn thinks the Gods want *her* to stop the Blood King."

"Gwendolyn would become as great a terror as the Blood King."

Eloise nodded. "I can certainly believe that."

"Your quest is exactly what Cueldea needs at this time. Gwendolyn will not save Cueldea. The Seven Sisters will not. Cueldea standing alone cannot stop the Blood King. His power is immense, and his sorceress wife fuels her Death Magic with the blood of entire horses. Only when Cueldea and the countries of Ifran join together to oppose him can the Blood King be stopped, with the help of the wizards of Insu and of Celeste...and her child."

"*What?*"

Zenia laughed. "Yes, Celeste has a tiny child in her, just beginning to form."

"How...who...who is the father?"

"The father is *her* father. They didn't know that when it happened, but now it's done."

"Oh dear Mother Goddess!" Eloise cried. "What kind of child will *that* be?"

"We shall see," said Zenia.

Chapter 24

Ilsa

Sighurd took the lead as they traveled down the road back to the East Highway. They were the same people that left Luteche together minus Edmund, but with the addition of Zenia and Ilsa. A villager offered two horses for the Pilgrim and her servant. Zenia blessed him and his family.

Ilsa let Eloise ride her horse because she'd never been on one, and she rode with Zenia instead. She could hardly contain her excitement. Only once before had she ever gone to Suedeche, and that was long ago before her injury. It seemed a wonderland to her then, and she was eager to see it again.

The River Sicana flowed along the outskirts of the city with docks and boats and ferries along its banks, then cut through the city itself. She remembered the city being huge as a child, but now it seemed more quaint. The castle of Duke Geoffrey loomed above on a hill. She tried to imagine what the lives of those who lived there were like.

They passed through streets and marketplaces, drawing attention everywhere they went. Ilsa was used to being stared at by people, but for the first time it was a pleasant experience. No more crutches, no more twisted legs, no more pitying stares or cruel smirks. People gazed at them with wonder, and it filled her with elation to be part of it.

They were received in the Great Hall of the castle of Suedeche. There were impressive chairs on the dais that commanded authority. She tried to imagine what Duke Geoffrey looked like sitting in one.

Geoffrey entered, dressed in finery she'd never seen, streaks of grey in his brown hair and beard. He looked every bit the duke he was, but he also seemed sad and haggard. She'd heard that his daughter had died, the one who became queen of Gallea, and wondered if that was why.

He came in almost apprehensively, gazing upon them with an expression that suggested concern, surprise, or even trepidation. He stopped at the chair, remaining standing, and placed his hand on the back of it, almost as if for support. He gazed at them for some time before he spoke.

"I couldn't believe what they told me, that a Pilgrim of Mother Goddess has honored me with her presence. But to have that Pilgrim be the nursemaid of my own daughter..."

He ignored the chair and walked down to them. First he hugged the Pilgrim. "Welcome, Zenia. It's good to see you again." Then he hugged Eloise. "You've returned to your homeland at last."

He turned to Ilsa. "And who is this beautiful woman?"

A thrill passed through her. She couldn't remember anyone ever calling her beautiful except her mother, and now the duke of the land had called her that. It was all she could do to keep from fainting.

"My name is Ilsa. I'm from Premveille. I serve the Pilgrim."

"Welcome to my castle, Ilsa. You must be quite the woman to have the honor of serving a Pilgrim."

He turned to the wizard and spoke in Ruic. "And Kasimir, welcome back. Have you had success in your quest?"

"I can speak Galleic now," he responded in Galleic, which seemed to please Geoffrey. "We found the girl, but we haven't been able to return her yet to her family."

"I pray the Gods will bless you with success."

"Sighurd has commissioned a new quest, which I've accepted. He speaks for us now."

Geoffrey raised his eyebrows and looked at Sighurd. "It seems much has changed since you came to me those years ago. I've heard rumors from Luteche. Rumors of the Beast appearing again. Rumors of a dragon attacking the castle."

"That's what we've come to discuss with you," said Sighurd.

Geoffrey's eyes narrowed. "Rumors that the dragon killed King Christian."

"*What?*" Sighurd and Thomas said in unison.

"It appears that is *not* one of the things you came to talk about."

"He was alive when we left," Sighurd said.

Geoffrey waved his arm toward an exit. "Let's speak more privately."

"How reliable are those rumors?" Sighurd said even before everyone had seated in the conference chamber.

"I've received reports from very reliable people."

"This is...shocking. It changes a lot of things."

"Why don't you tell me what you came to say," Geoffrey said. "Then we can go from there."

Zenia told Geoffrey the story of Tamara and Celeste and how the prince that Geoffrey thought was his grandson was the son of Christian's mistress. Kasimir told him about Celeste's leap at the Falls of Eircana. Sighurd told him about the dragon and the Beast attacking Gwendolyn. Kasimir told him about the new quest Sighurd had commissioned.

Eloise described Celeste's life from birth to when she fled Kasimir's men, how she determined that Celeste was the dragon, and the night the dragon and the Beast came to her affectionately.

Zenia told him about the vision Gwendolyn had shown her of the Blood King, and how Mother Goddess sent her back to find and protect Celeste and warn her of his coming.

Ilsa was beyond amazed. She could hardly believe what she heard. As a simple crippled girl in a simple village, she never dreamed people lived such astonishing lives. Part of her was shocked and frightened and wondered what she'd gotten herself into. But part of her was exhilarated that she could become a part of such magnificent stories.

Geoffrey listened in solemn silence. By the time they finished, his eyes glistened with tears that he had to wipe away. "I have a granddaughter," he said quietly, "not a grandson."

But soon his face darkened. "I allied with Gallea for protection from King Gunther and the sorceress Deirdre. His power looms over us, and the shadow of her tower casts a menacing pall over our land. My army joined with King Guillaume's to drive Gunther's armies back." He glanced at Zenia. "But we couldn't have stopped Deirdre without Gwendolyn's help."

He paused as he lowered his head and took a breath. "But Guillaume is dead, and now Christian is dead, with young Guillaume left to rule who is not even son of my blood as I've been told he was. Gwendolyn has caused the death of my daughter and forced my granddaughter into hiding for fear of her life, and all of Gallea lied to me about it."

Geoffrey trained his glaring eyes on Sighurd. "Even you."

Sighurd lowered his.

"I traveled to Luteche to meet my grandson," Geoffrey went on darkly. "I played with him and gave my love to him. Now I find out it was nothing but deceit."

"I had orders from my king," Sighurd said.

"My armies have stood alone on the border with Scaendelreic, as our alliance dictates, and for this I've been repaid with treachery." Geoffrey stood and imperially said, "The alliance between Suedeche and Gallea is broken."

A chill shot through Ilsa. These were overwhelming things to her, things bigger than any life she imagined for herself. What could she do to help in such sweeping events?

Serve my Pilgrim, she told herself. That's how she could make a small contribution.

Geoffrey looked at each of them in turn. "But now I'm free to form new alliances with new friends." He sat back down. "Sighurd, what do you believe will happen to Gallea, now that Christian is dead?"

"Prince Guillaume is king now, but only four years old. Gwendolyn will most certainly conspire to gain control."

"Yet my own granddaughter is of royal birth, and of an age...of a *maturity*... to rule." He looked at Eloise. "Thanks to your miraculous intervention."

She smiled back at him.

"Her claim to the throne is not strong," said Sighurd. "Celeste is the bastard daughter of the queen and a woodsman."

"Who happens to be the Beast," said Geoffrey.

"While Guillaume is the son of the king himself—"

"And a bastard himself."

"But no one in Gallea knows that except us," said Sighurd, "and no one in Gallea knows about the existence of Celeste. The truth will appear a self-serving lie if we try to advance her claim. A very unbelievable lie."

Geoffrey nodded. He turned to Kasimir. "How does Christian's death affect your quest?"

"It seems to me it'll be more challenging without the legitimacy of Christian with us."

"My thoughts too. Sighurd, as Captain of the Guard, you're the right hand man to the king. Am I correct that you would be the one to direct the appointment of a regent?"

"Yes."

"Gwendolyn would have no legitimate path to the regency until you return to Luteche?"

"That's correct. But I doubt that would stop her from trying."

"Then this is my recommendation." Geoffrey sat back and took a deep breath. "As duke of Suedeche, I officially recognize you, Sighurd, as the temporary regent of Gallea until you can arrange the affairs of your kingdom. I offer a new alliance with you as the representative of Gallea, and with whomever you duly recognize as the permanent regent until Guillaume comes of age. Do you accept?"

"On behalf of King Guillaume and Gallea, I accept your alliance."

"By this afternoon I can have fifty soldiers ready and enough skiffs to transport them and you down the River Sicana to Luteche. They'll symbolize my endorsement of you as regent and of our alliance. That will be the fastest way to travel back to Luteche...and the most unexpected."

Sighurd smiled and said, "That's very generous of you."

"I will have other men return your horses for you. Also, I will accompany you, to assure my message is clear." He looked around at everyone. "And I want to see my granddaughter."

He leaned forward and gazed at them intensely. "One more thing. To clear up

any controversy about who has claim to the throne and to stabilize the govern-
ment of our neighbors to the west, I offer my granddaughter Celeste as bride to
King Guillaume, as I offered my daughter Tamara to King Christian. She could
rule until he comes of age."

Sighurd looked at Eloise. She peered back with a somber expression and
said, "An interesting proposition we can consider."

"There would be no question of legitimacy," Geoffrey said. "The king would
be the son of the king, and the queen would be the daughter of the queen." He
turned to Kasimir. "Will all these things help with your quest?"

"Without question," Kasimir said. "A stable and legitimate rule in Luteche
along with support from Suedeche will go a long way to convincing the wizards
of Insu to make an alliance."

"Then it's settled," said Sighurd. "We return to Luteche on the river with
Geoffrey and his men. We march into the castle and declare our authority to
direct the affairs of Gallea until permanent rule can be established. We take Guillaume and Celeste into our protection. And we rely on our wizard and Pilgrim to
deal with Gwendolyn, who most certainly will resist our efforts."

"It sounds dangerous," said Faisal.

"Then let the Gods bless us all," said Geoffrey.

"They will," said Thomas. "Mother Goddess sent us her Pilgrim."

When the conference broke up, Ilsa joined Zenia at her side. She tried hard
to appear confident, but apprehension filled her.

Zenia must have noticed. She said, "That was a lot to take in all at once. How
are you feeling?"

"I'm...excited to be a part of it."

Zenia gazed at her with an amused expression. Ilsa realized she knew she
was hiding how she really felt. What a foolish thing to do, trying to pretend to a
Pilgrim!

"I'm terrified!" she blurted.

Zenia smiled and took her hand. "Let's go for a walk."

They walked through the gatehouse and into a garden alongside the castle.

"You feel like a small person caught in the middle of enormous events,"
Zenia said. "You're afraid you might be swallowed up by them."

That was exactly how she felt, she realized when Zenia said the words.

"If you like, you can return home. There'll be no shame in that."

The thought of returning to that dreary village after all she'd seen and heard
was unimaginable. Ever since she became a cripple, she never quite felt included. If she was going to feel out of place, she might as well feel out of place in
exciting places.

"I still want to see the world."

"Let me tell you a secret," Zenia said. "Everyone in that room started out a small person. Geoffrey was merely the duke of a small duchy tucked between two large kingdoms. Sighurd was the head guard for a king who was no older than you, charged with protecting him in a kingdom at peace with little danger. Eloise was the witch in that tiny village we visited. I was a timid apprentice, struggling to learn magic. Kasimir the wizard and his brother Faisal were apprentices themselves learning to be wizards. And Celeste was a little girl who played in the forest and splashed in a creek nearby and never had a care in her life."

They stopped to sit on a bench before a pool where fish swam.

"None of us were heroes," she continued. "None of us were caught up in enormous events. Until each of us, one by one, were thrown into circumstances that we never dreamed of. Just as you've never dreamed of facing the things we're about to face."

"But you became heroes."

Zenia smiled. "Yes, we did. But we never thought we would be. When the time came, we simply did what we had to do, and that's all it takes to become a hero."

She put her arm around Ilsa and squeezed. "It's alright to feel overwhelmed by the things we're facing. But don't feel overwhelmed by us. We're no different than you. When the time comes, you'll do what you have to do, and you'll become as much a hero as any of us." She kissed Ilsa on the cheek. "You're one of us now."

She wanted to believe, but it was so hard to imagine herself a hero. She was little crippled Ilsa, always left out of things because she couldn't do what others could do. They made her feel like she didn't deserve to do what others could do.

Her legs were whole now, but in her heart she still didn't feel like she deserved to be here.

"It's like...like...I'm still crippled in my mind."

"Do you have your dagger?"

Uncertain what Zenia intended, she pulled the dagger out and held it up.

"You said you're pretty good with it."

"I am."

"Show me."

Ilsa gazed at her for a moment, then started moving the dagger back and forth, slowly at first, then faster as she warmed up. She switched hands over and over, twirled the dagger and caught it and sliced at imaginary things in the air.

"That's very good," said Zenia. "But why are you sitting down?"

"I...I've always practiced sitting down."

"But you can stand now."

Ilsa looked at her, then stood up and walked a few steps away. She turned and took a deep breath. She began the same routine.

Zenia watched patiently, then said, "You're standing on your feet. Now *use* your feet."

She peered at her uncertainly, then swallowed and began again, attempting to step back and forth and side to side as if she were battling an opponent. She felt as clumsy and foolish as if she were still using crutches, and her handling of the dagger deteriorated.

"I don't know what to do with my feet!" she cried.

Zenia stood up. "But you *are* on your feet. You *are* using your feet." She walked up to her. "You're not crippled."

"But I *am*, if I don't know how to use my feet."

Zenia held out her hand in invitation. "Let's see what we can do about that."

Ilsa took her hand, and Zenia led her back into the castle. She brought her to where the guards of Luteche were. "Which one of you is the best knife fighter?" Zenia said.

Sighurd, Dietric, and Thomas looked at each other. "That would have to be Dietric," Sighurd said.

"Yes, Dietric," said Thomas.

"This young woman needs a little help with her footwork."

Dietric balked. "You want me to teach her knife fighting in an hour or two?"

"She already knows how to handle the knife," Zenia said. "She doesn't know what to do with her feet."

Dietric looked at Sighurd, who shrugged with an amused expression.

"Well," Dietric said. "Let me see what you *can* do."

She stood before them, eyes wide as she looked at them, and immense self-consciousness flooded over her. This was a terrible idea! She wanted to turn and flee.

But they looked at her in anticipation, Dietric, Thomas, Sighurd—and Zenia with a reassuring smile. They were all heroes in her mind, and she wanted to be counted among them one day. A hero wouldn't flee in terror because of embarrassment. A hero would...do what needs to be done.

She took a deep breath and held the dagger up. It trembled, and she realized it was herself who was trembling. She put the knife back down.

"Don't be embarrassed," Dietric said. "We all looked clumsy when we first started."

To her surprise, that made her feel a little better. She raised the dagger again and began her movements, very slowly, very deliberately, and slowly sped up. Her body became calmer and her moves more certain. As she relaxed, she tried moving her feet.

The guards watched quietly and without expression. At least they didn't smirk. At least they didn't laugh in derision. By the time she began to feel some confidence, Dietric said, "Okay, that's enough. You look better than I did when I started."

Such a small compliment, but it encouraged her.

For the rest of the morning until the call for the midday meal, Dietric gave her instructions and pointers and helped her polish her movements. They focused on her feet, moving them in concert with her hand. He explained when she'd want to do one thing and when another, depending on the circumstances and what her opponent was doing.

At the end, Dietric said, "Well, don't go charging into any battles just yet, but..." He nodded his head approvingly. "I'm impressed with how much you've improved with such little training."

She breathed heavily, as much from excitement as exertion. She could feel her face beaming and thought she probably had a silly smile on her face. But she didn't care.

As they went to the hall to eat, Zenia said, "How do you feel now?"

"I feel like a woman who was never crippled," she said with delight. "I feel like I *can* become a hero one day."

"How will you become a hero?"

"By...by doing what has to be done."

"Isn't that what you just did?"

She nodded enthusiastically.

"You won't become a hero one day," Zenia said. "You've already started becoming one."

After their midday meal, Eloise and Zenia and Ilsa took a walk along the rampart of the castle facing the city. Guards stationed there nodded at them and greeted them with "My Ladies" as they passed. Ilsa could feel that they included her in the greeting.

They stopped and leaned over to view the city and the River Sicana that flowed past, its ripples sparkling in the sunlight. Ilsa was almost in a daze as she looked out, standing beside a Pilgrim and a woman who had raised a daughter to become a dragon. It was like a dream to be included among them.

"Do you think they'll change tonight?" Eloise said. "Or will the moon no longer be full enough?"

"The legends say no," Zenia said, "but the legends say I should have been cursed. Yet I appeared before Mother Goddess, and she granted my request."

"You don't know?"

"The curse of the changeling doesn't come from us. It comes from an ancient source unknown to us."

Ilsa noted that Zenia referred to herself as if she were part of the Gods, which perhaps was true, being a demigod.

Eloise cast a spell and looked to the west. "I can't see her anywhere," she lamented.

"You're breath spell can't see very far," Zenia said.

"Can you cast a spell that sees farther?" Ilsa said.

"Spells are devices for mortals, a crutch to help them focus magical energy. I only need to choose to See." Zenia peered out to the west. "But I see nothing either."

"Dear Goddess, is she still alive?" Eloise said.

"There can be many reasons why an aura can't be seen. You used one of them while protecting Celeste."

"Thomas was right, wasn't he?" Eloise asked desperately. "Since Mother Goddess sent you, we're sure to be successful?"

"No," said Zenia flatly, shocking Ilsa. "We'll have to fight our best fight."

"They can't intervene?"

"They *won't* intervene." Zenia put her arm through Eloise's and squeezed. "How could mortals ever learn, ever develop if the Gods constantly meddled with their affairs? Our lives on earth are for becoming the best selves we can be. No coddled child ever grew to be a person of character."

"But they intervened by sending you!"

"I asked. I'm a part of this affair, and I sacrificed my life for it. I asked Mother Goddess to help Celeste, and her help was to send me back."

"So praying to the Gods is useless?"

"I asked, and she sent me back. Does that sound useless?"

Ilsa pondered this. It was a different view than she had of the Gods all her life. "So it *is* true that even you had to struggle to become a hero."

"It was so with the Seven Sisters of old," Zenia said. "Compassionate souls looked upon the earth they once lived on and asked Mother Goddess to help the world be a better place. Mother Goddess granted their request by bringing them together into the seven demigods that came to earth as the Seven Sisters. She sent them to do the work they requested of her."

Zenia chuckled. "Even they grew from their experience on earth. They tried to bless the world with magic, and learned through hard experience that mortals weren't ready for such things. They had to take it all back and left only a limited knowledge of magic behind."

"And even that limited amount has been abused by the Seven Sisters today," Eloise said.

"So their mission was a failure?" Ilsa asked in shock.

"Not at all!" said Zenia. " Before they came, the Onotrian Empire was a brutal place, as brutal as the empire of the Blood King. The Seven Sisters may have had to take the magic back, but their teachings, their influence, their example had an immense impact. Cueldea is a much more civilized place thanks to their efforts."

"But far from perfect," Eloise said.

Zenia smiled. "No, not perfect."

"I didn't want to say anything in front of the others," said Eloise. "It would only have complicated things. But I fear Gwendolyn isn't our only threat. I fear Deirdre knows too."

"She does," said Zenia with a matter-of-fact tone as if she were discussing the weather. "She's been watching us."

That alarmed Ilsa. "We're fighting Deirdre too?"

"I can sense her watching us. She's been watching me since I came to Vilnetal."

"Through *my* scrying globe, no doubt!" growled Eloise.

Zenia laughed. "Deirdre wouldn't see it that way."

"But you seem so unconcerned about it," Ilsa said.

"What is she but another old sorceress with limited magic? You weren't overly concerned about confronting Gwendolyn."

"But two sorceresses at once," Ilsa said.

"Do you think Deirdre would do that? Take us and Gwendolyn on at the same time?"

Eloise chuckled. "No, that wouldn't be her style. She'll wait until we deal with Gwendolyn, *then* swoop in."

"All we need to do is be ready for her when she does."

"If she's watching us," Ilsa asked, "should we be talking about what we know about her?"

"What will she do?" said Zenia. "Change her mind and try to take us and Gwendolyn on at the same time?"

"But now she'll know we know what she'll do."

Zenia squeezed Ilsa's arm. "I'm glad you're thinking these things through. Deirdre knows we're not fools and will anticipate many of the things she plans to do. We're not saying anything that'll surprise her."

Eloise put her arm around Zenia and pulled her close. "You make me feel hopeful, even after admitting we could lose. You learned well from your experiences. You've become the best daughter I could ever hope for."

"It's not only *my* experiences," Zenia said, returning the squeeze. "It's also Hereward's, and several other souls whom you don't even know."

Ilsa gazed at the river sparkling in the sun. She could barely remember what it was like trapped in that small village with nothing to experience but her mundane little life. It was like she had died and been reborn.

Almost like a Pilgrim.

Chapter 25

River Sicana

Celeste and Guillaume lay asleep on beds, Celeste with a gag over her mouth. With her Sight spell, Gwendolyn could see the Beast become a man again, stalking the corridors naked, continuing to circle around their location.

She also found Lucien still within the walls of the keep, stalking the Beast in the shadows. She didn't know whether to admire him for his courage or have contempt for his foolishness. Not until the Beast became a man again did he confront him with sword drawn.

The man stared him down solemnly and said, "I'll only become the wolf again and kill you."

"I have to protect the king," he said with determination in his face.

"I have no malice toward your king. I only want my daughter back."

Lucien's eyebrows flinched. "Your daughter?"

"Leave and I'll spare your life," the man said.

"Do it," Gwendolyn whispered. "Don't sacrifice yourself over my stupid order."

Lucien slowly backed away until he turned a corner, then fled.

Bernard watched her, wide-eyed, as she observed the man. "Is he coming?"

"He's trying. He doesn't know the way."

The man was in the unused chambers of the queen, where Tamara had spent lonely nights, where Christian banished Mariam to when she became too large to be desirable. The chambers that Zenia had stolen Mariam from.

He crept naked around the room, examining it in fine detail. She held her breath as he approached the mirror on the wall and peered into it for a moment. He began to feel along its edges. Before long he opened the mirror and crept down the passageway, pausing at each intersection, always choosing the fork that brought him closer to the safe room.

Gwendolyn panicked, even though he shouldn't be able to get in. Not only did she not want to lose Celeste, but the thought of confronting the man as the Beast terrified her. She thought of the amulet in her chest.

She drew it out, the gold locket on a chain, the Magic Eater. The last time she used it was during the war with Scaendelreic, cautiously to keep Deirdre from guessing she had it. She used it when she and Deirdre met privately to discuss an unofficial truce between their two kingdoms, to guarantee Deirdre couldn't ambush her with some devious magic. She wore it around her neck, hidden under her clothes, and quietly spoke the activation command before entering the room with Deirdre.

It was a good thing she had. Deirdre made a subtle attempt to use some kind of magic, an attempt Gwendolyn almost missed. At first it enraged her, but the confusion on Deirdre's face, then the frustration when nothing happened, was satisfying. Gwendolyn could see it in her eyes—that was the moment Deirdre truly resigned herself to a truce.

Gwendolyn never used it ever since, saving it for an emergency. That moment may have finally come.

Bernard peered at the amulet with curiosity. He knew of its existence, but had never seen it.

She slipped it over her head and tucked it inside her clothing. Using it would be a desperate act. She hoped, when she spoke the activation command, it would stifle Celeste's aura so the man couldn't detect her anymore. She hoped it would suppress Celeste's ability to call creatures to attack. But these were powers of the changeling, not of the magic of the Seven Sisters. She didn't know if the Magic Eater could eat such powers.

She couldn't begin to guess if it would suppress their ability to change.

For all she knew, it might do nothing more than rob Gwendolyn of the ability to cast any of her own spells. But she had to try. It was their only chance to escape without the Beast tracking them. She looked at the rug covering the middle of the floor. If the amulet failed, the Beast could follow and ambush them, and she wouldn't even have the power of Sight to see it coming.

"Celeste?" came a muffled voice through the stone wall. Bernard jumped.

Gwendolyn looked with Sight and found the man standing on the other side of the wall, facing the secret entrance.

"Gwendolyn," he called again, "your life for my daughter."

Bernard had an alarmed look, but Gwendolyn raised her hand to assure him, without feeling assured herself.

She spoke the amulet's activation command, *Thou shalt consume* in the Ancient Tongue. Immediately the man behind the wall became invisible as it consumed her Sight spell.

"Celeste!" the voice cried in consternation. "You witch! What have you done with her?"

Gwendolyn smiled with satisfaction. The Magic Eater did suppress her aura.

The man pounded on the wall. They were faint, powerless thumps. "Gwendolyn, I will tear you to shreds if you harm her!"

"I don't think he'll ever leave," Bernard whispered.

He was probably right. The man would be a threat for the entire nine months, along with Eloise, Sighurd, possibly even Kasimir and Deirdre.

"We have to leave Luteche," she said.

"Where will we go?"

She thought a moment and smiled. "Shall we return to Pretanica? Perhaps King John would appreciate a sorceress in his employ."

He gave her a wistful look. "Do you think they've forgotten by now?"

"Celeste!" the man shouted, beating his fists.

Celeste murmured and shifted. Her eyes fluttered open, and she looked about the room with alarm. She struggled to sit up, but with her hands tied behind her back could only turn sideways to look at the room.

Gwendolyn watched her apprehensively as she replaced her materials into the sack. "Bernard, gather up supplies from the pantry."

Celeste glared at her with an intense stare.

"Calling your little creatures?" Gwendolyn looked around and saw a spider lurking in a web in a corner near the ceiling. It didn't move. Celeste's face filled with dismay.

Gwendolyn, feeling relieved, came and sat on the bed next to her. "I'm tired of dealing with your efforts to escape. Bernard, bring a bottle of wine and a cup."

Bernard brought them and handed them to her.

"Since I can't cast a spell on you, I'll do it the old fashioned way." Gwendolyn pulled Celeste's gag down below her chin.

Immediately Celeste spoke a Flash spell. Gwendolyn waited with a satisfied smile. Nothing happened. Celeste's eyes widened with apprehension. She shouted *open* in the Ancient Tongue. The stones remained still.

"Help!" she screamed.

Guillaume jerked awake with a small cry. He sat up and rubbed his eyes.

Gwendolyn expected the man to call back, but there was no sound. He must have given up.

"I'm hungry," Guillaume murmured.

"Go over there and have Bernard find you something."

The boy and Bernard searched the pantry for something to eat.

"No one can get in, and you can't get out," Gwendolyn said to Celeste, twisting the cork out of the bottle. "You can't cast any spells in here, you can't call any creatures, and no one can see your aura." She poured wine into the cup. "There's nothing you can do, so you might as well calm down. Here, drink this."

Celeste glared at the cup, then at her.

Gwendolyn rolled her eyes and took a drink. "See? It's perfectly safe." She put the cup to Celeste's mouth. "Now drink. It'll help you relax."

Celeste spat on Gwendolyn's fingers. Bernard and Guillaume watched, frowning.

Holding back her anger, Gwendolyn switched the cup to her other hand and wiped her fingers on the blanket. Celeste jerked her legs up and knocked the cup out of her hand with her knees. It clattered to the floor, spilling the wine.

Fuming, Gwendolyn said, "Bernard, hold her down."

He forced Celeste back down and leaned on her as he held her head in place. "Hold her nose," Gwendolyn said as she hovered the bottle over her face.

"What are you doing?" Guillaume said.

Celeste struggled and kept her lips closed until the breath in her lungs exploded out. Gwendolyn stuffed the bottle in her mouth. Celeste made loud gulping sounds, then choked and coughed, spraying drops of wine all over Gwendolyn's face.

"Again!" Gwendolyn cried. The bottle went in, and Celeste gulped more until she coughed and sputtered.

"Again!" The third time, Celeste swallowed several times without choking.

Gwendolyn pulled the bottle away. "Have you ever had wine, Celeste?"

"I don't even know what it is," she said, still coughing.

"That should be enough then."

Bernard let her head go. She kept coughing for a while longer.

Gwendolyn strapped the sword and scabbard to her back where she could draw it quickly if necessary. Guillaume pressed his back into the corner as he stared at it.

"I feel sick," Celeste said.

"I imagine so," said Gwendolyn.

The wall reverberated with a loud crash, causing all of them to jump. Guillaume cried out.

"Help!" Celeste shrieked again.

"Celeste, I'm coming!" Another crash.

"He must have found a pickaxe," said Bernard.

Guillaume huddled down with his hands over his ears.

Gwendolyn slid the gag back into Celeste's mouth. "We need to leave now. Take her. Guillaume, come."

The boy remained bent over on the floor, shielding his ears.

She rushed over to the rug and rolled it back, revealing the trapdoor. "Guillaume! That's the Beast coming." She opened the door. "We have to run."

He looked up, saw the trapdoor, cringed as another blow crashed on the wall, then jumped up and ran over.

"Climb down," Gwendolyn said as she grabbed her sack of materials and the sack of provisions. He disappeared down the ladder.

Bernard wrapped the blanket around Celeste and carried her. She struggled, but Bernard held on tight.

The wall crashed again, and bits of gravel fell from it.

Gwendolyn went down the ladder next. Celeste kept struggling while Bernard climbed down, and Gwendolyn feared she might struggle out of his grasp and plummet. The last thing she needed now was for Celeste to try to kill herself a second time.

It was slow going for Bernard, and Gwendolyn reached the bottom well before him. He held tight to Celeste as he grappled with the rungs until he reached low enough to hand her off to Gwendolyn.

They were in a shallow cave that opened to the river. Its water flowed in, flooding the cave with a deep pool. An artificial platform was carved out of the rock wall that acted as the landing for the ladder and a dock for a skiff tied to it.

"Get in the boat," Gwendolyn commanded, and Guillaume climbed in. Bernard followed, and she handed Celeste to him. She placed the sacks in the boat, climbed in, and took Celeste into her lap, holding her tight as she continued to squirm.

A thunderous crash and a shout of "Celeste!" echoed down from above. The man had broken through.

Bernard paddled the boat out of the cave. The current of the water immediately caught them and pulled them downstream. Soon they passed the narrow waterfall from the moat.

Celeste retched. The vomit leaked around her gag. She started choking.

"Oh Gods!" Gwendolyn turned her face down and untied the gag.

"What's wrong with her?" said Guillaume.

Celeste coughed out the residue. "I'm sick."

"I'm sorry I had to do that, but I can't cast any Sleep spells on you. Now lean over the edge."

Celeste did so, and Gwendolyn splashed water from the river onto her mouth, then held a handful of water to her lips. "Drink this." Celeste slurped it in.

Gwendolyn swished the gag in the water and tied it back on. "Now be still! You're not helping yourself with all this squirming."

Celeste slumped forward and breathed heavily with her eyes closed. Bernard paddled, shooting the skiff swiftly down the river as it flowed north. Guillaume stared at Celeste with troubled eyes.

They approached the ferry. Gwendolyn said, "Guillaume, lie down in the boat." She didn't need to have anyone notice she was spiriting the king away. Several people with horses loaded up on the ferry on the west shore. They stared at the skiff as it went by. Gwendolyn turned away from them. She didn't need anyone noticing the sorceress of Luteche floating by either.

Before long Fenweald Forest loomed ahead. The River Sicana swept them into its haunting gloom.

———

Edmund swung the pickaxe for the blow that broke through the wall. He was glad now for all those years chopping wood that helped him focus and avoid the Change when it became difficult to resist. It gave him the muscles to save Celeste now.

"Celeste!" he shouted into the hole. There was no response.

He pounded until the hole widened enough to crawl through, then scrambled in, ignoring scratches from the jagged rock. When his head emerged, he found a large room, and the room was empty. Instantly he noticed the rolled up rug and the open trapdoor in the floor.

He crawled into the room and climbed down the ladder as quickly as he could. At the bottom was a cave and a platform and a pool from the river flowing in. Attached to the edge of the platform were some ropes that dangled and floated in the water. A boat, now gone. He cried out in anguish.

What could possibly have happened to Celeste? What happened to his sense of her presence? Had the witch killed her? Yet she had cried out to him.

He gauged the swift current of the river passing by the mouth of the cave. They probably traveled downstream. He dove into the pool and swam out.

He let the current push him down the river as he added to it with his strokes, keeping an eye out ahead and on either passing bank for a sign of the boat.

He came to a ferry floating across the river with people and horses on it. He swam up to it, and as the people gaped at him he remembered he was naked, but after all the times he'd been naked after changing back from the wolf, it didn't bother him.

"Did you see a boat go by," he called to them, "with a woman and a girl?"

One of the men nodded and pointed downriver.

Edmund pushed himself away from the ferry and swam on. In all his centuries of life, he'd never been this far west, having spent most of them hidden away in the forest. All he knew was the river emptied into the ocean somewhere ahead at a place called Sicana Harbor, a city within the duchy of Pretany.

Could that be where Gwendolyn was taking Celeste? Did she intend to leave Gallea entirely, sailing off to the Gods knew where?

He swam forward as fast as he could, keeping careful watch for a boat and a woman and a girl.

They launched the skiffs in the heat of the afternoon. Geoffrey, Sighurd, Kasimir, and Faisal rode in one in the middle of the caravan, Kasimir and Faisal wearing dark cloaks with hoods to hide their foreign appearance. Dietric, Thomas, Eloise, Zenia, and Ilsa rode in the skiff directly behind. Zenia also wore a dark cloak over her silk robe.

Ilsa had never ridden in a boat before. She was nervous and exhilarated. She never felt more alive.

The River Sicana veered quickly to the north from Suedeche. Within an hour it plunged into Fenweald Forest. The forest was sparse and cheery, but that didn't last long. The thick mass of trees closed in on them. The pines increased in number. The ground vegetation thickened. Ilsa had heard people say the forest was haunted, and now she believed it. She was glad there were fifty soldiers accompanying them.

The river made a long, wide arc to the west. By the time they could hear the thundering of the Falls of Eircana, the river had arced south, widening, spreading into the forest. Islands pockmarked it, and at the edges, trees arose from within its water. The river made a sharp crook west, much like a butcher's hook, then plunged into a gaping chasm on both sides to become a series of waterfalls that thundered loudly, disturbing Ilsa.

They beached on the north bank on the inner side of the crook. Geoffrey's soldiers portaged the skiffs along the northern cliffs for about a mile until they subsided back to the level of the river. By the time they were afloat again, the sun had set and the sky was darkening with a red glow.

The river flowed swiftly here, having narrowed. Mistress Moon rose and traveled across the sky as they paddled until it crossed the zenith above them by the time they saw the lights of the city of Luteche ahead. Before they left the forest, they pulled their boats ashore, hidden among the trees. They walked the rest of the way, swords ready.

Within a half hour, Sighurd, Kasimir, and Geoffrey presented themselves at the outer gatehouse with a wizard's attendant, a witch, two of the King's Guard, a Pilgrim and her servant, and fifty soldiers of Luteche standing behind them. By the look on the guards' faces, it must have been an impressive sight.

One of the guards came forward. "Captain Sighurd. Thank the Gods you're back."

"Lieutenant Lucien, is it true that King Christian is dead?"

"The dragon's breath got him."

"The dragon returned?"

"Gwendolyn brought a girl in, but she changed into a dragon in the Great Hall."

"Mother Goddess," Eloise murmured.

Gwendolyn did catch her! Ilsa thought with alarm.

"Where's that girl now?" said Sighurd.

"Gwendolyn took her after she changed back."

Ilsa tried to imagine all that. A girl about her own age captured by a sorceress and turning into a dragon inside a castle.

"And Guillaume. Where's he?" Sighurd asked.

"I brought him into the safe room. He's there now with Gwendolyn and the girl."

"Oh dear Mother Goddess!" Eloise said quietly.

"Open the gate and step aside."

"Captain, the Beast is still inside. He can change at any time."

"I know. Now step aside at once."

Lucien barked the command. Soon the portcullis slid open. The group from Suedeche entered.

The inner gate was also closed. Sighurd had to call multiple times before some guards crept down, looking around warily. "Let us in," he commanded.

"The Beast is—"

"I know. Do it!"

With the gate lifted, they came inside. The corridor that plunged into the keep was dark with no lanterns lit. Sighurd and Thomas grabbed torches from the walls of the gatehouse.

Sighurd said to the guards, "This is Duke Geoffrey of Suedeche, and these are his men. They've come as our allies to help me restore order in the kingdom. You will work with them."

Geoffrey commanded forty-five of his men to stay with the guards in the courtyard. He kept five of them with him as the group crept down the corridor along with some of the King's Guard.

When they entered the Great Hall, Ilsa gasped. The damage was shocking. A cool draft blasted in from a giant hole in the ceiling. The dragon must have tried to break through and escape. But it must not have succeeded, since the guard said Gwendolyn had Celeste in some room.

Eloise gazed about the keep with glassy eyes. Zenia gazed around too, then looked at Eloise and shook her head.

"The Beast and Celeste are gone from the castle," Zenia said. "I see nothing for miles."

"Light the lamps in here," Sighurd commanded the guards, "then gather everyone into the hall."

"Where can they be?" Eloise said. "Gods curse Gwendolyn if she killed them."

Kasimir said, "You masked Celeste's aura for years. Could Gwendolyn have done the same thing?"

"It's possible," said Zenia.

"Then how will we ever find her?" Faisal asked.

Sighurd looked up the staircase. "We start with Gwendolyn's chambers."

Edmund swam until exhausted, then sat on the shore resting. There was nothing around him but the encroaching forest. His body cried out for nourishment after all the swimming and the changes back and forth from man to Beast. He searched around until he found a snake slithering in the undergrowth. He grabbed it and broke its neck and devoured it raw.

His heart ached thinking of his daughter in the clutches of that wicked sorceress. He shouldn't have sent Tamara away all those years ago. From the things the Pilgrim and Eloise told him, it sounded like no one from the castle would have been too upset about losing her.

Then she and he and eventually Celeste could have lived a quiet life together with no one being the wiser of Celeste's existence and what she was. He could have taught Celeste to control her Change. Tamara would grow old and die, alas, but he and Celeste could have lived a long life together unplagued by loneliness.

He had to find her. He had to save her. He had to vanquish her enemies so she could live in peace. But he didn't even know where she was. He was playing a hunch, but for all he knew, he could be getting farther and farther away from her with every stroke in the river.

If she was even still alive.

He wept for a moment, then launched back into the river with a vengeance, swimming with mighty, desperate strokes, praying to the Gods he'd spurned for centuries that he was getting closer to her, not farther away.

Sighurd stood before the broken door to Gwendolyn's chambers with the others behind him. Dietric remained in the Great Hall to direct the clean-up activity.

Sighurd's torch flickered its light on the broken door lying on the floor. The rest of the room was dark with no lamps lit, an indication that no one had been there since nightfall.

Looking at the door, he said, "I'll wager the Beast has been here," then stepped in.

Gwendolyn's worktable was cluttered, her bed rumpled. Storage shelves seemed to have been emptied of a lot of materials that were once there when he came for Eloise's necklace. He noticed a square hole in the wall and went to it. Holding up the torch, he saw the four stones receded back. He felt around in it and found nothing.

"I guess we know where she hid her secrets." He took one more scan around the room. "My guess is she fled."

"Where?" Geoffrey said.

Sighurd went to the mirror on the wall and swung it open. He walked into a passageway hidden behind it. Everyone followed.

He navigated the passageway to the safe room entrance. A huge hole had been bashed through it, and a giant pickaxe sat abandoned on the floor. He peered into the room and saw the rug rolled back and the trapdoor open.

"Edmund was here," he said.

"Could he have rescued her?" Eloise asked hopefully.

He shook his head and squeezed through. Inside he found the pantry ransacked. On the floor near a bed was a pool of spilled wine, a cup lying on its side, and an open bottle.

As the others crawled in, he gestured to the trapdoor. "Gwendolyn had plenty of time to escape while he broke through the wall."

"The king's not here," Thomas said. "She must have taken him too."

"She's looking for legitimacy," Sighurd said. "She needs him to claim the regency." He went to the trapdoor. "Wait here."

He climbed in and descended the ladder, hopping his free hand from one rung to the next as he held the torch up with his other. When he reached the last few rungs, he looked about the cave and found what he expected. The boat was missing.

He worked his way back up. "The boat's gone. They couldn't go upriver with the falls. My guess is, she's fleeing with Celeste and Guillaume to Sicana Harbor."

"She could sail anywhere from there," Thomas said.

"Pretany's not an ally," Geoffrey said. "Won't they be suspicious if the sorceress of Gallea shows up alone with the king of Gallea?"

"If anyone even recognizes them," said Sighurd. "They may not know Christian is dead yet."

"They might not let them cross the border," Eloise said.

"With enough money, anyone can enter Pretany and buy passage anywhere," Thomas said.

"We need to chase them down immediately." Sighurd led them out of the room and down the passageway back to the Great Hall.

The lamps were lit. The guards and the soldiers of Suedeche were cleaning up the debris. The worst of it had been pushed against the walls.

Sighurd invited Geoffrey to sit on the one undamaged throne, then attempted to right the damaged one without success. He gave up and sat in Gwendolyn's chair.

Geoffrey spoke first. "I am Duke Geoffrey of Suedeche, ally to Gallea. Since King Christian has died and Guillaume is too young to rule, I recognize Captain Sighurd of the King's Guard as the acting regent until he can make permanent arrangements." He nodded to Sighurd.

"It appears Gwendolyn has abducted our king and may be fleeing the country by way of Sicana Harbor," Sighurd said. "This makes her a traitor. We'll travel down the river ourselves to get him back." He turned to Geoffrey. "May we bring half your men with, to help with any problems we have at the border?"

"You may bring half of my men and *me*," he said forcefully.

Sighurd smiled and turned back to the group. "Thomas will come with us. Dietric and Lucien will remain here and govern in my absence."

The official gathering ended. Dietric asked him, "What shall we do if Gwendolyn returns?"

"Go along with her as best you can, and send a messenger to us immediately. But protect Guillaume and Celeste at all costs." He smiled. "Perhaps Edmund is following her and can help you with that."

To his group Sighurd said, "Let's portage the skiffs past the falls."

Eloise shook her head. "I fear we'll be too late. I wish I'd stolen Deirdre's Flight spell."

"You wouldn't have it now anyway," Sighurd said.

Eloise scowled. "That's one I *would* have memorized."

Faisal, staring at one of the walls, grabbed Kasimir by the shoulder and said, "Brother!" He pointed to a rug piled in the corner. "Do you remember the stories Mother told us?"

Kasimir looked, and his eyes widened. "It's even a rug from Komshu," he said, grinning.

"What are you talking about?" Sighurd asked.

"Bring that rug out into the courtyard," Kasimir said. "Maybe we *can* steal Deirdre's Flight spell." He looked at Faisal. "I hope."

Guards carried the rug out. It was huge, having extended nearly up to the base of the ceiling and nearly down to the floor when it hung on the wall. They spread it out on the cobblestones, and Kasimir directed the group to sit on it.

"Mother Goddess," Eloise said, "are you doing what I think you're doing?"

"I'm going to try. I've never seen it done before."

Sighurd said to Geoffrey, "We'll meet you and your men in Sicana Harbor." To Lucien and Faisal he said, "You two go with them to represent Gallea and Insu."

Kasimir sat on the rug, and Sighurd, Thomas, Eloise, Zenia, and Ilsa joined him. Sighurd felt foolish and hoped whatever Kasimir intended would work so he wouldn't look foolish in front of his men.

Kasimir said to Faisal, "Come swiftly, Brother," then exposed his chest and plucked a starstone. As his trickle of blood activated it, he closed his eyes and spoke words of incantation. Sighurd held his breath, having no idea what to expect.

The shining gem burst and enveloped them all in a brief flash of light. The rug went rigid and shuddered, jostling everyone sitting on it. Ilsa gave out a yelp. Sighurd suddenly realized the rug was lifting them off the ground. "Great Father Sky!" he cried.

"Exactly," Faisal called up to him, grinning.

The occupants of the rug looked about with amazement. The men on the ground gaped at them. When the rug rose many feet above the walls of the courtyard, Kasimir said, "Which way to Sicana Harbor?"

"Follow the river north," Sighurd said as he pointed.

The rug accelerated, apparently controlled by Kasimir's mind, and flew over the wall, over the river, and over the trees of Fenweald Forest.

———

Bernard quietly paddled down the river. The moonlight cast a ghostly pall over everything. On either bank, the forest periodically approached and receded. There was nothing else but darkness around them, but for the sparkling of the stars.

Guillaume gazed around in silence. His face seemed to be filled with awe.

Celeste's head lay asleep in Gwendolyn's lap. Gwendolyn looked into her face. It was moist with perspiration, even though the night was pleasantly cool. She felt the girl's forehead. It was hot with a fever. This was more than the wine.

Gwendolyn untied her gag and dipped it in the water. Celeste didn't stir. She daubed at the perspiration on the girl's forehead, then daubed at the rest of her face. She dipped it in the water again and laid it across her forehead.

What disease had she caught? Gwendolyn whispered, "Don't you die on me, little one."

Did she dare risk deactivating the Magic Eater so she could cast a Sight spell and determine the malady, then cast a Healing spell? By now someone must have figured out where they'd gone. Certainly Sighurd, if he'd returned to Luteche by now. Would it matter if she confirmed their whereabouts to them? That wouldn't help them come any faster.

But there was always Deirdre. Gwendolyn had no idea if that bitch was aware of what happened tonight, but if she did, she assuredly would be watching. She could easily catch up with her Flying spell.

They voyaged down the river as the moon climbed high and shone down from above. Celeste moaned and squirmed, then gave off a small cry of discomfort. "Mother," she murmured.

Dreaming? Delirious? Gwendolyn dared not wait any longer. To the demons with Deirdre! She couldn't do anything to them with the Magic Eater activated.

She spoke the deactivation command, spoke a general Healing spell as quickly as she could, waited a moment for it to work, then reactivated the amulet. With any luck, she tried to tell herself, no one was looking during that short burst of Celeste's aura into the night. But she didn't believe it.

Celeste calmed down, eyes still closed. Gwendolyn thought her fever might have lessened, but didn't think the malady, whatever it was, had gone away with a mere breath spell. Hopefully it gave Celeste more time until it was safe for Gwendolyn to properly attend to her.

Several more times Edmund had to rest, then plunged on. Several times he caught a small animal and ate it raw to keep his strength up.

Suddenly he felt a pull ahead of him, farther down the river. It was Celeste! He was going the right direction. He redoubled his efforts, pushing hard against the water with each stroke.

As quickly as it came, the pull disappeared. He couldn't feel Celeste any-more. But she was still alive, and he was going in the right direction. Somehow the sorceress could switch her presence on and off.

He wanted to become the wolf and dash to her along the river bank. But without her pull, the wolf would probably wander aimlessly and end up Gods knew where, killing Gods knew who. He resigned himself to keep swimming. They couldn't flee forever. Eventually they'd come to the sea.

"I'm coming for you, Celeste," he called out.

Flying through the sky with the crisp night air blasting her face was exhila-rating. Ilsa pressed her fingers against the rug. It gave only a little, like pressing on a bed of fertile earth. She wanted to crawl to the edge and peer over, but didn't trust that the rug wouldn't bend under her weight and drop her to the ground.

"She stopped watching us," Zenia said all of a sudden.

"Deidre?" Eloise said.

Zenia nodded. "Her globe's gone dark."

"Dear Goddess, does that mean she's coming?" They looked at each other with concern.

The river meandered through the forest. Mistress Moon's pale face danced in its ripples. They followed the river for a long while as it cut through the forest in veering curves. The trees waved gently with a breeze vastly milder than the blast in Ilsa's face. She could smell the aromas of the forest.

Zenia jolted everyone by crying out, "I see her!"

"Celeste?" Kasimir said.

"Ahead on the river."

Eloise spoke a Sight spell. "I see her too." Suddenly her face went somber.

"It's gone again," Zenia said.

"But she's still alive," Eloise said hopefully.

"It looks like Gwendolyn *is* bringing her to the harbor," Zenia said.

"We'll find her there," Sighurd said with determination.

Guillaume slept on the floor of the skiff, and Celeste slept in Gwendolyn's arms. Ahead she could see where Fenweald Forest ended, with meadows and fields spread out beyond. This was where the border with Pretany began, divid-ing the River Sicana between the duchy of Pretany on the left and the kingdom of Gallea on the right. Pretany was a vassal state of Pretanica, left over from the time Pretanica crossed the Sea of Maneche to invade Gallea. Relations between Pretany and Gallea were not warm.

"Keep near the right shore," she told Bernard. "Let's stay inside Gallea."

He steered them over just as the Pretany outpost guarding the border came into view on the left. The guards watched them drift by with somber looks, but they had no authority past the middle of the river.

Gwendolyn estimated another two hours before they reached the highway along the seacoast that crossed from Gallea into Pretany over a large bridge across the River Sicana. The highway paralleled the seashore through Gallea until it came to the border with Brebannia in the north. That duchy also shared borders with Scaendelreic on the east and Scandia to the north. Brebannia remained neutral with the kingdoms surrounding it. Gwendolyn preferred to give the border guards of Pretany the impression they had come from there instead of Luteche.

Presently the river curved east from its northern course, then made a broad horseshoe arc to the west. Her plan was to beach the skiff and walk before they reached the highway. By then the sun should just be rising. They could cross the bridge appearing as if they traveled from Brebannia along the highway, and her gold coins should buy the privilege of entering Pretany and Sicana Harbor.

Then she'd arrange passage and find sanctuary in the island kingdom of Pretanica. It would be a homecoming of sorts for her and Bernard, even though King Richard, the king she served in her younger years, was dead. His younger brother John ruled in his stead, the brother who had rebelled against him while he was king. Gwendolyn and Bernard had fled to Luteche in those days. She'd have to play the penitent servant to John and get in his good graces, but that was something she had good experience in.

Chapter 26

Sicana Harbor

Gwendolyn let the boat get as close to the highway as she dared, gauging the distance by the lights from Sicana Harbor, then said, "Go ashore now."

She rummaged in her sack and scooped up a handful of gold coins and put them in the pocket of her dress as Bernard paddled and beached the skiff. Guillaume awoke from the jolt and sat up, groggy. "Where are we?"

Gwendolyn handed the sleeping Celeste to Bernard and helped Guillaume out of the boat. She crouched down before him and said, "Now listen to me. We're going into Pretany. Do you know Pretany?"

He shook his head, still rubbing his eyes.

"It's the country northwest of Luteche. They're not our friends."

"Then why are we going there?"

"There are ships there. We're going to ride one across the sea to an island kingdom. Would you like to go on a boat ride across the sea?"

He perked up and nodded.

"We have to pretend we're from a country that *is* friends with Pretany. It's called Brebannia. Can you do that? Can you pretend you're from Brebannia?"

"Be...Bebrannia?"

She smiled at him. "Close enough. Just keep quiet and act like a shy little boy when anyone talks to us. Can you do that?"

He nodded.

"Good boy!" She turned to Bernard and took Celeste so he could get out. "Leave the food. Just bring my sack of materials."

"What do we do with the boat?" he said.

"To the demons with the boat. We're nearly there." She wasn't concerned about someone from Luteche finding it soon. It wasn't like anyone there had Deirdre's Flight spell. It was Deirdre she was most concerned about, and she wanted to get away quickly without worrying about a boat.

Gwendolyn carried Celeste as Bernard carried the sack with one hand and held Guillaume's hand with the other. They walked to the highway, angling away from the mouth of the river so they'd enter the highway out of sight of any border guards.

The sun rose as they reached the highway. Far to the right in the direction of Brebannia, she saw a team of two horses pulling a wagon and a man driving them. "We're a family," she announced. "Guillaime, I'm your and Celeste's mother. Bernard is your father."

As the wagon approached, the driver eyed them with suspicion. He steered the horse to the far side of the road.

"Please, sir," Gwendolyn said in Ruic, in case he was from Brebannia. "My daughter's ill. Would you give us a ride into Sicana Harbor?"

He stopped the wagon, peering at them with a doubtful look. "I don't need any trouble at the border."

"Please, sir, she may die." She walked up to the man and shifted Celeste so he could see her face. "See how ill she looks?" She reached in her pocket, pulled out a gold coin, and set it on the seat next to him.

He looked at it warily.

"You can say we're your family."

"With two husbands?" he said, eyeing Bernard.

"He's my brother." She glanced at Guillaume, who stared at her with a confused look, but said nothing. She set another coin next to the other, studying the man. His brow knotted, and he frowned.

She placed a third coin. The corners of his mouth flickered with a smile.

She stepped back. "Can you help us?"

He scooped up the coins and pocketed them. "My wife doesn't carry a sword."

She'd forgotten about that! She put on a chagrined face. "Just for protection. I can hide it."

"You're the protector, not your brother?"

This man was beginning to irritate her. "It's easier for him to draw it from my back."

She felt foolish after saying it, and his face reflected skepticism, but he waved at the wagon full of produce under a tarpaulin. "Hide it back there somewhere. And the children."

Bernard climbed on the side of the wagon and untied a corner of the tarpaulin. He slid Gwendolyn's sack inside, then pushed vegetables aside and laid Guillaume, then Celeste in the empty space. "Don't make a sound," he said to the boy.

"Hurry up," said the man, looking at some travelers coming down the road from Sicana Harbor.

Bernard slid the scabbard and sword down between them and tied the corner back into place. He and Gwendolyn crowded on the seat beside the man.

"Won't they check your wagon?" she asked.

He whistled and jerked the reins to start the horses moving. "I've been going there for years and never gave them any trouble."

When they passed the travelers, they nodded. They reached the bridge, the largest one Gwendolyn had ever seen. All the traffic from the north came this way to the busiest harbor in the region. The mouth of the River Sicana spread wide on the seaward side of the bridge, becoming a bay as it joined with the sea. She wished Guillaume could see this impressive sight. But he'd have plenty thrills crossing the sea later.

Fishing boats dotted the water to the horizon. They were already out this early in the day. Gwendolyn began to feel the excitement of adventure, tainted only by concern for Celeste's health and the fear that Deirdre might suddenly appear.

Gods, she missed her Sight!

"What's your name?" she asked the man.

"Andries." A good Brebannian name. "And yours?"

"Genoveva," she said. It felt strange to use her birthname once again. But she certainly didn't want to advertise that the sorceress of Luteche was entering Pretany.

On the other side of the bridge were the border guards, and shortly after that the city began. The guards greeted the man warmly. "Who are these with you?"

"My sister and her husband," he said. "They want to see the city."

They waved him through. Gwendolyn smiled with satisfaction. She was surprised the border crossing had proven to be so effortless. She'd have lost more than three coins if she had to bribe the guards.

The Gods were blessing her today.

The moon was low ahead of them in the west. Its face reflected in the river sweeping past them as the rug flew above. Pinpricks of light on the horizon announced the nearing of Sicana Harbor. A sick feeling swept through Eloise. They'd seen no sign of Gwendolyn or Celeste along the river since that brief flash of her aura. Had they missed them somehow?

"What if they're not in the city?" Eloise said. "What if we missed them?"

"We didn't miss them," Zenia said, who'd been constantly sweeping the area with her form of Sight, "unless they're carrying the boat around with them on land."

"There's no reason to come this far down the river unless they're heading for Sicana Harbor," Sighurd said.

"What if they're tricking us into thinking they're going to Sicana Harbor," Eloise said, "but head toward Bebrannia instead? They could be shipping out from Seaxhavn."

Sighurd shot her a frown, but didn't answer at first. Finally he said, "If we don't find them in Sicana Harbor, then Kasimir flies us along the highway toward Brebannia."

Thomas pointed ahead. "We're approaching Pretany."

Eloise saw a border outpost with several guards on duty at this predawn hour. As they flew overheard, the guards looked up and pointed at them. A blast of a horn brought more guards scurrying out from the structures.

Everyone on the rug watched them somberly. Two horsemen burst from the gate and galloped down the road heading toward Sicana Harbor. "Couriers," said Thomas. "I think we've officially invaded Pretany."

"We'll have to sort it out later," said Sighurd. "Right now our focus is finding Celeste."

"They'll sound the alarm."

"We'll get there before them."

They flew on as the moon dipped down to the horizon and the first glow of dawn colored the sky to the east.

The rug suddenly shifted down a couple feet, causing everyone to sprawl. "What was that?" Eloise cried.

"The starstone is fading," Kasimir said.

"Will we make it to Sicana Harbor?" Sighurd asked.

Kasimir looked at Sighurd and didn't answer.

When the sun had just risen, Edmund found the boat. They hadn't even attempted to hide it. He looked in it and found a sack of food. Quickly he devoured enough to still his hunger. He found their tracks in the dirt leading away into a field, two adults and one child. The adult ones were too large for Celeste's feet, and the child's was too small.

He groaned in agony. Who was the adult with the sorceress? Who was the child? Where was Celeste? Was he even following the right people?

But he calmed himself and thought, of course Celeste wouldn't be walking. They'd have her restrained somehow and were probably carrying her. That encouraged him. Walking while carrying a young woman would slow them down. He broke into a run in the direction of the footprints, glad that no one was around. A naked man running through a field would attract more attention than he wanted.

He ran until he came to a farmhouse. A man and his young son were outside feeding pigs. He charged up to them, startling them. They backed away in fear.

It disturbed him to threaten innocent people, but he couldn't waste any time. He stood in a pose to emphasize his huge muscles and gave them his most frightening glare. "I need clothes!" he growled.

"Yes...yes, sir!" the man said with alarmed eyes and dragged his son with him into the cabin. Soon a pile of clothing flew out and the door slammed shut.

There was a pair of trousers that he could barely squeeze on and a shirt with buttons that was too small, so he let it hang open.

He ran, following a faint trampling of grasses through the fields that he hoped was them. Ahead he saw a wide road, and sitting stationary in the road a wagon pulled by two horses with a man driving it.

Two adults and a child stood next to it.

From this distance, and with her back to him, he couldn't be sure, but he thought the woman might be the one he'd seen briefly holding Celeste in the castle before he changed back into the wolf. The other adult, a man, and the child, a boy, he had no idea.

But the woman held something in her arms, something with a size and shape that could be a young woman.

Edmund crouched behind some bushes and watched. The man climbed up on the side of the wagon and pulled its tarpaulin back. He put the sack he held inside, then helped the boy climb up and disappear into the wagon.

The woman handed the bundle she held to the man. A head extended out from it, the head of a female with lustrous white-blonde hair.

Celeste!

He felt the tingling of the Change welling up inside him. It took great concentration to suppress it.

The wagon took off down the road. Edmund ran, angling to keep behind the wagon so they wouldn't notice him. They approached a great bridge that spanned the wide mouth of the river.

He had to think how to handle this. Becoming the Beast was out of the question in broad daylight with many people around, including Celeste. But if he attacked as a man, his rage could easily overwhelm him and invoke the Change before he could stop it.

He knew Celeste had to be alive, even though it confused him why he couldn't sense her. They wouldn't carry the body of a dead girl around with them. He could follow them and choose his time to rescue her.

As they stopped for the guards at the border, Edmund snuck into the river and swam across underneath the bridge. He crept up the embankment on the other side until he could just see them. Appearing dripping wet with soaked clothes would no doubt arouse the guards' suspicion, so he stealthily crept away from the bridge and circled around into the city.

He entered the first deserted alley he found and trotted through the streets of the city until he came to the main road that extended to the bridge. He peeked around the corner and saw the wagon pulling away from the guards. They'd pass right by him.

He pressed himself into the shadows as the wagon rattled past, then followed behind them, keeping out of sight.

———

"I see it!" Zenia cried. "The boat."

At first Eloise could see nothing, but as they traveled further and the sky brightened with sunrise and the expanse of the ocean came into view in the distance, she could just make out the shape of a skiff beached on the right bank of the river.

The rug shifted again, more violently.

"I'd better set us down now," Kasimir said.

"As close to the city as you can," Sighurd said.

The rug veered away from the river and headed straight for the city, which couldn't be more than a mile away. It was a sprawling aggregation of buildings and chaotic streets, as the harbor city was built up over the years a portion at a time. It seemed to shine with an unearthly light with the dawning sun's rays hitting it at a deep angle and the sea behind it glaring with sunlight. Seagulls screeched as they flew overhead.

The rug descended gradually, flying over fields and farmlands. The spell gave out a couple feet above the ground on the edge of a plot of thistly-headed artichokes growing in cultivated rows, dropping them to the ground with a jolt. A farmer's cabin was not far off, but no one seemed to have observed them.

"Roll the rug up and stash it in those bushes over there," Sighurd ordered. He turned to Eloise. "It would be best if we ran to the city."

She snarled at him. "I may be old, young man, but I'm spry! For Celeste, I can run."

They jogged at a steady pace along the small road leading away from the cabin toward the city. Without saying anything, they let Eloise lead the way. She fumed that they were condescending to her, letting her set the pace. If it weren't for the urgency to find Celeste, she'd stop and have words with them.

"Why is someone following you?" Andries said menacingly.

Gwendolyn and Bernard turned their heads to look behind them.

"Don't look back!" he barked.

"How do you know?" Gwendolyn said.

"He's been following us ever since I picked you up."

"But you never looked back."

He smirked. "You're pretty naive for a woman carrying a sword."

She wanted to get offended at that, but she didn't have time. "Is it a soldier?" she said.

"It's a man, wet from the river."

"What does he look like?"

"Black hair, back beard, a body that looks like it could lift boulders."

The blood ran from her face. The image flashed in her mind of the powerful man bounding through the forest for Celeste.

Andries looked at her, then reined the horses to a stop. "Get off!" he hissed.

"We can't get off here!" Bernard cried.

"I don't know what trouble you're in," Andries said, "but I can't have any part of it."

"That man will kill us and take our daughter."

"Get off now or I swear to the Gods—"

She grabbed his hand, pulled a small handful of coins out, and slapped them into his palm. "Get us to a safe place, then we'll get off."

He growled with his teeth clenched, but pocketed the coins and snapped the horses into a gallop. He turned them into the first cross street and galloped two more blocks, then turned again, and again. After several more turns that caused Gwendolyn to lose track of where they were, he stopped in front of a large building apart from the usual structures of the city and climbed down.

"This is an abandoned warehouse," he said as he whipped the tarpaulin aside, startling Guillaume and causing him to cry out. "There should be no one there *officially*." He grabbed the sword and tossed it on the ground. "You can use that to protect yourself from whatever *is* in there."

Gwendolyn and Bernard climbed down. She picked up the scabbard and strapped it on. Andries handed the sack to Bernard, then yanked Guillaume out, who gave off a squeal, and stood him on the ground. He turned, gaped at Celeste, then backed down off the wagon.

"I'm not touching her."

Bernard climbed up and pulled her out. Her face was deathly ashen and moist with perspiration. He stood her on her feet. She moaned in distress and buckled. He caught her and held her up.

Andries climbed on his wagon and shouted at the horses. They galloped away, leaving them coughing and wiping their eyes in a cloud of dust.

Bernard stared at the large double doors of the building, wide enough to drive a team of horses and a wagon through. The whole structure was rotting wood. One of the doors was ajar and askew, hanging a little off its hinge.

"What do you think's in there?" he said.

"Where are we?" whined Guillaume.

Gwendolyn went to the door and pulled. It gave off a loud, protesting creak. It's corner scraped against the ground. She looked in. There was a gaping hole in the ceiling with a stream of sunlight shining down onto the floor strewn with the wooden debris that had fallen from it. Everywhere else was pitch black.

"Come on," she said. Bernard lifted Celeste and carried her in. Gwendolyn grabbed the sack, took Guillaume's hand, and pulled him to the door.

"I don't want to go in there!" he cried.

She yanked him in with her and closed the door behind them as far as it would go. She turned around and tried to pierce the darkness with her eyes.

She heard scuttling around the walls. Some rats scurried through the bright spot of light on the floor. Rot and must and the stench of excrement permeated the air.

The first thing she made out in the blackness were eyes shimmering from the sunlight. There must have been a couple dozen pairs of them spread throughout the space to the right of the column of light. Soon dark silhouettes of humans materialized around the eyes as her vision sensitized. Some were sitting, some standing, some lying down. Those lying down rose up to a sitting position. Those sitting rose to their feet. Those standing took steps toward them.

"Bernard..." she said with a whimper. She drew the sword and held it out. Guillaume pressed against her, clinging hard. The figures stopped advancing.

How much more would the Gods demand of her? Why would they lead her here to die at the hands of the vermin of humanity?

The figures advanced again.

"Give me the sword," Bernard whispered. "I'll protect you."

She stood poised, fighting a sense of despair. Would the great sorceress Gwendolyn finally be defeated by the dregs of humanity? The two of them and one sword couldn't fight all of them off. A spell powerful enough to incapacitate them would take too much time to prepare as she rummaged through her sack for the necessary materials. And she'd have to deactivate the Magic Eater, allowing everyone pursuing her to know exactly where she was as she wasted time dealing with this human vermin.

She handed the sword to Bernard and put her arm around Celeste to prop her up.

Barely perceptible, Celeste whispered, "Now we both die." There was a hint of victory in her words.

This young vexation of a girl gloating over her brought her back to her senses. Die, would they? Maybe so, but she wasn't going down without a fight.

This was it, she decided. No fleeing to Pretanica. No groveling before King John as she waited for Celeste's child to be born. The dregs of society in this ruin of a building wouldn't defeat the great Gwendolyn, who stood up to Deirdre and the Seven Sisters. The accursed Beast searching for them wouldn't do it. Sighurd with all the legions of Gallea he could muster wouldn't do it. Deirdre with her scrying and flying wouldn't do it.

Gwendolyn had gotten greedy. The Gods gave her Celeste to stop the Blood King, and she'd lusted for more power, first with the Beast, now with his unborn child. She uttered a silent prayer of thankfulness to the Gods for Celeste's power and of penitence for her own lust.

It was time to drink Celeste's blood.

"Bernard, take this." She pulled the Magic Eater locket from around her neck and handed it to him. He gaped at her and took it. "Put it on." He slid it over his head. "Now listen to me. I'm going to back into the corner behind me. I want you to walk forward until I tell you to stop. Guillaume, you go with him."

"What are you doing, Mistress?" Bernard said.

"You'll see soon enough. Keep those vermin away from us."

She scooped up the sack and helped Celeste toward the corner, lying her down on the floor. As she went and as Bernard moved forward, she kept speaking Sight spells. When the distance between her and Bernard reached a certain point, her Sight flared before her.

"Stop!" she called.

Celeste's aura filled the space. Gwendolyn quickly spoke a Sleep spell on her and lowered her to the floor in the corner.

Bernard kept shifting the point of the sword back and forth as the figures advanced upon him. He began swinging threateningly. Guillaume hid behind him.

Gwendolyn stepped forward, raised her arms dramatically, and shouted in Pretanic, "I am Gwendolyn, the Sorceress of Luteche!" She cried out a Flash spell directed at no one specifically. It flashed and crackled before the advancing denizens. They cried out and drew back.

"You will leave this place and never come back!"

She fished the bag of gold coins out of the sack and threw it at the doors. It hit the floor and burst open, scattering coins. The figures ran for them and fought each other for them.

"Out of here!" she shouted, and threw another Flash spell at them. They flung the door open and ran out. In the sunlight, she saw long and matted hair and beards, filthy and tattered clothes, and diseased men and women smudged with the excrement of tawdry living fleeing the building.

Bernard ran and closed the door behind them.

Gwendolyn quickly pulled together the materials for as powerful a Warding spell as she could cast. She knew the Beast was moments away from coming for Celeste, now that her aura was out. "Get away from the door," she called to Bernard, "and stay away from me with that Magic Eater." He complied, and she burned the materials and cast the spell. "If any witch or sorceress comes, stay near them so they can't cast any spells."

She pulled out the container of materials she'd mixed together back in her chambers in Luteche—an eternity ago it seemed. She unrolled the scroll and weighted its corners down on the floor. She pulled out a stick and the knife, then sat down by Celeste and pulled her onto her lap. Deliriously Celeste murmured, "I'll kill you. I'll kill you." But she didn't wake up.

"No, you monster of a girl. I'll kill you."

She struggled to position Celeste with her legs propped up against the wall and her neck low to the ground. Gwendolyn would have to get into an awkward position to drink the blood as it oozed out. She never imagined this moment would be so undignified. Thank the Gods the world wouldn't see her like this.

Guillaume wandered over, studying them. "What are you doing to her?"

"You wanted me to kill her, didn't you?"

He shrugged.

Exasperated, she said, "Turn away. This will be frightening."

He didn't turn away. She grunted in frustration. "If you come near me, I'll kill you too."

He backed away with alarm in his eyes.

She turned Celeste's head so her tender neck showed. She could see the blood pulsing under the skin. A thrill shot through her. This was the moment! All her efforts and tribulations would finally come to a culmination.

She read the spell as she plunged the knife into Celeste's artery.

Edmund kept a steady, safe distance behind the wagon as it rolled leisurely through the city. The marketplaces were just beginning to open up and the streets became busy with people. Many of them stared at him, but walked by.

The wagon stopped. A lively discussion seemed to pass between the driver and the sorceress. Suddenly the wagon surged ahead at a gallop and turned a corner.

He broke into a desperate run, suppressing the tingling urge that welled up in him. The Beast couldn't find Celeste. It would only go on a killing rampage throughout the city.

He turned the corner, but the wagon was already out of sight. He ran to the next crossing, but could see nothing in either direction. He let out a howl of despair that almost sounded like the howl of a wolf, then dropped to his knees and wept.

"Edmund!" came a shout from behind him. He turned and saw Sighurd running to him with other familiar faces and two figures in dark cloaks with hoods drawn over their heads.

He stood up and grabbed Sighurd by his arms. "I had her!" He wiped his face with the sleeve of his still damp shirt. "I had her, and I lost her!"

One of the figures in a dark cloak threw back the hood and peered around. It was the Pilgrim. "I still can't see her," she said.

Sighurd turned to the others. "Spread out! Search for her."

"She was in a wagon pulled by horses," Edmund said.

They all rushed off in different directions.

The Pilgrim came up to Edmund and placed her hand on his cheek. Soothing warmth seemed to flow from it into him, calming him. "She's safe as long as I can't see her," she said. "Gwendolyn will have to negate whatever power she's using to hide Celeste before she can cast her spell."

"We need to search the docks. They could be trying to leave Pretany."

He and Zenia hurried to the harbor and walked along the docks, searching for any sign of Celeste or Gwendolyn or a wagon. Wagons there were plenty of, but none with a woman and a girl. The crowds in the area were becoming throngs as people came to board their ships. Edmund despaired when he saw how many ships there were and how many people crowded around them. Some of them were already casting off to sea.

"We'll never find her," he moaned.

Zenia had a tight look of concern as she gazed about the piers.

They continued to search, but Edmund was without hope. "Can't you see anything with your powers?"

"I can see every face in the crowd, but one at a time. I'm looking as fast as I can."

Edmund came to a jarring stop as he suddenly felt the pull of Celeste calling to him.

Zenia stopped when Edmund stopped. He faced the city, gazing intently. She looked where he looked.

"I see her!" she cried.

But the changeling glow was already forming around him. Citizens and sailors and travelers gasped, cried out, backed away as the misty glow intensified.

The Beast leaped out from the fog and the people around him scattered, screaming. It ignored them and charged straight to where Celeste's aura was.

Zenia ran after him as fast as she could, but he quickly disappeared into the city. As she ran, she passed dozens of people cowering off to the sides of the streets where the Beast had been. They formed an open path for her and a compass to where he'd gone.

She ran until she came to a huge dilapidated building. Celeste's aura was inside. The Beast pranced and howled before its large double doors, one of them hanging crookedly. Citizens of the city hovered in the distance on either side of the block, peering at him.

Eloise and Thomas came running and stopped short as they saw the Beast. Thomas drew his sword.

"Celeste's in there," Zenia called as she ran to the door. "Gwendolyn's casting her spell right now."

Eloise uttered a Sight spell. Sighurd appeared from around another corner, then Kasimir with his dark hood flung back.

Zenia reached out her hand to pull the crooked door open. Something repulsed it. "There's a Warding on the door."

"She's killing her!" Eloise cried.

The Beast stomped and howled behind Zenia. Rage welled up inside her as she saw Gwendolyn positioning herself to suck up the blood that spurted from Celeste's neck.

"Goddess, no!" Eloise shouted.

Zenia whipped off her cloak and let it drop to the ground. All the wrath she'd felt from the first moment she learned that Gwendolyn switched Tamara with Mariam until this moment when she could see Gwendolyn slurping the blood that pulsed from Celeste's neck flooded up inside her. She swept her arms out and blasted the door with her rage.

It exploded, sending chunks and splinters flying into the building. She marched in.

There was a great sphere of blindness in her Sight. In the middle of it, her natural eyes saw Bernard lying on the floor, bleeding with shards of wood piercing into his body. A young boy lay off to the right, unconscious or dead, with splinters and scratches.

Bernard shook his head and saw her, leaped up and charged with a sword pointed at her. The Beast bounded into the building and went straight for him. The man's shriek was cut off as the Beast lunged on him, knocking him back into the wall, bit into his face and tore the flesh.

Zenia turned toward Celeste. She was propped up against the wall upside down with her legs pointed to the ceiling and her body bent so her shoulders rested on the floor. Her aura was growing dim.

Gwendolyn lay sideways on the floor with her lips planted on Celeste's neck, slurping and swallowing. An aura similar to Celeste's surrounded her, slowly brightening. Gwendolyn turned to look at Zenia, her lips dripping blood, and her eyes widened in shock. Blood spurted from a gash in Celeste's neck with each heartbeat.

"Zenia!" Gwendolyn hissed. She snarled like a demon, an unholy sheen in her eyes. "You're too late!" She pressed her lips back onto Celeste's neck and continued to swallow.

Sighurd, Thomas, Kasimir, Eloise, and Ilsa rushed in and stopped in horror as they saw Gwendolyn and Celeste.

Zenia blasted out her passion with a sweep of her arms, tossing Gwendolyn up and away. She fell back against a wall and slid to the floor. Thomas and Kasimir ran toward her with swords out. Sighurd noticed the boy lying at the other end and headed to him. Eloise rushed to where Celeste lay slumped down.

"Heal her!" Zenia shouted, keeping her eyes on Gwendolyn.

Eloise dumped the contents of Gwendolyn's sack on the floor and grabbed up some weeds.

Gwendolyn gave out a roar of rage as she lifted herself to her feet. A fog formed around her. Thomas and Kasimir skidded to a stop. "Great Mabut, she's changing!" Kasimir cried.

Zenia gaped in shock, waiting to see what would come out.

Eloise stuffed the weeds into Gwendolyn's container of ashes and spoke a spell that cause them to burst into flame. She uttered a Healing spell.

From the fog rose white, scaly wings, then a head with a long snout and sharp teeth. The head lifted up on a serpentine neck, and a weak cry bleated from the creature.

The Beast howled.

"Attack!" Kasimir shouted. He and Thomas charged.

The head coiled back and shot forward.

"Get back!" Zenia shouted. "You can't fight dragon breath."

They dove to the side as it spewed out a puff of white vapor several feet that drifted up to the ceiling and dissipated.

The dragon spread its wings and lifted its head and trumpeted.

The Beast dashed to it, growling with blood dripping from its mouth, and howled as it pranced before the dragon.

"Why is it so small?" Kasimir said.

"Throw me a sword," Zenia said as she marched toward the dragon. She drifted into the background of her combined souls and let Hereward take over.

Thomas tossed his sword. Hereward reached out his hand and caught it. The dragon coiled and blasted. The Beast yelped and leaped back. The mist shot out stronger this time, surrounding Hereward. The vapor stung, and all the souls within him clung tightly together to keep from dissolving into swirls.

Hereward charged and swung at the creature's belly, barely slicing a gash through its scales.

Kasimir moved in, but Hereward cried, "Get away!"

"Hereward?" Thomas said.

The dragon flapped its wings and rose up, but bumped against the ceiling and came back down. The Beast growled with its eyes burning.

Kasimir dashed in and jabbed at the dragon, but had to leap aside as its head swung toward him with a hiss.

"Stay back!" Hereward cried angrily.

"I won't stand by and—"

"If you kill it, Celeste will die!"

"*What?*"

"Stay back!" Hereward repeated, then lunged in, slicing just under its neck.

The dragon blasted mist again. The pain was intense, and Hereward dropped to his hands and knees. His souls bound their vitalities together with all the power they had to keep intact. He didn't think they could survive another attack.

"We need to help you," Kasimir cried, taking steps toward him.

"*Stay away!*" Hereward shouted. "You can't help!" He lifted up on his knees and raised the sword.

The dragon's head dove down, and its teeth snapped at him. He swung the sword and whacked the snout, leaving a gash.

"Bring Celeste to me!" Hereward cried as he stood on his feet.

"No!" Eloise said. "She's barely alive."

Hereward plodded toward the dragon with all the strength he had. "Drag her to me! Hurry!"

Kasimir and Thomas rushed to Celeste and lifted her up. They carried her over.

The dragon's head swerved toward them. The Beast sprang and bit into its tail. The dragon screeched as it swung the tail and tossed the creature aside.

Hereward reached the dragon as Kasimir and Thomas lay Celeste next to him. "Now get back," Hereward said.

He drifted back and let Zenia return to the foreground. She looked up at the burning silver eyes of the dragon as its snout plunged down toward her with fangs bared.

"You can't have her!" she cried and rested one hand on Celeste's heart while she slapped the other hand against the dragon's belly. With all the longing her many souls could generate, she began pulling vitality from Gwendolyn and let it flow back into Celeste.

The dragon screeched, and the Beast pranced around barking. The dragon wings spread out and shuddered. They began to buckle, then shrivel. The dragon blasted another breath toward the ceiling, but it came out a weak flow of mist that dissipated quickly.

The entire dragon body shriveled down until it formed into the shape of a woman. The face took on the appearance of Gwendolyn, eyes widened in alarm.

"You demon from the netherworld, what are you doing?" she shrieked.

The glow of aura diminished around her and flared up around Celeste. Gwendolyn howled in anguish as her face contorted with horror. Her skin began to dry, to wrinkle, as if aging rapidly. Her hair blanched white and fell out in tufts. Pieces of the leathery flesh on her face and hands sloughed off and dropped like flakes, crumbling into dust on the floor. Her eyes rolled up into her skull until there was nothing but white.

The skin peeled away, then the muscles, and her organs began falling to the floor and shriveling up. Her flesh crumbled away and dried to dust until she was nothing but bones. Her skeleton clattered to the floor.

Zenia collapsed in exhaustion. Eloise rushed over and bundled Celeste up. The gash in her neck was gone. The Beast trotted over and nuzzled her, leaving streaks of blood on her cheek.

Sighurd came over to them carrying the boy in his arms.

Ilsa ran to Zenia and knelt before her, taking her head into her lap.

"Celeste needs nourishment," Zenia whispered between shallow breaths, "so her vitality can replace her blood."

"Celeste needs food!" Ilsa cried to the others. "She needs to replace her blood."

Sighurd lay the boy next to her. "Watch out for him. He's the king now. I'll get food." He headed for the door, but stopped as he peered out. "Soldiers are coming!" he cried as he backed in again.

Thomas and Kasimir ran to the door with swords ready.

"Ilsa," Sighurd said, "protect the king."

Wide-eyed, Ilsa lowered Zenia's head to the floor and stood. She grabbed the boy under his arms and dragged him into a dark corner where she hoped they'd be invisible in the shadows. The stench of the excrement watered her eyes. She sat next to him and checked his breathing. He was still alive. She drew her dagger out and watched.

Six soldiers marched in, swords out. Sighurd, Kasimir, and Thomas attacked three of them. The wolf roared with its eyes burning red and charged the others. The soldiers balked, but held their ground with swords extended at the wolf.

Eloise lay Celeste down and rushed to them, shouting, "Don't kill him! He's a man!"

The wolf leaped and fell upon the nearest soldier. His sword caught it on its side and put a gash in it. The Beast bit deep into the man's throat and tore it away. The man fell with his head dangling only by the spine.

Sighurd, Kasimir, and Thomas battled their soldiers as Eloise stood by distraught while the other two soldiers kept swinging their swords at the wolf.

Movement from above caught Ilsa's eye. To her shock, a woman with a colorful robe descended through the hole in the ceiling and landed next to Celeste.

"Eloise," Zenia croaked, but was too weak to catch her attention.

The woman picked Celeste up.

"She's got Celeste!" Ilsa shouted.

"Deirdre!" Eloise cried.

"Thank you for the gift." The woman ran and leaped and flew away through the hole.

"*Celeste!*" Eloise screamed.

The Beast howled and ran out the door.

"By all the Gods, no!" Kasimir shouted. He took one more swing at the soldier he fought and ran, tearing his upper garment open and holding his sword with one hand while yanking a gem from his chest with the other. He quickly spoke strange words as he dipped the stone in the blood that trickled out. It burst into a brilliance that encompassed him.

Ilsa gaped as he jumped and shot up and streaked through the hole in the ceiling.

Chapter 27

Flight Spells

As soon as the rug flew away, Geoffrey's men portaged and launched the skiffs into the River Sicana and paddled away from the castle with Geoffrey in the lead skiff. They moved swiftly with the current and the skilled paddlers who stroked in unison, paused for a restful moment, then stroked again, a technique that allowed them to continue for hours without tiring.

Geoffrey observed the landscape passing by. It was new to him, having never been further west than the city of Luteche. He enjoyed peaceful excursions up and down the River Sicana in Suedeche, and would have relished this adventurous journey through new territory if his bowels weren't aching with anxiety over his granddaughter. He was already grieving the loss of a grandson who never was. He didn't want to experience that with a second grandchild.

They passed a ferry, idle in the darkness of night. A flickering light shone from the window of the ferrymaster's cabin.

They swept into Fenweald Forest. The moon filled the shadowy terrain with a spectral glow. It reminded him of his youth when he and his siblings would float on the river with their ducal father on warm summer nights into the forest and back.

They traveled for hours until the sun rose, then traveled for hours more. They caused a skirmish as they passed the Pretany border outpost—twenty-five foreign military men sailing along their border. Many of the guards rushed to shore where their own skiffs sat ready, but they didn't launch. Geoffrey's boats had zoomed swiftly past, hugging the Gallean side.

By midmorning they came upon an abandoned skiff beached on the Gallean side of the river. It was a relief of sorts to him, an indication that they had chosen correctly coming this way. But now he had to face what he hadn't wanted to think about.

Entering Pretany with twenty-five soldiers would be an act of war. By all rights, he should have arranged their arrival diplomatically, explaining their purpose in advance. But he wouldn't have even begun the diplomatic process before Celeste would be dead or gone. It made him think of the old myths of Ellada of wars being fought and men dying over the abduction of a single woman.

"Come ashore on the left," he called to the steersman when they were close to the city.

The skiffs landed, and the men piled out. Geoffrey stood before them to give a speech he never thought he would give, with Lucien and Faisal on either side of him. His soldiers were good men, strong men, and sharp-witted. They understood the implications of what they were doing, but it was his duty to spell it out so they'd be ready to face it.

"Men, as of this moment we are an invading force in the Duchy of Pretany. We do this reluctantly, but necessarily. Intentional or not, Pretany is harboring the enemy of our ally, the sorceress Gwendolyn, who fled here for asylum with the king of Gallea and with the princess, my granddaughter."

He looked them over. Each of them stood crisp and proud with determination in their eyes.

"Our goal is not to vanquish or slaughter. Our goal is to rescue. But we may provoke an enemy today who has lain dormant all these years. It's no small matter, but pales in comparison to the trials we assuredly face in the coming conflicts with Scaendelreic and the Seven Sisters. You may well consider this the first confrontation in a sweeping war to come. We must stand firm with honor and do our duty. Will you stand with me, with our ally King Guillaume, and with the ambassador Kasimir of Insu?"

Each soldier drew his sword and held it high. "For the Gods and our homeland!" they shouted.

Geoffrey turned to Lucien. "Lieutenant, take command as representative of Gallea. We march into Sicana Harbor like we belong there. We find Gwendolyn and Celeste and engage in no combat unless forced to."

Lucien nodded and cried, "Forward, men!"

Kasimir willed the power of his spell to fly as fast as it could toward the distant figure fluttering with colors as varied as his starstones. The wind howled past him like a gale. A couple times he had to bat seagulls away with his sword. The dust in the wind stung his eyes.

This was the first time he pitted the magic of the wizards of Insu directly against the magic of the Seven Sisters. This was the moment he'd find out just how womanly their magic was. It would be a valuable test for the wizards back in Eranshar, but the only thing Kasimir cared for right now was to get Celeste back. Four years of dreary searching, the devastation of losing Celeste over the cliff when he had her, the treacherous scheming he faced in Luteche, the near success of Gwendolyn in drinking her blood, having Celeste once more in his possession only to have her snatched away by another sorceress, had driven him to the brink. He flew with rage boiling inside him.

A piercing howl came from behind him. He looked back and saw the Beast running, trying to keep up with him. Kasimir longed to grab Deirdre by the ankle and hurl her to the ground where the Beast could rip her apart. He wanted to chop her into pieces with his scimitar and feed her to the remaining six Sisters. He imagined a myriad of terrible deaths for her that he knew he couldn't visit on her as long as she held Celeste's life in her hands sailing through the air.

He could tell he was gaining on Deirdre, and he smiled grimly. Hers was the power of the weeds of Mistress Earth. His was the power of the stars of Father Sky. It came as no surprise to him that his power outstripped hers.

Deirdre clung to Celeste with one arm and extended the other to the side, letting her robe flap in the wind. Was that a necessary part of the spell, the robe catching the wind? Is using half her robe what slowed her down?

Enraged as he was, he had to think, to plan. He had no doubt, if Deirdre felt she'd lost, she'd drop Celeste to her death rather than let him have her. Or maybe drop her by accident as he attacked her. How could he confront her without letting that happen?

He cast a Sight spell to examine her. There was a glow of shimmering around her, whether only from her Flying spell or an additional Protection spell, he couldn't tell. He wasn't familiar with the signatures of womanly magic.

She drove forward relentlessly. She showed no sign of knowing he pursued her. From everything he'd heard people say in Cueldea, she apparently was the only one with a Flying spell. Perhaps she felt invincible in the sky.

But if she'd been watching all this time enough to know when to grab Celeste, she must have seen him cast the spell on the rug. She must know he'd be able to fly himself.

Perhaps she assumed his spell would be slower than hers, if she were judging by how swiftly the rug flew. The energy of his starstone then had vastly more mass to propel through the air, and he hadn't pushed it to the limit for safety's sake with multiple people riding on it. With himself alone, he pushed the speed of his flight half again as fast as he'd flown the rug.

He prayed her hubris would make her careless. He prayed he'd have the advantage of surprise. But he couldn't assume that. One thing he sensed about the sorceresses of the North—they were not careless.

His question was answered when she glanced back. If she hadn't known before, she knew now. She *would* attack. She had no choice. He plucked a starstone, activated it, and cast a spell of Protection around him.

Deirdre glanced back again. A blast of flames erupted behind her, swirling in the wind, and shot toward Kasimir, engulfing him. Reflexively he flinched. The flames frothed around his sphere of Protection. Without it he'd be glowing ashes fluttering to the ground right now.

He saw multiple rings of distortion in the air behind her growing and coming at him. They hit him with a thunderclap and a force that caused him to spiral out of control for an instant before he stabilized himself again.

The power of her spells disturbed him. Breath spells couldn't deliver that much force. It was all his sphere of Protection could do to keep their impact out. She must have stashed materials away on her person for energizing her spells.

He cursed her in frustration. She was prepared for pursuit. He'd acted impulsively without thought. She was encumbered by Celeste, but was probably willing to sacrifice her if necessary so no one else could possess her. With Gwendolyn gone, that alone would be a victory for the Seven Sisters.

Kasimir had no such option. He must keep Celeste alive. He needed to neutralize Deirdre's power without harming Celeste. He needed to think.

Suddenly she veered away in an arc that brought her around to face him. She extended a hand out toward him as her lips moved. Shafts of crackling light shot from her palm. They hit his sphere of Protection and scattered in a rainbow splash of streaming colors around it. Kasimir had no idea what those shafts of light would have done to him without the sphere of Protection.

When the streaming shafts of light cleared, Deirdre was a mere dozens of feet ahead and above him. With a predatory gleam on her face, she swooped down with a dagger in her free hand, ready to sink it deep into his back.

He dove down as her arm stabbed. The tip of her blade caught his dark robe and tore. He felt the sting of the point scrape across his skin, and he cried out. Deirdre swooped back up as he flailed to regain control and peer up at her. She climbed high as she circled around to head east again.

If she dropped Celeste now, I could catch her as she fell.

With that thought, he realized there was no way to take Deirdre on without the risk of her dropping Celeste. He knew what he needed to do. It would be a risk, but he couldn't think of any alternative. He needed to take drastic action.

He plucked a starstone and smeared it in the trickle of blood. It burst into a glow in his hand. Praying to Father Sky that its power would be enough, he spoke a Negation spell tightly focused around Deirdre so it wouldn't affect his Flying spell. A burst of energy formed around her, flashing and crackling as the power of her spells—Flying and whatever Protection spell she might have—ruptured and radiated into the air. With eyes wide open in terror, she dropped Celeste as she plummeted.

The speed that Celeste fell took him by surprise. He shot with all his might toward her, dropping his scimitar so both hands would be free. For an instant he wasn't sure he'd make it. At barely twice the height of a man above ground, he caught her and swooped back up.

Deirdre flailed and twisted as she plunged and hit hard on her back several feet away from a narrow road. Kasimir veered around and descended, landing next to her. Her eyes darted back and forth aimlessly, and her breathing was wheezing and laborious. Her head lolled to the side, and blood leaked from her mouth. He felt confident she wouldn't survive.

A howl in the distance came from behind him. He leaped into the air with Celeste and headed back to his scimitar. As he picked it up and slid it back into place, the Beast dashed toward them.

Kasimir was full of apprehension, but remembered the story Eloise told of the night where the dragon and Beast were affectionate to her. He stood waiting, hoping the Beast wouldn't attack him with Celeste in his arms, poised to launch back into the sky if needed.

But the Beast's red eyes were not glowing with their usual intensity, and his tongue flopped from his mouth with delight. He circled around them and reached his snout up to nuzzle Celeste. Kasimir laid her on the ground. The blanket wrapped around her had fallen open, exposing one of her breasts. He wrapped it back in place. The Beast wagged its tail and licked her cheek.

A glow of fog formed around the Beast. When it dissipated, Edmund lay on the ground naked and unconscious.

Kasimir removed his dark cloak and laid it over Edmund. He picked Celeste up. Her skin was ashen and swimming in perspiration. He felt the side of her face. It burned with a fever. He examined her with his Sight. He could see her vitality struggling to keep her alive.

Celeste needs food! rang in his ears in Ilsa's voice.

"I'm sorry, Edmund, but I have to go now. Come find us."

He launched back into the sky. As he flew, searching for a place that would have food, he wept with joy for holding Celeste in his arms at last, and with fear that she still might die.

As Lucien marched his small army into Sicana Harbor, inhabitants of the city stepped aside with alarm. He led the soldiers to the main part of town, congested with citizens and travelers and commerce. He halted the army and cried out in Ruic, "We are soldiers of Gallea and Suedeche. We are not here to attack. The princess of Gallea and granddaughter of Duke Geoffrey of Suedeche has been abducted and brought to Sicana Harbor. We only want to find her and return her safely."

The people stared at him as they murmured with expressions of fearfulness and mistrust. Some of them ran off.

"She was abducted by a sorceress. If anyone knows of her whereabouts, we'll amply reward you."

A man shouted back, "Did you bring that wolf with you?"

Lucien glanced at Faisal. Edmund must be in the city. "We have no wolf in our army." Technically it wasn't a lie.

The heavy footsteps of marching echoed off the walls of the buildings. "Move aside!" came a forceful command. The crowd separated to allow another small army of soldiers through.

An officer stepped forward. "You have violated the sovereignty of the Duke of Pretany. Withdraw immediately or we'll be forced to attack."

"Our princess has been abducted by a sorceress," Lucien called back. "We only want to find her and bring her home."

"You are an invading force," the officer countered. "Your scouts have already infiltrated us and brought with them an accursed creature." He gave a signal, and his soldiers drew their swords.

Lucien gave his own signal to draw swords. "We will not leave without our princess." The two armies stood face to face with weapons upraised.

The officer swung his arm forward. His army charged with a war cry.

"Engage!" Lucien shouted.

Eight more soldiers arrived at the warehouse. Speaking Ruic, an officer ordered, "Drop your weapons!"

Sighurd and Thomas complied. Ilsa huddled in the shadows with Guillaume, praying they wouldn't notice the two of them.

One of the soldiers grabbed Eloise and restrained her. "Let me go!" Eloise cried and gestured at the Pilgrim lying prostrate on the ground in the corner. "Can't you see she needs my help?"

The soldier released Eloise. He followed her as she ran over to Zenia and sat beside her, holding her head in her lap. "Are you alright?"

She tried to say something, but Eloise couldn't hear it.

Sighurd said, "I am Sighurd, Captain of the King's Guard in Luteche. We are here on a rescue mission—"

"You are the first wave of an invasion force and enemies of Duke Philip!" the officer shouted.

First wave of an invasion force? Ilsa dared hope that meant Duke Geoffrey had arrived with his men.

"What is this?" the soldier with Eloise said as he pointed his sword at Gwendolyn's skeleton.

"How would I know?" Eloise said. "It looks like it's been there forever."

Guillaume opened his eyes and made a soft moan. Ilsa clamped her hand over his mouth and looked at the soldiers in dismay. They didn't seem to notice.

The soldier kicked at the spilled contents of Gwendolyn's sack. The officer called, "What is that?"

"Witch's weeds, it looks like," the soldier said.

"Are they yours?" the officer asked Eloise.

"Yes, I'm a witch. I was trying to help her."

"Leave them." The officer pointed his sword at the torn man the wolf had attacked and asked Sighurd, "Who is that?"

"I don't know. He was here when we got here. The wolf ate him."

"We'll deal with that later. Bring them all." He marched out the door. Eloise and her soldier lifted Zenia to her feet. The other soldiers picked up the dropped weapons and escorted all of them out of the warehouse. Sighurd glanced at Ilsa and gave her a quick nod before he disappeared.

She breathed a sigh of relief when they'd gone, then stood up, trembling, and pulled Guillaume to his feet.

"What's going on?" Guillaume said.

"Our friends were captured." She ran to the door and peeked out, watching the group round a corner and disappear.

She went over to the torn body lying toward the back of the building, trying to hold down nausea from the sight of a faceless body of blood and gore.

Guillaume came up to her and, with a quaver in his voice, said, "Is that... Bernard?"

"The Beast got him." She picked up the sword lying there and hefted it with difficulty because of its weight. "I couldn't use this," she said and dropped it.

"That's a magic thing," Guillaume said, pointing to the locket around the body's neck.

"What?"

"It makes magic not work."

She gazed at it. "But how could Gwendolyn cast a spell with it here?"

"It works when you say one thing and stops when you say another."

"Is it working now?"

He shrugged his shoulders, then spoke something that sounded like witch's speech. "It's not working now."

"How did you know to say that?"

"I heard Gwendolyn say it."

She studied it and said, "Maybe we should bring it." Making a face of disgust, she used her thumb and forefinger to grab the chain around the neck and slide it off.

He looked around the building. "Where's Gwendolyn?"

She turned toward Gwendolyn's bones. "She's dead."

He looked where she looked. "*That's* her?" he said with alarm, pointing.

She covered his eyes and pulled him to her. "Don't look if it frightens you."

But he squirmed away and walked over to the remains, looked down and studied them. Ilsa came over and noticed the things spilled from the sorceress' sack. "We should bring all that too." She placed the locket and the other things inside the chest, and the chest inside the sack.

Guillaume said, "Did the dragon lady do this?"

"Gwendolyn stole the power from the dragon lady and turned into a dragon herself. But the Pilgrim gave Celeste the power back. Then the sorceress Deirdre flew in and stole her. The black wizard's chasing her now."

Still staring at the skeleton, he said, "I don't want to sail the ocean anymore. I want to go home."

"We will. But first we have to rescue our friends."

The words sent a chill through her spine as she uttered them. Never in her life had she dreamed of saying such a thing. She and a little boy rescuing people from soldiers in a strange country? It was insane! How would she ever succeed at such a thing?

What was she even doing here in this foreign land? Giant wolves eating people, wizards and sorceresses flying into the sky, a sorceress drinking someone's blood and turning into a dragon, a Pilgrim shriveling her to a skeleton, soldiers battling in a swordfight.

Sobs forced their way out, even though she tried to stop them. She dropped to the ground, burying her face into her knees as she hugged them, and rocked back and forth.

It was too much for her. She didn't belong here. With all her heart, she wished she'd stayed in Premveille with her mother. She wanted to see the world, but now that she had, it terrified her.

Guillaume stared at her, then walked up to her. He began patting her on her shoulder. She looked up and peered into his eyes, gazing back at her with complete trust.

"How do we rescue them?" he said.

She took deep breaths to calm herself. She felt ashamed, crying like a baby, wishing for home like a child. How would she get home anyway? She was miles and miles away from Suedeche, and she wasn't even sure if she could find her way back.

She tried to concentrate on the things Zenia told her. Heroes are just small people with the courage to do what has to be done. Well, she certainly qualified as a small person. But did she have the courage?

Zenia believed in her. Dietric told her she learned well when he taught her. Sighurd trusted her to protect the king. Everyone treated her like she was already a hero. Now she just had to treat herself that way.

But no matter how confident, no matter how brave, how could one girl with a dagger fight many soldiers with swords?

Then she realized, she didn't have to. Duke Geoffrey and his twenty-five soldiers and the Luteche guard and the wizard's brother must already be here. She only had to find them and tell them what happened. They could do the fighting.

"I want to go," Guillaume whined.

"We will," she said as she stood up and wiped her eyes. "We'll find the duke and his soldiers and rescue our friends, then we'll go back to Luteche."

She picked up the sack, took his hand, and sucked in a deep breath. She would choose to be brave. But she also learned in that moment that courage felt a lot like terror. Was this how all brave people felt? Afraid, but choosing to do what needed to be done anyway?

To her surprise, that made her feel better. Bravery was easier than she imagined. She didn't have to force herself to *feel* brave. She just had to *act* like she felt brave, no matter how scared she was.

She *would* be brave, and she *would* do what needed to be done. She *would* become a hero, even if a small one.

They walked out the door, checking to make sure no one was around. The Pilgrim's dark cloak still lay where she dropped it. Ilsa picked it up and put it on. It was a few inches too long and dragged on the ground.

She pulled the hood over her head. "Now act like we're normal people who live here," she told Guillaume, then headed out. An invasion force of over two dozen soldiers shouldn't be too hard to find.

"A young woman of Luteche was stolen and brought here to gain passage somewhere else," Sighurd said as the soldiers escorted them. "We came to bring her home."

"Where is this woman?" the officer said.

"Still in the hands of the abductor, fleeing further away while you detain us."

"You can discuss it with our commander."

This officer was no-nonsense, a trait Sighurd would normally admire if he weren't a victim of it. Thank the Gods Kasimir and Edmund got away so they could pursue Celeste. But he feared for Guillaume, protected only by an unseasoned young woman with a dagger, doing the job he should be doing.

He looked over at Zenia being propped up by Eloise and the soldier. Her silky Pilgrim clothing nearly shone in the sun.

"Are you feeling any better?" Eloise asked her.

Sighurd saw Zenia look at her with a faint smile and a twinkle in her eye. He suppressed his own smile and began watching for an opportunity.

The officer brought them to his commander. There were no introductions. The commander listened to a hushed report from the officer, then simply said, "Tell me why I shouldn't execute all of you."

"So you won't have a war with Gallea on your hands," Sighurd said.

"You already brought a war to us with your invasion."

Sighurd indicated the two women. "Do we look like an invasion force?"

"It's just a coincidence that you arrived right before some thirty soldiers came down the river and invaded us?"

"It's no coincidence. They're here to help us find the woman."

"They're fighting my army right now."

"It's Duke Geoffrey's soldiers, and now you also have a war with Suedeche."

"An ambassador from Insu is with them," Thomas said. "You also have a war with the Southern Wizards now."

The commander scowled, then turned to Zenia. "Who are you?"

She answered wearily, "I'm a Pilgrim of the Three Goddesses."

Suddenly she collapsed. The soldier and Eloise barely managed to catch her before she hit the floor.

"What's wrong with her?"

"She's ill," Eloise said.

"She's contagious," Sighurd said.

The soldier let her go and backed away. Eloise could do no more than help her land softly on one knee. The commander gaped at her with a disturbed look.

With Eloise's help, Zenia rose back to her feet and took precarious steps toward the commander. "Please...please help me."

The commander took several steps back. "Take her to a witch!"

Zenia pulled her arm away from Eloise's grasp and stood tall. She swept her arms out with a clap of thunder. A blast of wind shot out and knocked every Pretany soldier to the floor.

Sighurd said with awe, "I'm glad you're on our side."

"Let's go," she said. They grabbed their swords and rushed out.

"We need to find Guillaume at once," Sighurd said.

He led them back the direction they had come, but heard swords clanging and rushed to a crossroads where they could see. Lucien and the twenty-five warriors of Suedeche fought with a greater number of Pretany soldiers. Faisal stood alongside them, swinging his curved sword. Geoffrey remained behind them, his sword ready in case he needed it. Only the cramped space in the streets kept the Pretany soldiers from overrunning them.

"They're outnumbered," Thomas said. They need our help."

"We have to find the king!" Sighurd said. "We are the *King's* Guard."

"Go," Zenia said. To Eloise she said, "Wait here." She strode toward the skirmish.

Sighurd gaped at her for an instant, then he and Thomas headed for the warehouse.

Ilsa and Guillaume didn't make it to the first corner when two people appeared from around it. They were a man and a woman, ragged and filthy with hair that hadn't been groomed for ages. They had sores on their faces. Rotten teeth peered out from a jungle of beard on the man, and the woman had gaps in her leering smile.

Ilsa dropped back, pushing Guillaume with her. Fear washed through her, but she gripped the hilt of the dagger tightly and breathed deeply to calm herself. "I can do this. I can do this," she muttered under her breath.

The man said something in a strange language, probably Pretanic.

"I don't know what you're saying," Ilsa said in Ruic.

"Ah, foreigners," the man replied with a heavily accented Ruic.

"A pretty girl and a pretty boy lost in the city," said the woman. "The slavers will pay a price for them."

Ilsa's eyes went wide at the mention of slavers. For an instant an image flashed in her mind of her and Guillaume in chains being forced to do unspeakable things. Fear and anger battled within her. The anger won out.

"I'll be no slave for you," she growled.

The couple advanced menacingly with amused grins. Ilsa shoved Gwendolyn's sack into Guillaume's arms. "Hold that." She noticed two more filthy men creeping toward them from the other direction, closing them in. She backed herself and Guillaume up against a building and drew her dagger.

The woman's eyebrows raised. "The pretty girl has teeth! Be careful. You might hurt yourself."

"I'll kill you!" she hissed, trying hard not to tremble.

The couple paused an instant, studying her, then advanced again, keeping their eyes on the blade. The other two men never stopped approaching.

Ilsa lashed out at the couple with a broad swing. They jumped back with startled looks, and their grins turned into scowls. "Watch that, girl," the man said, "or I'll sample you myself before we sell you."

The two men creeping toward them stopped about twenty feet back and stood alert, watching. Ilsa realized she and Guillaume would be trapped if she didn't act fast.

The woman reached out a hand and said, "Give me the blade, girly, and we'll treat you nice."

Ilsa stared at the hand, then looked into the woman's eyes. She let her expression droop as if resigned, then slowly held the dagger out. The woman smiled with satisfaction and reached for it.

With blinding speed, Ilsa swept the blade up and caught the woman in her face. It sliced her upper lip, cleaving it in two like a cleft lip, and cut a deep gouge in her nose. She screamed and dropped to her knees with blood gushing all over her chin. The man knelt down to her.

"*Run!*" Ilsa cried in Galleic as she grabbed Guillaume's wrist and yanked him into movement. The sack flew out of his hands. The woman wailed, and the man tried to comfort her.

The two men gaped in shock for an instant before they dashed after them. As they passed the wailing woman, the man shouted, "We still get our share!"

Ilsa dragged Guillaume as fast as she could around the corner. Seconds later the two pursuers appeared behind them. As afraid as she was, she felt a thrill at being able to run on two healthy legs. It made her feel so alive. "I can do this! I can do this!" she chanted as she dashed through the streets.

The two pursuers charged after them. She couldn't run forever without tiring, especially dragging Guillaume with her. She had to confront them.

She stopped suddenly and faced them, pushing Guillaume behind her and holding the dagger out. The men slowed to a stop some several feet away and pulled their own wicked knives out. Ilsa eyed them and felt a chill run through her. For all her practicing, she'd never been in a knife fight in her life. How could she possibly win against two men?

Terror threatened to paralyze her, but she shook it off. She couldn't give in to that. It wasn't just her freedom at stake. It wasn't just her life. The Captain of the King's Guard had charged her with protecting the king himself, and she couldn't let either of them down.

"You're good with a blade, I'll give you that," the taller, uglier, filthier man said, "but it's over now. Lay your knife on the ground."

Ilsa studied him, his tangled hair and beard, his ragged and filthy clothes. She wrinkled her nose at the dark stain on his trousers around his crotch, trying not think what might have caused it. Blood, she hoped.

That thought led to another, and suddenly she knew what she could do. She couldn't take them both on at the same time, but...

"Come on, girl," the taller man growled. "We don't want to hurt you."

"Guillaume," she said, "run and hide. Quickly!" She pushed him, and he dashed away behind her.

"Get him!" the taller man said to the shorter.

The shorter man broke into a run. Ilsa whipped her dagger into her other hand, leaped and jabbed as he passed—right into his crotch. He buckled over with a great howl.

The taller man's eyes popped open, and he charged with his knife ready to plunge into her.

With a move straight out of Dietric's lessons, Ilsa whirled around full circle and swept the blade across his abdomen. His clothing and skin tore open, and a sheet of belly-wide blood oozed out. He bent over with a mighty groan.

Almost without thinking, she buried her dagger deep into his crotch. He cried out in anguish and dropped to the ground. Wet blood seeped into his trousers.

If it wasn't a blood stain before, it was now.

Ilsa stepped back, gaping at the two writhing men. She couldn't believe what she had done. Suddenly she remembered Guillaume and ran off to find him.

"Guillaume!" she cried. "Guillaume, it's safe. You can come out now."

Not a moment passed before his head popped out from around a barrel he'd hidden behind.

"Guillaume," she called, beckoning to him. He ran for her.

"Are those bad men gone?" he said.

She held up her bloody dagger. "They hurt too much to chase us now. Let's get out of here."

As they ran, a thrilling sensation flooded through her, a sensation she'd not felt before in her life. It was a wonderful sensation, one she wanted to feel over and over again. She tried to identify it, give it a name. It was a feeling of...of...

Power.

Sighurd and Thomas rounded the corner to the block where the warehouse was. A grimy couple sat on the ground leaning against a building toward the far corner. The woman howled, and the man held her.

They rushed to the door of the warehouse and ran inside. Sighurd peered about as he waited for his eyes to sensitize to the dark.

The space was empty. "Why didn't they stay here?" he cried.

"Maybe those vagrants out there saw something," Thomas said.

They went out and approached the couple. "Did you see a boy and a young woman?" Sighurd asked.

"She sliced her lip up," the man growled.

Sighurd peered with amazement at the sight of the bisected lip. "Really?"

"Where did they go?" Thomas said.

He pointed toward the corner.

Sighurd saw a sack lying in the street. "Isn't that Gwendolyn's magic?" He picked it up as they ran past and around the corner, checking down every side street and alley. They asked anyone they met, although there were few people about in the city. No doubt hiding from the clash of armies that had broken out.

"Why *did* she leave?" Thomas said.

"Probably didn't expect us to escape so quickly," said Sighurd. "Probably figured she was on her own."

They continued to search and stumbled across two men writhing on the ground with pools of blood. "What's this about?" Sighurd said.

They peered over the men. "What happened to you?" he asked in Ruic.

"Help us!" the taller one said. "We were attacked by marauding thugs."

Sighurd and Thomas looked at each other. "Were these thugs a girl and a small boy?" said Sighurd.

The dark glare the man gave him was confirmation enough for Sighurd.

"Probably wanted to sell them to slavers," Thomas said.

The man's glare deepened.

Sighurd peered at him with loathing. "Maybe someone will come along to help you before you bleed to death. I'll not waste my time on you." To Thomas he said, "Let's find them."

They hurried on. "Dietric's a better teacher than I thought," Sighurd said.

"Or Ilsa's a better student than you thought," said Thomas.

They searched several blocks, calling out, "Ilsa!" As they approached another corner, she dashed around it and ran straight into Thomas, who reflexively put his arms around her.

She fought him and backed away, crying, "Leave me alo—Thomas!" She threw herself back in his arms and hugged him tightly.

"Sighurd!" Guillaume cried and ran into his arms.

"Thank the Gods you're alright!" Sighurd said.

Thomas grasped Ilsa's wrist and held it up. "Look at this!"

Sighurd peered at the bloody dagger in her hand and shook his head. "Maybe *you* should be Captain of the King's Guard."

Her face went beet red as she smiled.

Zenia, hood down, strode forward with her arms extended. Eloise ignored her instruction and followed some paces behind, wishing she could help with something besides breath spells. But Zenia had her potent magic, as she demonstrated more than once now. She looked an imposing figure as a dazzling light formed around her and emanated from her. The sight made Eloise pause and stand in place.

In a voice so powerful, it almost sounded like many voices speaking at once, Zenia cried, "In the name of the Three Goddesses, cease this combat at once!"

Soldiers one after another turned and gaped. Some of the Pretany men fell to their knees. Lucien called out, "Hold, men!" The Suedeche soldiers stopped fighting and backed away a few steps.

"Drop your swords!" she commanded.

The ones kneeling let their weapons fall to the ground. More of the Pretany soldiers knelt, and some of the Suedeche soldiers did. Lucien and Faisal remained standing.

"They invaded our land!" the Pretany officer shouted. "Fight, you rogues!"

A few of the Pretany soldiers moved in on the Suedeche soldiers, including some that got up from kneeling.

Zenia's glow turned into a fiery sphere of brilliance. Flames seemed to flow from her arms and fingers and hair that fluttered violently as if caught in a storm. "Father Tanaris forbids this war."

The fighting stopped completely. Most of the Pretany soldiers dropped to their knees.

"Father Tanaris has charged you with defending Pretany!" the officer cried. "You *will* do your duty!"

The eyes of the soldiers wavered, uncertain. Some of them began to stand back up.

Sighurd and Thomas appeared beside Eloise. With them were Ilsa and Guillaume. "You're safe!" she cried softly, but their eyes were all on the scene before them.

Zenia's head turned toward them, and a faint smile crossed her lips. Softly so only they could hear, she said, "Time to end this."

She swept an arm at the officer. A whirlwind of flames leaped at him and knocked him into the air. He catapulted a short distance and landed with a cry. Many of his soldiers cried out too.

"Pretany soldiers, gather up your weapons and return to your homes," Zenia commanded. "Suedeche soldiers, return to your boats."

She walked through the armies. The soldiers scrambled to get out of her way. Lucien ordered the Suedeche soldiers to retreat. Both armies gathered up and assisted their wounded. Miraculously no one had been killed.

Eloise trotted up behind Zenia and followed her through the scattering men. Sighurd, Thomas, Ilsa, and Guillaume followed behind. They headed for the river, following Lucien, Faisal, Geoffrey, and the men of Suedeche.

"Where's Celeste?" Geoffrey asked Sighurd.

"Deirdre has her," he answered. "But Kasimir is chasing them."

"She can fly," Geoffrey said with alarm.

"So can he," Sighurd reassured him.

They boarded and launched the skiffs. With the extra people from the flying rug, they had to crowd in. The paddlers pushed hard against the current. The river flowed gradually here, slowing them down only a little.

As they paddled upriver, Ilsa felt almost in a dream. In mere days, she'd gone from a crippled young woman in a small village to the guardian of a king in a foreign land. She'd cut the lip of a woman and barely avoided getting herself and the king sold into slavery by incapacitating two dangerous men.

She peered at Zenia gazing off into the distance. She'd witnessed the Pilgrim blast open a door and spew fire at a soldier with a wave of her arm. Her mind spun at all the marvels she'd seen, at all the things she'd found the courage to do.

She wondered if she should feel bad about hurting those men and that woman. Never in her life had she dreamed she could do such things. Never in her life did she have the desire to do such things—even toward those who taunted her. She wondered if there was something wrong with her to not feel remorse now.

But she couldn't deny how she felt. A warm glow burned inside her that made her smile. She began a frightened girl and ended up a hero. A small hero, a tiny hero compared to those around her, but a hero nevertheless. In the midst of fear, she'd done what needed to be done. The king she was charged to protect was alive and well and going home. She had done her duty.

Eloise cast a spell and looked in the same direction as Zenia. "I see a glow, Celeste's aura mixed with the energy of the Flight spell."

"Kasimir is battling Deirdre now," said Zenia.

"Mother Goddess, help him," Eloise said.

Zenia kept gazing into the distance, a focused expression on her face. Geoffrey watched her with equal intensity.

They came to the skiff that Gwendolyn had fled in and stopped to load the extra people into it. Inside they found a sack of provisions left behind. They voyaged on, Zenia keeping watch in the distance.

"Since when did you become the Pilgrim of *three* goddesses?" Eloise said.

Without moving her eyes, she said, "They're the goddesses of Pretany."

"Aren't you concerned that you've stirred up the wrath of the Pretany Gods by pretending to speak for them?" Thomas asked Zenia.

"Their Gods *are* the Great Gods. The Pretanicans only perceive them differently. Father Tanaris is the name of their Sky God."

Thomas said, "Father Sky," and Faisal said, "Mabut," at the same time.

"The Three Goddesses are what they call Mother Goddess, Mistress Earth, and Granddaughter of Fortune. Together those three watch over and dictate the fortunes of humankind."

"Odd choices for the Three Goddesses," Eloise said.

"They don't know all the Great Gods," Zenia said. "They don't know about the Seven Sisters or any Pilgrims of the Seven Sisters." She smiled. "That's why I told them the Three Goddesses sent me—which is mostly true."

Her smile suddenly vanished, and she murmured, "Dear Goddess!"

"What?" Eloise cried.

Zenia's smile slowly came back as a broad grin. "He has Celeste! And Deirdre is dying."

Geoffrey's face brightened up. "Praise Father Sky!"

"Praise Mother Goddess!" Eloise cried and began a leap for joy, but sat suddenly back when the boat rocked and the paddlers protested. She looked at everyone with a chagrined smile. "Thank Mother Goddess. Thank Father Sky. Thank all the Great Gods! All of Celeste's enemies are gone!"

Zenia's grin disappeared. "But Celeste is also dying."

Chapter 28

Spell of Power

Kasimir landed with Celeste at the first farmhouse they encountered. The family was out working and fled into the cottage when they saw him coming.

He came to the door and beat hard on it. "Please!" he cried in Ruic. "She's ill and needs food."

No one came to the door.

He beat again. "I am a wizard of Insu. I am an ally of the king in Luteche on a mission for Gallea. Please help us."

A man called through the door, speaking foreign words.

Gods, he didn't know Ruic, and Kasimir didn't know Pretanic. He cast a spell of Sight. Celeste's vitality was weakening dangerously, trying to keep her alive with too little blood left in her. He had no time to handle this honorably.

He looked inside and saw the man's wife and children huddled behind him in fear. He tried the door and found it bolted. Giving off a sigh of exasperation, he spoke a breath spell that caused the man to buckle over with pain.

The children cried out and the wife tried to comfort him, but the door remained closed.

Desperate, he cast the spell of pain on the youngest child, a girl. She buckled over, crying. The mother gave a short scream and ran for the door, unbolted it, and swung it wide.

"Get back!" Kasimir cried.

His demeanor made clear what he wanted. The woman fell back.

He carried Celeste to where he saw food simmering in a pot over a fire and laid her on a nearby table. He grabbed a ladle of water from a bucket, lifted her head, and pressed it to her lips. "Drink, Celeste."

At first she did nothing, so he let a few drops slide out and wet her lips. Her tongue came out and licked it, then her lips parted so he could ease more into her mouth. She swallowed and coughed a little, then opened her mouth for more.

He gave her as much as she'd take in small sips. She opened her eyes just enough to look. She gave a feeble moan of distress at the sight of him.

"Gwendolyn is dead," he said to reassure her. "I'm here with your mother Eloise to save you."

Her eyes opened more and softened.

"Let me get you some food." He carefully lowered her head down and checked the pot. It was a broth with some kind of meat and various vegetables and grains in it. He found a bowl and a spoon and used the water ladle to fill it. He stirred and blew on it as he returned to Celeste, filled a spoonful with broth that he blew on again, then put it to her lips. She swallowed it. He took another spoonful, making sure to add a single pod of green bean, and let her take that in. She swallowed the broth and chewed and swallowed the green bean.

As he continued to feed her spoonfuls, the oldest child, a boy, said something to his parents. The father responded gruffly.

After the bowl was nearly empty, Celeste whispered hoarsely, "That's enough."

He gathered her up and turned to the family. "I can't repay you now, but I'll see that the king of Gallea sends you a token of our gratitude."

They looked at him without comprehension. He walked out the door.

Kasimir peered around, studying the landscape. Celeste seemed to have gone back to sleep. His Flying spell had faded away by then, so he needed to decide what to do next.

As he deliberated, a figure appeared in the distance, a man running toward them wearing a dark cloak. Kasimir was pleased Edmund caught up with them and started walking toward him.

Edmund came up and spent a moment leaning forward with his hands on his thighs, breathing hard.

"I'm sorry for leaving you," Kasimir said, "but Celeste was dying, and I couldn't wait for you to wake up."

He nodded. "How is she?" he said when he could breathe well enough to speak.

"I fed her." He nodded toward the farmhouse. "She's very weak. Her fever still burns, but her face seems to have more color to it." Her raspy breathing had quieted. He thought her vitality glowed with a little more strength.

"May I...hold her?"

Kasimir gently handed her to Edmund. She moaned softly, but kept her eyes closed. He gazed at her with great affection, but then his face clouded. Without looking at Kasimir, he said, "I'm afraid I've done a terrible thing, Wizard."

"As the Beast, you can't help the terrible things—"

"I did it as a man."

Kasimir studied him, waiting, but Edmund kept his gaze on Celeste. "What's this terrible thing?" he asked.

"I made love to...my daughter."

The revelation shocked Kasimir. "That's an abomination."

Edmund nodded. "I didn't know. She...she looked...she *felt*...so much like Tamara."

"Her real mother that you met and made love to in one night," Kasimir said sharply.

Edmund looked at him grimly.

"And how long after you met Celeste did you—"

Edmund's face turned sour, and his eyes began to smolder. He almost looked like the Beast he was. Kasimir took a step back.

"Have you ever gone a couple centuries without a woman?" Edmund growled.

"I've never had a woman at all."

Edmund's brow knotted. "Are you wizards sworn to celibacy?"

"No, no, it's not that." Kasimir tried to swallow his self-consciousness. "It...just...never came up."

The corners of Edmund's mouth twitched up. "I'm sorry for your affliction."

At first Kasimir was confused, then he realized. He tried to be angry, but a chuckle forced its way out despite himself. "That's not how I meant it."

They shared a smile, then Edmund became somber again. "I was once an honorable man with a wife and three beautiful children, longer ago than the fall of the Onotrian Empire. Before the Seven Sisters came."

"What happened to your family?"

Tears gleamed in Edmund's eyes. He shook his head as he bowed it.

"I'm sorry. You've lived such a strange and terrible life. The things you must have endured. I'm in no position to pass judgment on how you survived."

"Let's just get Celeste home. Do you know where the others are?"

"I left them at that abandoned building. After that, I don't know."

"I don't remember any abandoned building."

"That's right. Let me see if I can find Zenia's aura." Kasimir renewed his spell of Sight and gazed toward Sicana Harbor. He could see nothing there. "They've left the city." He scanned around until he saw the familiar glow off to the north. "There they are, near the River Sicana I think."

"Are they leaving us?"

"Wait! Zenia's moving *toward* us. She must see Celeste's aura."

"Which way?"

Kasimir pointed. Edmund immediately headed in that direction, still holding Celeste in his arms.

"Wait!" Kasimir cried and jogged up to him. "They're some miles away."

"So?"

"Are you going to carry her the whole way?"

Edmund scowled at him. "I'll manage."

Zenia saw Celeste's aura cease moving. "Pull over. Kasimir stopped flying."
The paddlers landed on the Pretany side.

"Hand me that sack of food," she said. "I'm going to him."

"Not alone," Sighurd said. To Geoffrey he said, "Will you guard Guillaume
while we're away?"

"I will not! I'm coming with you to see my granddaughter."

Lucien was left in charge of Geoffrey's men and Guillaume. "We'll wait for
you on the Gallean side," Lucien said.

Zenia said, "If I'm not mistaken, we should pass near where we hid the
rug. We could retrieve it on the way." She turned to Faisal. "If you think your
brother's willing to sacrifice another of his starstones."

"He won't be sacrificing his starstone," Faisal said. "He'll be sacrificing
mine." When everyone gave him a perplexed look, he said, "I'm a wizard too,
and this is my mage quest as much as his. He wears all the starstones because
he's the one Luteche wanted. When we return, I'll receive my starstones, but I'll
restore half to Kasimir of what he uses on this quest. So you see, I'm volunteer-
ing my own stone to fly us back."

"Then head to Luteche and await our return," Geoffrey said to Lucien. "Take
care of that young king of yours." He added with a smile, "He may yet become
my grandson after all."

Geoffrey's skiffs launched and paddled away, leaving Geoffrey, Faisal, Sighurd, Thomas, Zenia, and Ilsa on land. They worked their way south. Zenia
kept watch on Celeste's aura.

"Kasimir's coming right toward us," she said. "He must be watching me
with his Sight."

After several miles the farmhouse came into view, and from there they easily found the bushes where they stashed the rolled-up rug. Sighurd and Thomas
hefted it on their shoulders and carried it as they moved on.

Celeste gave off a disturbed moan. Kasimir looked and saw her eyes open
gazing at Edmund with consternation.

"I will never harm you, Daughter," Edmund said.

She looked over at Kasimir, which only increased her alarm. "Where are
we? Where's Mother?"

"We are walking through a field in Pretany, heading toward the Pilgrim right
now," Kasimir said. "I assume your mother is with her."

"Pilgrim?"

"Oh right. You don't know about her. Do you know who Zenia is?"

She nodded. "Mother told me the story. The Beast killed her." She gazed at

Edmund with an accusing look. "My father killed her."

Edmund looked at her with pursed lips.

"Your father can't help what he does as the Beast," Kasimir said.

She pierced Edmund with her gaze. "That's why he and I should kill ourselves." She looked at Kasimir. "You should have let me die."

"I will never let that happen," Edmund said.

"Nor will I," said Kasimir.

Celeste sighed, then said, "Who's this Pilgrim?"

"Zenia returned, sent to us as a Pilgrim of the Mother Goddess."

Her eyes opened wider. "Zenia's alive?"

"She's a demigod like the Seven Sisters of old," Kasimir said.

"And Gwendolyn is dead?"

"Yes. Do you remember what happened?"

"I remember a dark place and hoping the people there would kill her."

"She tried to steal your life. She nearly succeeded. But the Pilgrim restored your vitality."

"Gwendolyn is dead," she said as if trying to get used to the idea.

"Zenia shriveled her to bone as she restored the vitality she stole from you." Kasimir smiled. "I think you would have enjoyed seeing that."

A faint smile crossed her lips. "I do wish I could have seen that."

"I'd like to have seen that too," said Edmund.

"Then Deirdre tried to steal you," Kasimir went on, "but I chased her down and left her for dead. And here we are now, Princess."

"They're both dead," she said, then closed her eyes with a heavy sigh.

Kasimir leaned over her and brushed a strand of her illustrious hair from her face. "Rest well, young Princess. Your troubles at last are ended."

Her brow knotted with some concern. "I still feel sick."

When Eloise saw Kasimir and Edmund ahead with Celeste, she instructed Sighurd and Thomas to roll out the rug. Kasimir waved, and she and Geoffrey ran to them. Faisal walked toward them. Zenia sat on the rug and rummaged through the sack, selecting portions of food and handing them to Ilsa to lay out.

Eloise reached them first and, with tears streaming from her eyes, kissed Celeste's face and beamed at her with joy in her soul almost overwhelming her. "My beautiful, beautiful girl."

Celeste looked up. "Mother," she said weakly and pulled her arms out of the blanket to encircle her neck.

Eloise lifted her out of Edmund's arms and held her, weeping profusely. "Thank you, Mother Goddess, thank you."

Geoffrey came up and stroked her hair, eyes glistening. "As beautiful as the face of Mistress Moon." Celeste looked up at him. "Eyes glittering as the stars of Father Sky."

"Geoffrey," Eloise said, "meet Edmund, Celeste's father."

Geoffrey looked up and studied him, then nodded. He immediately returned his gaze to Celeste.

"We have a surprise for you, Celeste," Eloise said. "Meet the father of your mother Tamara. This is Duke Geoffrey, your grandfather."

Celeste put her arms around him and said, "My Mother Inside is happy to see you."

He looked at Eloise with confusion.

"Apparently when Tamara purified Celeste, her soul flowed into her. She speaks to Celeste with a voice inside her."

Geoffrey peered at Celeste with amazement. "My granddaughter *and* my daughter restored to me?" He could no longer hold his tears back.

Faisal said to Kasimir, "I've donated one of my starstones to fly us back."

"*Your* starstones?" Kasimir said with mock sternness. Faisal grinned.

"Take her," Eloise said to Geoffrey as she handed Celeste to him. "I've already had her four years."

"I see you have the rug ready," Kasimir said. "Let's bring her home."

They went back to the rug. Geoffrey laid Celeste on it and sat next to her. When she saw Zenia with her shining robe, she said, "Are you the Pilgrim Zenia? Oh, yes. My Mother Inside is happy to see you."

"Hello, Tamara." To Celeste she said, "Are you hungry?"

"I'm starving."

"Eat all the food you can. Gwendolyn drained most of the blood from you. Your vitality should be able to replace it quickly, but you'll need lots of nourishment."

Ilsa handed her a morsel of food. "Who are you?" Celeste asked.

She said with pride, "I'm Ilsa, servant of the Pilgrim."

Edmund sat nearby and reached a hand out to touch her, but pulled back. "Do I still frighten you?"

She peered at him as she chewed, then shook her head.

The rest of them sat on the rug. Kasimir plucked a starstone and cast the Flying spell. He willed the rug into the air, jostling everyone. Celeste cried through the food in her mouth, "Mother Goddess!"

Kasimir aimed the rug toward Luteche. Celeste kept devouring pieces of food that Ilsa handed her until she said, "That's all I can eat now."

"Are you feeling better?" Geoffrey said.

"I'm very tired, and I still feel sick." She lay back down and immediately went to sleep.

Eloise gazed at her with her heart bursting. How wonderful it was to see Celeste sleeping peacefully, free of danger for the first time in her short life. She felt a tremendous burden lift from her soul and dissolve away.

Zenia sat aloof, watching Celeste with that intense gaze that indicated she was looking with the eyes of Sight. "Something's wrong," she said.

Eloise's skin prickled. "Is she not recovering?"

"Her blood's replenishing just fine. It's something else."

Eloise uttered a spell and looked.

"There's a corruption inside her, conflicting with her vitality," Zenia said.

Eloise looked hard and thought she could see a flicker of disturbance in Celeste's gleaming aura. She gasped.

"It's her child in the womb," Zenia said.

"What?" several of them said in unison.

Zenia looked at them. "Celeste is with child."

"How? From whom?"

Edmund gaped at Celeste. Kasimir looked at him with shock.

"*Your* child," Eloise said, "with the same corruption you gave Celeste."

He gazed back ruefully.

Geoffrey's face went dark. "Celeste's father is the father of her child?" he roared.

"He didn't know," Kasimir said. "They had no idea they were father and daughter."

"How many of the women in my family are you going to defile, monster?" Geoffrey growled with a predatory gleam in his eyes.

"He loved Tamara, and he could sense her presence in Celeste. It was only natural—"

"Why are you defending him, Southerner?"

Kasimir's demeanor darkened. "Because I can't imagine what it was like to live the life he's lived. The isolation, the terrible guilt. For him to find even a moment of love in such a—"

"If you were my subject," Geoffrey said, glaring at Edmund, "I'd have you executed. But I exile you from Suedeche, and you will never see my granddaughter ag—"

"Grandfather!" Celeste said, her eyes open. "He's my father. I love him."

Geoffrey gaped at her.

"Tamara loves him. And we didn't know."

He fell silent, but continued to glare.

Celeste turned her eyes to Zenia. "My child is corrupt?"

"Your unborn child inherited from both of you," Zenia said. "Purity and corruption. Those two forces battle mightily inside you."

"That's why I feel sick?"

Zenia looked at her with a concerned expression. "I've never heard of such a pairing before, two changelings producing a child. It's poisoning your vitality. It will kill you."

"Gods curse you, Beast!" Geoffrey roared at Edmund.

"How soon?" Edmund said, ignoring him.

"Within a day, *maybe* two."

"Dear Goddess," Eloise whispered, her heart sinking.

"How can we save her?" Edmund said.

Zenia peered intensely into Edmund's eyes. "The child needs to go."

Edmund gaped at her with a wild look in his eyes. Celeste gazed at her in horror.

Eloise looked back and forth between them, her face drained of blood. "I don't understand. Tamara wasn't ill when she carried Celeste, was she?"

"Tamara was a normal mortal woman with a normal vitality," Zenia said. "Celeste has the vitality of a changeling, purified by Mistress Moon. There's a much greater conflict between her and the child's vitality. I'm afraid this baby will kill her."

"Then the child does need to go," Eloise said forlornly.

Scowling darkly, Geoffrey said, "Absolutely, to save my granddaughter."

Celeste gave him a stern look. "Do you wish they killed me when I was a corrupt baby, Grandfather?"

He peered at her with a troubled expression.

"I won't let you kill it," said Edmund.

"But the child will kill you," Kasimir said to her.

Weakly, Celeste struggled to sit up. Geoffrey helped her. She took Zenia's hands and gazed at her with intense eyes. "Zenia, please don't kill my baby." Her pleading voice seemed to have changed, as if someone else spoke through her.

Zenia and Eloise glanced at each other.

"Please, can't you draw the evil out?"

A thrill shot though Eloise. They were the words Tamara had pleaded with four years ago.

"Someone would have to die," Zenia said.

"I'll die," Edmund said. "I'm the cause of all this."

Celeste reached her arm out toward him. "No, Father. I don't want to lose you too."

"How can his life energy purify the child," Geoffrey said, "if he's the one that put the corruption there?"

Zenia said, "It was the undefiled love of a mother that purified Celeste."

"And healed that boy from the corruption of his disease," Eloise said.

"*I* love her," said Edmund. "Does that count for nothing?"

"The love of a mother *and* the energy of her life she sacrificed," Zenia said. "That's what worries me." She gazed at Celeste. "You were a fully developed baby when I cast that spell on you. This infant inside you has barely begun to grow. It's frail, and I fear the energy from that spell will be too much for it to endure. It might be too much for *you* in your weakened state."

"I will not risk my granddaughter to save a corrupt creature," Geoffrey said, eyes locked on Edmund.

"Celeste was as much a corrupt creature when she was born," Zenia said.

Geoffrey glared at her.

"How old is Celeste?" Kasimir said.

Eloise looked at him. His question seemed so out of place under the circumstances. Hesitantly she answered, "Sixteen."

"I mean how old in years?"

"Four," she said more assertively.

"She aged sixteen years in four years?"

"When I captured her aura inside her, the energy caused her to age four times faster."

Kasimir took a breath. "Then can we...is it possible to age a child in the womb nine months in one day?"

Everyone gaped at him in shock.

"She'd need nourishment," Zenia said. "More than replenishing her blood."

"It would take a profound amount of energy, I would think," Eloise said.

Kasimir glanced at his brother. "I think...maybe I can provide the energy." He gazed at Thomas. "You may get your wish after all."

Thomas perked up. "A Spell of Power?"

"But Zenia said that much energy might kill the child, and maybe Celeste," Eloise said.

"I think..." said Zenia, and paused as she deliberated. "Purifying the tiny infant in the womb would be an attack on half of what it is. Kasimir's spell will only make it do what it does naturally, but faster." She looked down at Celeste. "I'm only a Pilgrim, not a God. I can't promise you it's safe. But I think...I feel it can work."

"That's all the assurance you can give us, Pilgrim?" Geoffrey said. "We won't risk her life. The baby has to go."

"Enough of this!" Edmund said." The baby is ours. It's our choice. It's Celeste's choice."

Everyone fell silent. Celeste and Edmund gazed at each other.

Kasimir leaned toward Celeste. "Do you want me to age your child so it can be born in the morning?"

She nodded, not taking her eyes off Edmund.

"Celeste, please," Geoffrey said.

"Even if there's a chance you'll die?" Kasimir said.

Looking at Geoffrey, she said, "Mother Tamara died for me. I can't do anything less for my baby."

Geoffrey's head dropped. Kasimir nodded.

"Be ready with the food," Zenia said to Ilsa.

An incongruous laugh burst from Eloise through her glistening tears. "I love the irony! Gwendolyn provided the food for us to save Celeste and her child."

Kasimir and Faisal exchanged looks. Faisal pulled his dagger out. Kasimir plucked the last five stones from his chest and two more from his face, holding them in one hand. He ignored the trickles of blood that flowed and held out his other hand. Faisal took it, then looked at everyone in turn. "Brace yourselves. This will be...intense."

He sliced a gash across Kasimir's palm. Blood flowed out. Kasimir said to Celeste, "Start eating now."

Ilsa handed her a piece of food. Celeste bit into it.

Kasimir slapped his bleeding hand over the starstones in his palm and rubbed the blood into them. He spoke with forcefulness words in his wizard's tongue. Eloise wished she could understand them. Faisal shielded his eyes with his arm, and Eloise mimicked him.

The explosion of brilliance nearly blinded her anyway, and the blast of force knocked her back onto the rug. The clap of thunder caused her ears to ring.

"Father Sky!" Thomas cried out.

"Dear Goddess!" Eloise exclaimed.

Ilsa screamed.

The brightness seemed to blaze forever, then swirled around Celeste and shrank with a loud whoosh. Celeste gasped loudly as the energy swooped into her small frame and disappeared.

Everyone gaped in shock at each other, except for the two Southern wizards and Zenia, who watched Celeste. She sat trembling, eyes wide, gasping heavily.

"Every one of the Seven Sisters must have seen that," Eloise said.

"Six Sisters," Zenia said.

"It doesn't matter now," said Sighurd. "We began the war when we invaded Pretany."

"Are you alright?" Geoffrey asked Celeste.

Celeste shuddered all over. "It's...it's...my heart's pounding!"

Eloise reached over and felt her chest. "It's beating like the wings of a hummingbird."

"Moving blood to the baby as fast as it can," Zenia said.

Celeste clawed desperately at the sack of food. "I'm hungry!"

Ilsa dumped its contents onto the rug and pushed food toward her. Celeste grabbed a small loaf of bread and tore off pieces, stuffing them in her mouth.

"I don't like this," Eloise said, keeping her hand on Celeste's chest. "Her heart's going to burst."

Edmund peered at Eloise with an alarmed expression. "Please tell me you're exaggerating."

"I hope I'm exaggerating."

"This will kill her," Geoffrey said.

"Dear Mother Goddess," Eloise said. "All that power trapped inside! No wonder the infant will grow so fast."

"She's young...strong," Zenia said. "She has the vitality of Mistress Moon in her." Her eyes didn't look as sure as her words.

Sighurd peered at Celeste intently. "Its mother is a dragon. Its father is the Beast. I wonder what kind of changeling this child will be." He looked up at everyone.

"Whatever it is," Edmund said, "we'll care for it. I'll teach it to control its urge to change."

Everyone looked at him dubiously.

"I've lived with this curse for over two centuries. I can teach Celeste to control it. I can teach our child to control it. We'll go away and—"

"Going away isn't what our quest had in mind," Sighurd said.

"I suggest that's a concern for another day," Eloise said. "Children don't begin changing for many years. It took Celeste four years—sixteen effectively— before she changed. We'll have plenty of time to deal with that."

Faisal watched Celeste devouring food. She caught him looking as she ate, her eyes peering through low brows as she concentrated on her eating. "Perhaps this is a conversation for different ears," he said, keeping his eyes on her.

They grew silent, seeing who he was looking at.

The sun arced overhead and began its decline to the horizon. Celeste shifted her position, causing the blanket she was wrapped in to fall open. It revealed breasts larger than Eloise remembered her having. A distinct bulge had formed in her belly. Edmund pulled the blanket back over her body.

They came to the river as it wound its way back through the forest. They followed it the rest of the way to Luteche, passing over Geoffrey's skiffs returning to the castle. They were too focused on paddling to notice the rug flying overhead, but Lucien noticed and held his hand up in salute.

The food and the sunlight ran out before they reached the castle. Celeste lay back clutching her belly, now substantially larger. "It hurts," she said.

"Are you having the baby?" Thomas said.

"No, it just hurts."

Eloise adjusted the blanket to reveal her belly. Severe marks streaked along its sides, worse than any she'd ever seen on a pregnant woman in all her service as a witch. Eloise and Zenia exchanged looks. She covered Celeste's belly up.

Some time later they passed the ferry cabin, quiet in the shadows, even its window dark.

"Her body's getting thinner," Eloise said. "She'll be emaciated by the time we get to the castle."

It took few but anxious moments to reach Luteche. The castle perched on its rocky promontory framed by two waterfalls and the river flowing below, bathed in the glistening light of the moon, was an enchanting view. Eloise had never seen the castle this way before. She wished circumstances allowed her time to linger and admire it, but that was of no consequence now.

The rug flew over the courtyard. Celeste was asleep or unconscious. Her body was nearly skeletal but for her belly, and her skin pale. People in the courtyard below formed a ring around the rug as it sunk down.

Sighurd crawled to the edge and shouted, "Bring food now—immediately! Quickly, quickly!"

Men on the ground scattered.

The disconnected part of Deirdre knew she was in shock. She could feel the agony, but didn't care. For some reason, her eyes insisted on darting back and forth regardless of what she wanted to look at. Her head rolled to the side without her willing it, and something leaked from her mouth.

She fought to gain control of her eyes, and when she did, she focused on blue sky and white clouds. They brought back the memory of flying through the sky. She remembered carrying something as she did. She tried to move her arms to see if she still held that something, but they wouldn't respond.

She remembered there was a thing following her. Something malevolent. Something that wanted to steal the thing she carried. It had to be a human following her, she realized. Only humans, not things, would be interested in stealing something.

She also remembered the something she carried was human. A small human, light enough to carry as she flew.

She remembered anger and frustration. The human chasing her wasn't supposed to be able to chase her. Yet it had more power to fly than she had. It gained on her.

She had to do something. She remembered doing something. She threw a ball of fire at him. Yes, him. She remembered a black man. She threw a pulse of energy at him. She turned around to face him and threw a stream of light that should have shriveled him up into a desiccated, leathery carcass. All of it scattered around him in a burst of colors as if an impenetrable shield surrounded him.

While he was blinded by the stream of light, she pulled out her dagger and shot toward him, ready to bury it in his back. But he noticed just in time, and she only pricked him with its tip.

She could do nothing against his impenetrable shield. She panicked and flew up and around, heading again for her tower.

The next thing she remembered was waking up on the ground, trying to focus her eyes on the sky.

She tried to move her arms again. They refused. She tried to wiggle her toes. They refused. She tried to lift her head up. It moved, but a pain shot through her neck.

She tried opening her mouth. It obeyed. She tried speaking a word, a single word: "Help."

It came out, but she could barely hear it.

I'm going to die, she realized.

Tears formed in her eyes. She resented that useless tears worked so well when the important parts of her body refused to obey. What could she do, lying here helplessly?

She could speak. Speaking, she could cast a spell. She knew a spell, something useful to her now. A Healing spell.

She spoke it. She felt its power tingle through her. The pain seemed to lessen. But she still couldn't move arms or legs. Why?

She knew why. It was a breath spell, and her injuries were too great. She needed weeds, herbs, leaves, flowers, minerals to strengthen the spell. She had those things, tucked away in her pack. Without thinking, she reached to grab her pack. Her arm, her accursed arm, refused to move.

Useless tears flowed again. Her salvation, so close, yet so unattainable.

"Help!" she cried again. This time it came out louder and stronger, but still it seemed to blow away in the wind.

She closed her eyes. There was nothing to see but sky. She didn't want to see the mocking sky that she once had the power to fly through. She might as well lie in peace with the wind caressing her face, soothing her to death.

"Lady?" said a voice. It penetrated through fogs of sleep and delirium.

"Lady?" it said again. She realized it wasn't her homeland's tongue of Scaendlic. It was spoken in a man's voice. The black man, perhaps, who caused her demise?

Deirdre opened her eyes. The face was not black. The face was old and light colored, unlike the black man's youthful face. It peered over her with concern.

The face smiled. "Oh, I thought you were dead."

"Help me," she said in his language, trying to remember the name of it, trying to remember why she knew it.

"I'll bring you to a witch." He crouched down and started sliding his hands under her.

She remembered the pain in her neck. "No! No! Don't move me. I'm too broken up."

He pulled back in alarm. "Should I bring a witch to you?"

"I *am* a witch. But I can't move."

He looked at her perplexed. "What do you want me to do?"

"Is there a pack attached to me?"

He looked. "Yes, right here."

Did she detect a hint of avarice as he looked at it? "There's nothing of value in it except to witches. Only weeds and herbs."

A touch of disappointment colored his face.

"There's a bowl in it. Can you get the bowl out, and I'll tell you what things to mix in it?"

He got the bowl out. She told him what she needed for the spell. She had to describe what most of it looked like, since he was ignorant of the kinds of plants witches used. She made him hold up each item so she could be sure he had the right one.

It took an agonizing amount of time, but finally the mix was ready. She instructed him to pour oil on it from the flask in her pack, then get out one of the long thin sticks.

"Are any of my bones broken?"

He winced as he looked. "Yes."

"Will you set them straight so they can heal properly?"

The agony of his jostling her bones into place made her wish for the delirium to return. She had to keep coaxing him to set them as she cried out in pain.

"That's the best I can do," he said when finished.

"Hold the stick up in front of me."

He did, and she cast a spell that ignited it. He only flinched a little. Most people had seen witches ignite a stick with words.

"Set the oil on fire," she said. She couldn't see when he did it, but she could smell the aroma as it burned. She chanted the words to the Healing spell.

Its energy washed through her. She could feel the broken parts in her body coming together whole. When it was complete, she drew in a long, deep breath, then ventured a turn of her head. Her neck obliged with only a slight pain.

Now that she healed herself, she remembered everything. Celeste was the human in her grasp. The sorceress Gwendolyn wanted her for her power. Gwendolyn was dead, an event that thrilled Deirdre, but she still didn't want Celeste in the hands of Luteche or the thief-witch, and certainly not that wizard of Insu.

Deirdre stole Celeste. The wizard pursued her. She fought him, but his protective magic was too much. That disturbed her greatly. Could the wizards of the South be that powerful?

She remembered the name of the old man's language—Pretanic. She remembered she knew it because she had studied many languages in her long lifetime. She wanted to be able to communicate with people, and not everyone learned Ruic.

She couldn't remember anything after her attempt to bury the blade in the wizard's back. That memory was probably lost permanently. But waking up broken on the ground testified that he'd vanquished her and took Celeste.

Deirdre had failed.

She sat up, groaning at some residual soreness, and looked at the man, who gazed at her with awe after seeing her unable to move. She kissed his cheek. "Thank you. You saved my life. I wish I had something of value with me that I could repay you with."

He looked down at her arm. No, he looked at her sleeve. The sleeve of her colorful robe.

"I need this," she said regretfully.

His face frowned with disappointment.

"Let me check something." She rummaged through her pack and discovered she didn't have enough materials left to renew her Flight spell. "Am I still in Pretany?"

"Yes, my Lady."

It would be a long, dangerous journey back to Scaendelreic with Gallea in between without her Flight spell. It would probably take days to accumulate all the materials needed for it.

But maybe there was a better path to take.

The die had been cast. War was inevitable now. Deirdre would have to inform the Seven Sisters, and they'd have to make their move before Gallea with Celeste and Insu with Kasimir could prepare to make theirs. The Sisters would have to gather together all the lands of Cueldea to stand against Gallea and Insu. And Deirdre could begin that process right now.

Pretany and Scaendelreic had little interaction with one another, being separated by Scaendelreic's enemy, but that also meant there were no ill feelings between the two countries. Instead of returning directly to Scaendelreic, she could travel to Redonnes where the castle of Duke Philip of Pretany was. It would be a small beginning, forming an alliance with a small duchy, but it would be a beginning. Perhaps she could leverage that into an alliance with Pretanica itself, with promises of annexing all of Gallea to make up for their failed attempt when they invaded.

Yes, she would go to Redonnes. She wouldn't need her Flight spell or her robe today.

"Would your wife like this?" Deirdre asked the man, holding up her arm to display the robe.

"Yes, my Lady!" he replied enthusiastically.

Well that she should. It cost a stack of gold coins to have it made.

"If you can bring me to the duke's castle in Redonnes, it's yours."

His face brightened up. "I can take you by wagon. You can stay with us tonight and we'll leave in the morning."

"I look forward to meeting your wife."

He helped her to her feet, and they walked down the road that led to a cottage in the distance. Deirdre only had a small limp remaining from her injuries.

Chapter 29

Upyr

They fed Celeste as she lay on the rug in the courtyard until she was strong enough to move. They brought her to the queen's chambers that Tamara and Zenia had once occupied. Eloise could only imagine what it felt like for Zenia and Celeste with Tamara inside to be here together again. They didn't speak a word, since Celeste was busy eating as Edmund handed food to her and Zenia was by her side monitoring her, but Eloise could see an intimacy passing between the two women.

Geoffrey, Ilsa, Kasimir, Faisal, Sighurd, Dietric, and Thomas were there—everyone who had dedicated themselves to her protection. The blanket wrapped around her had been replaced with a shift. What little conversation they made was hushed, as everyone waited and watched Celeste's belly grow by the hour.

Eloise sat in tense silence, trying not to fidget. Would Celeste survive this ordeal? Would the baby? *Should* the baby? It was the product of two changelings. The product of incest.

She shook that thought out of her mind. It wasn't the baby's fault. It wasn't even Celeste and Edmund's fault, since they hadn't known they were father and daughter. And Celeste started out corrupt, but what a beautiful young women she became! Of course this baby deserved to live, to have a chance for a good life.

But who would they sacrifice to give it that chance?

"Great Gods," she muttered under her breath. *Why do you force such impossible choices on us?*

"What was that?" Thomas asked, sitting nearby. She shook her head.

She didn't want to face that issue. For the baby to live an uncorrupted life, someone else would have to die. Would someone volunteer? Edmund had, but he was the worst possible choice—wasn't he? He had his own corruption. Yet Zenia said it was the purity of the love Tamara had for her child that saved Celeste.

If it couldn't be Edmund, then they'd have to choose someone else. Who on

Mistress Earth would they choose? She looked about the room at everyone, trying to imagine who she would pick. Who was...expendable enough...

"Great Gods!" she muttered more forcibly. Thomas peered at her with a questioning look.

Everyone in the room sat in silence as tense as hers, except for Zenia and Edmund who doted over Celeste. Was everyone trying to avoid thinking about that same question as much as she was? If it was never mentioned, they could avoid having it become real.

I can't take this anymore! She had to do something to preoccupy herself.

The sack of Gwendolyn's magic sat on the floor beside her where she dropped it. Eloise picked it up and examined the contents of the chest. All Gwendolyn's precious magic seemed to be in it. How revealing it was to see what she'd accumulated over the years, and how disconcerting it was to wonder where she got it from.

A gold locket was the first thing she examined. Opening it revealed two sentences etched inside in the Ancient Tongue. The first was a command, *Thou shalt consume.* The second one was an observation, *Thou art satiated.* In reality, they must be the activation and deactivation commands for an amulet that consumed something, probably magical energy. This must be what Gwendolyn used to hide Celeste's aura—indeed, hide her whole group from the prying eyes of Sight. Eloise had an urge to try it out, but letting it consume Kasimir's Spell of Power was unthinkable.

There were other pieces of jewelry. Whether they were amulets or mere keepsakes, she couldn't tell, but hiding mere baubles alongside magical items seemed incongruous. There were no activation commands etched in these, but that was not uncommon for amulets. If they were magical, discovering their purpose and their commands would be daunting, since amulets gave off no aura to study. Even Gwendolyn may not have ever discovered their purpose.

The rest were scrolls. She examined a couple that were powerful versions of known spells that even witches cast, but the next one stood out. The title in the Ancient Tongue, translated literally, was *Thou Shalt See Extensively.* Very typical of how that language described profound things in almost mundane ways, as if great spells were a daily thing among the demigods—which was probably true. This spell echoed the literal title on every witch's copy of a normal Sight spell: *Thou Shalt See.* The list of materials needed for the spell was extensive and full of rare items. It was clearly a powerful spell. Eloise remembered Gwendolyn translated its name into Galleic as "Extended Sight."

Reading over the words of the spell revealed just how powerful it was. Phrases like *I shall see vast distances* and *I shall see what has been* and *I shall see what may become* revealed its extensiveness.

She wondered what things Gwendolyn had seen "extensively." Zenia had told her of the many nights the sorceress spent closed up in her chambers with a powerful magical aura shining. Many of those nights must have been exploring the East and the Blood King. Eloise shuddered at the thought. Chained in Gwendolyn's chambers, she was skeptical about Gwendolyn's excuse of the Blood King for stealing Celeste's power. But with what Zenia told her and with the spell in hand that proved Gwendolyn could see what she claimed to see, Eloise had to admit Gwendolyn must have had a clear understanding of the threat arising in the East. Perhaps she was legitimately alarmed. It could make her behavior more understandable, if not remotely excusable.

The Blood King was something Eloise would have to explore later.

The next spell was the Illusion spell Gwendolyn had cast on Mariam to appear as Tamara. Its title was *Thus shall it appear to be, evermore*. Eloise smiled at that one. Much more poetic than "Permanent Illusion spell."

The third one made her shudder. It was the spell that Gwendolyn tried to steal Celeste's vitality with. Its ingredients were extensive and worth a small fortune. Its text included instructions on how to cut a gash into the neck of the victim and consume the blood that oozed out. Its title was ominous: *Thou shalt poach the life vitality of thy enemy*. If there was ever a spell of Death Magic, this was it. The complete opposite of the Life Magic Eloise and Zenia had used to purify two children.

How did Gwendolyn get her hands on Death Magic?

Reading that one only contributed to her ediness. She packed everything back into the chest without reading the other scrolls. At least this trove of magic was a worthy replacement for the treasures Deirdre had taken from her. Eloise could be more useful to the quest than a village witch after all. She could share these things with Celeste, and together they could become rogue sorceresses. With Kasimir as their ally, and even Faisal, who revealed he was a wizard himself, they could stand against the Seven—the *Six* Sisters—and be an even more formidable challenge to the forces that threatened Cueldea.

I need to come up with a better name for us, she thought. "Rogue sorceress" fit Gwendolyn well, but that wouldn't do for her and Celeste. That implied illegitimacy, which Eloise was more inclined to attribute to the Seven Sisters. Six.

Four trays sat on the table in the room, all empty. A fifth tray, half-loaded, sat on Edmund's lap as he placed morsels into Celeste's mouth when she opened it. The food that girl had consumed!

When she wasn't eating, she slept.

Eloise looked over at Ilsa sitting in the corner watching Celeste with concern. Her hands fidgeted. She'd been the one in charge of feeding Celeste the entire journey back, but father Edmund had taken over that task when she was moved to this chamber. The Pilgrim Ilsa served sat next to father and daughter on the bed observing Celeste's condition. Maybe Ilsa felt out of place again, useless.

Eloise went over and sat next to her. "It was a wonderful thing you did, protecting the king while we were detained."

She looked up and smiled an appreciative smile. "I did my small part."

"It's no small part protecting the king. That was the duty of Sighurd and Thomas, and when they couldn't do it, you did. You fulfilled the duty of two grown men, trained soldiers."

Her eyes beamed. "I'm just happy to serve the Pilgrim."

"In serving the Pilgrim, you also serve our quest. You've proven you're as vital a part of it as any of us."

Ilsa grinned self-consciously. "I did what I had to do."

"You certainly did, and you did it with greater courage than most girls your age could muster."

"How's she doing?" Geoffrey asked Zenia.

She looked up from observing Celeste and nodded, but her face showed concern.

"Let's come closer to the others," Eloise said, "where you belong."

She and Ilsa brought their chairs closer to the bed, joining the rest of the group in their vigilance.

About two hours before sunrise, Celeste looked as if she were large enough for nine months to have passed. "How soon before she delivers?" Edmund asked.

"Less than an hour, I think," Zenia said, then knotted her brow as she peered deeply. "Or...maybe sooner."

Geoffrey looked at Kasimir with a scowl. "You said not until morning."

Looking apologetic, he said, "I've never cast a spell like this before. I've never even seen a Spell of Power cast. The amount of energy must have—"

"It's better this way," Zenia said. "The agitation in her child is increasing, affecting her vitality."

"She almost died when we ran out of food," Geoffrey said with a hint of accusation.

"But she didn't," Zenia said. "Instead of accusing Kasimir who saved her, I suggest we concern ourselves with the condition of the child when it's born. As stressful as this is on Celeste, it's infinitely more so for the poor infant."

The door opened and Lucien peered in. "You've returned," Sighurd said.

"Is she..." His eyes went wide when he saw Celeste's belly. "Great Gods, how is she—"

"What of Guillaume?" Sighurd said.

He paused an instant while gaping at Celeste before answering. "He's safely tucked in his chambers."

Sighurd nodded.

"How is she so large with child?" Lucien asked.

Sighurd said pointedly, "That's a tale better told over mugs of ale."

Lucien took a moment more to peer at Celeste, then closed the door.

Thomas, gazing at Celeste, said, "Do you think a monster will come out?"

"Celeste was no monster when she came out," Zenia said. "Just a newborn baby girl."

Eloise noticed she didn't mention the black eyes.

About a half hour later, the mirror on the wall eased open and Guillaume's head poked out. Sighurd looked up and said, "What are you doing here?"

"I wanted to see her."

"Where's Henrietta?"

Guillaume gazed at Celeste with wide eyes as he came into the room.

A woman followed after him, which Eloise assumed must be Henrietta. "I'm sorry, Captain. I turned my back only a moment..."

"Leave him be. The king should know what's going on in his kingdom."

She nodded and began to slink back, closing the mirror.

"Stay," Sighurd said. "As his nurse, you should know what's going on too. Just keep him out of the way."

She crept in and closed the mirror and headed for Guillaume, but he glanced back at her and walked away to stand at the foot of the bed. "What's wrong with her?" he said, eyeing Celeste's belly.

"She going to have a baby," Henrietta said, coming up behind and putting her hands on his shoulders.

A scowl crossed his face. "My mother died when I was born. Will she die?"

"She won't die," said Zenia. "Did you know you two are the same age?"

"That's stupid. She's old."

Zenia chuckled. "It's true. You were both born the same night."

"Why is she so old then?"

"It's a long story," said Zenia. "One day we'll tell you."

"Come, Guillaume," Henrietta said and steered him to some chairs.

Celeste gave out a moan and winced as she clutched her belly. "It hurts."

Dear Goddess, Eloise thought. Not already. "Is it starting?" She looked around disapprovingly. "I've never seen so many men at a birthing before."

"Thomas, Dietric," Sighurd said, "why don't you assist Lucien with...whatever he's up to."

Reluctantly they nodded and left.

Kasimir looked at Faisal. "Brother, perhaps..."

Faisal pursed his lips, stood and left the room.

"Well, that's better, I suppose," Eloise said, staring pointedly at the remaining men.

"I'm the Captain of the Guard," Sighurd said. "I should know what's going on in the kingdom too."

"It's my spell," said Kasimir. "I should monitor it."

Geoffrey's scowl made it clear he wasn't going anywhere.

She waved her hands as she stood and approached the bed. "At least back away and give us room. This is witch's work. Stand by the walls or something."

"I'm not moving," Edmund said firmly.

"Yes, you are," Zenia said. "You can stay at the head of the bed out of our way. Henrietta, Ilsa, fetch some clean cloths and some water."

The two women jumped up and left. The men moved to the edges of the room. Edmund stood and crouched down by the head of the bed.

Celeste cried out as she sat up and bent forward, both hands on her belly. Fluid burst from her loins, drenching her shift and the bedclothes. The odor filled the room. Eloise's heart leaped in shock. "It's too fast!"

"She's dying!" Guillaume cried and darted from his chair. He started to crawl onto the bed.

"I think he needs to leave the room," Zenia said.

Sighurd strode over and grabbed him by the waist.

"No, she's dying!" Guillaume cried, trying to wrench free.

"She's not dying," Sighurd said as he lifted the boy and plopped him back in the chair and sat next to him. "Having a baby just hurts."

Celeste fell back onto the bed with a sigh.

Zenia said, "Kasimir, I think your spell is making this baby come as fast as it grew."

Henrietta and Ilsa returned with cloths and water. "On the table," Eloise said.

Celeste howled in pain, buckling up with her arms hugging her legs. Eloise jumped up. "I'll fetch something from Gwendolyn's supplies for the pain."

"I don't think it'll do any good," Zenia said. "I tried that with Tamara, and it didn't work."

Eloise stood poised, uncertain.

Celeste fell back, weeping. "What's wrong with me?"

"It's just happening faster than usual," Zenia said soothingly.

"It hurts so much."

"She's really only four years old," Eloise said, tears filling her eyes. "She shouldn't have to go through this."

Edmund kissed Celeste on the cheek and stroked her hair. "Everything will be fine. Births always hurt like this."

Zenia turned to the men. "I really think it's best if you leave this to us now. Let her have her privacy."

Sighurd, Kasimir, and Geoffrey looked at one another. Eloise marched toward them, shooing them with her hands. "Out, all of you! There's nothing you can do for her now."

"We'll be right outside the door," Sighurd said. To Henrietta he said, "Take Guillaume back to his chambers."

The three men left, Geoffrey grumbling something under his breath.

"I want to see," Guillaume whined as Henrietta carried him out the door.

Edmund didn't budge. "I'm the father."

"That's fine," said Zenia, then caught Celeste as she buckled over with another pain. Zenia lifted Celeste's shift over her head and pulled it completely away. She slid two fingers into her and felt. "The head's about to show. Get on your feet, child, and squat down. This'll be over soon. Ilsa, help her."

Celeste cried out with another pain. Ilsa and Zenia helped her balance as she struggled to her feet on the bed and squatted. Edmund held her shoulders to steady her. Eloise watched with her knuckles in her mouth.

"Every time you feel pain," Zenia said, "squeeze down on the baby."

The next pain edged the crown of the head out. Flaming red hair appeared, wet and plastered to the scalp.

Celeste cried out again and pushed. Zenia guided the head out. It came too fast for Eloise's liking. She spoke a spell to strengthen Celeste's wall of flesh at the base of her birth canal and wondered if there was any chance this baby could come out without tearing the poor girl.

Zenia worked the lips carefully around the head as it emerged. The crown was completely out. The hair was thick, and the skin around the front of the child's scalp was pale.

Zenia held onto Celeste, speaking words of encouragement and affection into her ear. Ilsa held her up on the other side, using a cloth to daub her forehead. Sweat drenched Celeste's body. Her breasts heaved up and down with labored breaths.

Eloise noticed Edmund was becoming agitated. His skin was sleek with perspiration. "Edmund?" she said.

"I'm alright."

"Is this birth calling the wolf out? The last thing we need—"

"I'm controlling it," he said brusquely. "I was caught by surprise last time."

Celeste groaned and tensed, squeezing the muscles of her womb. The infant's eyes appeared, scrunched tightly closed. Eloise waited with apprehension for the eyes to open. The room was deathly silent except for Celeste's cries and Zenia's whisperings.

The nose appeared, then the mouth, thin-lipped and frowning. Ilsa's eyes bulged. Perhaps this was the first birth she'd witnessed. But she stoically kept doing her job.

The chin popped out, and Zenia carefully turned the head to the side. Shoulders emerged, and with one more shudder from Celeste, the infant's body slid out with a wash of birth fluid.

The child was sickly and frail. Its ribs pressed against its skin. Its arms and legs were thin. Male genitalia dangled from its loins.

"That poor thing," Eloise said. "He looks like he had a hard time in the womb."

Zenia took the child into her arms, studying it with an intense gaze. Celeste fell back with exhaustion into Edmund's arms.

Eloise spoke a Sight spell. The roiling aura of the child sent a chill through her. It was mottled with darkness and light grey patches flowing around as if fighting each other.

"Zenia, where's my baby?" Celeste said between heavy breaths.

The baby's mouth opened and let out a newborn wail. Tiny teeth lined his gums.

Eloise gaped. "Kasimir's spell gave him teeth!"

"He's still growing," Zenia said. "Irregularly."

"Give me my baby," Celeste said, trying to sit up.

Edmund pulled her into his chest. "It doesn't look well, sweetheart. I don't know if it'll survive."

"Give me my baby!" she cried again. The voice sounded as much like Tamara as it did Celeste.

The baby opened its mouth and let out a sickly croak. Its eyes blinked open. Burning red irises and heavily bloodshot whites peered out between the lids. Eloise gasped and peered at Zenia, who looked back at her with consternation.

The baby glared up at Zenia, its teeth opening and closing near her arms. She lowered the baby onto the bed and stepped back.

Celeste struggled against Edmund, but he held her tight. "Where's my baby?"

The infant flailed around until it rolled over on its belly and lifted itself up by trembling limbs. Its red eyes darted back and forth. Saliva drooled from between its teeth. It cried out like a bleating goat, saw the umbilical cord extending from its belly and pulled it into its mouth. The tiny teeth gnawed at it.

Ilsa screamed and backed away in horror. Disgusted, Eloise moved to pull the cord away, but Zenia stopped her. "Let it eat. It's still growing."

The cord broke in two. The child kept gnawing on the end connected to its own belly.

The door flew open and Geoffrey burst in, followed by Kasimir and Sighurd. "What's going on?" He took one look at the child, and horror crept across his face. "Kill it!" He drew his sword.

"Don't kill my baby," Celeste cried, struggling.

"It's still growing," Kasimir said in horror.

Eloise studied it up and down. It had to be two or three inches longer already. It continued to gnaw ravenously at its own piece of umbilical cord. "It must be starving like Celeste."

Celeste bit Edmund's arm. He grunted as he jerked. She pushed herself from him and sat up. Her jaw dropped and her eyes bulged at the sight of the baby gnawing at its own cord. She crawled over to it and reached a hand out.

The baby snapped at it. She pulled it back with a jerk. The red eyes glared at her.

"What's wrong with him?" she cried. "What's wrong with his eyes?"

Edmund tried to pull her back, but she pushed him away and peered at it. The umbilical cord dangled from her womb, its edge jagged and dripping blood where the baby had chewed through. "Can't you draw the evil out?" she pleaded.

Eloise swore she saw Tamara looking out from her eyes.

"Who would we sacrifice?" Zenia said.

"You'll sacrifice me!" Edmund cried, rushing toward Geoffrey. "Your sword."

Geoffrey pointed the sword at him and cried, "You'll corrupt it all the more. It needs to die."

Edmund stopped in his tracks, eyeing the sword.

The infant couldn't bend over far enough to consume any more of its umbilical cord. It looked up at Eloise, its mouth gaping. Hunger burned in its eyes.

"Zenia..." Eloise said apprehensively.

The child leaped from the bed and scampered on all fours at Eloise. She stumbled back and fell into her chair. It pounced on her. She grabbed it by its forearms and held it back as it snapped its teeth at her.

Geoffrey raised his sword, ready to strike, and marched toward Eloise. Zenia swept her arm out. The sword flew out of his hand and clattered against the wall and onto the floor.

The child wailed and squirmed and snapped. Ilsa rushed over and grabbed it from behind and deposited it on the bed, then quickly backed away.

Kasimir rested his hand on the hilt of his sword and said, "Zenia, can you purify it or not?"

"You will sacrifice me," Edmund said.

"No!" Celeste cried. "Not you, Father."

"You're the Beast!" Geoffrey growled.

Precariously the child rose up, standing on trembling legs. It had grown another couple of inches. It held its arms out, lifted its face, and wailed at the ceiling.

A pale yellow glow formed around it, engulfing it. Eloise's blood ran cold.

"Great Mabut, he's changing!" Kasimir said. "How is that possible?"

"He's already been changing," Eloise said with realization, "inside Celeste's womb when she changed."

The glow faded, and a shape zoomed up into the air. Leathery wings stretched out, mottled grey and yellow. Clawed fingers extended from the upper tips of each wing at the midway point. The eyes glowed red. The nose was a flat hog snout. Sharp teeth filled its mouth. The thick hair on the scalp was gone, but the entire body was covered with a short, sparse red fur. Long, naked catlike ears perched atop its head. Its legs were short and clawed. A rodent-like tail waggled behind it.

"*Kill it!*" Geoffrey shouted.

The creature swooped down at Kasimir. Its wingspan had to be at least three feet. Kasimir ducked and pulled his sword out as the creature veered past him with a piercing cry and zoomed up to the ceiling.

Edmund raced to Geoffrey's sword on the floor and grabbed it. He held the point of the sword to his throat and shouted, "Cast the spell, Zenia! Purify him!"

"Gods curse you, man!" Geoffrey cried.

"You can't just kill yourself," Zenia said. "It has to consume something from inside you."

"Then he can drink my blood." Edmund raised his eyes up to his son and beckoned. "Come to me, little one." He held the edge of the sword against his throat, ready to slide it across the flesh.

The creature circled the room. "Come to me," Edmund said.

It flew down toward him, but Geoffrey ran in front of him and flailed his hands out. "Scat!"

The creature shrieked at him and flew out the door.

Kasimir and Sighurd drew their swords.

"Don't kill my baby!" Celeste shouted as they ran out the door. "Zenia didn't kill me."

"What in the name of the Gods is that?" Kasimir heard Thomas cry out as he and Sighurd bolted from the chamber.

"It's in the Great Hall," Sighurd said. They ran to the stairs and down. The guards and the soldiers in the hall stood peering up with swords drawn.

The creature hung from a block on the edge of the hole in the ceiling, grasping with four clawed appendages. It twisted its head to look down at them and squealed. It let go and swooped down at Thomas. He raised his sword high. It veered to the side and circled around. Thomas turned, trying to follow it, but it pounced on his back and dug its claws into him. Its fangs sank deep into his neck. Blood spurted and the creature swallowed. Thomas shouted and dropped his sword, writhing as he tried to grab the creature.

Dietric charged with his sword. The creature looked up, blood dripping from its mouth, and hissed at him.

"Kill it!" cried Geoffrey as he descended the stairs.

The creature zoomed away and circled around the hall. Thomas dropped to his knees, clutching the wound on his shoulder. Blood spurted through his fingers. Dietric rushed to Thomas and ripped strips of cloth from his clothing to tend to the wound.

Sighurd, Kasimir, and Faisal danced around, jabbing their swords whenever the creature flew near. It gave off an angry screech and zoomed back up, flapped its leathery wings, and shot out of the Great Hall through the gaping hole in the ceiling and into the gloomy dark of predawn.

Dietric stared wide-eyed at the hole, then at Thomas. "Upyr," he murmured.

"What did you say?" Kasimir said.

"Upyr. An ancient legend in Vlachia and Rothenia. A flying changeling that drinks people's blood."

Screams of terror rang out from the courtyard. Sighurd shouted, "King's Guard with me!" and rushed down the corridor to the gatehouse. His and Geoffrey's men and Kasimir and Faisal charged after him.

Out in the courtyard, other guards peered toward the sky with swords up, following the flight of the upyr. As it plunged toward them, they bunched together and aimed their swordpoints at the creature, flailing them threateningly. The creature squawked in rage and arched back up, getting lost in the dark sky. Kasimir and the others joined them.

The creature dove again, trying to maneuver past the weapons, then shot up again. Its wingspan was now half again the size it was when the infant changed. It flew past the moon, low in the sky above the walls of the courtyard, its silhouette an ominous image.

The sight reminded Kasimir of the times the dragon silhouette had flown past the moon. "Remember, this is Celeste's son," he called to everyone.

"These are my men," Sighurd said. "How do we handle it if not kill it?"

"Wait for the moon to set?"

"And let how many be attacked?" Sighurd growled. "What about your stones, Wizard?"

Kasimir sighed. He'd tried his starstone against Hereward with only partial success. He'd overestimated the energy he needed when casting the Spell of Power, and now Celeste's baby continued to grow beyond the womb. He was hesitant to experiment again on an unknown outcome. "I can try."

The creature made one more dive and veered once more into the sky as Kasimir reached for a stone on his face. But this time the creature swooped away from the castle toward the city.

"Great Gods!" Sighurd shouted. "King's Guard, mount up!"

Everyone dashed for the livery. There were more men than horses. Those who mounted one galloped for the outer gate.

They pounded across the bridge over the River Sicana and rode into town. Sighurd split them up into four groups, each led by himself, Kasimir, Faisal, and Lucien.

The riders rode through the streets of the city of Luteche. Fortunately the hour was early and the streets nearly empty. But there were still a few early risers, and the commotion of men galloping through the city on horseback drew more people out. "Stay inside!" Kasimir shouted, but few heeded his warning.

The upyr was hard to track in the dark as it flitted through the structures in the city. The riders dashed around almost in a frenzy, trying to keep up with it, trying to threaten it away from the people of the city. Kasimir lost track of it entirely, and the men he led milled about, trying to relocate it.

A cry rang out, and Kasimir aimed for it. He found a beggar lying on the street with the creature's jaw clamped onto his neck sucking at the blood. Kasimir gave off a war cry and charged, swinging his scimitar to within a hair's breadth of the creature.

But to strike the creature would have been to chop the beggar's head off. The creature didn't budge. Kasimir whirled his horse around and leaped off, marching toward them. The upyr looked up at him and screeched with blood dripping from its fangs and mouth, then went back to sucking.

Kasimir jabbed at it with the point of his scimitar. That was enough to stop it from sucking and glare at him. He reached again for a starstone, but the creature cried out and took flight—straight for Kasimir. He ducked barely in time, and the creature launched into the sky and disappeared.

Faisal rode over to him. "Are you alright, Brother?"

He nodded quickly and remounted, shouting a command to one of Geoffrey's men to tend to the beggar. They charged in the direction the creature had disappeared.

"How are we going to stop this thing?" Faisal asked.

"I'm going to try a starstone," he answered. "If I can get it to hold in place long enough."

Dawn sent its first fingers of light above the horizon, doing little to lessen the shadows in the city. "Maybe the moon setting will save us," said Faisal.

"But it's not a full moon," Kasimir said.

Shouts and commotion ahead. They rode toward it, finding Lucien's group battling the upyr. Kasimir and Faisal entering the fray with their groups would have only caused more chaos in the confines of the city streets. They held back.

Kasimir peered toward the moon. How many other people would this monster attack before it set—a monster Kasimir had released with his Spell of Power?

Maybe we should have just killed it, he thought.

He considered plucking a starstone at last, but the way the creature dove and soared and darted in and out of swords and soldiers and structures made him doubt he could focus on it well enough to aim the energy at it.

The soldiers battling the upyr suddenly rushed away as the creature sailed off to another section of the city. Kasimir and company followed, but he despaired of being much use. Perhaps all they could do was stave it off until daylight. But would that even make a difference, since there was no full moon causing the change? Only Mabut knew when this creature would change back.

"Zenia didn't kill me," Celeste shouted as Kasimir and Sighurd ran out the door, followed by Geoffrey. She buckled over with more pain.

"What's wrong with her now?" Ilsa said.

Eloise said, "The caul still needs coming out."

"What in the name of the Gods is that?" a faint voice cried in the distance. Inhuman screeches echoed through the castle.

The cramp passed, and Celeste tried to slide off the bed.

"Oh no, you don't!" Eloise said as she pushed her back on. "We've got to get that caul out."

"Edmund...Father, take me to our son," she said.

"You're not finished yet," Edmund said.

"Then get this caul out of me!" She cried out with more pain.

In the next few moments, they worked the afterbirth out. *Gods above, that was fast*, Eloise marveled as she took the caul. Kasimir's spell again, no doubt.

"Now, Father, take me," said Celeste. Edmund lifted her into his arms.

"You just gave birth," Eloise said. "The hardest birthing anyone's ever been through."

"Then heal me, Mother."

Eloise spoke the same spell she gave every new mother to strengthen her after birth. A moment passed where Celeste's breathing seemed to calm, then she said, "Put me down."

Edmund gently lowered her. She stood on her legs, wobbly at first until she steadied them. He helped her slide the shift back on.

More shouts of commotion and unearthly screeches came from outside.

Celeste started walking to the door. Edmund rushed to her side to help. "I'll never forgive them if they kill our son," she said.

Zenia and Ilsa followed them out the door.

Eloise stood in the middle of the empty chamber holding the caul up, one that had contained the unborn child of two changelings. Only the Gods knew how much power was imbued within it. Only the Gods knew how much residual energy from Kasimir's spell lingered in it.

This was a caul to treasure. The powerful spells she could cast with it in service of their quest! She carried it over to where Gwendolyn's sack of magic lay and set it on the floor beside it, then headed after the others.

Father helped Celeste to the stairs. Her legs began to feel more sure, and the exhaustion she felt had waned with Mother's spell. "I can manage now," she told him.

He let her go, and she carefully held to the railing as she descended the stairs. She looked about with wonder at the gigantic room, larger than she'd ever imagined a room could be, and at the extensive damage in it. "What happened to this room?"

"You happened," Father said. "Gwendolyn put you here when you were about to change."

Geoffrey came up to her as he peered at a wounded soldier on the floor that another soldier tended to. He said softly, "We should have killed it. It's a monster and needs to be destroyed."

"You say that one more time, Grandfather," she said, "and the dragon will eat you alive."

Geoffrey looked at Father with alarm. Father chuckled.

Celeste headed to the soldier, but Zenia ran past her and dropped to her knees before him. Ilsa joined her.

The soldier tending him backed away to give her space. "It was an upyr," he said.

Zenia glanced up at him, then examined the wounded soldier. "Thomas, I can heal you, but..."

"I'm going to become *that*," he said, gesturing toward the hole in the ceiling.

"I'm sorry, Thomas," said Zenia.

But it wasn't Zenia. Celeste gaped as her face seemed to flow into the face of the soldier she had seen change into a wolf back at the falls.

"But your soul is not cursed," the soldier added. "You will kneel before Father Sky."

Zenia's face returned to normal as Celeste and Thomas stared at her in amazement.

"You have someone inside you too!" Celeste said.

"I have several someones inside," Zenia said. "Mother Goddess brought us together." To Thomas she said, "Would you like me to heal you?"

He deliberated, then nodded. "I'm still under my vow to serve in the King's Guard. But when the Change comes..." He shook his head. "I don't want anybody sacrificing themselves to save me."

"You can learn to resist the Change," said Father.

"You still need to train *me*," Celeste said, "like you promised."

He smiled at her, then his expression became somber. He lowered his eyes.

Zenia gripped Thomas by both shoulders and peered at him intensely. He peered back, and wonder spread across his face. Ilsa watched them both with a gleam in her eyes.

Zenia let go and slumped down as if exhausted. "You can remove that bandage now."

The other soldier jumped forward and unwound the strip of cloth. Underneath were stains of blood and unblemished skin.

"The Pilgrim healed me too," said Ilsa with a big grin.

"You've lost a lot of blood," Zenia said. "You'll need to eat, like Celeste."

"Where did my son go?" Celeste asked, looking around.

"It...*he*...flew into the night air," the soldier said. He pointed to the hole. "Sighurd and the rest chased after him."

With alarm, Celeste looked around. "How do I get out of here?"

Mother said, "Where do you think you're—"

But the soldier pointed toward the corridor, and Celeste ran down it, passing through a gate into a courtyard. Other soldiers stood about uncertainly, all with swords in hand, gazing up at the gloomy sky only beginning to be colored with the illumination of dawn.

"Where's my son?" she said to one of them.

"There's been no boy out here," he said.

"I mean...that flying...*creature*." It pained her to call him that.

"*That's* your son?" the soldier said.

"*Where is he?*"

"He flew away into the city."

She uttered a Sight spell and searched. Quickly she found the city beyond the river below the cliffs of the castle—a breathtaking sight to see so many cottages cramped together. She saw soldiers on horseback riding through the streets, flailing their swords at something.

She saw her son flying about erratically, surrounded by a roiling aura of black and grey, and shuddered. He *was* a monstrous sight, and so much larger now. "I see him," she said to Eloise. She turned and looked imploringly at the Pilgrim. "Zenia?"

"Someone will have to die."

She watched her son diving down and attacking. Soldiers on horseback charged him with their swords. "I've got to stop this," she murmured.

She reached out to her son, watching her aura extend out into the city.

Eloise studied her, then spoke a Sight spell. "What are you doing, Celeste?"

"Calling my son."

"You can't! It's too dangerous."

"My son won't harm me."

"You don't know that."

She reached until her aura touched him. *Come, my son. Come to me.*

Her aura surrounded him. His head jerked up immediately, and he cried out with a terrible shriek. He flapped his wings and rose into the air, screeching and writhing as if in pain. He flew up and down and swirled around as if trying to escape her aura.

Finally he turned his gaze in her direction and flew toward her.

"He's coming," Mother whispered with alarmed eyes, then shouted to the soldiers, "He's coming!"

They became alert, peering into the sky.

"What do we do when he gets here?" Geoffrey asked.

"We purify him," Celeste said.

Mother sighed. "It's not that easy. Who will we sacrifice?"

"Don't worry," Celeste said. "I know what to do. Tamara remembers."

"What does that mean?" Eloise said suspiciously.

Zenia came up to them, peering up toward her son. "This is a dangerous thing to do, and we're not ready."

Her son soared above the cliffs and circled above the courtyard, darting and thrashing within her aura and screeching viciously.

"Pull your aura away!" Zenia cried, studying him. "It attacks his dark aura and causes him harm."

Geoffrey hissed, "Let it harm him!"

Celeste immediately pulled back. Her son wavered in his flight and shook his head, darted about randomly, then looked down at her with fiery eyes.

Celeste stepped forward, watching him. "Mother, you know the spell."

Father pulled her back. "*No!* You're not sacrificing yourself."

She fought his grasp, but couldn't break free. "I'm his mother. I need to purify him as Mother Tamara purified me."

"You said he won't even harm you," Father said.

Her son locked his eyes on hers, then circled around and dove.

"He *will* harm her," Zenia said, studying her son. "Celeste's aura agitated him into a frenzy."

"I'm the cause of all this," Father said. "I loved Tamara and created you, then I loved you and created him. I'm the one that should be sacrificed."

"No, Father!" she said, clinging desperately to him. "No, Edmund," she said in a different voice. She wept profusely. "I love you."

"I love you too, Celeste...Tamara."

As Ilsa watched Celeste and Edmund argue, she knew what had to be done. She couldn't let Celeste die after so many had struggled to save her. She couldn't let Celeste lose her father. Ilsa may be one of the group, but she was the least of them. She was the one they could spare the most.

With everyone's attention on Edmund and Celeste, Ilsa crept out into the courtyard directly under the plummeting creature, trembling. *I can do this, I can do this*, she chanted in her mind. *This has to be done.*

Celeste continued to protest. Edmund called to somebody, "Protect her."

Ilsa walked out away from everyone else, open and exposed, and closed her eyes. She held her hands up and waited for the creature's teeth to sink into her. She shook uncontrollably, but stealed herself against the pain.

"Mother Goddess," she prayed quietly, "take me into your bosom."

Powerful hands gripped her shoulder. She was flung back to the ground, landing hard on her buttocks. It stung the tip of her spine.

"Not you, child," Edmund said and stood in front of her, his back to her, taking the same stance she'd taken. "Speak the spell!" he cried.

Zenia rushed forward and dragged Ilsa back.

The clatter of horse hooves sounded from the outer gatehouse, and Sighurd and his men galloped in.

"Stay back!" Edmund shouted to them, and they stopped.

"Father, I don't want to lose you!" Celeste cried, held back by Eloise.

"You won't lose me," Edmund called back. "I'll be inside our son, as Tamara is inside you."

The creature crashed into Edmund, knocking him to the ground. Its hideous mouth opened and its rows of fangs stabbed deep into the side of his neck. He cried out as his blood flowed and the creature sucked.

Celeste screamed and wept as she dropped to her knees.

"Gods, no!" Geoffrey cried.

"Speak the spell!" Edmund shouted.

Trembling, Eloise peered at Zenia, who nodded. Eloise uttered the words. Edmund lay motionless, not fighting the creature. It trembled as it devoured his blood. Edmund's moaning stopped, and he lay still.

"Father," Celeste whimpered, weeping profusely.

The creature straightened with a wild look in its red eyes. A strong wind swept in, thrashing the trees in the forest beyond the walls of the castle, and swirled in a vortex around the creature. It stretched its wings out, extended its neck, and shrieked an unearthly shriek to the sky. The wings shuddered. The body writhed. The creature shrieked again.

"What's happening?" Celeste cried.

"It's the corruption," Zenia said. "A turmoil of auras that have not existed before, swirling around like a whirlwind."

The creature shook and fell back and shrieked once more, writhing in pain.

"He's dying!" Zenia cried.

"Thank the Gods!" Geoffrey muttered.

 A pale yellow glow formed around the creature. Ilsa watched with dread, wondering what would happen next.

The glow disappeared. On the ground lay a child, no longer the infant Celeste had given birth to, but a small boy. The powerful wind whipped his red hair about. He jerked violently, writhing and howling.

"He's full of corruption," Zenia said. "We have to draw it out."

Eloise looked up in the sky. The sun had risen above the castle wall. "Master Sun!" she cried as she pointed.

Celeste stood up and looked to the east, then at her son.

"Yes," Zenia said. "Run to him, Celeste. Hold him up and pray to Master Sun to suck the corruption from him."

Celeste dashed to the creature and struggled to pick him up. Ilsa ran up to her and helped. They managed to stand with him in their arms, barely with his violent writhing.

"Master Sun!" Celeste shouted above the wind. "Please suck the corruption out of my son. Purify him as the Mistress Moon purified me. Take away his darkness and let him shine like me."

The wind around them became more violent, tossing Celeste's white blonde hair into her face, creating a vortex around the three of them. Foul smoke seemed to ooze from every pore of the child and engulf them.

A whirlwind of flames funneled down from the solar face, stretching in a blazing finger of fire to earth. The dark vortex reached up and the two swirls touched. Crackling explosions filled the sky as the air thundered with a vengeance.

It was all Ilsa could do not to scream. With eyes closed and teeth grit, she stood against the whirlwind and the storm of energy and fire surrounding them, concentrating on holding the boy up. She felt every hair on her body prickling, the power of the sun crackling all over her skin. It seemed to rage on and on. Would it never end? Would she be consumed by its power?

The child shuddered. Ilsa opened her eyes. The tree crowns in the nearby forest danced as if a storm raged. The horses of Sighurd and his men reared and neighed in consternation, nearly bucking them off. The air filled with fine, black particles that, one by one, burst into small flames with loud pops. The fiery solar funnel flowed throughout the courtyard, surrounding everyone. Many of them cried out.

The child seemed to breathe it into his nostrils. The pores all over his naked body seemed to suck it from the sky. In one great blast of energy as if a demon had given up the ghost, the darkness flew out in all directions and dissipated into the blue sky.

The wind subsided. Celeste and Ilsa stood trembling, holding a young boy in their arms, limp and eyes closed. His hair was a deep golden blond. His skin was smooth and sweet and a light golden brown, as if kissed by the sun. He sucked a deep breath in, and his eyes fluttered open. The irises were golden brown and glittered in the sunlight.

Ilsa backed away several steps, letting Celeste hold her son in her arms. She held her breath, full of emotion, as she watched mother peer at her son with a deep joy. What a glorious transformation!

The boy gazed at his mother. She set him on his feet, her arms trembling. His balance was precarious, but she steadied him until he found his footing, reaching half her height.

Those golden eyes peered at her, and her silvery eyes peered back. A thrill swept through Ilsa's body, and tears came to her eyes. *Her son is purified!* she cried out in her mind.

The boy smiled a loving smile and said, "Celeste."

She peered into his face intently. "Edmund?"

His expression changed, becoming every bit the little boy he was. "Mother?" he said as if coming out of a stupor.

She embraced him and wept.

Ilsa's heart pounded with joy. She clapped her hands with delight.

Celeste withdrew from the embrace. She grabbed the hem of her shift and pulled it high until it slid over her head, then tossed it away. Mother and son stood naked facing each other. A shimmering golden glow formed around them.

"Run, Ilsa!" Zenia cried.

Ilsa dashed back and stood beside Zenia. Celeste and the boy became two indistinct figures in the sphere.

"They're changing!" Sighurd cried as he and his men backed away.

"But into what?" Eloise said.

Ilsa gazed at them with anticipation, unable to breathe.

From the glow, two great creatures lifted their heads. Enormous wings unfolded and spread out wide. Where Celeste had stood, the white dragon rose up, proud with silvery scales glinting in the brilliance of the sun. Where the boy had stood, a mighty golden dragon arose, scales flashing reflections of sunlight that dazzled the eye.

The two dragons flapped their wings and shot into the sky. They zoomed and arced around one another in a dance of joy. The white dragon lifted her head, and from her mouth blasted a swirling white mist into the sky. The golden dragon lifted his head, and from his mouth blasted out a fierce orange flame. They swooped and rose and circled around each other and celebrated with joyous sprays of flame and mist.

Ilsa wept as she watched them, pressing against Zenia as the Pilgrim put her arm around her. "They look so happy together!"

Eloise came up to them and joined the hug. She peered up at the dragons and murmured, "My daughter. My sweet daughter."

Eloise's gaze fell upon Edmund's body, lying neglected. "Oh, poor Edmund." She rushed over to him and knelt down, brushing his black hair from his lifeless eyes. Zenia and Ilsa followed her.

Eloise leaned over and kissed his forehead. "Your soul is corrupt no more." Her tears dropped onto Edmund's brow. "Thank you for Celeste. Thank you for her son."

Sighurd dismounted and came over and put his hand on her shoulder. "We'll take care of his body. He'll be buried with the highest honors."

Eloise stood up and peered into the sky, watching the dragons frolic. All the others involved in Celeste's rescue joined her.

"Magnificent!" Geoffrey said as he gazed at the dragons, then said to Eloise, "Is that how you saved Celeste?"

"That's how Zenia saved her."

He hugged Zenia, then Eloise. "My house shall forever be in your debt. To all of you." He turned to Kasimir, "I regret ever having doubted you. You shall be honored in Suedeche from this time forth."

"I'm already honored to have you be part of our quest."

Ilsa watched the dragons fly off together toward the east where Fenweald Forest loomed.

"Where they first met," Eloise murmured.

Chapter 30

Blood King

Celeste awoke in the meadow where she first met Edmund. The sun was near midday. Near her lay her son, naked and sleeping. She scooted over to him and caressed his golden hair. She could see traces of Edmund in his face. Her Mother Tamara inside stirred, radiating warm emotions.

He's my son now, Celeste said to her.

I will still always love him, Tamara said.

So will I, said Celeste.

She looked up at the sun towering high in the sky. "Thank you, Master Sun," she whispered.

The boy's eyes fluttered open. He looked around, looked at Celeste, then sat up. He studied her for a long moment. "Who are you?" he finally said.

She had no experience with babies, but she knew enough to know they can't speak the same day they're born. It must be the influence of Edmund inside him, as Tamara influenced her to become knowledgeable beyond her years as a child.

"I'm Celeste, your mother."

He gazed at her with an odd expression, and she realized he and Edmund were having a conversation together.

"Who am I?" he finally said.

"You're my son, and that voice inside you is your father. He gave his life so you could live."

He took an even longer moment to think about that.

"His name is Edmund," she added.

His eyes brightened at her words, and a smile flickered on his lips.

"He remembers, doesn't he?"

The boy nodded. "What is my name?"

That caught her by surprise. She hadn't even thought of that. "I don't know. I haven't chosen one for you yet."

The pounding of horse hooves came from the trees at the edge of the meadow. Instinctively she tensed with fear, but forced herself to relax, remembering Gwendolyn was gone and the king's soldiers were now her friends.

Sighurd and Kasimir broke from the trees and galloped over to them. Her son clung to her with alarm.

"Don't be afraid," she said. "They're our friends."

He relaxed a little, but still clung to her.

Kasimir practically leaped from his horse. Sighurd dismounted more calmly. Kasimir knelt before her and took her hand. "Princess, I...I don't know what to say." Tears pooled in his eyes. "My quest has been fulfilled."

"Your old one," Sighurd said as he walked up. "We still have more of the new one to fulfill."

He laughed and said, "Of course."

To her Sighurd said, "We followed you as you flew. We thought you could use a ride home when you changed back."

She stood and brought her son to his feet. "Thank you." She looked around. "I know this meadow. It would have been a long walk."

Sighurd looked at her son and shook his head. "He's not even one day old yet."

"Who are they?" the boy said.

"This is Sighurd," Celeste said. "He's a captain of soldiers. And this is Kasimir, a wizard from another land."

The boy studied them for a moment, probably carrying on a conversation with his father about the strange words she used. "Why is he black?"

"All his people are black. It makes him very handsome, don't you think?"

"What are those things on his face?"

"These are my starstones," Kasimir said. "They have the power of the stars in them."

"What are stars?"

Sighurd chuckled. "You and Guillaume will get along very nicely."

"Tonight we'll show you the stars," Celeste said.

The boy looked at each of them. "All of you have names. I don't have a name."

She crouched down to his level. "Would you like to pick your name?"

"I don't know any names."

"Might I suggest..." Kasimir said tentatively. "How about Cyrus? It's a name from my country. In the Insan language, it means *Of the sun*."

Celeste smiled broadly. It was the perfect name for him. "Would you like that name?" she asked.

The boy looked into the sky, shielding his eyes. "Did I come from the sun?"

They all laughed. "That's a story I'll tell you back home," she said. "We have lots of things to talk about."

He thought and nodded. "My name is Cyrus."

"Is there anything I can do for you right now, Princess?" Sighurd asked.

"We're very hungry."

"Then let's get you back and fatten you two up. You look like you need it."

Celeste rode with Kasimir because Cyrus was still wary of the strange black man, so he chose to ride with Sighurd. They stopped by the cottage where Celeste and Mother had lived four years so they could eat the food left behind in the garden, and so they could find clothing to wear. Cyrus had to wear one of her shifts because there was nothing else for him.

She insisted they spend some time there, since she expected to never see the home of her childhood again. She told Cyrus stories of her life there. She told him how she met his father Edmund in the pool by the waterfall. She brought him to the top of her hill where they lay together gazing at the sky, and she showed him how she could call the animals by calling a rabbit and a deer.

They laughed at how uncomfortable Kasimir became when she told Cyrus how he chased her to the cliffs and she had to leap to escape him.

"I want to see the Falls of Eircana," he said when she described them to him.

"That's a journey for another day," Sighurd said. "I'm sure Geoffrey and Eloise are cursing my name already for delaying so long bringing you back."

Cyrus gazed at everything with wonder as they traveled down the wide highway through the forest. When they reached Luteche and he saw the castle towering over the cliffs and the waterfall splashing down to the river, he clapped his hands with joy and cried, "That's the most beautiful thing in the world!"

Celeste was elated at his delight with the wonders of the world. It allowed her to see everything with fresh eyes.

She was going to love being a mother.

When he first awoke, Cyrus met only a handful of people—his mother Celeste, Sighurd the man they called the Captain of the King's Guard, and Kasimir the strange wizard from someplace called Insu. It was easy to remember them all, especially with his Father Inside helping him. But at the castle he felt overwhelmed by the many people he was introduced to and who bundled him up in hugs and told him how happy they were to see him.

They all gathered around him when he walked through a gate into a large open space surrounded by walls with many round stones in the ground under his feet. There was a grandfather and a grandmother and a woman dressed all in white and some soldiers and another black man.

But the one he remembered most easily, the one that most intrigued him, was another boy that was about as tall as he was. His name was Guillaume. They stood before each other appraising one another.

"I'm the king," Guillaume said. "You have to obey me."

"I won't," Cyrus said, thinking the notion preposterous.

"You have to, or you'll be punished."

"I'll turn into a dragon and eat you."

Guillaume balked at that, then squinted his eyes and said, "Your mother is my sister. That makes me your uncle."

The woman in white crouched before them and put her arms around them. "How about you call each other friend?"

They looked at her, then looked at each other. Guillaume said, "You have girl's clothes on. Come on." He grabbed him by the arm and brought him into the castle.

They entered a giant room where a lot of people were cleaning up chunks of stone and damaged things. Cyrus looked up and saw a big hole in the ceiling. "What happened here?"

"Gwendolyn put your mother in here when she turned into a dragon." Guillaume brought him up a big staircase and down some corridors until they came into a room. "These are my chambers. You can wear some of my clothes."

He picked out some clothing and helped Cyrus put them on. "These are the clothes of a king. Don't tear them."

They had a meal in the giant room that evening. They called it the Great Hall. All the damage was cleaned away, and someone had put tables in the room. Lots of people he'd never seen before sat at them eating, but he and Mother and the other people who hugged him in the open space sat at tables at the front of the room. There was lots of food and hugs and talking and laughter.

He liked most of the food and spit out the things he didn't like. "Oh my!" the grandmother said, named Eloise. But Mother laughed.

The grandfather's name was Geoffrey. He was something called a duke. Father Inside said it was like a king but not as important. He marveled that a boy could be king while a grown man was only a duke. He decided he wanted to be a king someday.

When it got dark, they brought him out into the open space again and showed him the stars and the moon. He couldn't believe how dark the sky got after the bright day. It frightened him. That night he slept with Mother because she said she wanted to hold him all night. That made him happy. The castle was a big, dark place, and he didn't want to be alone in it.

Eloise sat at the worktable in Gwendolyn's chambers—*her* chambers now—as she and Zenia prepared the materials for the Extended Sight spell. They spent the day collecting the necessary ingredients, since Gwendolyn had all but emptied her shelves when she fled. Many chairs were set up around another table put there for the upcoming gathering.

When the materials were ready to burn and the scroll rolled out ready to read, Eloise looked around the room as they waited for the others to arrive. Her eyes landed on the chains attached to the wall. "That's the first thing I'm getting rid of."

"Have you figured out the commands yet?" Zenia said, pointing at the open secret compartment in the wall.

"I'm afraid to try. I might close it and never be able to open it again."

Zenia chuckled. "You could always use the Extended Sight to go back and hear what she says."

Eloise smiled mischievously. "I'm sure glad I have that spell. Makes up for losing my scrying globe." A thought suddenly occurred to her. "Deirdre's dead! That means—"

"That means it belongs to whoever replaces her," Zenia said as she slapped her hand.

Eloise tilted her head. "She had no apprentice. She hated apprentices." Her smile deepened. "Perhaps I should apply."

"You do and I'll ask Mother Goddess to curse you with warts all over your body."

A knock came to the door. "Come in," Zenia said.

Celeste entered with Cyrus, followed by Sighurd, Geoffrey, Kasimir, Faisal, Dietric, Thomas, Ilsa, and Guillaume—everyone related to the new quest.

"Come sit down," Zenia said.

When everyone was settled, she spoke. "When Gwendolyn fed me to the Beast, I vowed to kneel before Mother Goddess and beg her to let Celeste know about the threat in the East. I didn't know if I'd even appear before Mother Goddess, since the old legends say I'd be cursed." She smiled. "The legends were wrong, and I did appear before Mother Goddess. I made my request."

She rested her hand on Celeste's. "Mother Goddess granted it by sending me back to tell you myself." She looked at Kasimir. "This is *my* quest and my reason for being here. Everything I've done up to this point has been leading to this moment. Each of you are part of Kasimir's new quest." She turned to Guillaume and Cyrus. "Even you two."

Her mood became somber. "I struggled with whether I should let you boys see this. You're very young, and what I'm about to show you is very frightening and disturbing. But you, Guillaume, are the king, and you, Cyrus, are a changeling dragon that will stand with your mother in this war. You have the right and the need to know what you'll be facing. Are you ready to face this vision?"

Their expressions showed a mix of apprehension and excitement.

"Yes," said Guillaume.

"We are," said Cyrus.

Zenia addressed all of them again. "You think your quest is to unite the North and the South, but that's only the beginning. There's a much greater danger looming in the East, and you'll be facing it all too soon."

Kasimir and Faisal nodded. "We've met this threat," Faisal said.

"I want to show you so you can be prepared for it. Gwendolyn showed me before she killed me. She cast a powerful spell she called Extended Sight. I'll cast it on all of us now. The sensations you'll experience make normal Sight feel like a summer breeze. I hope to guide you through the chaos the best I can and show you the threat that's coming. Gwendolyn called him the Blood King."

The Blood King, echoed in Eloise's mind, remembering when Gwendolyn had uttered those words to her. She was afraid of what she might see, but she was also eager to see what Gwendolyn had seen that drove her to the extreme acts she committed. Maybe she could even learn to forgive Gwendolyn...now that she was dead.

Zenia nodded to her, and Eloise uttered the words to ignite the stick in her hand and dropped it in the bowl. The oil flamed high. Zenia read the words on the scroll forcefully. When she finished, the sensations of a Sight Eloise never dreamed existed blasted her with an almost physical force. A massive barrage of images and cacophony of sounds and floods of aromas bombarded her. She gasped with the onslaught.

Guillaume, Cyrus, and Ilsa cried out in shock.

"Listen to my voice," Zenia spoke through the uproar. "Follow my voice. Cyrus, Guillaume, can you see my face?"

She may have addressed the boys, but Eloise was thankful for her guidance or she would have been lost too. She followed Zenia's voice until her face formed within the chaos.

"Guillaume, can you see me?" Zenia called out. "Can you find me?"

"I see you!" he said triumphantly.

"Take my hand."

"Mother!" Cyrus cried. "Mother, I can't see you."

"I'm here," Celeste replied. "Listen to my voice. Hold out your hand. Follow my voice."

"Mother!"

"I'm here. Find my face. There...there, I've got you."

Zenia said, "Has everyone found me?"

Eloise and the others responded affirmatively.

"Do you see her?" Celeste said.

"I see her," said Cyrus.

"Follow me," Zenia said. "I'm bringing you east."

Images rushed past. They provided a sense of movement, but physically Eloise felt no movement. Time passed quickly, and yet it seemed forever, before Zenia brought them to a halt. The flashing images materialized into a sweeping steppe of grasslands and rolling hills. In the distance were snowcapped mountains. Two armies of thousands of men faced off from either end of a huge field, of a race she'd never seen before. A clear, sunny sky overlooked them. A man sat on a horse on a hill overlooking the armies, dressed in impressive armor.

"This is the Blood King," Zenia said. "His armies swear fealty to him by slicing their lips and kissing his feet with their blood."

Nine warriors rode out a short distance into the field, followed by nine men carrying vessels. A woman in a red tunic stepped out from the army and walked out, then raised her arms up.

"The woman is his sorceress wife," Zenia said.

At commands from the woman, the men on the horses climbed down, drew their swords and chopped the heads off their horses. They sat astride the bodies of the horses and held their swords in front of them. The men behind them poured the contents of the vessels over them and the horses.

Archers at the front of the army dipped their arrows in flaming pots and shot the warriors in the back. They and the horses flared up into tall flames. The burning warriors did not move or cry out.

The sorceress took a deep breath and broke into a fluid dance.

"I don't know where her people's magic comes from," Zenia said, "but they have the Death Magic the Seven Sisters took from us."

The sky darkened with angry clouds rushing in on the crest of a powerful gale. Rain deluged the field. Lightning sizzled down to the ground, catching the grass on fire and scorching the soldiers—but only the ones on the opposing army.

Zenia showed them the king's conquests throughout his land. She showed them his enemies boiled and suffocated. He spread south and east, his tactics and his wife's magic sweeping aside all other armies across the continent, conquering every kingdom on the way until his empire cut a swath across the northern half of the continent from the east shore to the borders of Komshu. The Blood King's armies must number in the hundreds of thousands.

"He invades Komshu at this moment," Zenia said. "He will conquer it, then he'll turn his sights to the West. He'll turn on us in Cueldea and Ifran."

She spoke a spell of Negation and the vision faded. Eloise looked around at everyone, seeing faces as troubled as her own heart felt. Cyrus clung to Celeste with a few tears dripping down his cheeks. Guillaume clung to Sighurd, shaking.

"Are you okay, Cyrus?" Zenia said, touching his arm.

He nodded, and his face went serene. "I'm taking care of him," he said in a different voice.

Celeste gazed at him and caressed his cheek with the back of her hand.

"And you, Guillaume?" Zenia asked.

Still shaking, he jut his chin out and said, "I'm going to kill that Blood King."

"That's my job," Sighurd said. "The king's job is to command me to kill him in your name."

"I command you to kill the Blood King."

"One day," Sighurd said with a smile.

"Gwendolyn, Gwendolyn," Eloise said, wiping at her own eyes. "If you hadn't craved power so much, we'd have joined with you to stop the Blood King. We could have started preparing for this four years ago."

"That's what you need to do now," Zenia said. "Sighurd, you must stand with Scaendelreic and Onotria and all the other kingdoms of Cueldea. Eloise, you must stand with the Six Sisters. Kasimir, Faisal, you must stand with Cueldea. Only then can you withstand the onslaught of the Blood King's armies and his wife's Death Magic."

The mood in the room was grave. Sighurd said, "How long?"

"I'd guess six months, maybe a year," Zenia said.

Everyone looked at each other. "An alliance with every country in the west, in just a few months?" Thomas said.

Zenia rolled up the scroll and handed it to Eloise. "Gwendolyn's powers are yours now. You have the power to show everyone what's coming, including the Six Sisters."

She took the scroll and stared at it. "If they don't kill me before I can show them. Even if they agree to join us, can I trust them?"

"They're not foolish. They'll understand the threat. And you have a formidable army backing you up. You have the Kingdom of Gallea..." She nodded to Sighurd, then Geoffrey. "...and the Duchy of Suedeche, the wizards of Insu..." She nodded to Kasimir and Faisal. "...and two dragons."

All eyes turned to Celeste and Cyrus. Celeste kept her eyes on her son as she stroked his hair.

"And you'll have Eloise, the Rogue Sorceress." Zenia grinned at her.

Eloise smiled back. "The weakest link in a strong chain. But I really have to think of a different title."

Zenia put her arm around Ilsa. "And my faithful servant, who was willing to give her life for Celeste and Cyrus."

Ilsa blushed.

"And a Pilgrim of Mother Goddess," said Thomas. "And Hereward."

Zenia peered at him poignantly. "My quest is over. I need to return to Mother Goddess."

"No!" Ilsa jumped up and hugged her.

"You'll abandon us now when our need is greatest?" said Thomas.

Zenia gently pulled Ilsa away. She gazed at her and at Thomas. "We're dead, Hereward and I. This is a quest for the living. The living created this situation. The living must end it. I could only come and warn you."

Ilsa sat back down with her tears still flowing.

"We have a lot to do," Sighurd said. "I suggest we begin making our plans."

He stood as a signal, and everyone in the room followed him out except Eloise, Zenia, Ilsa, Celeste, and Cyrus. They watched Celeste stroke Cyrus' hair as she gazed at him somberly.

"Celeste?" Eloise said as she studied her. "How are you feeling?"

She continued to stroke his air a few more times before answering. "I feel like I've lived more in the last few days than all those years in the forest. My son's lived years in a handful of days." She looked up at them. "Are we to never have a normal life? Are we now to become pawns for *your* cause?"

Eloise's heart sank. How could she say such a thing? What made it worse was the realization that maybe she was right. Maybe they *had* treated her exactly as Gwendolyn had.

"Dear Goddess," Eloise said as tears came out. "I'm so sorry." She went to her and knelt before her and Cyrus. "Say the word, sweetheart, and we'll leave Luteche. We'll go where we can live together without the cares of the world pressing in on us."

Zenia watched without expression.

"What do you think, Cyrus?" Celeste said as she lifted him to peer into his eyes. "Shall we go away together, or shall we fight the Blood King?"

"Will Guillaume fight the Blood King?"

"He and his whole army."

Cyrus squirmed out of her arms and dropped to the floor. He marched over to Zenia and looked up at her. "We'll fight the Blood King, my mother and I."

"Thank you, young man," Zenia said.

He went back to Celeste and took her hand, standing determined beside her.

"After what you showed us," Celeste said, "we can't turn our backs on the ones we love. We'll fight your battles for you as dragons. I'll marry that little boy and become queen of Gallea."

Eloise cringed. "You heard about that? I meant to talk to you."

"Word spreads in the castle." She stroked Cyrus' cheek with her hand. "But when it's over, we're going back to our cottage in the forest and live the life you gave me, Mother, for four happy years."

She stood and went to Eloise and kissed her on the cheek. "I love you, Mother, for loving me as your daughter."

She went to Zenia and kissed her. "I love you, Grandmother, for purifying me and giving your life for me."

She went to Ilsa and kissed her. "I love you, Servant of the Pilgrim, for feeding me when I was dying, and for being willing to give your life so I and my father wouldn't have to."

"I'm not a servant of the Pilgrim anymore," Ilsa said with tears glistening in her eyes. "She's leaving."

"Perhaps you can be the servant of two dragons," Zenia said.

Ilsa's eyebrows rose.

"Rather than being my servant," Celeste said, "perhaps you could be my friend. I've never had a friend before."

"Neither have I," Ilsa said with eyes shining, "for half my life."

Celeste took her hand and squeezed it, then gazed off into space. "I love you, Mother Tamara, for sacrificing your life for me." She kissed her son. "I love you for being a beautiful and brave boy."

Cyrus threw his arms around her neck. "I love you, Mother."

"I love you, Edmund," she said, "for giving me my life and my son's life."

"I love you, Celeste," Cyrus said in the other voice. "I love you, Tamara."

Eloise looked at everyone with a wide grin and wiped at her tears. "What a strange family we are!"

Ilsa accompanied Celeste and Eloise and Zenia through the outer gate of the castle and down the road that led to the bridge over the River Sicana, then along the East Highway. Celeste left Cyrus with Guillaume to play with his toy soldiers together. Night had fallen and Mistress Moon was low in the east, showing only a portion of her face. They continued until they left the city and stood at the edge of Fenweald Forest.

It was all Ilsa could do to keep from breaking out in sobs. She wondered if her own mother had felt this way when she left Premveille. She felt a strong desire to visit home and tell her of all the amazing things she'd experienced.

"Are you sure you can't stay and help us?" Eloise asked Zenia.

"How would mortals develop into demigods if the Gods constantly meddled in their affairs?" she said. "You have to learn to handle things yourselves. That's why Mother Goddess sent me instead of doing it herself."

"What if I just want to see you again?"

Zenia smiled and kissed her. "You will."

She turned and kissed Celeste. "It gives me great joy to see that all our sacrifices made it possible for you to become such a strong, beautiful woman, inside and out."

Celeste's tears flowed. "I'll always remember you, as the Pilgrim who restored my life when Gwendolyn took it, and through Tamara's memories, as the loving grandmother who gave her life to protect me." She kissed her back. "Thank Mistress Moon and Master Sun for me."

"I will." She turned to Ilsa and kissed her. "You are the best servant a Pilgrim could hope for."

"I only did what had to be done," she said, her eyes misting.

"And you're a hero because of it."

Zenia turned and walked down the highway into the forest, her white robe almost luminescent in the dark. Ilsa struggled and failed to keep her tears from falling as she and Eloise and Celeste lingered to watch her disappear around a bend in the road. They were almost ready to turn back to the castle when a blinding glow erupted through the trees. A shaft of brilliant light shot up into the night sky and soared to Mistress Moon where it disappeared in the glow of her face.

How Celeste Was Born

Once upon a time a storyteller named D. Michael married a woman who claimed to love him. Their relationship turned out to be rocky. They did not live happily ever after.

But before the end came, his wife expressed an interest in writing a novel together. D. Michael wasn't so sure that was the greatest idea, but he decided maybe working together would help strengthen their relationship. He asked her what kind of story she wanted to write.

She said she wanted it to be about a princess an evil sorceress was trying to capture, but three nice witches took her away and hid her in a cottage in a forest until she could grow up. When the princess became a woman, the witches wanted to celebrate her birthday by making her a cake and a new dress. But they couldn't agree on what color to make the dress, so they had a skirmish where each of them kept changing the color of the dress with their magic wands.

His wife gazed upon him in hopeful anticipation of what his reaction would be. But D. Michael said to her, "I think Walt Disney already did that one."

Having gotten past that small hurdle, he and his wife started working out a plot that would avoid landing them in court with the lawyers of Disney Corporation. They kept the princess and the sorceress and the cottage in the woods, but developed and wrote the story in a direction far away from the wife's original premise.

What was meant by developing and writing the story was that D. Michael, who after all was the storyteller in the family where his wife decidedly was *not*, would suggest ideas for her approval, then write that portion of the story and seek her approval again. She always approved them because, let's face it, D. Michael is a fine storyteller.

Through this belabored process, approximately one chapter was written before the marriage tanked and D. Michael came home from work one day to find his wife and her things had vanished into thin air. Or more accurately, had crossed two state borders to run home to momma.

This happened to be the very same day D. Michael's first published novel was released, *Brother Brigham*. The same glorious day he was heading over to his publisher's with great excitement to pick up his author copies. This was the very same first edition of the book that D. Michael dedicated to his wife with the words "who loves me more than I deserve."

It turned out, she loved him considerably less than he deserved.

It also turned out, that day was Halloween of 2007, which seemed oddly appropriate for such soul-shattering events.

THE END

But that was not THE END for *Celeste & the White Dragon*, the novel that grew out of that difficult birth with labor pains as great as what Celeste went through birthing Cyrus. One of the last communications I had with my soon-to-be exwife was, "I'm keeping Celeste and I'm gonna keep writing it." Her response was, "Go ahead. It's all yours."

I said that not to one-up her, but because by the time she left, this was no longer a mercy project to humor my wife. I had grown fond of the story and saw real potential in it, so I kept writing and kept writing. I had no idea how it would play out and no idea what the ending would be. I kept developing the story using the "Just In Time" manufacturing philosophy of planning the next chapter or two, then writing it, then wondering what should come next. I was at least halfway through the book before an ending finally began to formulate in my mind.

As a consequence, some interesting things happened along the way. Let me warn you right now...*SPOILERS AHEAD!* Do not continue reading this until you've finished reading the novel itself.

The first thing that happened was, when the Beast tears the liver out of Zenia, that was it. She was dead and never coming back. I had a writers group reading chapters as I pumped them out, and when they read that chapter, they screamed bloody murder. "You can't kill Zenia! She's the main character and we're invested in her!"

But one fellow said, "I don't believe she's dead. I think she's gonna come back somehow."

Well, she wasn't, but I didn't tell them that. And I didn't put any stock in their outrage over her death because I thought of Alfred Hitchcock's *Psycho* that testifies I most certainly *can* kill off the main character early on and get away with it.

Nevertheless that fellow got me to thinking, how could I bring her back? And the concept of the Pilgrim was born.

When it came time to write the chapter where child Celeste grows up, I did not know who Celeste was. I became acquainted with her as I wrote. I did not know what her powers were. I didn't know she had a Girl Inside until I discovered her existence while writing the chapter.

Another interesting development was where Kasimir came from. All the way until that chapter where Celeste grows up, he did not exist. After I wrote her chapter, I was clueless where to go next. And I had four years to account for what was going on in the world while Celeste grew up. Certainly Gwendolyn wasn't twiddling her thumbs all those years.

So what would she be doing? Searching for Celeste, of course. And how would she do it? Surely a high-positioned sorceress wouldn't go searching around herself. She'd have minions.

And in one instant, Kasimir and the Southern Continent and the Southern wizards were born.

But I didn't want my wizard to be a run-of-the-mill wizard with a staff he points and utters words and magic zaps out. Boring! (Sorry, Gandalf.) So I worked out how the magic of the Southern wizards functioned and devised the starstones, which is one cool idea if you ask me, and one cool image for when HBO picks the story up and makes a series out of it. [*Ahem!*]

But the biggest on-the-fly idea I came up with while writing the story was what motivates Gwendolyn altogether. There was no Blood King, and the Easterners were only an afterthought late in the novel when I realized I needed enemies for Celeste to battle in the sequel.

Gwendolyn's motive ended up being something called Dirty Magic, a thing she discovers in the future while using her Extended Sight. She discovers a modern technological society which she perceives in terms of magic instead of technology. She calls the technology Dirty Magic, and when she sees a nuclear war happen and wipe everything out, that becomes her motivation for amassing great power—to save the world from this dreadful future.

Yeah, I know. Pretty hokey, right?

I completed the novel and had my first readers read it and give me feedback, and they loved it. I figured I had something.

Somewhere around then, I became enamored of writing screenplays and producing films. For nine years I focused on that, and *Celeste* sat gathering dust on the shelf. I figured one day I'd do one more rewrite of it, then see about getting it published.

An interesting thing happened to me during the period of making movies. *Game of Thrones* happened to me. The first time I tried watching HBO's adaptation, I got lost in all the characters and couldn't figure out what was going on, so I gave up on it two or three episodes in. This in spite of being able to see Emilia Clarke nude, which is a powerful selling point!

A couple years went by with people raving about the series and with me being cynical about how unnecessarily complicated it was, yet people kept pestering me about how I *had* to try it again because they were *sure* I'd love it. So I broke down one day and gave it another try, determined to concentrate really hard and keep track of who was who and what was what.

I watched it...and watched it...and watched it... Well, let's just say I reached the point where I was ready to add George R. R. Martin to my pantheon of Gods in *Celeste*.

As a side note, were you aware that George's parents were pirates? That's why they named him George Arr Arr Martin.

I'm sure no one's ever thought of that joke before.

After that I decided I wanted to drag *Celeste* back off the shelf, dust it off, and work on it again. There was just one small problem. About as small as the problem Westeros faced with the coming of the White Walkers.

Celeste & the White Dragon sucked!

Hardly surprising, considering the slapdash way I wrote it. Oh, it was entertaining enough, and there were scenes in it that sparkled. But compared to *Game of Thrones*—good Lord! It felt to me like an inconsequential fantasy novel from the 1980s or something.

I had to up my game!

So instead of one more polishing rewrite, I realized I had to do a major overhaul. First thing I needed to was create a map. I never bothered to create a map the first time around. I only had a vague idea of the geography and the cultures of Celeste's world, and precious few place names, and it showed. It was a nebulous environment, incomplete. I mapped out Cueldea and Ifran and assigned craploads of place names everywhere. I developed a more thorough history leading up to the days of the novel and added languages to it, whereas before everyone just spoke the same "common" tongue.

I also desperately needed to develop the characters better. Kasimir no longer would appear out of thin air. I gave him a brother and a backstory and more sophisticated issues to deal with. I turned King Christian from a cardboard dunce into a meaningful character. I vastly fleshed out Edmund as a character. I introduced a brand-spanking-new character freshly minted, Ilsa, who breathed more fire into a few chapters.

Equally critical was changing Gwendolyn's character. She wasn't quite a two-dimensional villain, but she was closer to it than I cared for her to be, and that motivation of the Dirty Magic had to go. That's when I turned back to the Easterners and promoted them into the Major Threat and not an afterthought. The Blood King worked much better to drive Gwendolyn's actions.

I also needed to give my villain Gwendolyn a much more dramatic ending, so I tossed her death scene out and fabricated an entirely new death scene worthy of her villainy.

Something totally unrelated to all this helped me enrich Celeste's world even more. Long before her story was a twinkle in my eye, I'd been developing a completely separate fantasy world with its own continent and magic system and history. I mapped that one out in detail and developed a history for every country in it. I had three—count them, three—pantheons of Gods in it, and multiple humanoid species. To this date I've written a whopping three chapters of what was supposed to be a major fantasy series.

While writing *Celeste*, it occurred to me that a prequel to it could make a fascinating story in and of itself, and of course a sequel was a virtual requirement. What started out a stand-alone novel morphed into a trilogy. But once I thought of *Celeste* as more than one novel, I started thinking, you know, I can see a way to connect it with the utterly unrelated other series, placing them both in the same universe. There could even be an entire novel's worth of telling the story of how they're connected.

This on top of plans for a trilogy telling the story of the Blood King.

Once I started seeing all these connections and how to synthesize them into one mega-series, the cross-pollination of meshing their individual worlds into a consistent whole aided me in enriching the worlds of each of them. I reimagined how magic in Celeste's world worked, who the Great Gods were, and exactly what the Pilgrim and the Seven Sisters were, and that pathetic little first version I wrote beginning with my exwife got lost in the dust. I just hope the Gods smile on me and let me live long enough to write them all.

So did my efforts pay off? I struggled to get my story into the same league as *Game of Thrones*, or *A Song of Ice and Fire*, depending on which version you prefer. Did I succeed?

Only you, Dear Reader, can judge that. I'd be content if it's considered in the same ballpark, or even the next neighborhood over. I only know that my efforts transformed my first version into something vastly greater, to the point where I will never allow the original version to see the light of day. I couldn't stand the embarrassment.

One more small detail. There's a second sorceress in *Celeste* besides Gwendolyn, who is as equally questionable of character as Gwendolyn is, who represents the conniving, power-hungry Seven Sisters in the book. When it came to naming her, I decided to indulge my bitterness over my failed marriage just a teensy bit. I named her after the nasty exwife who came up with the seed of the story idea in the first place.

I named her Deirdre.

D. Michael Martindale is a storyteller. It doesn't matter which medium the story is told in—whether it be film or television or books or music—what's important is telling stories that people enjoy.

He was born in Minnesota and has been telling stories since before he could write. He started out by drawing comic strips and having his mother fill in the dialog balloons for him. He developed a taste for science fiction and fantasy, and although he's written screenplays in all sorts of genres, he continues to gravitate back to speculative fiction.

Martindale earned an Associate Degree in Film Production at Salt Lake Community College and a Bachelor Degree in Screenwriting and Cinematography at Utah Valley University.

For a period of time, he focused on telling stories about his religious community, Mormons. He considered the quality of Mormon literature subpar and preachy and wanted to tell stories about his people that he'd want to read, quality stories that were honest and edgy and not the least bit preachy. He's glad to see that the quality of Mormon art has been improving over the years.

He served three years on the board of the Association for Mormon Letters, a nonprofit organization that promotes Mormon literature and other arts, and acted as their Writers Conference chairperson for four years. He wrote a number of articles and book and film reviews for their literary journal *Irreantum.*

He worked for a time as a staff writer for *The Sugar Beet*, an Internet publication of Mormon satire patterned after the infamous website *The Onion*. Many of these online articles of alleged Mormon "news" were eventually collected into the popular book *The Mormon Tabernacle Enquirer*.

The editor of *The Mormon Tabernacle Enquirer* decided to start his own publishing company, Zarahemla Books, and chose as its flagship publication Martindale's second novel *Brother Brigham*, which he categorizes as "Mormon speculative fiction." *Brother Brigham* went on to receive substantial critical acclaim and was even used as reading material in a college comparative religion class one semester. He also had a science fiction short story "Bokev Momen" published in the anthology *Monsters and Mormons*, which is included in his collection of short stories *Twisted Mind*.

Inspired by *Jesus Christ Superstar*, he composed the musical *General Prophet Joseph Smith*, based on the events leading up to the assassination of the Mormon prophet Joseph Smith. He produced a concept album recording of it on CDs, and is currently developing a film adaptation of it. He calls it "Les Mis for Mormons."

Martindale has written two other novels. His first, *The Power of the Seeker*, is the beginning installment of a science fiction series called *The Reincarnate*. It remains unpublished, and he describes it as "crap." He may rewrite it someday. His third novel is a fantasy called *Celeste & the White Dragon* which he's in the process of bringing to publication. It's the first volume in a series, as of yet untitled.

He's already writing the first draft of his fourth novel, the prequel to *Celeste & the White Dragon*, which currently has the title *Seven Sisters*, but he makes no guarantee that title will remain the same. He envisions more volumes to the series and wonders if he'll live long enough to produce them all.

For nine years Martindale has focused on screenwriting and film making as a director and editor. Film is his favorite medium in which to tell stories. He wrote, produced, directed, and edited eight short films and a feature-length fantasy film called *Geeks and Goblins, Elves and Elliot*. He has multiple other screenplays ready to be developed into feature-length films, including an adaptation of his short story "Solar Butterfly" that also appears in *Twisted Mind*. Additionally, he's been on the development team for three television/web series.

He resides in Salt Lake City, Utah, and is the father of three grown children and the grandfather of the best granddaughter in the world. Do not debate him on this.

Twisted Mind:
6 Science Fiction Stories
by D. Michael Martindale

From the twisted mind of D. Michael comes six science fiction stories that disrupt the status quo of our world in the spirit of The Twilight Zone and Black Mirror. Whether the new world that arises is better or worse is a question each individual will have to decide for themselves.

A Growth in the Backyard
Eternal Rectangle
Solar Butterfly
Bokev Momen
Mary Mother of Nanites
Eyes of the Beholder
Bonus story: **Time Forks**

twistedstories.worldsmithstories.com

Twisted Soul
4 Slipstream Novellas
by D. Michael Martindale

From the twisted soul of D. Michael come four slipstream novellas that explore the twists and turns of human spirituality and psychic powers. The hidden worlds they reveal may inspire or disturb, but the souls that experience them will never be the same again.

Alexandra
A Face in the Window
First Mormons in the Moon
Godblind
Bonus novelette: **The Dreamcatcher**

twisted.worldsmithstories.com

Brother Brigham
by D. Michael Martindale

Like many young boys, C.H. Young grew up with an imaginary friend. In his case, it was his ancestor Brigham Young—or rather, "Brother Brigham" as C.H. knew him. During his formative years, Brother Brigham filled the boy's head with grand expectations of an important mission in life.

Now grown up with a wife and two young sons, C.H. has sacrificed his dreams to earn a living for his family. Brother Brigham is just a distant memory—until one day he returns in a most unexpected way. As Brother Brigham's appearances and instructions grow increasingly bold, C.H. struggles to hold together his faith, his marriage, and his sanity.

brotherbrigham.worldsmithstories.com